THE CLASSIC DUNGEON
DESIGN GUIDE III

A BLACK LABEL FANTASY RPG SUPPLEMENT

BY KENT DAVID KELLY

CASTLE OLDSKULL

The Classic Dungeon Design Guide III
The Black Label Edition

A **Basic** / **Expert** / **Advanced**
Compatible Supplement For Classic Fantasy Role-Playing Games

CREATED BY

Kent David Kelly

© 2012-2023

WONDERLAND IMPRINTS

Only the Finest Works of Fantasy

OSR

The Old School Renaissance

New Innovations, Classic Games

TABLE OF CONTENTS

CHAPTER I:

INTRODUCTION

DESCRIPTION

Enchanted fountains shadowed by gargoyle sentries,

Tricksy nymphs cavorting in crystal pools,

Unholy altars, sacred shrines,

Undiscovered treasure vaults,

Thousands upon thousands of wondrous rooms

Filled with treasure, tricks, magic and eldritch horror,

All awaiting your heroes' intrepid discovery ...

What greater mysteries await far below,

For only the most dauntless magi

And fearless warlords to ever find?

~

Continuing the proud tradition of *The Classic Dungeon Design Guide (Books I and II)*, Book III provides you with a nearly endless array of dungeon room types which you can use to build any size, plan and theme of dungeon you desire. This is the largest and most extensive dictionary of dungeon rooms in existence, featuring over 1,300 unique entries and 6 matrixed D1000 generation tables for the appropriate thematic structuring of underworld strongholds, ruins, temples, tombs, cave labyrinths, and more.

The exhaustively complete matrix tables allow you to build thematic dungeons with ease, just using room size consideration, floor planning, and random die rolls. When coupled with the dungeon content generation systems featured in Book II, you will now have everything you need to create an infinite number of instant dungeon rooms with instant contents and unique features.

In this massive tome you will also find many detailed real-world examples of layouts and room arrangements for caves, dungeons, manor houses, castles, and catacombs; and underworld lore that explains how to turn random results into coherently structured underworlds (such as deep dwarven undercities, arenas, hideouts, haunted fanes, and more).

So what are you waiting for? This book is the perfect companion to *The Classic Dungeon Design Guides I and II*, and has been specially designed to serve both as a learning grimoire and as a tabletop go-to book for design and for sandbox play. After all, if you're going to dare to delve into the netherworld, you should probably take not just a lantern and an elvish sword of great antiquity; you should also carry the ultimate guidebook with you along the way ...

Another classic and epic Fantasy Role-Playing Game Supplement from Wonderland Imprints, *Only the Finest Works of Fantasy*. (85,500 words, 209 pages.)

TWISTY LITTLE PASSAGES

Welcome once again to *The Classic Dungeon Design Guide* series of supplements for old school Fantasy Role-Playing Games (FRPGs). This series is devoted to pulling together several decades' worth of Game Mastering advice, turning a maelstrom of historical reality, fantasy fiction, play experience and classic film into a clean, usable set of random tables for your dungeon designs and game play. This is volume three, and I assume from the beginning that you own and have read the initial companion volumes, *Book I* (CDDG1) and *Book II* (CDDG2). If you have not, you can certainly still derive value from this work, but you may get frustrated when I leap quickly through topics, cite prior sources, or repeatedly reference intricate subjects which have already been covered in deep detail earlier on. A little agility may be required on your part so that you do not become lost along the way.

So what is it that you will find chronicled in Book III? This is a supplement intended for the Game Master who wants to create the best, most amusing, most varied, most compelling, and most *amazing* dungeons in the world. You only need this book if you want your players to never forget you, to never forgive you, and to praise your insidious dungeons to the high heavens and deepest Hells forevermore. (Hopefully, that's just about all of us).

Specifically, this book is all about rooms and semi-realistic dungeon themes with an emphasis on intriguing details that make players want to explore. Too many "classic" dungeons feature a mix of about 10 different room types (guardroom, storeroom, vault, secret room, monster lair, etc.) with only minor variations on a very basic theme, and I want to fix that. We will dive into history, folklore, architecture, weird fiction, spelunking lore, and more as we make sure that every possible room type is considered at length and offered to you in an easily used set of random tables for rapid and sensible dungeon design.

Herein, I will give you an absolutely disgusting amount of information about room types that you can use to distinguish and improve all of your maps and dungeon floorplans, whether they be strongholds, crypts, temples, magical labyrinths, haunted houses or cave systems. All of those archetypal designs are covered in detail here. We already treated this topic glancingly in Books I and II, particularly with the Purely Random Room Generation system. There I provided you with lists of hundreds of room types, laid out for D100 percentile rolls. You could roll up guardrooms, storerooms, halls, cells, and treasure vaults with ease. Pretty great, right?

Well, I heard back from a lot of people over the years that they didn't like the fact that I listed the room types with no definitions whatsoever. I also heard that they didn't know what an ambulatory was, much less a buttery or a salt room (go figure). I encouraged many a fan and fellow Game Master to hit the books, to go online and to look for their own answers. Unlearn what you have learned, do or do not, there is no try, am I right? But the retorts came back that I should write yet another monstrously-paginated guide detailing all of the different room types from a dungeon designer's perspective.

And here we are.

As I conducted my "room research" over the years, I gradually came to realize a few things:

[1] Not Enough Rooms: In writing Book One, I very clearly hadn't provided *nearly* enough room types for you to play with. I gave GMs there about 500 room classifications, but in playing more dungeon modules, reading more novels, and plowing through more architectural encyclopedias I realized that I had missed about 800 subtypes which should have been included. Many of these were contingent upon archetype, a unique mix of fantasy and reality, or highly specialized. All of these differentiators needed to be detailed.

[2] Too Many Time Periods: This kind of guide was actually needed, because many people were getting confused over what types of rooms would exist in a magical medieval setting, vs. room types that only exist in modern industrial times. It was a lot of work to reconfigure reality to fit the fantasy milieu in a meaningful and coherent manner. People were using the same room types over and over again, but no one was actually looking at classical Roman ruins, ancient Egyptian temples, medieval nunneries or tholos tombs to figure out how these things were actually constructed. In other words, the game that should always be dedicated to honoring the best of the past had devolved to the point that it was only honoring the past of itself.

[3] Not Enough Modern Compendiums: There were cultures and time periods that had unique names for rooms, and unique types of rooms, that would be fascinating to put into an FRPG setting. But most of that information was hidden away in academic books that were out of print.

[4] Lacking Verisimilitude: There were next to zero quality guidelines for Game Masters in regard to designing historically-based dungeon floor plans in a reasonable manner, as opposed to just creating a funhouse dungeon with random rooms everywhere. And, most distressingly:

[5] A Distinct Lack of Dungeon Lore: For a game that's supposed to be all about dungeons, there was very little information on the history and tangibility of realistic dungeons proper, what they were, why they existed, or summaries on how to replicate them and use their most interesting details in a fantasy setting.

So, the 40-page, 10,000-word supplement I was initially going to write gradually blossomed over the years to encompass close to 80,000 words demanding 270+ pages. All of the in-depth research work has been done for you; the creative endeavors remain for you to indulge in.

So what will you find here *now*? Basically, all of the fruits of my research are now offered to you in a succinct and organized format. Here you'll find the largest selection of dungeon rooms ever written, presented as a massive master table of over 1,300 selections. You'll find an extensive list of castle types, dozens of floor plans, lists of real-world dungeons and tombs, and lots of advice on turning wild random dungeon design results into practical layouts ready for play. What you won't find here is a list of potential dungeon room *contents*. We've already covered that to a basic degree in Book I, and with special depth in Book II (which is solely devoted to that topic). But as an extra bonus, you'll also find a nifty appendix at the back that ties the dungeon design systems in all three *Dungeon Design Guide* books into a single master system, which you can use to create any dungeon you've ever desired with just this trilogy and a couple of ten-sided dice. We're all equipped. The Dvergar caravans are ready to depart for the dungeons deep. So let's get moving!

CHAPTER II:
DUNGEON ROOMS

HOW TO USE THIS BOOK

So what can you do to ensure that your dungeon has the maximum amount of variety and unusual locations? Simply, you need to maximize the number of room types available for your consideration. But this really shouldn't just be a completely random hodgepodge, from laboratory to bathroom to arena and back again; you need a way to control the randomness of the results, using thematic constraints as discussed in Book I of *The Classic Dungeon Design Guide*.

In Book I, The Cyclopedia of Dungeon Rooms, we touched on the idea of how the vast majority of dungeons can be classified as belonging to one of six major archetypes: **[1]** Cave Systems, **[2]** Dungeons (or Prisons), **[3]** "Haunted" Manor Houses, **[4]** Strongholds (or Castles), **[5]** Temples or **[6]** Tombs. Each of these archetypes had a random selection of room names, for example (for Dungeons) ranging from Abattoir to Workpit. That's a good system for naming rooms at random, but it doesn't really tell you anything about the room or what it's meant to be. What do you do when you need more detail and guidance before you can design your new room concept?

Enter the Labyrinth Lexicon. This chapter provides you with an extreme expansion of Book I's random generation system. You can now decide how much detail you want to add to your dungeon creation process. Book I's simple and abstract system is best used when you just want to come up with a room name and make all of the details yourself. It's certainly useful, but sometimes it's not enough. (For example, new players will be charmed by whatever you throw at them, but veteran players will express frustration if unusual features in the dungeon turn out to be design shortcuts rather than deep and explorable features that reward player discovery.) The far more complete Labyrinth Lexicon system by contrast will come in handy when you want to know the random room's size, description, unique distinctions, a bit of detail, and the room's

relation to other rooms throughout the dungeon level.

There are several different ways that you can use the Labyrinth Lexicon, depending on how much of the heavy lifting you want to do yourself and how much you want the random generation systems to take the wheel. You will find that there are three general approaches that you can take toward using the Labyrinth Lexicon, which we can term the Hard Way, the Middle Path, and the Easy Shortcut.

THE MASTER'S WAY

The most "hands on" way to use the Lexicon is to read through on your own, until you find an interesting-sounding and mysterious room type that you want to use. No dice are required; just scan, select and go.

Refer also to *The Classic Dungeon Design Guide, Book I,* particularly the section entitled Thematic Sub-Regions for Dungeon Levels. That special system will allow you to (for example) roll up a Temple dungeon level with branching Tomb and Stronghold areas.

THE JOURNEYMAN'S PATH

The intermediate approach involves using a pre-existing dungeon map, and coming up with a randomly-selected function for a room which has no description. Where do these dungeon maps come from? Basically, they're from six different selection paths:

[1] Your Own Map. If you've drawn up your own dungeon map, but you don't know how to populate it, you can roll on the Lexicon tables to help you out. You just need to decide if your map is a Cave System, Dungeon, Manor House, Stronghold, Temple or Tomb and roll on the appropriate column for logical selection.

[2] A Classic Dungeon Module Map. This is a fun method to use with veteran players especially, because they might recognize your source material and still be surprised by the unusual changes they find at every turn. You just pull an old dungeon module off your bookshelf (or your hard drive) and look at the keyed and numbered map, but nothing else. So if you have a map of the Hill Fort of the Highland Giant Chief, or The Moathouse in the Borderwilds, or Gray Mist Mountain or whatever, just gauge the size of each room — Tiny, Small, Medium, Large, or Huge, as discussed in the next section — and keep rolling randomly until you find a new room description that makes sense. This "remixing" process keeps the old dungeons fresh, by keeping the maps and scrubbing out the old contents to concoct a new adventure setting.

[3] Output from a Random Dungeon Generator. Refer to Book I, Chapter 5, Section 4 for general information on these online random map generation systems. You can also search on Google for "random dungeon generator" and see what new stuff comes up; programmers are creating interesting new map creation methods all the time. Make a random numbered map, print it, and fill it using the Lexicon.

[4] Dungeon Geomorphs. These are the rearrangeable print map sections, which can be connected to one another and/or rotated to create new dungeon layouts quickly. The original ones were created by TSR in the 1970s, and you can find them compiled in print as product 9048. On various publisher websites, you can also check out (unaffiliated with Wonderland Imprints) the Dungeons in Blue series, the Inked Adventures Hand-Drawn Geomorph Tiles, and similar products to create quick geomorphic layouts. Just print, number the rooms, and use the Lexicon herein to generate the room types.

[5] Someone Else's Dungeon. There are many erstwhile Game Masters out there who generously share their own maps online. Do a Google (Large) image search for "cool dungeon map," print out your favorite, and start rolling up room types using the Lexicon.

[6] A Real-World Locale. This option takes a bit of research, but you can find real-world castles, temples, tombs, and other useful floor plans everywhere you like. I provide a nice selection of useful places (such as the Palace of Versailles) later on in this book. The details I can provide you here are necessarily partial, but feel free to go looking for more detailed real-world lore online!

THE PRENTICE'S SHORTCUT

The easiest way to use the Lexicon is to just take 1D1000 and start rolling on the Lexicon Table without rhyme or reason. The results might not always be great, because random is random; but just keep rolling until you're satisfied with the results. You're 100% guaranteed a new dungeon design that will be like no other in the world!

Making sense of the random results will cause you to flex your creative muscles, and you will find that half of the dungeon writes itself due to the justifications which all of the random room transitions require.

DETERMINING ROOM SIZES

Whichever use method you decide upon, before you can effectively use the Labyrinth Lexicon for random dungeon room generation you need to know the codes for room size. The Lexicon uses the following simple system to classify all rooms into five size-based thematic clusters: Tiny, Small, Medium, Large and Huge.

~

Tiny: This is the smallest size of room that is still worthwhile as being considered separately from other rooms. If you're using a piece of graph paper for your dungeon map, and the scale of that map is 1 square = 10', then a Tiny room fills 1 or 2 squares. That could mean a square cell (10'x10'), or a small rectangular area (10'x20'), or an irregularly-shaped area of 200 sq. ft. or less.

Small: A Small room usually has few furnishings, and only a few monsters (if any). The space is too small for ranged combat, since melee range occurs by default. A Small room fills 3 to 7 squares at the 10' scale. That could mean a square room of 20'x20', a rectangular room that's 15'x30', or an irregularly-shaped area of 300 to 700 sq. ft.

Medium: In an average dungeon, most of the closely-packed rooms will be Medium in size. There might a bit of ranged combat or spell casting at the beginning of an encounter, but due to the cramped conditions melee will quickly follow. A Medium room fills 8 to 19 squares at the 10' scale. That could mean a square room of 30'x30', a rectangular room that's 20'x40', or an irregularly-shaped area of 800 to 1,900 sq. ft.

Large: Large rooms tend to be major encounter areas, set pieces, or central locales with many passageways and niches branching off from them. There is enough room for ranged combat and troop maneuverability, but things are still close enough that a quick charge will close the distance. A Large room fills 20 to 50 squares at the 10' scale. That could mean a square room of 50'x50', a rectangular room that's 30'x70', or an irregularly-shaped area of 2,000 to 5,000 sq. ft.

Huge: This is the largest type of space that I recommend for most dungeons, and if you're using random generation you will want to keep these areas at a minimum (to avoid from filling your map too quickly). A Huge room fills 51 to 100 squares at the 10' scale. That could mean a square room of 80'x80' or 100'x100', a rectangular room that's 60'x120', or an irregularly-shaped area of 5,100 to 10,000 sq. ft.

(As always, subterranean rooms in the game world are larger than they would be in real life.)

~

So how do these sizes determine your dungeon map design? That's entirely dependent on whether you already have a map that you're populating with details, or if you're using the Labyrinth Lexicon to design the dungeon for you.

If you have an existing map, then you can count the number of squares in each room before you roll the dice. For example, if your dungeon room is 16 squares, that's a Medium room based on the descriptions I provided above. Therefore you would roll 1D1000 in the Labyrinth Lexicon tables and keep rolling until you came up with a room that you like that has the "Medium" classification. Or, if you don't want to reroll at all, you can simply read through the Lexicon beginning with the room type that you rolled, and then read down through further entries until you reach one that is designated as Medium.

If you don't have a map yet, and you are now drawing one based on what the Labyrinth Lexicon is telling you, then you just roll 1D1000 and decide on a specific size based on (a) what you want your map to look like and (b) how much space you have on your paper. Consider the following example room type from the Lexicon:

Annex Warren

(Tiny, Small, or Medium)

A poorly-planned excavation (abandoned due to imminent collapse?) adjacent to a cave or cavern.

The room name appears first, in bold. Then we have the parenthetical notation (Tiny, Small, or Medium). This means that an Annex Warren (by definition) will never be Large or Huge. So which of the three possible sizes do you choose? I usually recommend going with Medium if you don't know what to do. Or, you can decide at random, for example using 1D6 (1 or 2 = Tiny, 3 or 4 = Small, 5 or 6 = Medium). Hereafter you will find a handy summary including all of the information above, so you can determine the room size of any location at a glance. You'll probably find that you memorize this information once you use the Lexicon a few dozen times.

TINY ROOM DESIGNATIONS

Area in Square Footage: 50' to 200'

Area in 10' x 10' Map Squares: 1 or 2

Example Room Dimensions:

- ❖ 7' Diameter Circle (<1 square)
- ❖ 10' x 10' Square (1 square)
- ❖ 10' x 20' Rectangle (2 squares)

SMALL ROOM DESIGNATIONS

Area in Square Footage: 201' to 600'

Area in 10' x 10' Map Squares: 3 to 6

Example Room Dimensions:

- ❖ 20' Diameter Circle (~3 squares)
- ❖ 10' x 40' Rectangle (4 squares)
- ❖ 20' x 20' Square (4 squares)
- ❖ 15' x 30' Rectangle (4.5 squares)
- ❖ 25' x 25' Square (5.25 squares)
- ❖ 20' x 30' Rectangle (6 squares)

MEDIUM ROOM DESIGNATIONS

Area in Square Footage: 601' to 1,200'

Area in 10' x 10' Map Squares: 7 to 12

Example Room Dimensions:

- ❖ 30' Diameter Circle (~7 squares)
- ❖ 20' x 40' Rectangle (8 squares)
- ❖ 30' x 30' Square (9 squares)
- ❖ 20' x 50' Rectangle (10 squares)
- ❖ 25' x 40' Rectangle (10 squares)
- ❖ 30' x 40' Rectangle (12 squares)

LARGE ROOM DESIGNATIONS

Area in Square Footage: 1,201' to 4,000'

Area in 10' x 10' Map Squares: 13 to 40

Example Room Dimensions:

- ❖ 40' Diameter Circle (~12.5 squares)
- ❖ 40' x 40' Square (16 squares)
- ❖ 30' x 60' Rectangle (18 squares)
- ❖ 30' x 70' Rectangle (21 squares)
- ❖ 50' x 50' Square (25 squares)
- ❖ 60' Diameter Circle (~28 squares)
- ❖ 40' x 80' Rectangle (32 squares)

HUGE ROOM DESIGNATIONS

Area in Square Footage: 4,001' to 10,000'

Area in 10' x 10' Map Squares: 41 to 100

Example Room Dimensions:

- ❖ 50' x 90' Rectangle (45 squares)
- ❖ 70' x 70' Square (49 squares)
- ❖ 60' x 120' Rectangle (72 squares)
- ❖ 90' Diameter Circle (~63.5 squares)
- ❖ 80' x 80' Square (64 squares)
- ❖ 100' Diameter Circle (~78.5 squares)
- ❖ 70' x 120' Rectangle (84 squares)

DEFINING ROOMS AND CHAMBERS

So, you may still be wondering: What exactly is a room? That's easy, and the definition is deliberately gamist and unrealistic: A "room" is a keyed feature on your map, separated from other keyed features by some kind of space or transition area (e.g., a wall, door, archway, corridor, etc.). A "room" by this definition can be a bedchamber, cavern, or even a separate outbuilding adjacent to a castle ruin. If it has a number assigned to it, it's a room.

And what is a chamber? That's a little trickier. The term is too vague to be very useful here as a technical term. Various definitions are offered in the literature, and they are often conflicting. Some writers focus on security (the specific number of entrances, or archways vs. doors), while others focus on access (with rooms being encountered "earlier" and chambers being more interior). But there is no one true definition.

Therefore, the exact differentiation between a chamber and a room remains a common question of expert dispute, relating to any space's size, function, entryways, access, and other variables.

Herein, I dodge all of that technicality and move forward with a gamist Gygaxian approach: chambers are usually small, and rooms are usually medium-sized, with halls being larger than either. You can get more technical if you like, but I believe this general distinction fits very well within the game and the definitions for rooms given in printed dungeon scenarios.

DUNGEONS IN DECAY: ORIGINAL vs. CURRENT USE

Whenever you are designing a new dungeon randomly, you need to consider the conflicting concepts of the **Original Room Usage** (builder intent) and then also the **Current Room Usage** (use by the dungeon denizens).

The Original Room Usage is the purpose that the room was first designed for, and the Current Room Usage is what it is currently being used for. You can certainly have A = B whenever you want to, but this distinction can help you figure out why two strange room types might be adjacent to one another.

For example, let us say that a manor house was built for a wealthy family of wizards. There are three rooms adjacent to one another: A dining room, a library, and a guardroom. These are the Original Room Usage delineations.

Centuries later, the manor house might well still be standing (due to magic and repairs and repurposing), even though the wizards have long since died out. The dining room might be a storage room, filled with rubble and boxes; the library could be a wraith's lair, haunted by one of the former wizards; and the guardroom could be a treasure vault, where a madman stashed some gold and later died there, unable to part with his riches do to an ancestral curse.

When we stop to consider the Original and the Current use, we now have a brief story for each room's history, and we can also justify random results where (for example) a treasure vault appears adjacent to a dining room with no rhyme or reason.

As long as you make sure that your dungeons are old, partially destroyed (before the PCs ever even get there), repaired, repurposed, enlarged, and taken over by different generations of monsters and NPCs, you can easily turn random results into interesting bits of dungeon history.

As always, you can reroll results that simply don't work together at all; but I encourage you to ask yourself whether the "roll that just doesn't fit" is an Original Room Usage, or a Current Room Usage.

Why is that room type there, and what does it mean? That's for you (and the adventurous players) to figure out. Remember that you can always justify the existence of a strange room type by the inclusion of an even stranger monster!

~

Here is a brief set of examples to show the designation of seven original-intent room types, and some thoughts about what might happen to those rooms over time.

~

[1] Bedroom / Quarters: The room probably had one or more beds, and various furnishings (table, chair, mirror, armoire, chest, etc.). The room's comforts would fall to decay quickly if not cared for, and the room might be repurposed for storage, as a garbage pit, or even a prison.

[2] Guardroom: The room probably has good lines of sight, and/or peepholes in the doors, and/or a weapons rack. This makes an ideal monster lair, and some kind of intelligent monster may have converted the guardroom into a living area.

If the room was never converted and the guards were wiped out, there may well be hacked doors, splintered racks, bloodstains, etc.

[3] Library: The room would be filled with shelves, books, tables and light sources. The room could have caught fire, and turned into a scorched chamber filled with ashes; or the books could have been protected by a powerful NPC or monster; or the room might also now be used (by unintelligent monsters) as a warren, with the shelves serving as sub-lairs for families of beetles, slimes, spiders, or whatever.

[4] Pool or Fountain Room: The room had a source of fresh water originally, either naturally occurring or as a decoration.

After ruin, the fresh water would be in demand by monsters … either those who want to drink the water, or aquatic monsters who come up from below when the floor works decay. The room could be (for example) the crumbling entrance to an underground stream.

[5] Storeroom: The boxes could fall to ruin, or their contents could be plundered. The containers could be shoved aside to make room for bedding for humanoids, or to create a defensive barrier.

[6] Shrine Chamber: The shrine was originally devoted to a god, demon, or angel that was worshipped by wealthy and/or devout NPCs. Over time, the shrine might have been defaced by enemies, or protected by like-minded creatures, or it might have fallen into ruin while the original divine (or unholy) aura remains, giving the room a "strange feeling" and ambient light.

[7] Treasure Vault: The treasure is probably either plundered, or is guarded by a powerful monster who took the room over.

If the treasure was trapped, the discharge of the trap may have destroyed part of the room.

The room may have been reinforced, re-locked, or walled up and made secret and/or defensible.

(Etc.)

~

Use this guide as a general reference, so that you can repurpose rooms that "don't fit" into something that works for your overall dungeon design.

And remember, the Original Room Usage can always be "unknown" if you don't know why the room came to be ... that's history you can always come up with later when there is need.

(The D1000 tables for generating random rooms for each of the six major dungeon archetypes appear hereafter.)

CHAPTER III:
RANDOM ROOM TABLES

CAVE SYSTEM ROOMS

For random rooms appearing in a cave system, roll 1D1000 and consult the following table.

TABLE 1
CAVE SYSTEM ROOMS

[001 to 003] Abzu (Huge)

[004 to 006] Access Cave (Small or Medium)

[007 to 009] Access Cavern (Large)

[010 to 012] Acidic Cave (Small or Medium)

[013 to 015] Acidic Cavern (Large)

[016 to 017] Adamantite Delve (Medium or Large)

[018 to 020] Annex Warren (Tiny, Small, or Medium)

[021 to 023] Antecavern (Small or Medium)

[024 to 026] Antrum (Medium)

[027 to 029] Antrum Cavern (Small or Medium)

[030 to 032] Apse Cavelet (Small)

[033 to 035] Arena Cave (Medium or Large)

[036 to 038] Arena Cavern (Huge)

[039 to 040] Ash Pit (Small or Medium)

[041 to 042] Ashen Abyss (Large or Huge)

[043 to 045] Atrium Cave (Medium or Large)

[046 to 048] Atrium Cavern (Huge)

[049 to 051] Audience Cavern (Large or Huge)

[052 to 054] Augury Cave (Small or Medium)

[055 to 057] Auxiliary Cave (Small or Medium)

[058 to 060] Basalt Cave (Small or Medium)

[061 to 063] Basalt Cavern (Large or Huge)

[064 to 065] Biaw (Large or Huge)

[066 to 068] Blocked Cave (Small or Medium, but with accessible area Tiny)

[069 to 070] Blocked Cavern (Small or Medium, but with accessible area Tiny)

[071 to 073] Bone-Filled Cave (Small or Medium)

[074 to 076] Bone-Filled Cavern (Large or Huge)

[077 to 079] Boulder Cave (Small or Medium)

[080 to 082] Boulder Cavern (Large or Huge)

[083 to 084] Burrow (Tiny or Small)

[085] Burrow Maze (Huge)

[086 to 087] Burrow Warren (Large)

[088 to 090] Cave (Small or Medium)

[091 to 092] Cave of Ancestors (Small or Medium)

[093 to 095] Cave of Ashes (Small or Medium)

[096 to 098] Cave of Bones (Small or Medium)

[099 to 101] Cave of Columns (Small or Medium)

[102 to 104] Cave of Echoes (Small)

[105 to 107] Cave of Husks (Small or Medium)

[108 to 110] Cave of Meetings (Small or Medium)

[111 to 113] Cave of Paintings (Small or Medium)

[114 to 116] Cave of Pools (Small or Medium)

[117 to 119] Cave of Residual Magic, Elemental Air (Small, Medium, or Large)

[120 to 122] Cave of Residual Magic, Elemental Earth (Small, Medium, or Large)

[123 to 125] Cave of Residual Magic, Elemental Fire (Small, Medium, or Large)

[126 to 128] Cave of Residual Magic, Elemental Water (Small, Medium, or Large)

[129 to 131] Cave of Skulls (Small or Medium)

[132 to 134] Cave of Slaughter (Small or Medium)

[135 to 137] Cave of Stalactites (Small or Medium)

[138 to 139] Cave of Stalagmites (Small or Medium)

[140 to 142] Cave of the Dead (Small or Medium)

[143 to 145] Cave of Unmined Gemstones (Small or Medium)

[146 to 148] Cave of Unmined Metals, Adamantite (Small or Medium)

[149 to 151] Cave of Unmined Metals, Copper (Small or Medium)

[152 to 154] Cave of Unmined Metals, Electrum (Small or Medium)

[155 to 157] Cave of Unmined Metals, Gold (Small or Medium)

[158 to 160] Cave of Unmined Metals, Iron (Small or Medium)

[161 to 163] Cave of Unmined Metals, Lead (Small or Medium)

[164 to 166] Cave of Unmined Metals, Mithral (Small or Medium)

[167 to 169] Cave of Unmined Metals, Platinum (Small or Medium)

[170 to 172] Cave of Unmined Metals, Silver (Small or Medium)

[173 to 175] Cave of Unmined Metals, Tin (Small or Medium)

[176 to 180] Cave of Unmined Metals, Various (Small or Medium)

[181 to 182] Cave Temple (Small or Medium)

[183 to 185] Cavelet (Tiny or Small)

[186 to 188] Cavern (Large or Huge)

[189 to 191] Cavern of Ancestral Memory (Large or Huge)

[192 to 194] Cavern of Ashes (Large or Huge)

[195 to 197] Cavern of Bones (Large or Huge)

[198 to 200] Cavern of Columns (Large or Huge)

[201 to 203] Cavern of Echoes (Large or Huge)

[204 to 206] Cavern of Husks (Large or Huge)

[207 to 209] Cavern of Slaughter (Large or Huge)

[210 to 212] Cavern of the Gatherings (Large or Huge)

[213 to 215] Cavern of the Piping Ones (Large or Huge)

[216 to 218] Cavern Temple (Large or Huge)

[219 to 221] Cavity (Tiny, Small, Medium, or Large)

[222 to 223] Cesspit (Tiny, Small, or Medium)

[224 to 226] Cesspit Cavern (Large or Huge)

[227 to 228] Cesspool (Tiny, Small, or Medium)

[229 to 231] Cesspool Cavern (Large or Huge)

[232 to 233] Chasm (Large or Huge)

[234 to 236] Chiming Cave (Small or Medium)

[237 to 238] Clay Cave (Small or Medium)

[239 to 241] Clay-Filled Cavern (Large or Huge)

[242 to 244] Coal Cave (Small or Medium)

[245 to 247] Coal Cavern (Large or Huge)

[248 to 250] Collapsed Cavern (Large or Huge)

[251 to 252] Combat Pit (Small or Medium)

[253 to 254] Concealed Cave (Small or Medium)

[255 to 257] Concealed Cavern (Large or Huge)

[258 to 260] Copper Cave (Small or Medium)

[261 to 263] Copper Cavern (Large or Huge)

[264 to 265] Crawlspace (Tiny, Small, or Medium)

[266] Crevice (Tiny or Small)

[267 to 269] Crumbling Cave (Small or Medium)

[270 to 272] Crumbling Cavern (Large or Huge)

[273 to 275] Crystal Cave (Small or Medium)

[276 to 278] Crystal Garden (Large or Huge)

[279 to 280] Cul-de-Sac (Tiny or Small)

[281 to 282] Cyst (Small, Medium, or Large)

[283 to 285] Dead End Cave (Small)

[286 to 288] Death Cavern (Large or Huge)

[289 to 290] Delve (Large or Huge)

[291 to 292] Den (Small or Medium)

[293 to 294] Diorite Cave (Small or Medium)

[295 to 297] Diorite Cavern (Large or Huge)

[298 to 299] Drowning Pool (Small or Medium)

[300 to 301] Dry Well (Small or Medium, size being vertical)

[302 to 303] Dueling Pit (Small or Medium)

[304] Dueling Pit Matrix (Small)

[305 to 306] Dust Pit (Tiny, Small, or Medium)

[307 to 309] Echoing Cave (Tiny, Small, or Medium)

[310 to 312] Echoing Cavern (Large or Huge)

[313 to 314] Egg Chamber (Small, Medium, or Large)

[315 to 317] Electrum Cave (Small or Medium)

[318 to 320] Electrum Cavern (Large or Huge)

[321 to 323] Elemental Vortex, Air (Tiny, Small, Medium, Large, or Huge)

[324 to 326] Elemental Vortex, Ash (Tiny, Small, Medium, Large, or Huge)

[327 to 329] Elemental Vortex, Dust (Tiny, Small, Medium, Large, or Huge)

[330 to 332] Elemental Vortex, Earth (Tiny, Small, Medium, Large, or Huge)

[333 to 334] Elemental Vortex, Fire (Tiny, Small, Medium, Large, or Huge)

[335 to 337] Elemental Vortex, Ice (Tiny, Small, Medium, Large, or Huge)

[338 to 340] Elemental Vortex, Lightning (Tiny, Small, Medium, Large, or Huge)

[341 to 344] Elemental Vortex, Magma (Tiny, Small, Medium, Large, or Huge)

[345 to 347] Elemental Vortex, Mist (Tiny, Small, Medium, Large, or Huge)

[348 to 350] Elemental Vortex, Steam (Tiny, Small, Medium, Large, or Huge)

[351 to 353] Elemental Vortex, Water (Tiny, Small, Medium, Large, or Huge)

[354 to 355] Enchanted Grotto (Small, Medium, or Large)

[356 to 357] Enclave (Large or Huge)

[358 to 359] Excavation (Large or Huge)

[360] Firepit (Tiny or Small)

[361 to 362] Fissure (Small, Medium, or Large)

[363 to 364] Fissure, Ceiling (Small, Medium, or Large)

[365 to 366] Fissure, Wall / Fissure Vault (Medium, Large, or Huge)

[367 to 368] Flooded Cave (Small or Medium)

[369 to 371] Flooded Cavern (Large or Huge)

[372 to 374] Food Cave (Tiny, Small, or Medium)

[375 to 376] Formicary (Large or Huge)

[377] Foss (Medium, Large, or Huge)

[378 to 379] Fountain Grotto (Small, Medium, or Large)

[380 to 381] Fungal Garden (Medium, Large, or Huge)

[382 to 384] Gallery (Cavern) (Large or Huge)

[385 to 387] Gas-Filled Cave (Small or Medium)

[388 to 390] Gas-Filled Cavern (Large or Huge)

[391 to 393] Gem Lode (Tiny or Small)

[394 to 396] Gemstone Cave (Small or Medium)

[397 to 399] Gemstone Cavern (Large or Huge)

[400 to 402] Geode Cave (Tiny or Small)

[403 to 405] Geode Cavern (Medium or Large)

[406] Geode Mine (Tiny, Small, Medium, or Large)

[407 to 409] Geothermal Cave (Small or Medium)

[410 to 412] Geothermal Cavern (Large or Huge)

[413 to 415] Geyser Cave (Small or Medium)

[416 to 418] Geyser Cavern (Large or Huge)

[419 to 421] Glittering Cave (Small or Medium)

[422 to 424] Glittering Gallery (Large or Huge)

[435 to 427] Gold Cave (Small or Medium)

[428 to 430] Gold Cavern (Large or Huge)

[431 to 433] Grand Cavern (Huge)

[434 to 436] Great Adamantite Delve (Huge)

[437 to 438] Gren (Tiny)

[439 to 440] Grof (Tiny or Small)

[441 to 442] Grot (Tiny or Small)

[443 to 444] Grotto (Medium or Large)

[445 to 446] Guano Cave (Small or Medium)

[447 to 449] Guano Cavern (Small)

[450 to 452] Guard Cave (Small or Medium)

[453 to 455] Guard Cavern (Large or Huge)

[456 to 458] Gypsum Cave (Small or Medium)

[459 to 461] Gypsum Cavern (Large or Huge)

[462 to 463] Hatchery (Small, Medium, or Large)

[464 to 465] Hell Mouth (Medium, Large, or Huge)

[466 to 467] Hellir (Small, Medium, or Large)

[468 to 470] Hole (Tiny or Small)

[471 to 472] Hollow (Tiny or Small)

[473] Hollowed Trash Heap (Large or Huge)

[474] Hollowed Wall (Tiny, Small, or Medium)

[475 to 476] Hylr (Small or Medium)

[477 to 478] Ice Cave (Small or Medium)

[479 to 480] Ice Cavern (Large or Huge)

[481 to 482] Idol Grotto (Small, Medium, or Large)

[483 to 485] Iron Cave (Small or Medium)

[485 to 488] Iron Cavern (Large or Huge)

[489 to 491] Jewel Cave (Small or Medium)

[492 to 493] Jewel Cavern (Large or Huge)

[494 to 496] Labyrinthine Cavern (Large or Huge)

[497 to 498] Labyrinthine Warrens (Huge)

[499 to 502] Lair (Tiny, Small, Medium, Large, or Huge)

[503 to 505] Lava / Magma Cave (Small or Medium)

[506 to 507] Lava / Magma Cavern (Large or Huge)

[508 to 509] Leaching Cesspool (Small, Medium, or Large)

[510 to 512] Lead Cave (Small or Medium)

[513 to 515] Lead Cavern (Large or Huge)

[516] Leap (Tiny, Small, or Medium)

[517 to 519] Limestone Cave (Small or Medium)

[520 to 522] Limestone Cavern (Small or Medium)

[523 to 525] Littered Cave (Small or Medium)

[526 to 528] Littered Cavern (Large or Huge)

[529 to 531] Low-Ceilinged Cave (Small or Medium)

[532 to 533] Low-Ceilinged Cavern (Large or Huge)

[534 to 536] Majestic Aerie (Huge)

[537 to 538] Mass Grave (Large or Huge)

[539 to 540] Mine (Large or Huge)

[541 to 542] Mine Shaft (Small or Medium)

[543 to 545] Mined Cave (Small or Medium)

[546 to 548] Mined Cavern (Large or Huge)

[549 to 551] Misty Cave (Small or Medium)

[552 to 554] Misty Cavern (Large or Huge)

[555 to 557] Mold-Filled Cave (Small)

[558 to 560] Mold-Filled Cavern (Medium or Large)

[561 to 563] Moss-Filled Cave (Small or Medium)

[564 to 565] Moss-Filled Cavern (Large or Huge)

[566 to 568] Mud Cave (Small or Medium)

[569 to 571] Mud Cavern (Large or Huge)

[572 to 574] Mushroom Cave (Small or Medium)

[575 to 576] Mushroom Forest (Large or Huge)

[577 to 578] Natatorium (Large or Huge)

[579 to 580] Natural Amphitheater (Large or Huge)

[581 to 583] Nest (Tiny, Small, or Medium)

[584 to 585] Nether (Large or Huge)

[586 to 587] Netherworld (Huge)

[588 to 589] Netherworld Descent (Huge)

[590 to 592] Niched Cave (Small or Medium)

[593 to 595] Niched Cavern (Large or Huge)

[596 to 598] Oracular Cave (Small or Medium)

[599 to 601] Oracular Cavern (Large or Huge)

[602 to 604] Ossuary Cave (Small or Medium)

[605 to 607] Ossuary Cavern (Large or Huge)

[608 to 609] Overlook (Small or Medium)

[610 to 612] Painted Cavern (Large or Huge)

[613 to 615] Phosphorescent Cave (Small or Medium)

[616] Phosphorescent Cavern (Large or Huge)

[617 to 618] Pit (Tiny or Small)

[619 to 621] Pit Cave (Small or Medium)

[622 to 624] Pit Cavern (Large or Huge)

[625 to 627] Platinum Cave (Small or Medium)

[628 to 629] Platinum Cavern (Large or Huge)

[630 to 631] Plunge (Small, Medium, or Large)

[632 to 634] Pool (Tiny, Small, or Medium)

[635 to 637] Pool Cave (Small or Medium)

[638 to 640] Pool Cavern (Large or Huge)

[641 to 644] Puffball Cave (Small or Medium)

[645 to 646] Puffball Cavern (Large or Huge)

[647 to 649] Quarry (Small, Medium, or Large)

[650 to 652] Quarry Cavern (Large or Huge)

[653 to 654] Quarry Shaft (Small or Medium)

[655 to 657] Quicksand Cave (Small or Medium)

[658 to 659] Quicksand Cavern (Large or Huge)

[660 to 662] Quicksand Pit (Tiny, Small, or Medium)

[663 to 664] Reflecting Pool (Tiny, Small, or Medium)

[665 to 666] Refuse Pit (Tiny, Small, or Medium)

[667 to 668] Reservoir (Large or Huge)

[669 to 670] Roost (Tiny, Small, or Medium)

[671 to 673] Rubble-Filled Cave (Small or Medium)

[674 to 676] Rubble-Filled Cavern (Large or Huge)

[677 to 679] Runic Cave (Small or Medium)

[680 to 682] Runic Cavern (Large or Huge)

[683 to 684] Sacrificial Grotto (Small or Medium)

[685 to 686] Sacrificial Pool (Tiny, Small, or Medium)

[687 to 689] Salt Cave (Small or Medium)

[690 to 692] Salt Cavern (Large or Huge)

[693 to 694] Salt Mine (Medium, Large, or Huge)

[695 to 697] Sand Cave (Small or Medium)

[698 to 699] Sand Cavern (Large or Huge)

[700 to 701] Sandpit (Small, Medium, or Large)

[702 to 704] Sandstone Cave (Small or Medium)

[705 to 707] Sandstone Cavern (Large or Huge)

[708 to 709] Secret Cyst (Tiny, Small, Medium, or Large)

[710 to 711] Secret Grotto (Small or Medium)

[712 to 714] Shaft Cave (Small or Medium)

[715 to 717] Shaft Cavern (Large or Huge)

[718 to 720] Shunned Cave (Small or Medium)

[721 to 723] Shunned Cavern (Large or Huge)

[724 to 726] Silver Cave (Small or Medium)

[727 to 728] Silver Cavern (Large or Huge)

[729 to 731] Sinkhole (Small, Medium, Large, or Huge)

[732 to 733] Skull Cavern (Large or Huge)

[734] Slave Pit (Tiny, Small, or Medium)

[735 to 737] Slime Cave (Small or Medium)

[738 to 739] Slime Cavern (Large or Huge)

[740 to 742] Sloping Cave (Small or Medium)

[743 to 745] Sloping Cavern (Large or Huge)

[746 to 747] Sludge Pit (Tiny, Small, or Medium)

[748 to 750] Spur Cave (Small or Medium)

[751 to 753] Spur Cavern (Large or Huge)

[754 to 756] Stalactite Cave (Small or Medium)

[757 to 759] Stalactite Cavern (Large or Huge)

[760 to 762] Stalagmite Cave (Small)

[763 to 765] Stalagmite Cavern (Large or Huge)

[766 to 768] Steam Cave (Small or Medium)

[769 to 771] Steam Cavern (Large or Huge)

[772 to 774] Storage Cave (Small or Medium)

[775 to 777] Storage Cavern (Large or Huge)

[778 to 780] Stream Cave (Small or Medium)

[781 to 783] Stream Cavern (Large or Huge)

[784 to 785] Stricture (Tiny or Small)

[786 to 788] Submerged Cave (Small or Medium)

[789 to 790] Submerged Cavern (Large or Huge)

[791 to 793] Sulfur Cave (Small or Medium)

[794 to 796] Sulfur Cavern (Large or Huge)

[797 to 798] Tar Pit (Small, Tiny, or Medium)

[799 to 801] Temple Cavern (Large or Huge)

[802 to 803] Torture Pit(s) (Small, Medium, or Large, with Large implying multiple pits)

[804 to 806] Treasure Cave (Small or Medium)

[807 to 808] Treasure Cavern (Large or Huge)

[809 to 810] Underground Lake (Large or Huge)

[811] Underground Mausoleum (Huge)

[812 to 813] Underground Palace (Huge)

[814 to 815] Underground Pyramid (Huge)

[816 to 817] Underground River (Huge)

[818 to 819] Underground Swamp (Huge)

[820] Underground Ziggurat (Huge)

[821 to 822] Undervault (Large or Huge)

[823 to 825] Underwater Cave (Small or Medium)

[826 to 828] Underwater Cavern (Large or Huge)

[829 to 831] Unstable Cave (Small or Medium)

[832 to 835] Unstable Cavern (Large or Huge)

[836 to 838] Vaulted Cave (Small or Medium)

[839 to 841] Vaulted Cavern (Large or Huge)

[842 to 843] Verdigris Cave (Small or Medium)

[844 to 845] Verdigris Cavern (Large or Huge)

[846 to 847] Vertical Cave (Small or Medium)

[848 to 849] Vertical Cavern (Large or Huge)

[850 to 851] Volcanic Cave (Small or Medium)

[852 to 853] Volcanic Cavern (Large or Huge)

[854 to 855] Warren (Tiny or Small)

[856 to 858] Warrens (Medium, Large, or Huge)

[859 to 861] Water Cave (Small or Medium)

[862 to 864] Water Cavern (Large or Huge)

[865 to 867] Waterfall Cavern (Large or Huge)

[868 to 870] Webbed Cave (Small or Medium)

[871 to 873] Webbed Cavern (Large or Huge)

[874 to 876] Wharf Cavern (Large)

[877 to 879] Whirlpool Cave (Small or Medium)

[880 to 882] Whirlpool Cavern (Large or Huge)

[883 to 885] Winch Cavern (Medium or Large)

[886 to 888] Winch Pit (Tiny or Small)

[889 to 891] Wine Cave (Small or Medium)

[892 to 894] Wine Cavern (Large or Huge)

[895 to 897] Workpit (Tiny or Small)

[898 to 900] Ziggurat Cavern (Large or Huge)

[901 to 909] Cavern Sub-Region: Dungeon Chambers. Roll on the Dungeon Room Table for the next 1D4+1 rooms (rerolling any results of 901 to 000), and then return to this table.

[910 to 915] Cavern Sub-Region: Dungeon Vaults. Roll on the Dungeon Room Table for the next 2D4 rooms (rerolling any results of 901 to 000), and then return to this table.

[916 to 918] Cavern Sub-Region: Extensive Dungeon Vaults. Roll on the Dungeon Room Table for the next 2D6+1 rooms (rerolling any results of 901 to 000), and then return to this table.

[919 to 927] Cavern Sub-Region: Manorial Chambers. Roll on the Manor House Room Table for the next 1D4+1 rooms (rerolling any results of 901 to 000), and then return to this table.

[928 to 933] Cavern Sub-Region: Furnished Cavern Lair. Roll on Manor House Room Table for the next 2D4 rooms (rerolling any results of 901 to 000), and then return to this table.

[934 to 936] Cavern Sub-Region: Underground Manor. Roll on Manor House Room Table for the next 2D6+1 rooms (rerolling any results of 901 to 000), and then return to this table.

[937 to 945] Cavern Sub-Region: Stronghold Caves. Roll on the Stronghold Room Table for the next 1D4+1 rooms (rerolling any results of 901 to 000), and then return to this table.

[946 to 951] Cavern Sub-Region: Fortified Caverns. Roll on the Stronghold Room Table for the next 2D4 rooms (rerolling any results of 901 to 000), and then return to this table.

[952 to 954] Cavern Sub-Region: Monster Stronghold. Roll on the Stronghold Room Table for the next 2D6+1 rooms (rerolling any results of 901 to 000), and then return to this table.

[955 to 963] Cavern Sub-Region: Cavern Fane. Roll on the Temple Room Table for the next 1D4+1 rooms (rerolling any results of 901 to 000), and then return to this table.

[964 to 969] Cavern Sub-Region: Sacred Caverns. Roll on the Temple Room Table for the next 2D4 rooms (rerolling any results of 901 to 000), and then return to this table.

[970 to 972] Cavern Sub-Region: Subterranean Temple. Roll on the Temple Room Table for the next 2D6+1 rooms (rerolling any results of 901 to 000), and then return to this table.

[973 to 981] Cavern Sub-Region: Chthonic Crypt. Roll on the Tomb Room Table for the next 1D4+1 rooms (rerolling any results of 901 to 000), and then return to this table.

[982 to 987] Cavern Sub-Region: Burial Caverns. Roll on the Tomb Room Table for the next 2D4 rooms (rerolling any results of 901 to 000), and then return to this table.

[988 to 990] Cavern Sub-Region: Excavated Tombs. Roll on the Tomb Room Table for the next 2D6+1 rooms (rerolling any results of 901 to 000), and then return to this table.

[991 to 995] Cavern Sub-Region: Eerie Caves. Roll on the Evocative Random Rooms Table (refer to *The Classic Dungeon Design Guide, Book I*) for the next 1D4+1 rooms (rerolling any results of 901 to 000), and then return to this table.

[996 to 998] Cavern Sub-Region: Strange Caverns. Roll on the Evocative Random Rooms Table (refer to *The Classic Dungeon Design Guide, Book I*) for the next 2D4 rooms (rerolling any results of 901 to 000), and then return to this table.

[999 to 000] Cavern Sub-Region: Enigmatic Region. Roll on the Evocative Random Rooms Table (refer to *The Classic Dungeon Design Guide, Book I*) for the next 2D6+1 rooms (rerolling any results of 901 to 000), and then return to this table.

DUNGEON ROOMS

For random rooms appearing in a dungeon or prison environment, roll 1D1000 and consult the following table.

TABLE 2

DUNGEON ROOMS

[001 to 002] Abattoir (Small or Medium)

[003] Abreuvoir (Medium, Large, or Huge)

[004 to 005] Absis (Small)

[006] Aerarium / Ancient Aerary (Medium or Large)

[007] Aerarium Chamber (Small or Medium)

[008 to 009] Aerary (Medium or Large)

[010 to 011] Aerary Chamber (Small)

[012] Af-Hus (Tiny or Small)

[013] Ah Hwt / Ahu Hewet (Small or Medium)

[014] Air Chamber (Small)

[015 to 016] Air Room (Medium)

[017] Ala (Tiny or Small)

[018] Alae, plural (Medium or Large)

[019 to 020] Alcove (Tiny or Small)

[021 to 022] Alcove Succession (Medium or Large)

[023] Alhacena (Tiny or Small)

[024] Alhacena Succession (Medium or Large)

[025 to 026] Almonerium (Medium or Large)

[027] Almonry (Medium)

[028 to 029] Almonry Chamber (Small)

[030] Almonry Hall (Large)

[031 to 032] Altar Chamber (Small)

[033 to 034] Altar Room (Medium)

[035] Ambitus (Medium or Large, with a Tiny or Small enclosure)

[036] Ambry (Small or Medium)

[037 to 038] Ambry Chamber (Tiny or Small)

[039] Ambulatory (Medium)

[040 to 041] Ancestral Chamber (Small or Medium)

[042] Ancestral Hall (Large or Huge)

[043] Anddyri (Small, Medium, or Large)

[044 to 045] Annex (Tiny, Small, or Medium)

[046] Annex Labyrinth (Large or Huge)

[047 to 048] Antechamber (Small)

[049 to 050] Anteroom (Medium)

[051 to 052] Aperture (Tiny)

[053] Apotheca (Small or Medium)

[054 to 055] Apse (Small)

[056] Apse Room (Medium)

[057] Arboretum (Large)

[058 to 059] Archive (Medium, Large, or Huge)

[060] Arena (Medium, Large, or Huge)

[061 to 062] Armory (Medium)

[063] Armory and Forge (Large or Huge)

[064 to 065] Armory Chamber (Small)

[066 to 067] Arsenal (Large)

[068] Arsenal and Forge (Large or Huge)

[069] Arsenal Chamber (Small)

[070 to 071] Ash Pit (Small or Medium)

[071] Ashen Abyss (Large or Huge)

[073] Aslukku (Small or Medium)

[074] At Iwf / Atu Iwef (Medium or Large)

[075 to 076] Auxiliary Chamber (Tiny or Small)

[077] Auxiliary Room (Medium)

[078] Bailey (Medium, Large, or Huge)

[079 to 080] Balnea (Small or Medium)

[081] Balnearium (Small or Medium)

[082] Barbican (Large)

[083 to 084] Barracks (Medium or Large)

[085 to 086] Barracks Hall (Huge)

[087] Barrow (Small or Medium)

[088] Barrow Crypt (Small, Medium, or Large)

[089 to 090] Bastion (Medium or Large)

[091] Bawm (Small, Medium, or Large)

[092 to 093] Bay (Tiny or Small)

[094] Bay Succession (Medium or Large)

[095 to 096] Beast Crypt (Tiny, Small, or Medium)

[097 to 098] Beast Pit (Small or Medium)

[099] Belfry (Medium or Large)

[100] Biaw (Large or Huge)

[101] Bodega (Small)

[102] Bone House (Large or Huge)

[103 to 104] Bone Pit (Small or Medium)

[105 to 106] Bouleuterion (Large or Huge)

[107] Bourse (Small, Medium, or Large)

[108] Breezeway (Medium or Large)

[109 to 110] Burial Chamber (Tiny or Small)

[111 to 112] Burial Room (Medium)

[113 to 114] Burial Vault (Large or Huge)

[115] Burrow (Tiny or Small)

[116] Burrow Maze (Huge)

[117] Burrow Warren (Large)

[118] Buru (Small or Medium)

[119 to 120] Butchery (Small)

[121 to 122] Cache Chamber (Small)

[123] Cache Room (Medium or Large)

[124 to 125] Cage (Tiny, Small, or Medium)

[126] Cage Matrix (Large or Huge)

[127 to 128] Camba (Small or Medium)

[129] Carcer (Medium, Large, or Huge)

[130] Cascade Hall (Large or Huge)

[131] Cascade Room (Small)

[132] Casemate (Small or Medium)

[133] Catabulum (Medium or Large)

[134 to 135] Catacomb (Tiny or Small)

[136] Catacombs, plural

[137] Catacumba (Tiny or Small)

[138] Catacumbae, plural

[139] Cavea (Small, Medium, or Large)

[140 to 141] Cell (Tiny or Small)

[142 to 143] Cell Block (Medium or Large)

[144] Cellae, plural (Medium or Large)

[145] Cellar (Small or Medium)

[146 to 147] Cellarage (Large or Huge)

[148 to 149] Cellula (Tiny or Small)

[150] Cenotaph (Small)

[151 to 152] Ceremonial Chamber (Small)

[153] Ceremonial Hall (Large or Huge)

[154 to 155] Ceremonial Room (Medium or Large)

[156 to 157] Cesspit (Tiny, Small, or Medium)

[158] Cesspool (Tiny, Small, or Medium)

[159 to 160] Chamber (Small)

[161] Chamber Barrow (Small)

[162] Chamber of Catafalques (Small or Medium)

[163] Chamber Tomb (Small, Medium, or Large)

[64 to 165] Chambers, plural (Medium, Large, or Huge)

[166] Chandlery (Small or Medium)

[167] Chantier (Small, Medium, or Large)

[168] Char Cellar (Tiny, Small, or Medium)

[169 to 170] Charnel House (Medium, Large, or Huge)

[171] Chasm (Large or Huge)

[172] Chrismographion (Small)

[173] Chrismographium (Small)

[174 to 175] Cinerarium (Medium, Large, or Huge)

[176 to 177] Cistern (Small, Medium, Large, or Huge)

[178 to 179] Cistern Room (Small or Medium)

[180] Cloaca (Medium, Large, or Huge)

[181] Clockwork Room (Small or Medium)

[182 to 183] Coal Room (Small, Medium, or Large)

[184] Coemeterium, plural Coemeteria (Smell or Medium)

[185] Coldroom (Small or Medium)

[186 to 187] Collapsed Room (Small, Medium, or Large, with the accessible area being Tiny or Small)

[188] Colonnade Hall (Large or Huge)

[189 to 190] Colonnade Room (Medium)

[191 to 192] Combat Pit (Small or Medium)

[193] Commandery (Medium or Large)

[194 to 195] Common Room (Medium, Large, or Huge)

[196 to 197] Communal Quarters (Medium, Large, or Huge)

[198] Compluvium Chamber (Small)

[199] Compluvium Hall (Large)

[200] Compluvium Room (Medium)

[201 to 202] Concealed Chamber (Small)

[203 to 204] Concealed Room (Medium or Large)

[205 to 206] Conclave (Medium or Large)

[207] Conclavium (Medium or Large)

[208] Conditivum (Small or Medium)

[209 to 210] Conjuring Chamber (Small or Medium)

[211] Conservatory (Medium or Large)

[212 to 213] Control Room (Small or Medium)

[214] Corycaeum (Small, Medium, or Large)

[215] Counting Room (Small or Medium)

[216 to 217] Crawlspace (Tiny, Small, or Medium)

[218] Crematorium (Small or Medium)

[219 to 220] Crevice (Tiny or Small)

[221] Crowde (Tiny, Small, or Medium)

[222] Crypt (Tiny, Small, or Medium)

[223 to 224] Cubicle (Tiny)

[225] Cubicula, plural (Small, Medium, or Large)

[226 to 227] Cubiculum (Tiny or Small)

[228] Cubiculum Cineraria (Tiny)

[229] Cul-de-Sac (Tiny or Small)

[230 to 231] Cyst (Small, Medium, or Large)

[232] Cyzicene Hall (Large or Huge)

[233 to 234] Dais Chamber (Small or Medium)

[235 to 236] Dais Room (Medium or Large)

[237] Darkroom (Small, Medium, or Large)

[238 to 239] Dead End (Tiny or Small)

[240] Defiled Tomb (Small, Medium, or Large)

[241] Delve (Large or Huge)

[242 to 243] Den (Small or Medium)

[244] Depository (Medium or Large)

[245 to 246] Divination Chamber (Small)

[247] Divination Hall (Large or Huge)

[248 to 249] Divination Room (Medium)

[250 to 251] Domed Chamber (Small)

[252] Domed Hall (Large or Huge)

[253] Domed Room (Medium)

[254 to 255] Donjon (Small, Medium, or Large, with Large implying multiple rooms and chambers)

[256] Drawbridge / Drawbridge Chamber (Small)

[257] Drowning Pool (Small or Medium)

[258 to 259] Dry Well (Small or Medium, size being vertical)

[260] Drying Room (Small or Medium)

[261 to 262] Dueling Pit (Small or Medium)

[263] Dueling Pit Matrix (Small)

[264 to 265] Dungeon (Small, Medium, or Large, with Large implying multiple rooms and chambers)

[266] Dungeon Court (Large or Huge)

[267] Dust Pit (Tiny, Small, or Medium)

[268] Earth Cellar (Small, Medium, or Large)

[269 to 270] Echo Chamber (Small or Medium)

[271] Echoing Vault (Small)

[272] Egg Chamber (Small, Medium, or Large)

[273 to 274] Embalming Chamber (Small or Medium)

[275] Embalming Room (Large)

[276] Enchanted Grotto (Small, Medium, or Large)

[277] Enclave (Large or Huge)

[278] Enclosed Loggia (Medium or Large)

[279 to 280] Enclosure (Small or Medium, with a Tiny internal space)

[281] Enterclose (Tiny or Small)

[282] Entrance Hall (Medium, Large, or Huge)

[283 to 284] Entry / Entryway (Small or Medium)

[285 to 286] Entry Hall (Medium or Large)

[287] Episcenium (Tiny or Small)

[288] Excavation (Large or Huge)

[289 to 290] Excavation Room (Small or Medium)

[291] Excubitorium (Small or Medium)

[292] Execution Chamber (Small)

[293] Execution Hall (Large or Huge)

[294] Execution Room (Medium)

[295 to 296] Experimentation Chamber (Small)

[297] Experimentation Vault (Medium or Large)

[298] Fallen Angelic Shrine (Small or Medium)

[299 to 300] False Tomb (Small, Medium, or Large)

[301] False Treasure Room (Small or Medium)

[302] False Treasure Vault (Medium or Large)

[303 to 304] Fane (Medium or Large)

[305 to 306] Feretorium (Small or Medium)

[307] Feretory (Small or Medium)

[308 to 309] Firepit (Tiny or Small)

[310] Fissure (Small, Medium, or Large)

[311] Fissure, Ceiling (Small, Medium, or Large)

[312 to 313] Fissure, Wall / Fissure Vault (Medium, Large, or Huge)

[314] Flooded Hall (Large or Huge)

[315 to 316] Flooded Room (Small or Medium)

[317 to 318] Forbidden Chamber (Small or Medium)

[319] Forbidden Vault (Large)

[320 to 321] Forge (Small, Medium, or Large)

[322] Formicary (Large or Huge)

[323 to 324] Fornix Chamber (Small)

[325] Fornix Hall (Large or Huge)

[326] Fornix Room (Medium)

[327 to 328] Foss (Medium, Large, or Huge)

[329] Fosse Chamber (Small)

[330] Fosse Room (Medium)

[331 to 332] Foundry (Small, Medium, or Large)

[333 to 334] Fountain Chamber (Small)

[335] Fountain Grotto (Small, Medium, or Large)

[336] Fountain Hall (Large or Huge)

[337 to 338] Fountain Room (Medium)

[339 to 340] Fumarium (Tiny or Small)

[341] Fumigatory (Tiny, Small, or Medium)

[342] Fundament (Small or Medium)

[343] Fundament Room (Medium or Large)

[344 to 345] Funerary Chapel (Small or Medium)

[346] Funerary Workshop (Small or Medium)

[347 to 348] Funereal Crowde (Small or Medium)

[349 to 350] Fungal Garden (Medium, Large, or Huge)

[351] Fungarium (Small, Medium, or Large)

[352 to 353] Gaol (Small, Medium, or Large, with Large implying many cells)

[354] Garderobe (Tiny or Small)

[355 to 356] Garderobe Chamber (Small or Medium)

[357] Gardr (Small, Medium, or Large)

[358] Garret (Tiny, Small, or Medium)

[359 to 360] Garrison (Medium or Large)

[361] Gate Chamber (Medium)

[362] Gate Room (Large)

[363] Gauntlet (Medium or Large)

[364] Geode Mine (Tiny, Small, Medium, or Large)

[365] Grand Aerarium (Large or Huge)

[366 to 367] Grand Aerary (Large or Huge)

[368] Grand Arena (Huge)

[369 to 370] Grand Armory (Large or Huge)

[371] Grand Armory and Forge (Large or Huge)

[372 to 373] Grand Arsenal (Large or Huge)

[374] Grand Arsenal and Forge (Large or Huge)

[375] Grand Aviary (Large or Huge)

[376 to 377] Great Abattoir (Large or Huge)

[378 to 379] Great Almonry (Large)

[380] Great Andron (Large or Huge)

[381 to 382] Great Hall (Large or Huge)

[383] Gren (Tiny)

[384 to 385] Grinding Chamber (Small)

[386] Grinding Room (Medium or Large)

[387] Grof (Tiny or Small)

[388] Grot (Tiny or Small)

[389 to 390] Grotto (Medium or Large)

[390 to 391] Guard Chamber (Small)

[392 to 393] Guard Post (Tiny or Small)

[394 to 395] Guardroom (Medium)

[396] Guild Hall (Large or Huge)

[397] Guild Room (Medium)

[398 to 399] Hall (Large or Huge)

[400] Hall of Bones (Large or Huge)

[401] Hall of Challenge (Large or Huge)

[402] Hall of Contemplation (Large or Huge)

[403 to 404] Hall of Doors (Large or Huge)

[405] Hall of Healing (Large or Huge)

[406] Hall of Honor (Large or Huge)

[407 to 408] Hall of Pools (Large or Huge)

[409 to 410] Hall of Runes (Large or Huge)

[411] Hall of Souls (Large or Huge)

[412] Hall of Statuary (Large or Huge)

[413 to 414] Hall of the Dead (Large or Huge)

[415] Hamr (Small or Medium)

[416 to 417] Hastarium (Medium)

[418 to 419] Hatchery (Small, Medium, or Large)

[420] Haugr (Tiny, Small, Medium, or Large)

[421 to 422] Hell Mouth (Medium, Large, or Huge)

[423] Herbarium (Small or Medium)

[424 to 425] Hermitage (Tiny, Small, or Medium)

[426] Heroum (Tiny, Small, or Medium)

[427 to 428] Hideout (Medium or Large)

[429 to 430] Hiding Place (Tiny or Small)

[431 to 432] Hole (Tiny or Small)

[433 to 434] Hollow (Tiny or Small)

[435] Hollowed Trash Heap (Large or Huge)

[436] Hollowed Wall (Tiny, Small, or Medium)

[437] Holr (Small or Medium)

[438] Hrt / Heret (Large)

[439] Hwt Ka / Hewet Ka (Small or Medium)

[440] Hylr (Small or Medium)

[441] Hypocaust (Medium)

[442 to 443] Hypocaust Chamber (Tiny or Small)

[444 to 445] Hypogeum (Small, Medium, or Large)

[446 to 447] Hypostyle Hall (Large or Huge)

[448 to 449] Ice Chamber (Small)

[450] Icehouse (Medium)

[451 to 452] Idol Grotto (Small, Medium, or Large)

[453] Ikw / Ikew (Large or Huge)

[454 to 455] Illusory Chamber (Small)

[456 to 457] Illusory Room (Medium or Large)

[458] Imht / Imehet (Small or Medium)

[459] Imnt / Imenet (Tiny, Small, or Medium)

[460 to 461] Impluvium Chamber (Small)

[462] Impluvium Hall (Large or Huge)

[463 to 464] Impluvium Room (Medium)

[465] Inquisition / Inquisitorial Chamber

[466] Internment Chamber

[467 to 468] Interrogation Chamber (Tiny or Small)

[469] Interrogation Room (Small or Medium)

[470] Isittu (Small, Medium, or Large)

[471] Itima (Small or Medium)

[472 to 473] Jail (Small, Medium, or Large, with Large implying many cells)

[474 to 475] Junk Room (Small or Medium)

[476] Karmu (Small, Medium, or Large)

[477 to 478] Keep (Large or Huge)

[479] Kelda (Small or Medium)

[480] Kila (Small, Medium, or Large)

[481] Kimah (Small, Medium, or Large)

[482] Kukku (Small, Medium, or Large)

[483 to 484] Laboratory (Alchemical) (Small, Medium, or Large)

[485] Laboratory (Magical) (Small, Medium, or Large)

[486 to 487] Labyrinth (Large or Huge)

[488 to 489] Lair (Tiny, Small, Medium, Large, or Huge)

[490] Landing (Tiny or Small)

[491] Lararium (Tiny or Small)

[492] Larder (Medium)

[493] Larder Chamber (Small)

[494] Latrine (Tiny)

[495 to 496] Latrine Chamber (Small or Medium)

[497] Lazarette (Tiny, Small, Medium, or Large)

[498 to 499] Leaching Cesspool (Small, Medium, or Large)

[500] Leap (Tiny, Small, or Medium)

[501 to 502] Lookout (Tiny, Small, or Medium)

[503] Lumber Room (Small or Medium)

[504] Makkuri (Small, Medium, or Large)

[505 to 506] Manufactorium (Large or Huge)

[507] Manufactory (Large or Huge)

[508] Manzazu (Small, Medium, or Large)

[509 to 510] Map Chamber (Small)

[511] Map Room (Medium)

[512] Martyrium (Tiny, Small, or Medium)

[513] Mass Grave (Large or Huge)

[514 to 515] Mausoleum (Large or Huge)

[516 to 517] Maze (Large or Huge)

[518 to 519] Mechanical Room (Small or Medium)

[520 to 521] Meditation Chamber (Small or Medium)

[522] Mestaku (Tiny)

[523] Metroon (Small, Medium, or Large)

[524 to 525] Mine (Large or Huge)

[526 to 527] Mine Shaft (Small or Medium)

[528] Moat / Moat Vault (Medium or Large)

[529] Moat Hall (Large or Huge)

[530] Monastic Cell (Tiny)

[531] Monster Crypt (Tiny, Small, or Medium)

[532] Morgue (Small or Medium)

[533 to 534] Mortuary Chapel

[535] Msxnt / Mesixenet (Large or Huge)

[536] Mtwn / Metwen (Large or Huge)

[537 to 538] Murder Room (Tiny, Small, or Medium)

[539 to 540] Mushroom Cellar (Small or Medium)

[541] Narthex (Medium, Large, or Huge)

[542] Natatorium (Large or Huge)

[542 to 544] Necropolis (Large or Huge)

[545] Nest (Tiny, Small, or Medium)

[546 to 547] Nether (Large or Huge)

[548 to 549] Netherworld (Huge)

[550 to 551] Netherworld Descent (Huge)

[552] Niche (Tiny)

[553] Niched Room (Small or Medium)

[554] Obelisk Chamber (Small or Medium)

[555] Obelisk Hall (Large or Huge)

[556 to 557] Observation Chamber (Small or Medium)

[558] Offering Chamber (Small)

[559 to 560] Oil Cellar (Small or Medium)

[561] Opisthodomos (Small or Medium)

[562] Oracular Chamber (Small or Medium)

[563] Ossuary (Tiny)

[564] Ossuary Chamber (Small)

[565] Ossuary Room (Medium or Large)

[566] Oubliette (Tiny)

[567 to 568] Oubliette Room (Small, Medium, or Large)

[569 to 570] Outpost (Small, Medium, or Large)

[571] Overlook (Small or Medium)

[572 to 573] Pallet Chamber (Tiny or Small)

[574 to 575] Pen (Tiny, Small, or Medium, with Medium implying a number of pens in a single location)

[576] Penaria (Small or Medium)

[577 to 578] Pergula (Tiny, Small, or Medium)

[579] Peristyle (Small, Medium, or Large, surrounding a smaller interior)

[580] Peristylium (Small, Medium, or Large, surrounding a smaller interior)

[581 to 582] Pit (Tiny or Small)

[583 to 584] Pit Chamber (Small)

[585 to 586] Pit Room (Medium)

[587] Ploutonion (Small or Medium)

[588] Plundered Tomb (Small, Medium, or Large)

[589 to 590] Plundered Vault (Medium, Large, or Huge)

[591] Plunge (Small, Medium, or Large)

[592] Pool (Tiny, Small, or Medium)

[593 to 594] Pool Chamber (Small)

[595] Pool Room (Medium or Large)

[596 to 597] Portcullis Chamber

[598 to 599] Potionry (Small or Medium)

[600] Pr Hd / Per Hed (Small, Medium, or Large)

[601] Pr Nfr / Per Nefer (Small or Medium)

[602] Priest Hole (Tiny or Small)

[603 to 604] Prison (Small, Medium, or Large)

[605] Prison Block (Medium, Large, or Huge)

[606] Prison Cell (Tiny)

[607 to 608] Prison Chamber (Small)

[609] Prison Hall (Large or Huge)

[610 to 611] Privy (Tiny or Small)

[612] Procoeton (Small)

[613] Procoetum (Small)

[614 to 615] Protective Ditch (Small, Medium, or Large)

[616 to 617] Proving Ground, plural Proving Grounds (Medium, Large, or Huge, with Huge being plural)

[618 to 619] Pump Room (Small or Medium)

[620] Puteus (Small, Medium, or Large)

[621 to 622] Pyre Chamber (Small)

[623] Pyre Room (Medium or Large)

[624] Quarry (Small, Medium, or Large)

[625 to 626] Quarry Shaft (Small or Medium)

[627 to 628] Quarters (Small, Medium, or Large)

[629 to 630] Quarters, Solitary (Tiny or Small)

[631] Quicksand Pit (Tiny, Small, or Medium)

[632] Quppu (Tiny, Small, or Medium)

[633] Recess (Tiny or Small, with an adjacent Small, Medium, or Large space)

[634 to 635] Redoubt (Small, Medium, or Large)

[636] Reflecting Pool (Tiny, Small, or Medium)

[637] Refuge (Small, Medium, or Large)

[638 to 639] Refuse Pit (Tiny, Small, or Medium)

[640 to 641] Reservoir (Large or Huge)

[642 to 643] Revolving Chamber (Small or Medium)

[644] Riding Hall (Large or Huge)

[645 to 646] Room (Small or Medium)

[647] Room of Pools (Large or Huge)

[648] Room of Slaughter (Small, Medium, or Large)

[649 to 650] Room of Unknown Purpose (Tiny, Small, Medium, Large, or Huge)

[651] Roost (Tiny, Small, or Medium)

[652] Root Cellar (Small or Medium)

[653] Rotating Room (Small or Medium)

[654 to 655] Rotting Chamber (Small)

[656] Rotting Room (Medium or Large)

[657 to 658] Rotunda (Small, Medium, or Large)

[659] Royal Tomb (Large or Huge)

[660 to 661] Rubble-Filled Room / Ruined Room (Small or Medium)

[662 to 663] Ruined Chamber (Small)

[664] Ruined Hall (Large or Huge)

[665] Rum (Small or Medium)

[666 to 667] Runic Chamber (Small or Medium)

[668] Sacred Abattoir (Small, Medium, or Large)

[669 to 670] Sacred Crypt (Small)

[671] Sacred Tomb (Medium or Large)

[672 to 673] Sacrificial Chamber (Small or Medium)

[674] Sacrificial Grotto (Small or Medium)

[675 to 676] Sacrificial Pool (Tiny, Small, or Medium)

[677] Sacrificial Vault (Large or Huge)

[678] Sarcophagus Room (Medium or Large)

[679] Safe Room (Small or Medium)

[680] Salt Cellar (Small or Medium)

[681] Salt Chamber (Small)

[682 to 683] Salt Mine (Medium, Large, or Huge)

[684 to 685] Salt Room (Medium)

[686] Sandpit (Small, Medium, or Large)

[687 to 688] Sarcophagus Chamber (Small or Medium)

[689 to 690] Scrapheap (Small, Medium, or Large)

[691] Scullery (Small or Medium)

[692 to 693] Sealed Tomb (Small, Medium, or Large)

[694] Secret Crypt (Small, Medium, or Large)

[695] Secret Cyst (Tiny, Small, Medium, or Large)

[696 to 697] Secret Grotto (Small or Medium)

[698 to 699] Secret Guardroom (Small or Medium)

[700 to 701] Secret Room (Tiny, Small, Medium, or Large)

[702] Secret Tomb (Small, Medium, or Large)

[703 to 704] Sepulcher / Sepulchre

[705 to 706] Sepulchral Cell (Tiny)

[707] Sepulchral Chapel (Small, Medium, or Large)

[708] Sepulchral Hall (Large or Huge)

[709] Sepulchral Heroum (Small or Medium, perhaps in a Medium, Large, or Huge surrounding space)

[710 to 711] Servant's Quarters / Servants' Quarters (Tiny, Small, or Medium)

[712 to 713] Sewer (Small, Medium, Large, or Huge)

[714] Shambles (Small or Medium)

[715] Shanty / Shanties (Tiny, Small, or Medium)

[716] Shelter (Tiny or Small)

[717 to 718] Shrine (Small or Medium)

[719 to 720] Shrine Chamber (Small)

[721 to 722] Shrine Room (Medium or Large)

[723] Sibitti (Small, Medium, or Large, with Large implying multiple cells)

[724 to 725] Sinkhole (Small, Medium, Large, or Huge)

[726] Skinning Room (Small or Medium)

[727 to 728] Slave Chamber (Tiny, Small, or Medium)

[729 to 730] Slave Pit (Tiny, Small, or Medium)

[731] Slaves' Tomb (Small, Medium, or Large)

[732 to 733] Sleeping Chamber (Small)

[734] Sleeping Room (Medium)

[735 to 736] Sludge Pit (Tiny, Small, or Medium)

[737] Smelter (Small, Medium, or Large)

[738] Smithy (Small, Medium or Large)

[739] Smoke Room (Small or Medium)

[740 to 741] Spiral Labyrinth (Medium, Large, or Huge)

[742] Stable (Small, Medium, or Large)

[743] Stair Chamber (Small)

[744 to 745] Stairway Room (Medium)

[746 to 747] Statuary (Small, Medium, or Large)

[748] Steinn (Small, Medium, or Large)

[749] Stockpile Room (Small or Medium)

[750] Storage Chamber (Small)

[751 to 752] Storage Room / Storeroom (Small or Medium)

[753] Storeroom – Alchemical (Small or Medium)

[754] Storeroom – Alcohol / Wine (Small or Medium)

[755 to 756] Storeroom – Armor (Small or Medium)

[757 to 758] Storeroom – Box Room (Small or Medium)

[759] Storeroom – Butchered Meat (Small or Medium)

[760] Storeroom – Ceremonial (Small or Medium)

[761 to 762] Storeroom – Char / Coal (Small or Medium)

[763 to 764] Storeroom – Construction (Small or Medium)

[765] Storeroom – Drink (Small or Medium)

[766 to 767] Storeroom – Dry Goods (Small or Medium)

[768] Storeroom – Embalming (Small or Medium)

[769 to 770] Storeroom – Equipment Room (Small or Medium)

[771] Storeroom – Failed Experiments (Small or Medium)

[772] Storeroom – Foodstuffs (Small or Medium)

[773] Storeroom – Herbs and Spices (Small or Medium)

[774] Storeroom – Ice (Small or Medium)

[775] Storeroom – Lumber (Small or Medium)

[776 to 777] Storeroom – Masonry (Small or Medium)

[778 to 779] Storeroom – Oil (Small or Medium)

[780] Storeroom – Reagents (Small or Medium)

[781] Storeroom – Salt (Small or Medium)

[782 to 783] Storeroom – Sundries (Small or Medium)

[784 to 785] Storeroom – Tools and Gear (Small or Medium)

[786] Storeroom – Water (Small or Medium)

[787 to 788] Storeroom – Weapons (Small or Medium)

[789] Stricture (Tiny or Small)

[790 to 791] Strongroom (Small)

[792] Sub-Basement (Tiny, Small, or Medium)

[793] Sub-Cellar (Tiny, Small, or Medium)

[794 to 795] Submerged Chamber (Small)

[796] Submerged Hall (Large or Huge)

[797 to 798] Submerged Room (Medium)

[799 to 800] Summoning Chamber (Small)

[801] Summoning Gauntlet (Medium, Large, or Huge)

[802] Summoning Room (Medium or Large)

[803] Tack Room (Small or Medium)

[804 to 805] Tank (Small, Medium, Large, or Huge)

[806 to 807] Tar Pit (Small, Tiny, or Medium)

[808] Taum (Tiny, Small, or Medium)

[809 to 810] Teleportation Chamber (Tiny, Small, or Medium)

[811 to 812] Terminus (Tiny, Small, or Medium)

[813] Tholos (Small, Medium, or Large)

[814] Threshold (Tiny, Small, Medium, or Large)

[815] Throne Room (Medium or Large)

[816 to 817] Tomb (Medium or Large)

[818 to 819] Tomb Chamber (Small)

[820] Tomb Shaft (Tiny, Small, or Medium)

[821] Tool Room (Small or Medium)

[822 to 823] Torture Chamber (Small, Medium, or Large)

[824 to 825] Torture Pit(s) (Small, Medium, or Large, with Large implying multiple pits)

[826 to 827] Treasure Chamber (Small or Medium)

[828 to 829] Treasure Vault (Medium or Large)

[830] Undercroft (Small, Medium, Large, or Huge)

[831] Undercroft (Special) (Small, Medium, Large, or Huge)

[832] Underground Lake (Large or Huge)

[833 to 834] Underground Mausoleum (Huge)

[835] Underground Palace (Huge)

[836] Underground Pyramid (Huge)

[837 to 838] Underground River (Huge)

[839] Underground Swamp (Huge)

[840] Underground Ziggurat (Huge)

[841] Undervault (Large or Huge)

[842 to 843] Unfinished Chamber (Small)

[844] Unfinished Hall (Large or Huge)

[845] Unfinished Room (Medium)

[846 to 847] Unfinished Tomb (Small, Medium, or Large)

[848] Utility Chamber (Small)

[849 to 850] Utility Room (Medium or Large)

[851 to 852] Vault (Small, Medium, or Large)

[853] Vaulted Chamber (Small or Medium)

[854] Vaulted Hall (Large or Huge)

[855 to 856] Vaulted Room (Medium or Large)

[857] Vestibule (Small or Medium)

[858] Vestibulum (Small or Medium)

[859] Vigil (Tiny, Small, or Medium)

[860 to 861] Walled-Up Chamber (Small)

[862 to 863] Walled-Up Corridor (Small or Medium)

[864 to 865] Walled-Up Room (Medium or Large)

[866] Ward (Medium or Large)

[867 to 868] Warren (Tiny or Small)

[869 to 870] Warrens (Medium, Large, or Huge)

[871] Wasi (Small, Medium, or Large)

[872 to 873] Watchroom (Tiny, Small, or Medium)

[874 to 875] Well (Tiny, Small, or Medium)

[876 to 877] Well Room (Small or Medium)

[878 to 879] Winch Pit (Tiny or Small)

[880 to 881] Winch Room (Medium or Large)

[882] Wine Cellar (Small or Medium)

[883] Wine Vault (Small, Medium, or Large)

[884 to 885] Wizard's Laboratory (Small, Medium, or Large)

[886 to 887] Wizard's Workroom (Small or Medium)

[888] Wndwt / Wenedewet (Small)

[889 to 891] Work Chamber (Small)

[891 to 892] Workers' Hall (Large or Huge)

[893 to 894] Workpit (Tiny or Small)

[895 to 896] Workroom (Medium or Large)

[897] Workshop (Medium or Large)

[898] Xnrt / Xeneret (Small or Medium)

[899] Ziggurat Hall (Large or Huge)

[900] Zoo (or Menagerie) (Large or Huge)

[901 to 909] Dungeon Sub-Region: Dungeon Grottoes. Roll on the Cave Room Table for the next 1D4+1 rooms (rerolling any results of 901 to 000), and then return to this table.

[910 to 915] Dungeon Sub-Region: Excavated Caves. Roll on the Cave Room Table for the next 2D4 rooms (rerolling any results of 901 to 000), and then return to this table.

[916 to 918] Dungeon Sub-Region: Cave Labyrinth. Roll on the Cave Room Table for the next 2D6+1 rooms (rerolling any results of 901 to 000), and then return to this table.

[919 to 927] Dungeon Sub-Region: Secret Furnished Rooms. Roll on the Manor House Room Table for the next 1D4+1 rooms (rerolling any results of 901 to 000), and then return to this table.

[928 to 933] Dungeon Sub-Region: Cultic Manor. Roll on Manor House Room Table for the next 2D4 rooms (rerolling any results of 901 to 000), and then return to this table.

[934 to 936] Dungeon Sub-Region: Cabal's Secret Manor. Roll on Manor House Room Table for the next 2D6+1 rooms (rerolling any results of 901 to 000), and then return to this table.

[937 to 945] Dungeon Sub-Region: Guardian Halls. Roll on the Stronghold Room Table for the next 1D4+1 rooms (rerolling any results of 901 to 000), and then return to this table.

[946 to 951] Dungeon Sub-Region: Dungeon Holdfast. Roll on the Stronghold Room Table for the next 2D4 rooms (rerolling any results of 901 to 000), and then return to this table.

[952 to 954] Dungeon Sub-Region: Dungeon Stronghold. Roll on the Stronghold Room Table for the next 2D6+1 rooms (rerolling any results of 901 to 000), and then return to this table.

[955 to 963] Dungeon Sub-Region: Cultic Fane. Roll on the Temple Room Table for the next 1D4+1 rooms (rerolling any results of 901 to 000), and then return to this table.

[964 to 969] Dungeon Sub-Region: Underground Fane. Roll on the Temple Room Table for the next 2D4 rooms (rerolling any results of 901 to 000), and then return to this table.

[970 to 972] Dungeon Sub-Region: Underground Temple. Roll on the Temple Room Table for the next 2D6+1 rooms (rerolling any results of 901 to 000), and then return to this table.

[973 to 981] Dungeon Sub-Region: Dungeon Crypt. Roll on the Tomb Room Table for the next 1D4+1 rooms (rerolling any results of 901 to 000), and then return to this table.

[982 to 987] Dungeon Sub-Region: Dungeon Barrows. Roll on the Tomb Room Table for the next 2D4 rooms (rerolling any results of 901 to 000), and then return to this table.

[998 to 990] Dungeon Sub-Region: Extensive Dungeon Tombs. Roll on the Tomb Room Table for the next 2D6+1 rooms (rerolling any results of 901 to 000), and then return to this table.

[991 to 995] Dungeon Sub-Region: Strange Chambers. Roll on the Evocative Random Rooms Table (refer to *The Classic Dungeon Design Guide, Book I*) for the next 1D4+1 rooms (rerolling any results of 901 to 000), and then return to this table.

[996 to 998] Dungeon Sub-Region: Eerie Domain. Roll on the Evocative Random Rooms Table (refer to *The Classic Dungeon Design Guide, Book I*) for the next 2D4 rooms (rerolling any results of 901 to 000), and then return to this table.

[999 to 000] Dungeon Sub-Region: Eldritch Vaults. Roll on the Evocative Random Rooms Table (refer to *The Classic Dungeon Design Guide, Book I*) for the next 2D6+1 rooms (rerolling any results of 901 to 000), and then return to this table.

MANOR HOUSE ROOMS

Note that there are two types of manor houses which should be considered: the *palatial*, and the *gentrified*.

A *palatial* manor house will be positively huge, and you can use the room sizes and square footage indicated for other dungeon types as noted earlier in this tome. But for a *gentrified* (smaller) manor house, you will probably want to use 5' x 5' map squares instead of 10' x 10'. This means that hallways that are one square wide will be 5' wide instead of 10'. Similarly, a small room (of 3 to 6 squares) would consist of 3 to 6 5'-wide squares, instead of 3 to 6 10'-wide squares.

You can use this reduced scale for gentrified houses if the massive (palatial) room results bother you. The gentrified scale is more realistic; the palatial scale is more epic, and in line with the presentation of haunted mansions and such in many classic dungeon modules. Either scale will suit your manorial environments well.

~

For random rooms appearing in a haunted and/or ruined manor house, roll 1D1000 and consult the following table.

TABLE 3

MANOR HOUSE ROOMS

[001 to 002] Accommodation (Small)

[003 to 004] Accommodations, plural (Medium or Large)

[005] Af-Hus (Tiny or Small)

[006 to 007] Ala (Tiny or Small)

[008 to 009] Alae, plural (Medium or Large)

[010 to 011] Alcove (Tiny or Small)

[012 to 013] Alcove Succession (Medium or Large)

[014 to 015] Ale Cellar (Small or Medium)

[016 to 017] Aleatorium (Small or Medium)

[018 to 019] Alhacena (Tiny or Small)

[020 to 021] Alhacena Succession (Medium or Large)

[022 to 023] Alipterion (Medium or Large)

[024 to 025] Alipterium (Medium or Large)

[026 to 027] Altar Chamber (Small)

[028 to 029] Altar Room (Medium)

[030 to 031] Ambry (Small or Medium)

[032 to 033] Ambry Chamber (Tiny or Small)

[034 to 035] Ambulatory (Medium)

[036 to 037] Amphitheater (Large or Huge)

[038 to 039] Anatomical Theater (Medium, Large, or Huge)

[040 to 041] Ancestral Chamber (Small or Medium)

[042 to 043] Ancestral Hall (Large or Huge)

[044 to 045] Anddyri (Small, Medium, or Large)

[046 to 047] Angelic Shrine (Small or Medium)

[048 to 049] Annex (Tiny, Small, or Medium)

[050 to 051] Annex Labyrinth (Large or Huge)

[052 to 053] Antecabinet (Small)

[054 to 055] Antechamber (Small)

[056 to 057] Anteroom (Medium)

[058] Apartments, plural (Medium or Large)

[059 to 060] Aperture (Tiny)

[061 to 062] Apotheca (Small or Medium)

[063 to 064] Apothecarium (Small or Medium)

[065 to 066] Apothecary (Small or Medium)

[067 to 068] Apse (Small)

[069 to 070] Apse Room (Medium)

[071 to 072] Aquarium (Medium, Large, or Huge)

[073 to 074] Arboretum (Large)

[075 to 076] Archive (Medium, Large, or Huge)

[077 to 078] Armorial Chamber (Medium)

[079 to 080] Armorial Hall (Large or Huge)

[081 to 082] Armory Chamber (Small)

[083 to 084] Arsenal Chamber (Small)

[085 to 086] Art Gallery (Medium, Large, or Huge)

[087] Artisan's Chamber (Small or Medium)

[088 to 089] Artisan's Room (Medium or Large)

[090] Astrarium Chamber (Medium)

[091 to 092] Astrarium Room (Large)

[093 to 094] Atelier (Small or Medium)

[095 to 096] Athanor Chamber (Small)

[097 to 098] Athanor Room (Medium or Large)

[099 to 100] Atrium (Large or Huge)

[101 to 102] Atrium Chamber (Small or Medium)

[103 to 104] Attic (Medium or Large)

[105 to 106] Attic Space (Small)

[107 to 108] Augury Chamber (Small)

[109 to 110] Augury Room (Medium)

[111 to 112] Bakery (Small or Medium)

[113 to 114] Ballroom (Large or Huge)

[115 to 116] Balnea (Small or Medium)

[117 to 118] Balnearium (Small or Medium)

[119 to 120] Banquet Hall (Large or Huge)

[121 to 122] Banquet Room (Medium)

[123 to 124] Basement (Medium or Large)

[125] Basement Space (Small)

[126 to 127] Bath (Small, Medium, or Large)

[128 to 129] Bath Room / Bathroom (Small or Medium)

[130] Bathhouse (Medium or Large)

[131 to 132] Bay (Tiny or Small)

[133 to 134] Bay Succession (Medium or Large)

[135 to 136] Bedchamber (Small)

[137 to 138] Bedroom (Small or Medium)

[139 to 140] Bodega (Small)

[141 to 142] Boudoir (Small or Medium)

[143 to 144] Bower (Small)

[145 to 146] Breezeway (Medium or Large)

[147 to 148] Buttery (Small or Medium)

[149 to 150] Cabinet (Small)

[151 to 152] Calefactorium (Small, Medium, or Large)

[153 to 154] Calefactory (Small, Medium, or Large)

[155 to 156] Camba (Small or Medium)

[157 to 158] Cartographer's Hall (Large or Huge)

[159 to 160] Cavaedium (Large or Huge)

[161 to 162] Cella Olearia (Medium or Large)

[163 to 164] Cella Vinaria (Small, Medium, or Large)

[165 to 166] Cellar (Small or Medium)

[167 to 168] Cellarage (Large or Huge)

[169 to 170] Cellula (Tiny or Small)

[171] Cenaculum (Medium or Large)

[172 to 173] Cenatio (Medium)

[174 to 175] Chamber (Small)

[176 to 177] Chambers, plural (Medium, Large, or Huge)

[178] Chandlery (Small or Medium)

[179 to 180] Charter Room (Small or Medium)

[181 to 182] Chartophylacium (Medium, Large, or Huge)

[183 to 184] Cheese Cellar (Small or Medium)

[185 to 186] Chimney Corner (Tiny or Small)

[187 to 188] Cistern (Small, Medium, Large, or Huge)

[189 to 190] Cistern Room (Small or Medium)

[191 to 192] Cloak Room (Small or Medium)

[193 to 194] Clockwork Room (Small or Medium)

[195 to 196] Coal Room (Small, Medium, or Large)

[197 to 198] Coenaculum (Small or Medium)

[199 to 200] Coenatio (Medium or Large)

[201 to 202] Coldroom (Small or Medium)

[203 to 204] Comfort Room (Tiny or Small)

[205 to 206] Concealed Chamber (Small)

[207 to 208] Concealed Room (Medium or Large)

[209 to 210] Conclave (Medium or Large)

[211 to 212] Conclavium (Medium or Large)

[213 to 214] Conjuring Chamber (Small or Medium)

[215 to 216] Conservatory (Medium or Large)

[217 to 218] Control Room (Small or Medium)

[219] Courtyard (Medium or Large if subterranean, otherwise Large or Huge)

[220 to 221] Crafter's Room (Small or Medium)

[222 to 223] Crawlspace (Tiny, Small, or Medium)

[224 to 225] Crowde (Tiny, Small, or Medium)

[226 to 227] Cubicle (Tiny)

[228 to 229] Cubicula, plural (Small, Medium, or Large)

[230 to 231] Cubiculum (Tiny or Small)

[232 to 233] Culina (Medium)

[234 to 235] Cupboard (Tiny)

[236 to 237] Dairy Chamber (Small or Medium)

[238 to 239] Dairy Room (Medium or Large)

[240 to 241] Dais Chamber (Small or Medium)

[242] Dais Room (Medium or Large)

[243 to 244] Darkroom (Small, Medium, or Large)

[245 to 246] Dayroom (Small or Medium)

[247 to 248] Dead End (Tiny or Small)

[249 to 250] Den (Small or Medium)

[251 to 252] Depository (Medium or Large)

[253 to 254] Dining Chamber (Small)

[255 to 256] Dining Hall (Large or Huge)

[257 to 258] Dining Room (Medium)

[259] Distillery (Medium or Large)

[260 to 261] Divination Chamber (Small)

[262 to 263] Domed Chamber (Small)

[264 to 265] Domed Hall (Large or Huge)

[266 to 267] Domed Room (Medium)

[268 to 269] Domicile (Small or Medium)

[270 to 271] Drawing Chamber (Small)

[272 to 273] Drawing Room (Medium)

[274 to 275] Dressing Chamber (Small)

[276 to 277] Dressing Room (Medium)

[278 to 279] Earth Cellar (Small, Medium, or Large)

[281 to 281] Elaeothesium (Small or Medium)

[282] Eldaskali (Large or Huge)

[283 to 284] Enclosed Loggia (Medium or Large)

[285 to 286] Enclosure (Small or Medium, with a Tiny internal space)

[287 to 288] Enterclose (Tiny or Small)

[289 to 290] Entertaining Room (Medium or Large)

[291 to 292] Entry / Entryway (Small or Medium)

[293 to 294] Entry Hall (Medium or Large)

[295 to 296] Ewery (Tiny or Small)

[297 to 298] Excubitorium (Small or Medium)

[299] Exedra (Small or Medium)

[300 to 301] Experimentation Chamber (Small)

[302 to 303] Experimentation Vault (Medium or Large)

[304 to 305] Fainting Room (Small or Medium)

[306 to 307] Family Room (Small or Medium)

[308 to 309] Feast Hall (Large or Huge)

[310 to 311] Forbidden Chamber (Small or Medium)

[312 to 313] Forbidden Vault (Large)

[314 to 315] Fornix Chamber (Small)

[316] Fornix Hall (Large or Huge)

[317 to 318] Fornix Room (Medium)

[319 to 320] Fountain Chamber (Small)

[321 to 322] Fountain Hall (Large or Huge)

[323 to 324] Fountain Room (Medium)

[325 to 326] Foyer (Small or Medium)

[327 to 328] Fresco Gallery (Large)

[329 to 330] Fresco Room (Small or Medium)

[331 to 332] Frigidarium (Small, Medium, or Large)

[333 to 334] Front Room (Small or Medium)

[335 to 336] Fumarium (Tiny or Small)

[337 to 338] Fumigatory (Tiny, Small, or Medium)

[339 to 340] Function Hall (Large or Huge)

[341 to 342] Function Room (Medium)

[343 to 344] Fungarium (Small, Medium, or Large)

[345 to 346] Galleria (Medium, Large, or Huge)

[347 to 348] Gallery (Display) (Medium, Large, or Huge)

[349 to 350] Gambling Room (Medium)

[351 to 352] Game Room (Small, Medium, or Large)

[353 to 354] Garden (Medium or Large)

[355 to 356] Garderobe (Tiny or Small)

[357 to 358] Garret (Tiny, Small, or Medium)

[359 to 360] Gate Chamber (Medium)

[361 to 362] Gate Room (Large)

[363 to 364] Goods Hall (Medium or Large)

[365] Granary (Small or Medium)

[366 to 367] Grand Aquarium (Large or Huge)

[368 to 369] Grand Arboretum (Large or Huge)

[370 to 371] Grand Gallery (Display) (Small)

[372 to 373] Grand Salon (Large or Huge)

[374 to 375] Grapery (Small, Medium, or Large)

[376 to 377] Great Chamber (Large or Huge)

[378] Great Kitchen (Large or Huge)

[379 to 380] Great Room (Large)

[381] Greenhouse (Small, Medium, or Large)

[382 to 383] Guard Chamber (Small)

[384 to 385] Guard Post (Tiny or Small)

[386 to 387] Guardroom (Medium)

[388 to 389] Guest Chamber (Small)

[390 to 391] Guestroom (Small or Medium)

[393 to 393] Hall (Large or Huge)

[394 to 395] Hall of Doors (Large or Huge)

[396 to 397] Hall of Honor (Large or Huge)

[398 to 399] Hall of Mirrors (Large or Huge)

[400 to 401] Hall of Reverence (Large or Huge)

[402 to 403] Hall of Runes (Large or Huge)

[404 to 405] Hall of Statuary (Large or Huge)

[406 to 407] Hall of Tapestries (Large or Huge)

[408] Harem (Small, Medium, or Large)

[409 to 410] Harness Chamber (Small)

[411] Harness Hall (Large or Huge)

[412 to 413] Harness Room (Medium)

[414 to 415] Haven (Small or Medium)

[416 to 417] Hearth Chamber (Small)

[418 to 419] Hearth Hall (Large or Huge)

[420 to 421] Hearth Room (Medium)

[422 to 423] Herbarium (Small or Medium)

[424 to 425] Heroum (Tiny, Small, or Medium)

[426 to 427] Horological Hall (Large or Huge)

[428 to 429] Horologium (Small or Medium)

[430 to 431] Hospitalium (Small)

[432 to 433] Hospitium (Medium)

[434 to 435] Hostel (Medium or Large)

[436 to 437] Hunters' Hall (Large or Huge)

[438 to 439] Hus (Small or Medium)

[440 to 441] Hylr (Small or Medium)

[442 to 443] Hypocaust (Medium)

[444 to 445] Hypocaust Chamber (Tiny or Small)

[446 to 447] Hypogeum (Small, Medium, or Large)

[448 to 449] Hypostyle Hall (Large or Huge)

[450 to 451] Ice Chamber (Small)

[452 to 453] Icehouse (Medium)

[454 to 455] Idol Grotto (Small, Medium, or Large)

[456 to 457] Illusory Chamber (Small)

[458 to 459] Illusory Room (Medium or Large)

[460 to 461] Immense Archive (Huge)

[462 to 463] Impluvium Chamber (Small)

[464] Impluvium Hall (Large or Huge)

[465 to 466] Impluvium Room (Medium)

[467 to 468] Inscription Chamber (Small)

[469 to 470] Instrument Chamber (Small)

[471 to 472] Instrument Room (Medium)

[473 to 474] Junk Room (Small or Medium)

[475 to 476] Kelda (Small or Medium)

[477 to 478] Kitchen (Medium)

[479 to 480] Kitchen Chamber (Small)

[481 to 482] Kneipe (Small or Medium)

[483 to 484] Laboratory (Alchemical) (Small, Medium, or Large)

[485 to 486] Laboratory (Magical) (Small, Medium, or Large)

[487 to 488] Laconicum (Small, Medium, or Large)

[489 to 490] Lady's Chamber (Small or Medium)

[491 to 492] Lair (Tiny, Small, Medium, Large, or Huge)

[493 to 494] Landing (Tiny or Small)

[495 to 496] Lararium (Tiny or Small)

[497 to 498] Larder (Medium)

[499 to 500] Larder Chamber (Small)

[501 to 502] Launderer's Room / Laundry Room (Small or Medium)

[503 to 504] Lavatorium (Small or Medium)

[505 to 506] Lavatory (Small or Medium)

[507 to 508] Library (Medium, Large, or Huge)

[509 to 510] Lightwell (Tiny, Small, or Medium)

[511 to 512] Living Room (Small or Medium)

[513] Lobby (Small, Medium, or Large)

[514 to 515] Loft (Tiny, Small, or Medium)

[516 to 517] Lokrekkja (Tiny)

[518 to 519] Long Gallery (Large or Huge)

[520] Lopt (Large or Huge)

[521 to 522] Lord's Chamber (Small or Medium)

[523 to 524] Lounge (Small or Medium)

[525 to 526] Lumber Room (Small or Medium)

[527 to 528] Map Chamber (Small)

[529 to 530] Map Room (Medium)

[531 to 532] Mechanical Room (Small or Medium)

[533 to 534] Meeting Room (Small or Medium)

[535 to 536] Memorial Chamber (Small or Medium)

[537 to 538] Mezzanine (Small or Medium, a subspace within an area that is Large or Huge)

[539 to 540] Monument Room (Large)

[541 to 542] Muniment Room (Small or Medium)

[543 to 544] Museum (Large or Huge)

[545 to 546] Mushroom Cellar (Small or Medium)

[547 to 548] Music Chamber (Small)

[549 to 550] Music Room (Medium)

[551 to 552] Narthex (Medium, Large, or Huge)

[553 to 554] Necessarium (Tiny or Small)

[555 to 556] Niche (Tiny)

[557 to 558] Niched Room (Small or Medium)

[559 to 560] Nursery (Small or Medium)

[561] Observatory (Small, Medium, or Large)

[562 to 563] Occus (Small)

[564 to 565] Oecus (Medium or Large)

[566 to 567] Office (Tiny, Small, or Medium)

[568] Oil Cellar (Small or Medium)

[569 to 570] Oil Press Room (Small or Medium)

[571 to 572] Oracular Chamber (Small or Medium)

[573 to 574] Painting Gallery (Large or Huge)

[575 to 576] Pallet Chamber (Tiny or Small)

[577 to 578] Pantry (Small or Medium)

[579 to 580] Parlatorium (Small or Medium)

[581 to 582] Parlor (Small or Medium)

[583 to 584] Penaria (Small or Medium)

[585 to 586] Pergula (Tiny, Small, or Medium)

[587 to 588] Peristyle (Small, Medium, or Large, surrounding a smaller interior)

[589 to 590] Peristylium (Small, Medium, or Large, surrounding a smaller interior)

[591 to 592] Planetarium (Large or Huge)

[593] Playroom (Small or Medium)

[594 to 595] Ploutonion (Small or Medium)

[596 to 597] Poison Garden (Small, Medium, or Large)

[598 to 599] Potionry (Small or Medium)

[600 to 601] Priest Hole (Tiny or Small)

[602 to 603] Privy (Tiny or Small)

[604 to 605] Procoeton (Small)

[606 to 607] Procoetum (Small)

[608 to 609] Psychomanteum (Small or Medium)

[610 to 611] Quarters (Small, Medium, or Large)

[612 to 613] Quarters, Solitary (Tiny or Small)

[614 to 615] Reading Chamber (Tiny or Small)

[616 to 617] Reading Room (Small or Medium)

[618 to 619] Receiving Room (Medium)

[620 to 621] Reception Chamber (Small)

[622 to 623] Reception Hall (Large or Huge)

[624 to 625] Reception Room (Small or Medium)

[626] Recess (Tiny or Small, with an adjacent Small, Medium, or Large space)

[627 to 628] Recreation Chamber (Small)

[629 to 630] Recreation Hall (Large or Huge)

[631 to 632] Recreation Room (Medium)

[633 to 634] Refectorium (Small or Medium)

[635 to 636] Refuge (Small, Medium, or Large)

[637] Repository (Small or Medium)

[638 to 639] Reredorter (Small or Medium)

[640 to 641] Retreat (Small or Medium)

[642 to 643] Revolving Chamber (Small or Medium)

[644 to 645] Room (Small or Medium)

[646 to 647] Room of Unknown Purpose (Tiny, Small, Medium, Large, or Huge)

[648 to 649] Root Cellar (Small or Medium)

[650 to 651] Rotating Room (Small or Medium)

[652 to 653] Rotunda (Small, Medium, or Large)

[654 to 655] Royal Chamber / Noble's Chamber (Small or Medium)

[656 to 657] Rum (Small or Medium)

[658 to 659] Runic Chamber (Small or Medium)

[660 to 661] Safe Room (Small or Medium)

[662 to 663] Salon (Small or Medium)

[664 to 665] Salt Cellar (Small or Medium)

[666 to 667] Salt Chamber (Small)

[668 to 669] Salt Room (Medium)

[670 to 671] Sauna (Small or Medium)

[672 to 673] Schola (Small or Medium)

[674 to 675] Scullery (Small or Medium)

[676 to 677] Secret Guardroom (Small or Medium)

[678 to 679] Secret Room (Tiny, Small, Medium, or Large)

[680 to 681] Servant's Quarters / Servants' Quarters (Tiny, Small, or Medium)

[682 to 683] Servants' Hall (Medium, Large, or Huge)

[684 to 685] Servery (Tiny, Small, or Medium)

[686] Sewing Room (Small or Medium)

[687 to 688] Shrine (Small or Medium)

[689 to 690] Shrine Chamber (Small)

[691 to 692] Shrine Room (Medium or Large)

[693 to 694] Sick Chamber (Small)

[695 to 696] Sick Room (Medium or Large)

[697 to 698] Sitting Room (Small or Medium)

[699 to 700] Sleeping Chamber (Small)

[701] Smithy (Small, Medium or Large)

[702 to 703] Smoke Room (Small or Medium)

[704 to 705] Solar (Small or Medium)

[706 to 707] Solarium (Small, Medium, or Large)

[708 to 709] Spear Closet (Tiny or Small)

[710 to 711] Spoliarium (Small)

[712 to 713] Stair Chamber (Small)

[714 to 715] Stairway Room (Medium)

[716 to 717] State Chamber (Small or Medium)

[718 to 719] State Room (Large or Huge)

[720 to 721] Statuary (Small, Medium, or Large)

[722 to 723] Still Room (Small or Medium)

[724 to 725] Stockpile Room (Small or Medium)

[726 to 727] Stofa (Small or Medium)

[728 to 729] Storage Chamber (Small)

[730 to 731] Storage Room / Storeroom (Small or Medium)

[732 to 733] Storeroom – Alchemical (Small or Medium)

[734 to 735] Storeroom – Alcohol / Wine (Small or Medium)

[736 to 737] Storeroom – Armor (Small or Medium)

[738 to 739] Storeroom – Box Room (Small or Medium)

[740] Storeroom – Butchered Meat (Small or Medium)

[741 to 742] Storeroom – Char / Coal (Small or Medium)

[743 to 744] Storeroom – Cheese (Small or Medium)

[745 to 746] Storeroom – Drink (Small or Medium)

[747 to 748] Storeroom – Dry Goods (Small or Medium)

[749 to 750] Storeroom – Failed Experiments (Small or Medium)

[751 to 752] Storeroom – Foodstuffs (Small or Medium)

[753 to 754] Storeroom – Furniture (Small or Medium)

[755 to 756] Storeroom – Herbs and Spices (Small or Medium)

[757 to 758] Storeroom – Ice (Small or Medium)

[759 to 760] Storeroom – Lumber (Small or Medium)

[761 to 762] Storeroom – Oil (Small or Medium)

[763 to 764] Storeroom – Reagents (Small or Medium)

[765 to 766] Storeroom – Salt (Small or Medium)

[767 to 768] Storeroom – Sundries (Small or Medium)

[769 to 770] Storeroom – Tools and Gear (Small or Medium)

[771 to 772] Storeroom – Water (Small or Medium)

[773 to 774] Storm Cellar (Small or Medium)

[775 to 776] Stricture (Tiny or Small)

[777 to 778] Strongroom (Small)

[779 to 780] Studio (Small)

[781 to 782] Study (Small or Medium)

[783 to 784] Sub-Basement (Tiny, Small, or Medium)

[785 to 786] Sub-Cellar (Tiny, Small, or Medium)

[787 to 788] Suite (Medium)

[789 to 790] Suite Chamber (Small)

[791 to 792] Summoning Chamber (Small)

[793 to 794] Summoning Room (Medium or Large)

[795 to 796] Sunroom (Small or Medium)

[797] Svefnhus (Small or Medium)

[798 to 799] Tablinum (Small or Medium)

[800 to 801] Tabulinum (Small)

[802 to 803] Tack Room (Small or Medium)

[804 to 805] Taxidermy Hall (Small, Medium, or Large)

[806 to 807] Teleportation Chamber (Tiny, Small, or Medium)

[808 to 809] Tepidarium (Small, Medium, or Large)

[810 to 811] Thalamium (Small or Medium)

[812 to 813] Thalamos (Small or Medium)

[814 to 815] Theater (Large or Huge)

[816 to 817] Tholos (Small, Medium, or Large)

[818 to 819] Threshold (Tiny, Small, Medium, or Large)

[820 to 821] Torcularium (Small)

[822] Tower / Tower Chamber (Small, Medium, Large, or Huge, with the Huge variant being almost wholly subterranean)

[823 to 824] Treasure Chamber (Small or Medium)

[825 to 826] Treasure Vault (Medium or Large)

[827 to 828] Triclinium (Small or Medium)

[829 to 830] Trophy Hall (Large or Huge)

[831 to 832] Trophy Room (Small or Medium)

[833 to 834] Turret / Turret Vault (Small, Medium, or Large)

[835 to 836] Utility Chamber (Small)

[837 to 838] Utility Room (Medium or Large)

[839 to 840] Vault (Small, Medium, or Large)

[841 to 842] Vaulted Chamber (Small or Medium)

[843 to 844] Vaulted Hall (Large or Huge)

[845 to 846] Vaulted Room (Medium or Large)

[847 to 848] Vestiary (Tiny, Small, or Medium)

[849 to 850] Vestibule (Small or Medium)

[851 to 852] Vestibulum (Small or Medium)

[853 to 854] Vigil (Tiny, Small, or Medium)

[855 to 856] Vinery (Small, Medium, or Large)

[857 to 858] Waiting Chamber (Small)

[859 to 860] Waiting Room (Medium or Large)

[861 to 862] Walk-In Closet (Tiny or Small)

[863 to 864] Walled-Up Chamber (Small)

[865 to 866] Walled-Up Corridor (Small or Medium)

[867 to 868] Walled-Up Room (Medium or Large)

[869 to 870] Wardrobe (Tiny)

[871 to 872] Wardrobe Room (Small or Medium)

[873 to 874] Warming Room (Small, Medium, or Large)

[875 to 876] Washroom (Tiny, Small, or Medium)

[877 to 878] Watchroom (Tiny, Small, or Medium)

[879 to 880] Weaving Room (Small or Medium)

[881 to 882] Well (Tiny, Small, or Medium)

[883 to 884] Well Room (Small or Medium)

[885 to 886] Wine Cellar (Small or Medium)

[887 to 888] Wine Vault (Small, Medium, or Large)

[889 to 890] Withdrawing Chamber (Small)

[891 to 892] Withdrawing Room (Medium)

[893 to 894] Wizard's Laboratory (Small, Medium, or Large)

[895 to 896] Wizard's Workroom (Small or Medium)

[897] Xenodocheion (Small, Medium, or Large)

[898] Xenodocheum (Small, Medium, or Large)

[899 to 900] Zoo (or Menagerie) (Large or Huge)

[901 to 909] Manor House Sub-Region: Artificial Grottoes. Roll on the Cave Room Table for the next 1D4+1 rooms (rerolling any results of 901 to 000), and then return to this table.

[910 to 915] Manor House Sub-Region: Elaborate Artificial Grottoes. Roll on the Cave Room Table for the next 2D4 rooms (rerolling any results of 901 to 000), and then return to this table.

[916 to 918] Manor House Sub-Region: Collapsed Understructure. Roll on the Cave Room Table for the next 2D6+1 rooms (rerolling any results of 901 to 000), and then return to this table.

[919 to 927] Manor House Sub-Region: Forbidden Chambers. Roll on the Dungeon Room Table for the next 1D4+1 rooms (rerolling any results of 901 to 000), and then return to this table.

[928 to 933] Manor House Sub-Region: Walled-Up Vaults. Roll on Dungeon Room Table for the next 2D4 rooms (rerolling any results of 901 to 000), and then return to this table.

[934 to 936] Manor House Sub-Region: Haunted Dungeon Vaults. Roll on Dungeon Room Table for the next 2D6+1 rooms (rerolling any results of 901 to 000), and then return to this table.

[937 to 945] Manor House Sub-Region: Secure Rooms. Roll on the Stronghold Room

Table for the next 1D4+1 rooms (rerolling any results of 901 to 000), and then return to this table.

[946 to 951] Manor House Sub-Region: Manorial Donjon. Roll on the Stronghold Room Table for the next 2D4 rooms (rerolling any results of 901 to 000), and then return to this table.

[952 to 954] Manor House Sub-Region: Manorial Keep. Roll on the Stronghold Room Table for the next 2D6+1 rooms (rerolling any results of 901 to 000), and then return to this table.

[955 to 963] Manor House Sub-Region: Sacred Chambers. Roll on the Temple Room Table for the next 1D4+1 rooms (rerolling any results of 901 to 000), and then return to this table.

[964 to 969] Manor House Sub-Region: Ancestral Fane. Roll on the Temple Room Table for the next 2D4 rooms (rerolling any results of 901 to 000), and then return to this table.

[970 to 972] Manor House Sub-Region: Ancestral Temple. Roll on the Temple Room Table for the next 2D6+1 rooms (rerolling any results of 901 to 000), and then return to this table.

[973 to 981] Manor House Sub-Region: Family Crypt. Roll on the Tomb Room Table for the next 1D4+1 rooms (rerolling any results of 901 to 000), and then return to this table.

[982 to 987] Manor House Sub-Region: Familial Tombs. Roll on the Tomb Room Table for the next 2D4 rooms (rerolling any results of 901 to 000), and then return to this table.

[988 to 990] Manor House Sub-Region: Ancestral Mausoleum. Roll on the Tomb Room Table for the next 2D6+1 rooms (rerolling any results of 901 to 000), and then return to this table.

[991 to 995] Manor House Sub-Region: Eerie Rooms. Roll on the Evocative Random Rooms Table (refer to The Classic Dungeon Design Guide, Book I) for the next 1D4+1 rooms (rerolling any results of 901 to 000), and then return to this table.

[996 to 998] Manor House Sub-Region: Haunted Chambers. Roll on the Evocative Random Rooms Table (refer to The Classic Dungeon Design Guide, Book I) for the next 2D4 rooms (rerolling any results of 901 to 000), and then return to this table.

[999 to 000] Manor House Sub-Region: Halls of Madness. Roll on the Evocative Random Rooms Table (refer to The Classic Dungeon Design Guide, Book I) for the next 2D6+1 rooms (rerolling any results of 901 to 000), and then return to this table.

STRONGHOLD ROOMS

There are many different types of strongholds, with the relatively size of a fortress generally depending upon a noble's station. Please refer to the *Game World Generator* supplement if you would care to see full details on Oldskull nobility and holdings, by a ruler's (or a steward's, or a castellan's) title, heritage, and experience level.

Strongholds can be epic in size, or they can be baronial or relatively small (with the majority of the dungeon being situated underground, beneath the fortified structure).

Note too that if you as the Game Master prefer realistic strongholds, the rooms on average will be smaller than they are on classic dungeon maps; in that case, you might then want to use the square footage for *gentrified* manorial room sizes as given in the Manor House section prior.

For random rooms appearing in a stronghold or fortress, roll 1D1000 and consult the following table.

TABLE 4

STRONGHOLD ROOMS

[001 to 002] Abreuvoir (Medium, Large, or Huge)

[003] Access Chamber (Small)

[004 to 005] Access Room (Medium)

[006] Accommodation (Small)

[007 to 008] Accommodations, plural (Medium or Large)

[009] Aerarium / Ancient Aerary (Medium or Large)

[010 to 011] Aerarium Chamber (Small or Medium)

[012 to 013] Aerary (Medium or Large)

[014] Aerary Chamber (Small)

[015] Af-Hus (Tiny or Small)

[016 to 017] Air Chamber (Small)

[018] Air Room (Medium)

[019 to 020] Ala (Tiny or Small)

[021] Alae, plural (Medium or Large)

[022 to 023] Alcove (Tiny or Small)

[024] Alcove Succession (Medium or Large)

[025 to 026] Ale Cellar (Small or Medium)

[027] Aleatorium (Small or Medium)

[028 to 029] Alhacena (Tiny or Small)

[030] Alhacena Succession (Medium or Large)

[031 to 032] Ambry (Small or Medium)

[033] Ambry Chamber (Tiny or Small)

[034 to 035] Ambulatory (Medium)

[036] Amphithalamoi, plural (Medium or Large)

[037 to 038] Amphithalamos (Small or Medium)

[039 to 040] Amphithalamus (Small or Medium)

[041 to 042] Ancestral Chamber (Small or Medium)

[043 to 044] Ancestral Hall (Large or Huge)

[045] Anddyri (Small, Medium, or Large)

[046] Andron (Small or Medium)

[047] Annex (Tiny, Small, or Medium)

[048] Annex Labyrinth (Large or Huge)

[049] Antecabinet (Small)

[050 to 051] Antechamber (Small)

[052] Anteroom (Medium)

[053 to 054] Aperture (Tiny)

[055] Apotheca (Small or Medium)

[056 to 057] Apothecarium (Small or Medium)

[058 to 059] Apothecary (Small or Medium)

[060 to 061] Apse (Small)

[062] Apse Room (Medium)

[063 to 064] Archive (Medium, Large, or Huge)

[065 to 066] Arena (Medium, Large, or Huge)

[067 to 068] Armorial Chamber (Medium)

[069] Armorial Hall (Large or Huge)

[070 to 071] Armory (Medium)

[072] Armory and Forge (Large or Huge)

[073 to 074] Armory Chamber (Small)

[075] Arryt (Large or Huge)

[076 to 077] Arsenal (Large)

[078 to 079] Arsenal and Forge (Large or Huge)

[080 to 081] Arsenal Chamber (Small)

[082] Artisan's Chamber (Small or Medium)

[083] Artisan's Room (Medium or Large)

[084 to 085] Assembly Chamber (Small or Medium)

[086 to 087] Assembly Hall (Large or Huge)

[088] Athanor Chamber (Small)

[089 to 090] Athanor Room (Medium or Large)

[091] Atrium (Large or Huge)

[092 to 093] Atrium Chamber (Small or Medium)

[094 to 095] Audience Chamber (Small)

[096 to 097] Audience Hall (Large or Huge)

[098 to 099] Audience Room (Medium)

[100] Auditorium (Huge)

[101] Aula (Medium or Large)

[102 to 103] Aula Regia (Huge)

[104] Auxiliary Chamber (Tiny or Small)

[105] Auxiliary Room (Medium)

[106 to 107] Bailey (Medium, Large, or Huge)

[108] Balnea (Small or Medium)

[109 to 110] Balnearium (Small or Medium)

[111 to 112] Banquet Hall (Large or Huge)

[113] Banquet Room (Medium)

[114 to 115] Barbican (Large)

[116 to 117] Barracks (Medium or Large)

[118 to 119] Barracks Hall (Huge)

[120 to 121] Bastion (Medium or Large)

[122] Bawm (Small, Medium, or Large)

[123] Bay (Tiny or Small)

[124] Bay Succession (Medium or Large)

[125] Beast Pit (Small or Medium)

[126] Bedchamber (Small)

[127] Bedroom (Small or Medium)

[128] Belfry (Medium or Large)

[129] Bell Tower (Medium, Large, or Huge)

[130] Bleeding Chamber (Small)

[131 to 132] Bleeding Room (Medium)

[133] Bodega (Small)

[134 to 135] Boudoir (Small or Medium)

[136 to 137] Bouleuterion (Large or Huge)

[138 to 139] Bourse (Small, Medium, or Large)

[140] Bower (Small)

[141] Breezeway (Medium or Large)

[142 to 143] Brewery (Medium, Large, or Huge)

[144 to 145] Butchery (Small)

[146] Buttery (Small or Medium)

[147] Cabinet (Small)

[148 to 149] Cache Chamber (Small)

[150 to 151] Cache Room (Medium or Large)

[152 to 153] Cage (Tiny, Small, or Medium)

[154] Cage Matrix (Large or Huge)

[155] Caldarium (Small, Medium, or Large)

[156 to 157] Calefactorium (Small, Medium, or Large)

[158] Calefactory (Small, Medium, or Large)

[159 to 160] Camba (Small or Medium)

[161 to 162] Carcer (Medium, Large, or Huge)

[163 to 164] Cartographer's Hall (Large or Huge)

[165 to 166] Casemate (Small or Medium)

[167] Catabulum (Medium or Large)

[168] Cavaedium (Large or Huge)

[169 to 170] Cavea (Small, Medium, or Large)

[171] Cell (Tiny or Small)

[172 to 173] Cell Block (Medium or Large)

[174] Cella Vinaria (Small, Medium, or Large)

[175 to 176] Cellae, plural (Medium or Large)

[177 to 178] Cellula (Tiny or Small)

[179] Cesspit (Tiny, Small, or Medium)

[180] Cesspool (Tiny, Small, or Medium)

[181 to 182] Chamber (Small)

[183 to 184] Chambers, plural (Medium, Large, or Huge)

[185 to 186] Chandlery (Small or Medium)

[187] Chantier (Small, Medium, or Large)

[188] Chapter House (Medium, Large, or Huge)

[189] Chapter Room (Small or Medium)

[190] Char Cellar (Tiny, Small, or Medium)

[191 to 192] Charter Room (Small or Medium)

[193 to 194] Chartophylacium (Medium, Large, or Huge)

[195] Cheese Cellar (Small or Medium)

[196 to 197] Cistern (Small, Medium, Large, or Huge)

[198 to 199] Cistern Room (Small or Medium)

[200] Classroom (Medium or Large)

[201] Clinic (Medium or Large)

[202] Cloaca (Medium, Large, or Huge)

[203] Cloak Room (Small or Medium)

[204 to 205] Clockwork Room (Small or Medium)

[206 to 207] Coal Room (Small, Medium, or Large)

[208 to 209] Coldroom (Small or Medium)

[210 to 211] Colonnade Hall (Large or Huge)

[212 to 213] Colonnade Room (Medium)

[214 to 215] Combat Pit (Small or Medium)

[216 to 217] Commandery (Medium or Large)

[218 to 219] Common Room (Medium, Large, or Huge)

[220] Communal Quarters (Medium, Large, or Huge)

[221] Compluvium Chamber (Small)

[222] Compluvium Hall (Large)

[223] Compluvium Room (Medium)

[224] Concealed Chamber (Small)

[225 to 226] Concealed Room (Medium or Large)

[227 to 228] Conclave (Medium or Large)

[229 to 230] Conclavium (Medium or Large)

[231] Conjuring Chamber (Small or Medium)

[232 to 233] Control Room (Small or Medium)

[234] Corycaeum (Small, Medium, or Large)

[235 to 236] Council Chamber / Counsel Chamber

[237 to 238] Council Hall / Counsel Hall (Large)

[239 to 240] Council Room / Counsel Room (Medium)

[241 to 242] Counting Room (Small or Medium)

[243 to 244] Court (Large or Huge)

[245 to 246] Courtyard (Medium or Large if subterranean, otherwise Large or Huge)

[247] Crafter's Room (Small or Medium)

[248] Crowde (Tiny, Small, or Medium)

[249 to 250] Cubicle (Tiny)

[251 to 252] Cubicula, plural (Small, Medium, or Large)

[253 to 254] Cubiculum (Tiny or Small)

[255] Dairy Chamber (Small or Medium)

[256] Dairy Room (Medium or Large)

[257 to 258] Dais Chamber (Small or Medium)

[259 to 260] Dais Room (Medium or Large)

[261] Dead End (Tiny or Small)

[262 to 263] Depository (Medium or Large)

[264 to 265] Dining Chamber (Small)

[266 to 267] Dining Hall (Large or Huge)

[268] Dining Room (Medium)

[269] Distillery (Medium or Large)

[270] Divination Chamber (Small)

[271 to 272] Domed Chamber (Small)

[273] Domed Hall (Large or Huge)

[274 to 275] Domed Room (Medium)

[276] Domicile (Small or Medium)

[277 to 278] Donjon (Small, Medium, or Large, with Large implying multiple rooms and chambers)

[279] Dormitory (Large or Huge)

[280 to 281] Drawbridge / Drawbridge Chamber (Small)

[282] Drawing Chamber (Small)

[283] Drawing Room (Medium)

[284 to 285] Drill Hall (Large or Huge)

[286] Drying Room (Small or Medium)

[287 to 288] Dueling Pit (Small or Medium)

[289 to 290] Dueling Pit Matrix (Small)

[291] Dungeon (Small, Medium, or Large, with Large implying multiple rooms and chambers)

[292] Eldaskali (Large or Huge)

[293] Enclosed Loggia (Medium or Large)

[294 to 295] Enclosure (Small or Medium, with a Tiny internal space)

[296] Enterclose (Tiny or Small)

[297 to 298] Entrance Hall (Medium, Large, or Huge)

[299 to 300] Entry / Entryway (Small or Medium)

[301 to 302] Entry Hall (Medium or Large)

[303] Ephebeum (Medium)

[304] Episcenium (Tiny or Small)

[305 to 306] Excubitorium (Small or Medium)

[307] Execution Chamber (Small)

[308] Execution Hall (Large or Huge)

[309 to 310] Execution Room (Medium)

[311 to 312] Exercise Room (Small, Medium, or Large)

[313] False Treasure Room (Small or Medium)

[314] False Treasure Vault (Medium or Large)

[315 to 316] Feast Hall (Large or Huge)

[317 to 318] Firepit (Tiny or Small)

[319] Flooded Hall (Large or Huge)

[320] Flooded Room (Small or Medium)

[321 to 322] Forbidden Chamber (Small or Medium)

[323 to 324] Forbidden Vault (Large)

[325 to 326] Forecourt (Medium or Large)

[327 to 328] Forge (Small, Medium, or Large)

[329] Fornix Chamber (Small)

[330] Fornix Hall (Large or Huge)

[331 to 332] Fornix Room (Medium)

[333 to 334] Fosse Chamber (Small)

[335] Fosse Room (Medium)

[336 to 337] Foundry (Small, Medium, or Large)

[338 to 339] Fountain Chamber (Small)

[340] Fountain Hall (Large or Huge)

[341 to 342] Fountain Room (Medium)

[353 to 344] Foyer (Small or Medium)

[345 to 346] Frater (Small, Medium, or Large)

[347] Fresco Gallery (Large)

[348] Fresco Room (Small or Medium)

[349] Frigidarium (Small, Medium, or Large)

[350] Fumarium (Tiny or Small)

[351 to 352] Fumigatory (Tiny, Small, or Medium)

[353] Function Hall (Large or Huge)

[354 to 355] Function Room (Medium)

[356 to 357] Fundament (Small or Medium)

[358 to 359] Fundament Room (Medium or Large)

[360 to 361] Gallery (Display) (Medium, Large, or Huge)

[362] Gambling Hall (Large)

[363] Gambling Room (Medium)

[364] Game Room (Small, Medium, or Large)

[365 to 366] Gaol (Small, Medium, or Large, with Large implying many cells)

[367 to 368] Garden (Medium or Large)

[369 to 370] Garderobe (Tiny or Small)

[371 to 372] Garderobe Chamber (Small or Medium)

[373] Gardr (Small, Medium, or Large)

[374 to 375] Garrison (Medium or Large)

[376 to 377] Gate Chamber (Medium)

[378 to 379] Gate Room (Large)

[380 to 381] Gatehouse (Medium or Large)

[382 to 383] Gauntlet (Medium or Large)

[384] Goods Hall (Medium or Large)

[385] Granary (Small or Medium)

[386] Grand Aerarium (Large or Huge)

[387] Grand Aerary (Large or Huge)

[388] Grand Arena (Huge)

[389 to 390] Grand Armory (Large or Huge)

[391 to 392] Grand Armory and Forge (Large or Huge)

[393 to 394] Grand Arsenal (Large or Huge)

[395 to 396] Grand Arsenal and Forge (Large or Huge)

[397] Grand Aviary (Large or Huge)

[398 to 399] Grand Gallery (Display) (Small)

[400] Grand Salon (Large or Huge)

[401] Great Andron (Large or Huge)

[402 to 403] Great Chamber (Large or Huge)

[404 to 405] Great Hall (Large or Huge)

[406] Great Kitchen (Large or Huge)

[407] Grinding Chamber (Small)

[408] Grinding Room (Medium or Large)

[409 to 410] Guard Chamber (Small)

[411 to 412] Guard Hall (Large or Huge)

[413 to 414] Guard Post (Tiny or Small)

[415 to 416] Guardroom (Medium)

[417] Guest Chamber (Small)

[418] Guestroom (Small or Medium)

[419] Guild Hall (Large or Huge)

[420] Guild Room (Medium)

[421] Gymnasium (Large)

[422] Gynaeceum (Medium or Large)

[423 to 424] Hall (Large or Huge)

[425 to 426] Hall of Assembly (Large or Huge)

[427 to 428] Hall of Challenge (Large or Huge)

[429 to 430] Hall of Doors (Large or Huge)

[431 to 432] Hall of Honor (Large or Huge)

[433 to 434] Hall of Judgment (Large or Huge)

[435] Hall of Reverence (Large or Huge)

[436 to 437] Hall of Runes (Large or Huge)

[438 to 439] Hall of Statuary (Large or Huge)

[440] Hall of Tapestries (Large or Huge)

[441] Hamr (Small or Medium)

[442 to 443] Harness Room (Medium)

[444 to 445] Hastarium (Medium)

[446] Hearth Chamber (Small)

[447 to 448] Hearth Hall (Large or Huge)

[449 to 450] Hearth Room (Medium)

[451 to 452] Heroum (Tiny, Small, or Medium)

[453] Hideout (Medium or Large)

[454 to 455] Hiding Place (Tiny or Small)

[456] Holl (Large or Huge)

[457] Horological Hall (Large or Huge)

[458] Horologium (Small or Medium)

[459] Horreum (Small, Medium, or Large)

[460 to 461] Hospitalium (Small)

[462 to 463] Hospitium (Medium)

[464 to 465] Hostel (Medium or Large)

[466 to 467] Hunters' Hall (Large or Huge)

[468 to 469] Hus (Small or Medium)

[470] Hylr (Small or Medium)

[471 to 472] Hypocaust (Medium)

[473 to 474] Hypocaust Chamber (Tiny or Small)

[475 to 476] Hypogeum (Small, Medium, or Large)

[477 to 478] Hypostyle Hall (Large or Huge)

[479] Ice Chamber (Small)

[480] Icehouse (Medium)

[481] Idol Grotto (Small, Medium, or Large)

[482] Illusory Chamber (Small)

[483] Illusory Room (Medium or Large)

[484 to 485] Immense Archive (Huge)

[486 to 487] Impluvium Chamber (Small)

[488 to 489] Impluvium Hall (Large or Huge)

[490] Impluvium Room (Medium)

[491] Infirmary (Medium or Large)

[492 to 493] Inquisition / Inquisitorial Chamber

[494] Inscription Chamber (Small)

[495] Instrument Chamber (Small)

[496 to 497] Interrogation Chamber (Tiny or Small)

[498 to 499] Interrogation Room (Small or Medium)

[500] Isi (Medium or Large)

[501 to 502] Jail (Small, Medium, or Large, with Large implying many cells)

[503] Junk Room (Small or Medium)

[504 to 505] Keep (Large or Huge)

[506] Kelda (Small or Medium)

[507 to 508] Kitchen (Medium)

[509 to 510] Kitchen Chamber (Small)

[511] Kneipe (Small or Medium)

[512 to 513] Knights' Hall (Medium, Large, or Huge)

[514] Laconicum (Small, Medium, or Large)

[515 to 516] Lady's Chamber (Small or Medium)

[517] Lair (Tiny, Small, Medium, Large, or Huge)

[518 to 519] Landing (Tiny or Small)

[520 to 521] Larder (Medium)

[522] Larder Chamber (Small)

[523 to 524] Latrine (Tiny)

[525 to 526] Latrine Chamber (Small or Medium)

[527] Lavatorium (Small or Medium)

[528] Lavatory (Small or Medium)

[529 to 530] Library (Medium, Large, or Huge)

[531 to 532] Lightwell (Tiny, Small, or Medium)

[533] Loft (Tiny, Small, or Medium)

[534] Lokrekkja (Tiny)

[535] Long Gallery (Large or Huge)

[536 to 537] Lookout (Tiny, Small, or Medium)

[538] Lopt (Large or Huge)

[539 to 540] Lord's Chamber (Small or Medium)

[541] Lumber Room (Small or Medium)

[542 to 543] Manufactorium (Large or Huge)

[544 to 545] Manufactory (Large or Huge)

[546 to 547] Map Chamber (Small)

[548 to 549] Map Room (Medium)

[550] Mechanical Room (Small or Medium)

[551 to 552] Meeting Room (Small or Medium)

[553 to 554] Megaron (Large or Huge)

[555 to 556] Mess Hall (Large or Huge)

[557] Mezzanine (Small or Medium, a subspace within an area that is Large or Huge)

[558] Mezzanine Hall (Large or Huge)

[559 to 560] Moat / Moat Vault (Medium or Large)

[561 to 562] Moat Hall (Large or Huge)

[563] Monument Hall (Huge)

[564] Monument Room (Large)

[565] Moot Hall (Large or Huge)

[566 to 567] Motte (Medium, Large, or Huge)

[568] Mtwn / Metwen (Large or Huge)

[569 to 570] Muniment Hall (Large or Huge)

[571] Muniment Room (Small or Medium)

[572 to 573] Murder Room (Tiny, Small, or Medium)

[574] Museum (Large or Huge)

[575] Music Chamber (Small)

[576] Music Room (Medium)

[577 to 578] Narthex (Medium, Large, or Huge)

[579] Naumachia (Large or Huge)

[580] Necessarium (Tiny or Small)

[581 to 582] Niche (Tiny)

[583 to 584] Niched Room (Small or Medium)

[585 to 586] Observation Chamber (Small or Medium)

[587 to 588] Occus (Small)

[589] Oecus (Medium or Large)

[590 to 591] Office (Tiny, Small, or Medium)

[592 to 593] Oil Cellar (Small or Medium)

[594] Oil Press Room (Small or Medium)

[595] Oracular Chamber (Small or Medium)

[596 to 597] Outpost (Small, Medium, or Large)

[598] Overlook (Small or Medium)

[599 to 600] Palatial Hall (Huge)

[601] Pallet Chamber (Tiny or Small)

[602] Pantry (Small or Medium)

[603] Parlatorium (Small or Medium)

[604] Pastophorium (Small)

[605 to 606] Pen (Tiny, Small, or Medium, with Medium implying a number of pens in a single location)

[607] Penaria (Small or Medium)

[608] Pergula (Tiny, Small, or Medium)

[609] Peristyle (Small, Medium, or Large, surrounding a smaller interior)

[610] Peristylium (Small, Medium, or Large, surrounding a smaller interior)

[611 to 612] Pit (Tiny or Small)

[613 to 614] Pit Chamber (Small)

[615 to 616] Pit Room (Medium)

[617 to 618] Planning Room (Small or Medium)

[619 to 620] Portcullis Chamber

[621] Priest Hole (Tiny or Small)

[622 to 623] Prison (Small, Medium, or Large)

[624 to 625] Prison Block (Medium, Large, or Huge)

[626 to 627] Prison Cell (Tiny)

[628 to 629] Prison Chamber (Small)

[630 to 631] Prison Hall (Large or Huge)

[632 to 633] Privy (Tiny or Small)

[634] Procoeton (Small)

[635] Procoetum (Small)

[636 to 637] Protective Ditch (Small, Medium, or Large)

[638] Prothyron (Small or Medium)

[639 to 640] Proving Ground, plural Proving Grounds (Medium, Large, or Huge, with Huge being plural)

[641] Pump Room (Small or Medium)

[642] Puteus (Small, Medium, or Large)

[643 to 644] Quarters (Small, Medium, or Large)

[645 to 646] Quarters, Solitary (Tiny or Small)

[647 to 648] Reception Chamber (Small)

[649 to 650] Reception Hall (Large or Huge)

[651 to 652] Reception Room (Small or Medium)

[653] Recess (Tiny or Small, with an adjacent Small, Medium, or Large space)

[654 to 655] Redoubt (Small, Medium, or Large)

[656 to 657] Refuge (Small, Medium, or Large)

[658] Repository (Small or Medium)

[659 to 660] Retreat (Small or Medium)

[661] Revolving Chamber (Small or Medium)

[662 to 663] Riding Hall (Large or Huge)

[664] Room (Small or Medium)

[665 to 666] Room of Slaughter (Small, Medium, or Large)

[667] Room of Unknown Purpose (Tiny, Small, Medium, Large, or Huge)

[668] Roost (Tiny, Small, or Medium)

[669] Root Cellar (Small or Medium)

[670 to 671] Rotating Room (Small or Medium)

[672] Rotunda (Small, Medium, or Large)

[673 to 674] Royal Chamber / Noble's Chamber (Small or Medium)

[675] Rum (Small or Medium)

[676 to 677] Safe Room (Small or Medium)

[678] Salr (Large or Huge)

[679] Salt Cellar (Small or Medium)

[680] Salt Chamber (Small)

[681 to 682] Salt Room (Medium)

[683] Sauna (Small or Medium)

[684] Scrapheap (Small, Medium, or Large)

[685] Scriptorium (Medium or Large)

[686 to 687] Scullery (Small or Medium)

[688 to 689] Secret Guardroom (Small or Medium)

[690 to 691] Secret Room (Tiny, Small, Medium, or Large)

[692] Sellaria (Large)

[693 to 694] Seraglio (Small or Medium)

[695 to 696] Servant's Quarters / Servants' Quarters (Tiny, Small, or Medium)

[697 to 698] Servants' Hall (Medium, Large, or Huge)

[699 to 700] Servery (Tiny, Small, or Medium)

[701 to 702] Sewer (Small, Medium, Large, or Huge)

[703 to 704] Shelter (Tiny or Small)

[705] Shop (Small or Medium)

[706] Shrine (Small or Medium)

[707] Shrine Chamber (Small)

[708] Shrine Room (Medium or Large)

[709] Skali (Small, Medium, or Large)

[710] Skinning Room (Small or Medium)

[711 to 712] Slave Chamber (Tiny, Small, or Medium)

[713 to 714] Sleeping Chamber (Small)

[715 to 716] Sleeping Hall (Large)

[717 to 718] Sleeping Room (Medium)

[719 to 720] Smelter (Small, Medium, or Large)

[721 to 722] Smithy (Small, Medium or Large)

[723 to 724] Smoke Room (Small or Medium)

[725 to 726] Spoliarium (Small)

[727 to 728] Squires' Hall (Medium or Large)

[729 to 730] Stable (Small, Medium, or Large)

[731 to 732] Stair Chamber (Small)

[733 to 734] Stairway Room (Medium)

[735] State Chamber (Small or Medium)

[736] State Room (Large or Huge)

[737] Statuary (Small, Medium, or Large)

[738] Steinn (Small, Medium, or Large)

[739] Still Room (Small or Medium)

[740 to 741] Stockpile Room (Small or Medium)

[742] Stofa (Small or Medium)

[743 to 744] Storage Chamber (Small)

[745 to 746] Storage Room / Storeroom (Small or Medium)

[747 to 748] Storeroom – Alcohol / Wine (Small or Medium)

[749 to 750] Storeroom – Armor (Small or Medium)

[751] Storeroom – Box Room (Small or Medium)

[752] Storeroom – Butchered Meat (Small or Medium)

[753] Storeroom – Char / Coal (Small or Medium)

[754] Storeroom – Cheese (Small or Medium)

[755 to 756] Storeroom – Construction (Small or Medium)

[757] Storeroom – Drink (Small or Medium)

[758 to 759] Storeroom – Dry Goods (Small or Medium)

[760 to 761] Storeroom – Equipment Room (Small or Medium)

[762 to 763] Storeroom – Foodstuffs (Small or Medium)

[764] Storeroom – Furniture (Small or Medium)

[765] Storeroom – Herbs and Spices (Small or Medium)

[766] Storeroom – Ice (Small or Medium)

[767] Storeroom – Lumber (Small or Medium)

[768 to 769] Storeroom – Masonry (Small or Medium)

[770] Storeroom – Oil (Small or Medium)

[771] Storeroom – Salt (Small or Medium)

[772] Storeroom – Sundries (Small or Medium)

[773 to 774] Storeroom – Tools and Gear (Small or Medium)

[775 to 776] Storeroom – Water (Small or Medium)

[777 to 778] Storeroom – Weapons (Small or Medium)

[779 to 780] Stricture (Tiny or Small)

[781 to 782] Strongroom (Small)

[783 to 784] Study (Small or Medium)

[785] Sudatorium (Small, Medium, or Large)

[785] Suite (Medium)

[787 to 788] Suite Chamber (Small)

[789 to 790] Summoning Gauntlet (Medium, Large, or Huge)

[791] Svefnhus (Small or Medium)

[792] Tablinum (Small or Medium)

[793 to 794] Tabulinum (Small)

[795 to 796] Tack Room (Small or Medium)

[797 to 798] Tank (Small, Medium, Large, or Huge)

[799 to 800] Taxidermy Hall (Small, Medium, or Large)

[801] Teleportation Chamber (Tiny, Small, or Medium)

[802] Tepidarium (Small, Medium, or Large)

[803] Thalamium (Small or Medium)

[804] Thalamos (Small or Medium)

[805 to 806] Therma (Large or Huge)

[807] Thermopolium (Small or Medium)

[808] Tholos (Small, Medium, or Large)

[809 to 810] Threshold (Tiny, Small, Medium, or Large)

[811 to 812] Throne Hall (Huge)

[813 to 814] Throne Room (Medium or Large)

[815 to 816] Tool Room (Small or Medium)

[817] Torcularium (Small)

[818 to 819] Torture Chamber (Small, Medium, or Large)

[820] Torture Pit(s) (Small, Medium, or Large, with Large implying multiple pits)

[821 to 822] Tower / Tower Chamber (Small, Medium, Large, or Huge, with the Huge variant being almost wholly subterranean)

[823 to 824] Training Hall (Large or Huge)

[825 to 826] Training Room (Medium or Large)

[827 to 828] Treasure Chamber (Small or Medium)

[829] Treasure Vault (Medium or Large)

[830 to 831] Treasury (Medium or Large)

[832 to 833] Trophy Hall (Large or Huge)

[834 to 835] Trophy Room (Small or Medium)

[836 to 837] Turret / Turret Vault (Small, Medium, or Large)

[838] Unfinished Chamber (Small)

[839] Unfinished Hall (Large or Huge)

[840] Unfinished Room (Medium)

[841] Utility Chamber (Small)

[842 to 843] Utility Room (Medium or Large)

[844] Vault (Small, Medium, or Large)

[845 to 846] Vaulted Chamber (Small or Medium)

[847 to 848] Vaulted Hall (Large or Huge)

[849 to 850] Vaulted Room (Medium or Large)

[851] Vestibule (Small or Medium)

[852] Vestibulum (Small or Medium)

[853] Vigil (Tiny, Small, or Medium)

[854] Vinery (Small, Medium, or Large)

[855] Walled-Up Chamber (Small)

[856] Walled-Up Corridor (Small or Medium)

[857] Walled-Up Room (Medium or Large)

[858 to 859] War Room (Medium or Large)

[860 to 861] Ward (Medium or Large)

[862] Warming Room (Small, Medium, or Large)

[863 to 864] Washroom (Tiny, Small, or Medium)

[865 to 866] Watchroom (Tiny, Small, or Medium)

[867 to 868] Weaving Room (Small or Medium)

[869 to 870] Well (Tiny, Small, or Medium)

[871 to 872] Well Room (Small or Medium)

[873 to 874] Winch Pit (Tiny or Small)

[875 to 876] Winch Room (Medium or Large)

[877 to 878] Wine Cellar (Small or Medium)

[879 to 880] Wine Vault (Small, Medium, or Large)

[881 to 882] Withdrawing Chamber (Small)

[883 to 884] Withdrawing Room (Medium)

[885 to 886] Work Chamber (Small)

[887 to 888] Workers' Hall (Large or Huge)

[889 to 890] Workpit (Tiny or Small)

[891 to 892] Workroom (Medium or Large)

[893 to 894] Workshop (Medium or Large)

[895] Wsxt / Wesixet (Large or Huge)

[896] Xenodocheion (Small, Medium, or Large)

[897] Xenodocheum (Small, Medium, or Large)

[898] Xnr / Xener (Small or Medium)

[899] Ziggurat Hall (Large or Huge)

[900] Zoo (or Menagerie) (Large or Huge)

[901 to 909] Stronghold Sub-Region: Fortified Grottoes. Roll on the Cave Room Table for the next 1D4+1 rooms (rerolling any results of 901 to 000), and then return to this table.

[910 to 915] Stronghold Sub-Region: Extensive Fortified Grottoes. Roll on the Cave Room Table for the next 2D4 rooms (rerolling any results of 901 to 000), and then return to this table.

[916 to 918] Stronghold Sub-Region: Hidden Cave Fortress. Roll on the Cave Room Table for the next 2D6+1 rooms (rerolling any results of 901 to 000), and then return to this table.

[919 to 927] Stronghold Sub-Region: Donjon Chambers. Roll on the Dungeon Room Table for the next 1D4+1 rooms (rerolling any results of 901 to 000), and then return to this table.

[928 to 933] Stronghold Sub-Region: Donjon Holdfast. Roll on Dungeon Room Table for the next 2D4 rooms (rerolling any results of 901 to 000), and then return to this table.

[934 to 936] Stronghold Sub-Region: Donjon Keep. Roll on Dungeon Room Table for the next 2D6+1 rooms (rerolling any results of 901 to 000), and then return to this table.

[937 to 945] Stronghold Sub-Region: Furnished Chambers. Roll on the Manor House Room Table for the next 1D4+1 rooms (rerolling any results of 901 to 000), and then return to this table.

[946 to 951] Stronghold Sub-Region: Noble Abodes. Roll on the Manor House Room Table for the next 2D4 rooms (rerolling any results of 901 to 000), and then return to this table.

[952 to 954] Stronghold Sub-Region: Regal Suites. Roll on the Manor House Room Table for the next 2D6+1 rooms (rerolling any results of 901 to 000), and then return to this table.

[955 to 963] Stronghold Sub-Region: Chaplain Chambers. Roll on the Temple Room Table for the next 1D4+1 rooms (rerolling any results of 901 to 000), and then return to this table.

[964 to 969] Stronghold Sub-Region: Noble's Fane. Roll on the Temple Room Table for the next 2D4 rooms (rerolling any results of 901 to 000), and then return to this table.

[970 to 972] Stronghold Sub-Region: Ruler's Sacred Temple. Roll on the Temple Room Table for the next 2D6+1 rooms (rerolling any results of 901 to 000), and then return to this table.

[973 to 981] Stronghold Sub-Region: Champion's Crypts. Roll on the Tomb Room Table for the next 1D4+1 rooms (rerolling any results of 901 to 000), and then return to this table.

[982 to 987] Stronghold Sub-Region: Noble Crypts. Roll on the Tomb Room Table for the next 2D4 rooms (rerolling any results of 901 to 000), and then return to this table.

[988 to 990] Stronghold Sub-Region: Lordly Tombs. Roll on the Tomb Room Table for the next 2D6+1 rooms (rerolling any results of 901 to 000), and then return to this table.

[991 to 995] Stronghold Sub-Region: Enigmatic Vaults. Roll on the Evocative Random Rooms Table (refer to The Classic Dungeon Design Guide, Book I) for the next 1D4+1 rooms (rerolling any results of 901 to 000), and then return to this table.

[996 to 998] Stronghold Sub-Region: Secret Ancestral Hold. Roll on the Evocative Random Rooms Table (refer to The Classic Dungeon Design Guide, Book I) for the next 2D4 rooms (rerolling any results of 901 to 000), and then return to this table.

[999 to 000] Stronghold Sub-Region: Forbidden Ancestral Bastion. Roll on the

Evocative Random Rooms Table (refer to The Classic Dungeon Design Guide, Book I) for the next 2D6+1 rooms (rerolling any results of 901 to 000), and then return to this table.

TEMPLE ROOMS

For random rooms appearing in a temple or fane, roll 1D1000 and consult the following table.

TABLE 5

TEMPLE ROOMS

[001] Abreuvoir (Medium, Large, or Huge)

[002 to 003] Absis (Small)

[004] Access Chamber (Small)

[005] Access Room (Medium)

[006 to 007] Accommodation (Small)

[008] Accommodations, plural (Medium or Large)

[009] Adyton (Small or Medium)

[010] Adytum (Small or Medium)

[011 to 012] Aerarium / Ancient Aerary (Medium or Large)

[013 to 014] Aerarium Chamber (Small or Medium)

[015] Aerary (Medium or Large)

[016] Aerary Chamber (Small)

[017] Af-Hus (Tiny or Small)

[018] Agiasterion (Medium or Large)

[019] Agiasterium (Medium or Large)

[020] Ah / Ahu (Large or Huge)

[021 to 022] Air Chamber (Small)

[023 to 024] Air Room (Medium)

[025] Ala (Tiny or Small)

[026] Alae, plural (Medium or Large)

[027 to 028] Alcove (Tiny or Small)

[029 to 030] Alcove Succession (Medium or Large)

[031] Ale Cellar (Small or Medium)

[032] Alhacena (Tiny or Small)

[033] Alhacena Succession (Medium or Large)

[034] Alipterion (Medium or Large)

[035] Alipterium (Medium or Large)

[036] Almonerium (Medium or Large)

[037] Almonry (Medium)

[038] Almonry Chamber (Small)

[039] Almonry Hall (Large)

[040] Altar Chamber (Small)

[041 to 042] Altar Room (Medium)

[043] Ambitus (Medium or Large, with a Tiny or Small enclosure)

[044] Ambry (Small or Medium)

[045] Ambry Chamber (Tiny or Small)

[046 to 047] Ambulatory (Medium)

[048 to 049] Amphithalamoi, plural (Medium or Large)

[050] Amphithalamos (Small or Medium)

[051 to 052] Amphithalamus (Small or Medium)

[053] Amphitheater (Large or Huge)

[054 to 055] Ancestral Chamber (Small or Medium)

[056] Ancestral Hall (Large or Huge)

[057 to 058] Anchorage (Small)

[059] Anddyri (Small, Medium, or Large)

[060] Andron (Small or Medium)

[061] Angelic Shrine (Small or Medium)

[062] Annex (Tiny, Small, or Medium)

[063] Annex Labyrinth (Large or Huge)

[064] Anointing Chamber (Small)

[065] Anointing Room (Medium)

[066 to 067] Antecabinet (Small)

[068 to 069] Antechamber (Small)

[070] Antechapel (Small or Medium)

[071 to 072] Anteroom (Medium)

[073] Aperture (Tiny)

[074] Apodyterium (Small or Medium)

[075] Apotheca (Small or Medium)

[076 to 077] Apothecarium (Small or Medium)

[078] Apothecary (Small or Medium)

[079] Apse (Small)

[080] Apse Room (Medium)

[081] Apsidal Chapel (Small)

[082] Arboretum (Large)

[083 to 084] Archive (Medium, Large, or Huge)

[085] Arcosolium (Tiny or Small)

[086 to 087] Armory (Medium)

[088] Arryt (Large or Huge)

[089] Artisan's Chamber (Small or Medium)

[090] Artisan's Room (Medium or Large)

[091] Aslukku (Small or Medium)

[092 to 093] Assemblage (Medium, Large, or Huge)

[094 to 095] Assembly Chamber (Small or Medium)

[096] Assembly Hall (Large or Huge)

[097] Astrarium Chamber (Medium)

[098] Astrarium Room (Large)

[099] Asylum (Small, Medium, or Large)

[100] At Iwf / Atu Iwef (Medium or Large)

[101] Atrium (Large or Huge)

[102] Atrium Chamber (Small or Medium)

[103 to 104] Audience Chamber (Small)

[105 to 106] Audience Hall (Large or Huge)

[107] Audience Room (Medium)

[108] Auditorium (Huge)

[109] Augury Chamber (Small)

[110] Augury Room (Medium)

[111] Aula (Medium or Large)

[112 to 113] Aula Regia (Huge)

[114] Axnwty / Axenwety (Small, Medium, or Large)

[115 to 116] Balnea (Small or Medium)

[117] Balnearium (Small or Medium)

[118] Barag (Small or Medium)

[119] Basilica (Large or Huge)

[120] Bath (Small, Medium, or Large)

[121] Bath Room / Bathroom (Small or Medium)

[122] Bathhouse (Medium or Large)

[123] Bay (Tiny or Small)

[124] Bay Succession (Medium or Large)

[125] Bedchamber (Small)

[126] Bedroom (Small or Medium)

[127] Belfry (Medium or Large)

[128] Bell Tower (Medium, Large, or Huge)

[129] Bema (Medium or Large)

[130 to 131] Bleeding Chamber (Small)

[132] Bleeding Room (Medium)

[133] Bodega (Small)

[134] Bone House (Large or Huge)

[135] Bouleuterion (Large or Huge)

[136 to 137] Bourse (Small, Medium, or Large)

[138 to 139] Breezeway (Medium or Large)

[140 to 141] Brewery (Medium, Large, or Huge)

[142] Bursary (Medium or Large)

[143] Buru (Small or Medium)

[144] Cabinet (Small)

[145 to 146] Cache Chamber (Small)

[147] Cache Room (Medium or Large)

[148] Caged Chantry (Small, Medium, or Large)

[149 to 150] Caged Chapel (Small)

[151] Caldarium (Small, Medium, or Large)

[152] Calefactorium (Small, Medium, or Large)

[153] Calefactory (Small, Medium, or Large)

[154] Camba (Small or Medium)

[155] Cantoris (Small)

[156] Cascade Hall (Large or Huge)

[157] Cascade Room (Small)

[158] Catacomb (Tiny or Small)

[159 to 160] Catacombs, plural

[161] Catacumba (Tiny or Small)

[162] Catacumbae, plural

[163] Cavaedium (Large or Huge)

[164 to 165] Celestial Hall (Large or Huge)

[166] Cella (Medium or Large)

[167] Cella Olearia (Medium or Large)

[168] Cella Vinaria (Small, Medium, or Large)

[169] Cellula (Tiny or Small)

[170] Cenotaph (Small)

[171] Ceremonial Chamber (Small)

[172] Ceremonial Hall (Large or Huge)

[173 to 174] Ceremonial Room (Medium or Large)

[175] Ceroma (Small or Medium)

[176 to 177] Chamber (Small)

[178] Chamber of Revelation (Small)

[179] Chambers, plural (Medium, Large, or Huge)

[180] Chancel (Small or Medium)

[181] Chandlery (Small or Medium)

[182 to 183] Chantier (Small, Medium, or Large)

[184] Chantry (Medium or Large)

[185] Chapel (Small or Medium, inside an enclosing Large or Huge area)

[186] Chapel Hall (Large, inside an enclosing Huge area)

[187 to 188] Chapter House (Medium, Large, or Huge)

[189] Chapter Room (Small or Medium)

[190] Char Cellar (Tiny, Small, or Medium)

[191 to 192] Charter Room (Small or Medium)

[193] Chartophylacium (Medium, Large, or Huge)

[194] Choir (Small or Medium)

[195] Chrismographion (Small)

[196] Chrismographium (Small)

[197 to 198] Cimeliarch (Medium or Large)

[199] Cinerarium (Medium, Large, or Huge)

[200] Cistern (Small, Medium, Large, or Huge)

[201 to 202] Cistern Room (Small or Medium)

[203] Classroom (Medium or Large)

[204 to 205] Clinic (Medium or Large)

[206 to 207] Cloaca (Medium, Large, or Huge)

[208] Cloak Room (Small or Medium)

[209] Clockwork Room (Small or Medium)

[210 to 211] Cloister (Medium, Large, or Huge)

[212 to 213] Coal Room (Small, Medium, or Large)

[214] Coemeterium, plural Coemeteria (Smell or Medium)

[215] Coldroom (Small or Medium)

[216] Colonnade Hall (Large or Huge)

[217] Colonnade Room (Medium)

[218] Columbarium (Large or Huge)

[219] Common Room (Medium, Large, or Huge)

[220 to 221] Communal Quarters (Medium, Large, or Huge)

[222] Compluvium Chamber (Small)

[223] Compluvium Hall (Large)

[224] Compluvium Room (Medium)

[225] Concealed Chamber (Small)

[226 to 227] Concealed Room (Medium or Large)

[228 to 229] Conclave (Medium or Large)

[230] Conclavium (Medium or Large)

[231] Confessional (Tiny or Small)

[232] Conjuring Chamber (Small or Medium)

[233] Conservatory (Medium or Large)

[234] Control Room (Small or Medium)

[235] Convocation Room (Medium or Large)

[236] Court (Large or Huge)

[237 to 238] Courtyard (Medium or Large if subterranean, otherwise Large or Huge)

[239 to 240] Crafter's Room (Small or Medium)

[241] Crowde (Tiny, Small, or Medium)

[242 to 243] Cubicle (Tiny)

[244] Cubicula, plural (Small, Medium, or Large)

[245] Cubiculum (Tiny or Small)

[246] Cyzicene Hall (Large or Huge)

[247] Dairy Chamber (Small or Medium)

[248] Dairy Room (Medium or Large)

[249 to 250] Dais Chamber (Small or Medium)

[251] Dais Room (Medium or Large)

[252] Dead End (Tiny or Small)

[253] Delubrum (Medium or Large)

[254 to 255] Depository (Medium or Large)

[256] Diaconia (Medium or Large)

[257] Diaconicon (Medium or Large)

[258] Diaconicum (Medium or Large)

[259 to 260] Dining Chamber (Small)

[261] Dining Hall (Large or Huge)

[262 to 263] Dining Room (Medium)

[264] Distillery (Medium or Large)

[265] Divination Chamber (Small)

[266] Divination Hall (Large or Huge)

[267 to 268] Divination Room (Medium)

[269] Domed Chamber (Small)

[270 to 271] Domed Hall (Large or Huge)

[272] Domed Room (Medium)

[273] Domicile (Small or Medium)

[274] Dormitory (Large or Huge)

[275 to 276] Dorter (Large or Huge)

[277] Drawing Chamber (Small)

[278] Drawing Room (Medium)

[279] Dressing Chamber (Small)

[280] Dressing Room (Medium)

[281 to 282] Drowning Pool (Small or Medium)

[283] Drying Room (Small or Medium)

[284] Dulli (Small or Medium)

[285] Elaeothesium (Small or Medium)

[286] Eldaskali (Large or Huge)

[287] Emasu (Small or Medium)

[288 to 289] Embalming Chamber (Small or Medium)

[290] Embalming Room (Large)

[291] Enchanted Grotto (Small, Medium, or Large)

[292] Enclosed Loggia (Medium or Large)

[293] Enclosure (Small or Medium, with a Tiny internal space)

[294] Enterclose (Tiny or Small)

[295] Entertaining Room (Medium or Large)

[296] Entrance Hall (Medium, Large, or Huge)

[297 to 298] Entry / Entryway (Small or Medium)

[299 to 300] Entry Hall (Medium or Large)

[301] Ephebeum (Medium)

[302] Episcenium (Tiny or Small)

[303] Ersi (Small or Medium)

[304] Ewery (Tiny or Small)

[305] Excubitorium (Small or Medium)

[306] Exercise Room (Small, Medium, or Large)

[307] Fallen Angelic Shrine (Small or Medium)

[308] False Treasure Room (Small or Medium)

[309] False Treasure Vault (Medium or Large)

[310 to 311] Fane (Medium or Large)

[312] Favissa (Small, Medium, or Large)

[313 to 314] Feast Hall (Large or Huge)

[315] Feretorium (Small or Medium)

[316] Feretory (Small or Medium)

[317] Firepit (Tiny or Small)

[318] Flooded Hall (Large or Huge)

[319] Flooded Room (Small or Medium)

[320 to 321] Forbidden Chamber (Small or Medium)

[322] Forbidden Vault (Large)

[323] Forge (Small, Medium, or Large)

[324] Fornix Chamber (Small)

[325] Fornix Hall (Large or Huge)

[326] Fornix Room (Medium)

[327] Fosse Room (Medium)

[328] Foundry (Small, Medium, or Large)

[329 to 330] Fountain Chamber (Small)

[331] Fountain Grotto (Small, Medium, or Large)

[332] Fountain Hall (Large or Huge)

[333 to 334] Fountain Room (Medium)

[335] Foyer (Small or Medium)

[336] Frater (Small, Medium, or Large)

[337 to 338] Fresco Gallery (Large)

[339] Fresco Room (Small or Medium)

[340] Frigidarium (Small, Medium, or Large)

[341] Fumarium (Tiny or Small)

[342] Fumigatory (Tiny, Small, or Medium)

[343 to 344] Function Hall (Large or Huge)

[345 to 346] Function Room (Medium)

[347] Fundament (Small or Medium)

[348] Fundament Room (Medium or Large)

[349 to 350] Funerary Chapel (Small or Medium)

[351] Funerary Workshop (Small or Medium)

[352] Funereal Crowde (Small or Medium)

[353] Fungarium (Small, Medium, or Large)

[354] Galininu (Small or Medium)

[355 to 356] Gallery (Display) (Medium, Large, or Huge)

[357] Gambling Hall (Large)

[358] Gambling Room (Medium)

[359] Game Room (Small, Medium, or Large)

[360] Ganunmahu (Small or Medium)

[361] Garden (Medium or Large)

[362] Garderobe (Tiny or Small)

[363] Garderobe Chamber (Small or Medium)

[364 to 365] Gate Chamber (Medium)

[366] Gate Room (Large)

[367] Goods Hall (Medium or Large)

[368 to 369] Granary (Small or Medium)

[370 to 371] Grand Aerary (Large or Huge)

[372] Grand Aquarium (Large or Huge)

[373 to 374] Grand Arboretum (Large or Huge)

[375] Grand Aviary (Large or Huge)

[376] Grand Gallery (Display) (Small)

[377] Grand Salon (Large or Huge)

[378] Grapery (Small, Medium, or Large)

[379 to 380] Great Adyton (Large or Huge)

[381] Great Almonry (Large)

[382 to 383] Great Chamber (Large or Huge)

[348] Great Kitchen (Large or Huge)

[385] Great Room (Large)

[386] Grinding Chamber (Small)

[387] Grinding Room (Medium or Large)

[388] Grot (Tiny or Small)

[389] Grotto (Medium or Large)

[390 to 391] Guard Chamber (Small)

[392] Guard Post (Tiny or Small)

[393] Guardroom (Medium)

[394] Guest Chamber (Small)

[395] Guestroom (Small or Medium)

[396 to 397] Gymnasium (Large)

[398] Gynaeceum (Medium or Large)

[399] Hall (Large or Huge)

[400] Hall of Assembly (Large or Huge)

[401] Hall of Bones (Large or Huge)

[402] Hall of Contemplation (Large or Huge)

[403] Hall of Doors (Large or Huge)

[404 to 405] Hall of Healing (Large or Huge)

[406] Hall of Immortal Judgment

[407] Hall of Judgment (Large or Huge)

[408] Hall of Mourners (Large or Huge)

[409] Hall of Offerings (Large or Huge)

[410] Hall of Pools (Large or Huge)

[411] Hall of Repentance (Large or Huge)

[412] Hall of Resurrection (Large or Huge)

[413 to 414] Hall of Reverence (Large or Huge)

[415] Hall of Runes (Large or Huge)

[416] Hall of Souls (Large or Huge)

[417] Hall of Statuary (Large or Huge)

[418] Hall of Tapestries (Large or Huge)

[419 to 420] Hall of the Dead (Large or Huge)

[421] Harem (Small, Medium, or Large)

[422] Harness Chamber (Small)

[423] Harness Hall (Large or Huge)

[424] Hastarium (Medium)

[425] Haven (Small or Medium)

[426] Hearth Chamber (Small)

[427 to 428] Hearth Hall (Large or Huge)

[429] Hearth Room (Medium)

[430] Helieum (Large or Huge)

[431] Hell Mouth (Medium, Large, or Huge)

[432] Herbarium (Small or Medium)

[433] Hermitage (Tiny, Small, or Medium)

[434] Heroum (Tiny, Small, or Medium)

[435] Hieron (Medium, Large, or Huge)

[436] Holl (Large or Huge)

[437] Horological Hall (Large or Huge)

[438 to 439] Horologium (Small or Medium)

[440] Horreum (Small, Medium, or Large)

[441 to 442] Hospitalium (Small)

[443] Hospitium (Medium)

[444] Hostel (Medium or Large)

[445] Hrt Ib / Heret Ib (Large or Huge)

[446 to 447] Hursu (Tiny, Small, or Medium)

[448] Hus (Small or Medium)

[449] Hwt / Hewet (Large or Huge)

[450] Hwt Ka / Hewet Ka (Small or Medium)

[451] Hylr (Small or Medium)

[452] Hypocaust (Medium)

[463] Hypocaust Chamber (Tiny or Small)

[454] Hypogeum (Small, Medium, or Large)

[455 to 456] Hypostyle Hall (Large or Huge)

[457] Ice Chamber (Small)

[458] Icehouse (Medium)

[459 to 460] Idol Grotto (Small, Medium, or Large)

[461] Idrt / Idret (Large or Huge)

[462] Illusory Chamber (Small)

[463] Illusory Room (Medium or Large)

[464] Immense Archive (Huge)

[465] Imnt / Imenet (Tiny, Small, or Medium)

[466 to 467] Impluvium Chamber (Small)

[468] Impluvium Hall (Large or Huge)

[469 to 470] Impluvium Room (Medium)

[471 to 472] Infirmary (Medium or Large)

[473] Inner Chamber (Tiny, Small, or Medium)

[474] Inner Ward (Small or Medium)

[475 to 476] Inquisition / Inquisitorial Chamber

[477 to 478] Inscription Chamber (Small)

[479] Instrument Chamber (Small)

[480] Instrument Room (Medium)

[481] Internment Chamber

[482] Ipa (Small or Medium)

[483] Isi (Medium or Large)

[484] Isittu (Small, Medium, or Large)

[485] Itima (Small or Medium)

[486] Iwnn / Iwenen (Small or Medium)

[487] Iwnyt / Iwenyt (Small)

[488] Junk Room (Small or Medium)

[489] Kelda (Small or Medium)

[490 to 491] Kitchen (Medium)

[492 to 493] Kitchen Chamber (Small)

[494 to 495] Kosmeterion (Tiny, Small, or Medium)

[496] Kukku (Small, Medium, or Large)

[497] Kummu (Small or Medium)

[498] Kunukku (Small or Medium)

[499 to 500] Labyrinth (Large or Huge)

[501] Laconicum (Small, Medium, or Large)

[502] Lady's Chamber (Small or Medium)

[503] Lair (Tiny, Small, Medium, Large, or Huge)

[504] Landing (Tiny or Small)

[505 to 506] Lararium (Tiny or Small)

[507] Larder (Medium)

[508] Larder Chamber (Small)

[509 to 510] Lavatorium (Small or Medium)

[511] Lavatory (Small or Medium)

[512] Lazarette (Tiny, Small, Medium, or Large)

[513] Leprosarium (Small, Medium, or Large)

[514] Lesser Almonry (Small)

[515 to 516] Library (Medium, Large, or Huge)

[517] Lightwell (Tiny, Small, or Medium)

[518] Locutorium (Small or Medium)

[519] Loft (Tiny, Small, or Medium)

[520] Lokrekkja (Tiny)

[521] Long Gallery (Large or Huge)

[522] Lookout (Tiny, Small, or Medium)

[523] Lopt (Large or Huge)

[524 to 525] Lord's Chamber (Small or Medium)

[526] Lumber Room (Small or Medium)

[527] Lyceum (Large or Huge)

[528] Makkuri (Small, Medium, or Large)

[529] Manufactorium (Large or Huge)

[530] Manufactory (Large or Huge)

[531] Manzazu (Small, Medium, or Large)

[532 to 533] Map Chamber (Small)

[534] Map Room (Medium)

[535 to 536] Martyrium (Tiny, Small, or Medium)

[537] Marw / Marew (Small)

[538] Massaku (Small, Medium, or Large)

[539 to 540] Mausoleum (Large or Huge)

[541] Maze (Large or Huge)

[542] Mechanical Room (Small or Medium)

[543] Meditation Chamber (Small or Medium)

[544] Meeting Room (Small or Medium)

[545] Megaron (Large or Huge)

[546 to 547] Memorial Chamber (Small or Medium)

[548] Mesitu (Tiny or Small)

[549 to 550] Metroon (Small, Medium, or Large)

[551] Mezzanine (Small or Medium, a subspace within an area that is Large or Huge)

[552] Mezzanine Hall (Large or Huge)

[553] Mihat (Small or Medium)

[554] Misericord (Small or Medium)

[555] Monastic Cell (Tiny)

[556] Monument Hall (Huge)

[557] Monument Room (Large)

[558] Moot Hall (Large or Huge)

[559] Mortuary Chapel

[560] Msxn / Mesixen (Small or Medium)

[561] Msxnt / Mesixenet (Large or Huge)

[562 to 563] Muniment Hall (Large or Huge)

[564] Muniment Room (Small or Medium)

[565] Museum (Large or Huge)

[566] Mushroom Cellar (Small or Medium)

[567] Music Chamber (Small)

[568] Music Room (Medium)

[569] Naos (Medium, Large, or Huge)

[570] Narthex (Medium, Large, or Huge)

[571] Naspaku (Small or Medium)

[572] Nat (Small or Medium)

[573] Natatorium (Large or Huge)

[574] Nave (Small or Medium)

[575 to 576] Necessarium (Tiny or Small)

[577] Nht / Nehet (Small)

[578] Niche (Tiny)

[579] Niched Room (Small or Medium)

[580 to 581] Novitiate (Small)

[582] Nymphaeum (Small, Medium, or Large)

[583] Obelisk Chamber (Small or Medium)

[584] Obelisk Hall (Large or Huge)

[585] Oblatorium (Small)

[586] Observation Chamber (Small or Medium)

[587] Observatory (Small, Medium, or Large)

[588] Occus (Small)

[589] Oecus (Medium or Large)

[590 to 591] Offering Chamber (Small)

[592] Offertorium (Small)

[593] Oil Cellar (Small or Medium)

[594] Oil Press Room (Small or Medium)

[595] Opisthodomos (Small or Medium)

[596] Oracular Chamber (Small or Medium)

[597] Oratory (Small or Medium)

[598] Ossuary (Tiny)

[599] Ossuary Chamber (Small)

[600] Ossuary Room (Medium or Large)

[601] Palatial Hall (Huge)

[602] Pallet Chamber (Tiny or Small)

[603] Pantry (Small or Medium)

[604] Parakki (Small or Medium)

[605 to 606] Parlatorium (Small or Medium)

[607] Parlor (Small or Medium)

[608] Parthenon (Huge)

[609] Pastophorium (Small)

[610] Penaria (Small or Medium)

[611] Pergula (Tiny, Small, or Medium)

[612 to 613] Peristyle (Small, Medium, or Large, surrounding a smaller interior)

[614] Peristylium (Small, Medium, or Large, surrounding a smaller interior)

[615] Piristi (Small or Medium)

[616] Planning Room (Small or Medium)

[617 to 618] Ploutonion (Small or Medium)

[619] Poison Garden (Small, Medium, or Large)

[620] Pool (Tiny, Small, or Medium)

[621 to 622] Pool Chamber (Small)

[623 to 624] Pool Room (Medium or Large)

[625 to 626] Portcullis Chamber

[627] Potionry (Small or Medium)

[628] Pr Dwat / Per Dewat (Small)

[629] Pr Hd / Per Hed (Small, Medium, or Large)

[630] Pr Mdat / Per Medat (Medium or Large)

[631] Pr Nfr / Per Nefer (Small or Medium)

[632] Priest Hole (Tiny or Small)

[633 to 634] Privy (Tiny or Small)

[635] Procoeton (Small)

[636] Procoetum (Small)

[637] Propylaeum (Small or Medium)

[638] Prostas (Small or Medium)

[639] Prothyron (Small or Medium)

[640] Pulvinarium (Medium or Large)

[641] Pump Room (Small or Medium)

[642 to 643] Purification Chamber (Small or Medium)

[644 to 645] Puteus (Small, Medium, or Large)

[646 to 647] Quarters (Small, Medium, or Large)

[648 to 649] Quarters, Solitary (Tiny or Small)

[650] Quppu (Tiny, Small, or Medium)

[651] Rdw / Redew (Small or Medium)

[652] Reading Chamber (Tiny or Small)

[653] Reading Room (Small or Medium)

[654 to 655] Reception Chamber (Small)

[656] Reception Hall (Large or Huge)

[657] Reception Room (Small or Medium)

[658] Recess (Tiny or Small, with an adjacent Small, Medium, or Large space)

[659] Refectorium (Small or Medium)

[660 to 661] Refectory (Small, Medium, or Large)

[662] Reflecting Pool (Tiny, Small, or Medium)

[663] Reflecting Room (Small or Medium)

[664] Refuge (Small, Medium, or Large)

[665 to 666] Reliquary (Tiny, Small, or Medium)

[667] Repository (Small or Medium)

[668] Reredorter (Small or Medium)

[669] Reservoir (Large or Huge)

[670] Retreat (Small or Medium)

[671 to 672] Ritual Hall (Large or Huge)

[673] Robing Room (Tiny, Small, or Medium)

[674] Room (Small or Medium)

[675 to 676] Room of Pools (Large or Huge)

[677] Room of Unknown Purpose (Tiny, Small, Medium, Large, or Huge)

[678] Rotating Room (Small or Medium)

[679] Rotunda (Small, Medium, or Large)

[680] Royal Chamber / Noble's Chamber (Small or Medium)

[681] Rugbu (Tiny, Small, or Medium)

[682] Rum (Small or Medium)

[683 to 684] Runic Chamber (Small or Medium)

[685] Rwyt / Reweyet (Small)

[686 to 687] Sacrarium (Small or Medium)

[688 to 689] Sacred Abattoir (Small, Medium, or Large)

[690] Sacred Crypt (Small)

[691] Sacred Tomb (Medium or Large)

[692 to 693] Sacrificial Chamber (Small or Medium)

[694] Sacrificial Grotto (Small or Medium)

[695] Sacrificial Pool (Tiny, Small, or Medium)

[696] Sacrificial Vault (Large or Huge)

[697 to 698] Sacristy (Small or Medium)

[699] Safe Room (Small or Medium)

[700] Salon (Small or Medium)

[701] Salt Cellar (Small or Medium)

[702] Salt Chamber (Small)

[703] Salt Room (Medium)

[704 to 705] Sanctuary (Small or Medium)

[706 to 707] Sanctum (Small or Medium)

[708 to 709] Sanctum Sanctorum (Small or Medium)

[710] Sarcophagus Chamber (Small or Medium)

[711] Sarcophagus Room (Medium or Large)

[712] Sauna (Small or Medium)

[713] Schola (Small or Medium)

[714 to 715] Scriptorium (Medium or Large)

[716] Scullery (Small or Medium)

[717] Sealed Tomb (Small, Medium, or Large)

[718 to 719] Secret Crypt (Small, Medium, or Large)

[720 to 721] Secret Guardroom (Small or Medium)

[722] Secret Room (Tiny, Small, Medium, or Large)

[723 to 724] Secret Tomb (Small, Medium, or Large)

[725] Sellaria (Large)

[726 to 727] Seminary (Small or Medium)

[728] Sepulchral Chapel (Small, Medium, or Large)

[729] Sepulchral Hall (Large or Huge)

[730] Sepulchral Heroum (Small or Medium, perhaps in a Medium, Large, or Huge surrounding space)

[731 to 732] Servant's Quarters / Servants' Quarters (Tiny, Small, or Medium)

[733 to 734] Servants' Hall (Medium, Large, or Huge)

[735] Servery (Tiny, Small, or Medium)

[736] Set (Small or Medium)

[737] Shop (Small or Medium)

[737 to 738] Shrine (Small or Medium)

[739 to 740] Shrine Chamber (Small)

[741 to 742] Shrine Room (Medium or Large)

[743] Sick Chamber (Small)

[744] Sick Room (Medium or Large)

[745] Simmiltu (Tiny, Small, or Medium)

[746] Skenotheke (Small or Medium)

[747] Slave Chamber (Tiny, Small, or Medium)

[748] Sleeping Chamber (Small)

[749 to 750] Sleeping Hall (Large)

[751] Sleeping Room (Medium)

[752] Smithy (Small, Medium or Large)

[753] Smoke Room (Small or Medium)

[754] Solarium (Small, Medium, or Large)

[755] Spiral Labyrinth (Medium, Large, or Huge)

[756] Spoliarium (Small)

[757] Stair Chamber (Small)

[758] Stairway Room (Medium)

[759] Statuary (Small, Medium, or Large)

[760] Still Room (Small or Medium)

[761 to 762] Stockpile Room (Small or Medium)

[763 to 764] Storage Chamber (Small)

[765 to 766] Storage Room / Storeroom (Small or Medium)

[767] Storeroom – Alchemical (Small or Medium)

[768] Storeroom – Alcohol / Wine (Small or Medium)

[769] Storeroom – Armor (Small or Medium)

[770] Storeroom – Box Room (Small or Medium)

[771 to 772] Storeroom – Ceremonial (Small or Medium)

[773] Storeroom – Char / Coal (Small or Medium)

[774] Storeroom – Cheese (Small or Medium)

[775] Storeroom – Drink (Small or Medium)

[776 to 777] Storeroom – Dry Goods (Small or Medium)

[778 to 779] Storeroom – Embalming (Small or Medium)

[780] Storeroom – Foodstuffs (Small or Medium)

[781] Storeroom – Furniture (Small or Medium)

[782 to 783] Storeroom – Herbs and Spices (Small or Medium)

[784] Storeroom – Ice (Small or Medium)

[785] Storeroom – Lumber (Small or Medium)

[786] Storeroom – Masonry (Small or Medium)

[787] Storeroom – Oil (Small or Medium)

[788] Storeroom – Reagents (Small or Medium)

[789] Storeroom – Salt (Small or Medium)

[790] Storeroom – Sundries (Small or Medium)

[791] Storeroom – Tools and Gear (Small or Medium)

[792] Storeroom – Water (Small or Medium)

[793] Stricture (Tiny or Small)

[794 to 795] Strongroom (Small)

[796 to 797] Submerged Chamber (Small)

[798] Submerged Hall (Large or Huge)

[799] Submerged Room (Medium)

[800] Sudatorium (Small, Medium, or Large)

[801 to 802] Suite (Medium)

[803] Suite Chamber (Small)

[804] Summoning Chamber (Small)

[805] Summoning Room (Medium or Large)

[806] Sunroom (Small or Medium)

[807] Tablinum (Small or Medium)

[808] Tabulinum (Small)

[809] Tank (Small, Medium, Large, or Huge)

[810] Taum (Tiny, Small, or Medium)

[811] Teleportation Chamber (Tiny, Small, or Medium)

[812 to 813] Temple (Medium, Large, or Huge)

[814 to 815] Templum (Large or Huge)

[816] Tepidarium (Small, Medium, or Large)

[817] Terminus (Tiny, Small, or Medium)

[818] Thalamium (Small or Medium)

[819] Thalamos (Small or Medium)

[820] Theater (Large or Huge)

[821] Therma (Large or Huge)

[822] Tholos (Small, Medium, or Large)

[823] Threshold (Tiny, Small, Medium, or Large)

[824] Tool Room (Small or Medium)

[825] Torcularium (Small)

[826 to 827] Treasure Chamber (Small or Medium)

[828 to 829] Treasure Vault (Medium or Large)

[830] Tuppi (Small, Medium, or Large)

[831] Turrinum (Small, Medium, or Large)

[832 to 833] Unctorium (Small)

[834 to 835] Unctuarium (Small or Medium)

[836 to 837] Undercroft (Small, Medium, Large, or Huge)

[838 to 839] Undercroft (Special) (Small, Medium, Large, or Huge)

[840] Urbatu (Small)

[841] Ursu (Small or Medium)

[842] Usgidum (Tiny or Small)

[843] Utility Chamber (Small)

[844] Utility Room (Medium or Large)

[845] Vault (Small, Medium, or Large)

[846] Vaulted Chamber (Small or Medium)

[847] Vaulted Hall (Large or Huge)

[848 to 849] Vaulted Room (Medium or Large)

[850] Vestiary (Tiny, Small, or Medium)

[851 to 852] Vestibule (Small or Medium)

[853] Vestibulum (Small or Medium)

[854 to 855] Vestry (Small or Medium)

[856 to 857] Vigil (Tiny, Small, or Medium)

[858] Vinery (Small, Medium, or Large)

[859] Wadyt (Large or Huge)

[860] Waiting Chamber (Small)

[861] Waiting Room (Medium or Large)

[862] Walled-Up Chamber (Small)

[863] Walled-Up Corridor (Small or Medium)

[864] Walled-Up Room (Medium or Large)

[865 to 866] Ward (Medium or Large)

[867] Warming Room (Small, Medium, or Large)

[868] Washroom (Tiny, Small, or Medium)

[869] Watchroom (Tiny, Small, or Medium)

[870] Wda / Weda (Small or Medium)

[871] Weaving Room (Small or Medium)

[872 to 873] Well (Tiny, Small, or Medium)

[874 to 875] Well Room (Small or Medium)

[876 to 877] Wine Cellar (Small or Medium)

[878] Wine Vault (Small, Medium, or Large)

[879 to 880] Withdrawing Chamber (Small)

[881] Withdrawing Room (Medium)

[882] Wndwt / Wenedewet (Small)

[883 to 884] Work Chamber (Small)

[885] Workers' Hall (Large or Huge)

[886 to 887] Workroom (Medium or Large)

[888 to 889] Workshop (Medium or Large)

[890] Wsxt / Wesixet (Large or Huge)

[891] Xawt / Xawet (Small or Medium)

[892] Xenodocheion (Small, Medium, or Large)

[893] Xenodocheum (Small, Medium, or Large)

[894] Xnmt / Xenemet (Small, Medium, or Large)

[895] Xnr / Xener (Small or Medium)

[896] Xnrt / Xeneret (Small or Medium)

[897] Xnty / Xenety (Small or Medium)

[898] Zaggu (Small or Medium)

[899] Ziggurat Hall (Large or Huge)

[900] Zoo (or Menagerie) (Large or Huge)

[901 to 909] Temple Sub-Region: Sacred Grottoes. Roll on the Cave Room Table for the next 1D4+1 rooms (rerolling any results of 901 to 000), and then return to this table.

[910 to 915] Temple Sub-Region: Forbidden Caves. Roll on the Cave Room Table for the next 2D4 rooms (rerolling any results of 901 to 000), and then return to this table.

[916 to 918] Temple Sub-Region: God-Sworn Caverns. Roll on the Cave Room Table for the next 2D6+1 rooms (rerolling any results of 901 to 000), and then return to this table.

[919 to 927] Temple Sub-Region: Forbidden Chambers. Roll on the Dungeon Room Table for the next 1D4+1 rooms (rerolling any results of 901 to 000), and then return to this table.

[928 to 933] Temple Sub-Region: Vaults of the Damned. Roll on Dungeon Room Table for the next 2D4 rooms (rerolling any results of 901 to 000), and then return to this table.

[934 to 936] Temple Sub-Region: Domain of the Impure / Unworthy. Roll on Dungeon Room Table for the next 2D6+1 rooms (rerolling any results of 901 to 000), and then return to this table.

[937 to 945] Temple Sub-Region: Cantors' Chambers. Roll on the Manor House Room Table for the next 1D4+1 rooms (rerolling any results of 901 to 000), and then return to this table.

[946 to 951] Temple Sub-Region: High Priest's Sanctums. Roll on the Manor House Room Table for the next 2D4 rooms (rerolling any results of 901 to 000), and then return to this table.

[952 to 954] Temple Sub-Region: Immortal Sanctuary. Roll on the Manor

House Room Table for the next 2D6+1 rooms (rerolling any results of 901 to 000), and then return to this table.

[955 to 963] Temple Sub-Region: Protected Chambers. Roll on the Stronghold Room Table for the next 1D4+1 rooms (rerolling any results of 901 to 000), and then return to this table.

[964 to 969] Temple Sub-Region: Guardian Halls. Roll on the Stronghold Room Table for the next 2D4 rooms (rerolling any results of 901 to 000), and then return to this table.

[970 to 972] Temple Sub-Region: Sacred Holdfast. Roll on the Stronghold Room Table for the next 2D6+1 rooms (rerolling any results of 901 to 000), and then return to this table.

[973 to 981] Temple Sub-Region: Holy / Unholy Crypts. Roll on the Tomb Room Table for the next 1D4+1 rooms (rerolling any results of 901 to 000), and then return to this table.

[982 to 987] Temple Sub-Region: Sepulchers of the Martyrs. Roll on the Tomb Room Table for the next 2D4 rooms (rerolling any results of 901 to 000), and then return to this table.

[988 to 990] Temple Sub-Region: Sacred Underhalls. Roll on the Tomb Room Table for the next 2D6+1 rooms (rerolling any results of 901 to 000), and then return to this table.

[991 to 995] Temple Sub-Region: Ancient Overbuilt Structures. Roll on the Evocative Random Rooms Table (refer to *The Classic Dungeon Design Guide, Book I*) for the next 1D4+1 rooms (rerolling any results of 901 to 000), and then return to this table.

[996 to 998] Temple Sub-Region: Ornate Halls. Roll on the Evocative Random Rooms Table (refer to *The Classic Dungeon Design Guide, Book I*) for the next 2D4 rooms (rerolling any results of 901 to 000), and then return to this table.

[999 to 000] Temple Sub-Region: Halls of the Mysteries. Roll on the Evocative Random Rooms Table (refer to *The Classic Dungeon Design Guide, Book I*) for the next 2D6+1 rooms (rerolling any results of 901 to 000), and then return to this table.

TOMB ROOMS

For random rooms appearing in a tomb or series of catacombs, roll 1D1000 and consult the following table.

TABLE 6

TOMB ROOMS

[001 to 003] Absis (Small)

[004 to 006] Aerarium / Ancient Aerary (Medium or Large)

[007 to 008] Aerarium Chamber (Small or Medium)

[009 to 011] Aerary (Medium or Large)

[012 to 014] Aerary Chamber (Small)

[015 to 017] Af-Hus (Tiny or Small)

[018 to 020] Ah Hwt / Ahu Hewet (Small or Medium)

[021 to 023] Air Chamber (Small)

[024 to 025] Air Room (Medium)

[026 to 027] Ala (Tiny or Small)

[028 to 030] Alae, plural (Medium or Large)

[031 to 033] Alcove (Tiny or Small)

[034 to 035] Alcove Succession (Medium or Large)

[036 to 038] Alhacena (Tiny or Small)

[039 to 040] Alhacena Succession (Medium or Large)

[041 to 043] Altar Chamber (Small)

[044 to 045] Altar Room (Medium)

[046 to 048] Ambitus (Medium or Large, with a Tiny or Small enclosure)

[049 to 051] Ambulatory (Medium)

[052 to 053] Ancestral Chamber (Small or Medium)

[054 to 056] Ancestral Hall (Large or Huge)

[057 to 058] Anddyri (Small, Medium, or Large)

[059 to 060] Angelic Shrine (Small or Medium)

[061 to 063] Annex (Tiny, Small, or Medium)

[064 to 065] Annex Labyrinth (Large or Huge)

[066 to 068] Antechamber (Small)

[069 to 070] Anteroom (Medium)

[071 to 072] Aperture (Tiny)

[073 to 075] Apse (Small)

[076 to 077] Apse Room (Medium)

[078 to 080] Arcosolium (Tiny or Small)

[081 to 082] Arryt (Large or Huge)

[083 to 085] Ash Pit (Small or Medium)

[086 to 088] Ashen Abyss (Large or Huge)

[089 to 091] Aslukku (Small or Medium)

[092 to 093] Barrow (Small or Medium)

[094 to 095] Barrow Crypt (Small, Medium, or Large)

[096 to 097] Bay (Tiny or Small)

[098 to 100] Bay Succession (Medium or Large)

[101 to 103] Beast Crypt (Tiny, Small, or Medium)

[104 to 105] Bone House (Large or Huge)

[106 to 107] Bone Pit (Small or Medium)

[108 to 109] Burial Chamber (Tiny or Small)

[110 to 112] Burial Room (Medium)

[113 to 115] Burial Vault (Large or Huge)

[116 to 117] Buried Longship (Large or Huge)

[118 to 119] Burrow (Tiny or Small)

[120 to 121] Burrow Maze (Huge)

[122 to 124] Burrow Warren (Large)

[125 to 127] Catacomb (Tiny or Small)

[128 to 129] Catacombs, plural

[130 to 132] Catacumba (Tiny or Small)

[133 to 134] Catacumbae, plural

[135 to 136] Cella (Medium or Large)

[137 to 139] Cellula (Tiny or Small)

[140 to 142] Cenotaph (Small)

[143 to 144] Ceremonial Chamber (Small)

[145 to 146] Ceremonial Hall (Large or Huge)

[147 to 149] Ceremonial Room (Medium or Large)

[150 to 151] Ceroma (Small or Medium)

[152 to 154] Cesspit (Tiny, Small, or Medium)

[155 to 156] Cesspool (Tiny, Small, or Medium)

[157 to 158] Chamber (Small)

[159 to 160] Chamber Barrow (Small)

[161 to 162] Chamber of Catafalques (Small or Medium)

[163 to 165] Chamber Tomb (Small, Medium, or Large)

[166 to 167] Chambers, plural (Medium, Large, or Huge)

[168 to 170] Chantier (Small, Medium, or Large)

[171 to 172] Char Cellar (Tiny, Small, or Medium)

[173 to 174] Charnel House (Medium, Large, or Huge)

[175 to 176] Cinerarium (Medium, Large, or Huge)

[177 to 179] Cistern (Small, Medium, Large, or Huge)

[180 to 181] Cistern Room (Small or Medium)

[182 to 184] Cistvaen (Small or Medium)

[185 to 187] Cloaca (Medium, Large, or Huge)

[188 to 189] Coemeterium, plural Coemeteria (Smell or Medium)

[190 to 192] Collapsed Room (Small, Medium, or Large, with the accessible area being Tiny or Small)

[193 to 194] Colonnade Hall (Large or Huge)

[195 to 197] Colonnade Room (Medium)

[198 to 200] Columbarium (Large or Huge)

[201 to 202] Concealed Chamber (Small)

[203 to 204] Concealed Room (Medium or Large)

[205 to 207] Conditivum (Small or Medium)

[208 to 210] Crematorium (Small or Medium)

[211 to 213] Crowde (Tiny, Small, or Medium)

[214 to 215] Crypt (Tiny, Small, or Medium)

[216 to 218] Cubicle (Tiny)

[219 to 220] Cubicula, plural (Small, Medium, or Large)

[221 to 222] Cubiculum (Tiny or Small)

[223 to 225] Cubiculum Cineraria (Tiny)

[226 to 227] Cul-de-Sac (Tiny or Small)

[228 to 230] Cyst (Small, Medium, or Large)

[231 to 233] Dais Chamber (Small or Medium)

[234 to 235] Dais Room (Medium or Large)

[236 to 237] Darkroom (Small, Medium, or Large)

[238 to 240] Dead End (Tiny or Small)

[241 to 243] Defiled Tomb (Small, Medium, or Large)

[244 to 246] Domed Chamber (Small)

[247 to 249] Domed Hall (Large or Huge)

[250 to 251] Domed Room (Medium)

[252 to 253] Drowning Pool (Small or Medium)

[254 to 255] Dry Well (Small or Medium, size being vertical)

[256 to 258] Dungeon (Small, Medium, or Large, with Large implying multiple rooms and chambers)

[259 to 261] Dust Pit (Tiny, Small, or Medium)

[262 to 263] Echo Chamber (Small or Medium)

[264 to 266] Echoing Vault (Small)

[267 to 269] Embalming Chamber (Small or Medium)

[270 to 272] Embalming Room (Large)

[273 to 274] Enchanted Grotto (Small, Medium, or Large)

[275 to 276] Enclosed Loggia (Medium or Large)

[277 to 278] Enclosure (Small or Medium, with a Tiny internal space)

[279 to 281] Enterclose (Tiny or Small)

[282 to 283] Entrance Hall (Medium, Large, or Huge)

[284 to 285] Entry / Entryway (Small or Medium)

[286 to 288] Entry Hall (Medium or Large)

[289 to 290] Episcenium (Tiny or Small)

[291 to 292] Excavation (Large or Huge)

[293 to 294] Excavation Room (Small or Medium)

[295 to 296] Execution Chamber (Small)

[297 to 299] Execution Hall (Large or Huge)

[300 to 301] Execution Room (Medium)

[302 to 303] Fallen Angelic Shrine (Small or Medium)

[304 to 306] False Tomb (Small, Medium, or Large)

[307 to 309] False Treasure Room (Small or Medium)

[310 to 311] False Treasure Vault (Medium or Large)

[312 to 313] Feretorium (Small or Medium)

[314 to 316] Feretory (Small or Medium)

[317 to 318] Firepit (Tiny or Small)

[319 to 320] Fissure, Ceiling (Small, Medium, or Large)

[321 to 323] Fissure, Wall / Fissure Vault (Medium, Large, or Huge)

[324 to 325] Flooded Hall (Large or Huge)

[326 to 328] Flooded Room (Small or Medium)

[329 to 330] Forbidden Chamber (Small or Medium)

[331 to 332] Forbidden Vault (Large)

[333 to 334] Fornix Chamber (Small)

[335 to 337] Fornix Hall (Large or Huge)

[338 to 339] Fornix Room (Medium)

[340 to 342] Fountain Chamber (Small)

[343 to 345] Fountain Grotto (Small, Medium, or Large)

[346 to 347] Fountain Hall (Large or Huge)

[348 to 349] Fountain Room (Medium)

[350 to 351] Fresco Gallery (Large)

[352 to 354] Fresco Room (Small or Medium)

[355 to 357] Fundament (Small or Medium)

[328 to 359] Fundament Room (Medium or Large)

[360 to 361] Funerary Chapel (Small or Medium)

[362 to 364] Funerary Workshop (Small or Medium)

[365 to 367] Funereal Crowde (Small or Medium)

[368 to 370] Gate Chamber (Medium)

[371 to 372] Gate Room (Large)

[373 to 374] Grand Aerarium (Large or Huge)

[375 to 376] Grand Aerary (Large or Huge)

[377 to 378] Great Abattoir (Large or Huge)

[379 to 380] Gren (Tiny)

[381 to 382] Grof (Tiny or Small)

[383 to 384] Grot (Tiny or Small)

[385 to 387] Grotto (Medium or Large)

[388 to 390] Hall (Large or Huge)

[391 to 393] Hall of Bones (Large or Huge)

[394 to 396] Hall of Doors (Large or Huge)

[397 to 398] Hall of Mourners (Large or Huge)

[399 to 401] Hall of Offerings (Large or Huge)

[402 to 404] Hall of Pools (Large or Huge)

[405 to 406] Hall of Resurrection (Large or Huge)

[407 to 408] Hall of Reverence (Large or Huge)

[409 to 411] Hall of Runes (Large or Huge)

[412 to 414] Hall of Souls (Large or Huge)

[2415 to 416] Hall of Statuary (Large or Huge)

[417 to 419] Hall of the Dead (Large or Huge)

[420 to 421] Haugr (Tiny, Small, Medium, or Large)

[422 to 424] Hell Mouth (Medium, Large, or Huge)

[425 to 427] Heroum (Tiny, Small, or Medium)

[428 to 430] Hole (Tiny or Small)

[431 to 433] Hollow (Tiny or Small)

[434 to 435] Hollowed Wall (Tiny, Small, or Medium)

[436 to 438] Holr (Small or Medium)

[439 to 440] Hrt / Heret (Large)

[441 to 442] Hrt Ib / Heret Ib (Large or Huge)

[443 to 445] Hwt Ka / Hewet Ka (Small or Medium)

[446 to 447] Hylr (Small or Medium)

[448 to 449] Hypogeum (Small, Medium, or Large)

[450 to 452] Hypostyle Hall (Large or Huge)

[453 to 454] Ibw / Ibiw (Tiny, Small, or Medium)

[455 to 457] Idol Grotto (Small, Medium, or Large)

[458 to 459] Idrt / Idret (Large or Huge)

[460 to 461] Ikw / Ikew (Large or Huge)

[462 to 463] Illusory Chamber (Small)

[464 to 466] Illusory Room (Medium or Large)

[467 to 469] Imht / Imehet (Small or Medium)

[470 to 471] Imnt / Imenet (Tiny, Small, or Medium)

[472 to 473] Impluvium Chamber (Small)

[474 to 476] Impluvium Hall (Large or Huge)

[477 to 478] Impluvium Room (Medium)

[479 to 481] Internment Chamber

[482 to 483] Isittu (Small, Medium, or Large)

[484 to 486] Itima (Small or Medium)

[487 to 489] Iwnyt / Iwenyt (Small)

[490 to 492] Karmu (Small, Medium, or Large)

[493 to 495] Kelda (Small or Medium)

[496 to 497] Kila (Small, Medium, or Large)

[498 to 499] Kimah (Small, Medium, or Large)

[500 to 501] Kukku (Small, Medium, or Large)

[502 to 503] Kummu (Small or Medium)

[504 to 505] Kunukku (Small or Medium)

[506 to 508] Labyrinth (Large or Huge)

[509 to 510] Lair (Tiny, Small, Medium, Large, or Huge)

[511 to 512] Landing (Tiny or Small)

[513 to 514] Lararium (Tiny or Small)

[515 to 516] Leaching Cesspool (Small, Medium, or Large)

[517 to 518] Leap (Tiny, Small, or Medium)

[519 to 520] Makkuri (Small, Medium, or Large)

[521 to 522] Manzazu (Small, Medium, or Large)

[523 to 525] Martyrium (Tiny, Small, or Medium)

[526 to 527] Mass Grave (Large or Huge)

[528 to 529] Mausoleum (Large or Huge)

[530 to 531] Maze (Large or Huge)

[532 to 533] Memorial Chamber (Small or Medium)

[534 to 536] Mestaku (Tiny)

[537 to 538] Metroon (Small, Medium, or Large)

[539 to 541] Mihat (Small or Medium)

[542 to 543] Monster Crypt (Tiny, Small, or Medium)

[544 to 546] Morgue (Small or Medium)

[547 to 549] Mortuary Chapel

[550 to 552] Msxn / Mesixen (Small or Medium)

[553 to 554] Msxnt / Mesixenet (Large or Huge)

[555 to 556] Narthex (Medium, Large, or Huge)

[557 to 558] Naspaku (Small or Medium)

[559 to 560] Natatorium (Large or Huge)

[561 to 563] Necropolis (Large or Huge)

[564 to 565] Nether (Large or Huge)

[566 to 568] Netherworld (Huge)

[569 to 570] Netherworld Descent (Huge)

[571 to 572] Niche (Tiny)

[573 to 574] Niched Room (Small or Medium)

[575 to 576] Obelisk Chamber (Small or Medium)

[577 to 578] Obelisk Hall (Large or Huge)

[579 to 581] Offering Chamber (Small)

[582 to 584] Oil Cellar (Small or Medium)

[585 to 586] Opisthodomos (Small or Medium)

[587 to 588] Oracular Chamber (Small or Medium)

[589 to 591] Ossuary (Tiny)

[592 to 593] Ossuary Chamber (Small)

[594 to 595] Ossuary Room (Medium or Large)

[596 to 597] Oubliette (Tiny)

[598 to 599] Oubliette Room (Small, Medium, or Large)

[600 to 601] Pastophorium (Small)

[602 to 603] Pergula (Tiny, Small, or Medium)

[604 to 605] Pit (Tiny or Small)

[606 to 608] Pit Chamber (Small)

[609 to 610] Pit Room (Medium)

[611 to 613] Ploutonion (Small or Medium)

[614 to 616] Plundered Tomb (Small, Medium, or Large)

[617 to 618] Plundered Vault (Medium, Large, or Huge)

[619 to 620] Plunge (Small, Medium, or Large)

[621 to 622] Pool (Tiny, Small, or Medium)

[623 to 625] Pool Chamber (Small)

[626 to 627] Pool Room (Medium or Large)

[628 to 630] Portcullis Chamber

[631 to 633] Pr Hd / Per Hed (Small, Medium, or Large)

[634 to 635] Pr Nfr / Per Nefer (Small or Medium)

[636 to 637] Procoeton (Small)

[638 to 640] Procoetum (Small)

[641 to 643] Pyre Chamber (Small)

[644 to 646] Pyre Room (Medium or Large)

[647 to 648] Rdw / Redew (Small or Medium)

[649 to 650] Recess (Tiny or Small, with an adjacent Small, Medium, or Large space)

[651 to 652] Reflecting Pool (Tiny, Small, or Medium)

[653 to 655] Refuse Pit (Tiny, Small, or Medium)

[656 to 658] Reliquary (Tiny, Small, or Medium)

[659 to 661] Reservoir (Large or Huge)

[662 to 663] Revolving Chamber (Small or Medium)

[664 to 665] Room (Small or Medium)

[666 to 667] Room of Pools (Large or Huge)

[668 to 670] Room of Unknown Purpose (Tiny, Small, Medium, Large, or Huge)

[671 to 672] Rotating Room (Small or Medium)

[673 to 675] Rotting Chamber (Small)

[676 to 678] Rotting Room (Medium or Large)

[679 to 681] Rotunda (Small, Medium, or Large)

[682 to 684] Royal Tomb (Large or Huge)

[685 to 686] Rubble-Filled Room / Ruined Room (Small or Medium)

[687 to 689] Ruined Chamber (Small)

[690 to 691] Ruined Hall (Large or Huge)

[692 to 694] Rum (Small or Medium)

[695 to 697] Runic Chamber (Small or Medium)

[698 to 700] Sacred Abattoir (Small, Medium, or Large)

[701 to 703] Sacred Crypt (Small)

[704 to 705] Sacred Tomb (Medium or Large)

[706 to 707] Sacrificial Chamber (Small or Medium)

[708 to 709] Sacrificial Grotto (Small or Medium)

[710 to 712] Sacrificial Pool (Tiny, Small, or Medium)

[713 to 715] Sacrificial Vault (Large or Huge)

[716 to 718] Sandpit (Small, Medium, or Large)

[719 to 721] Sarcophagus Chamber (Small or Medium)

[722 to 723] Sarcophagus Room (Medium or Large)

[724 to 726] Scrapheap (Small, Medium, or Large)

[727 to 729] Sealed Tomb (Small, Medium, or Large)

[730 to 732] Secret Crypt (Small, Medium, or Large)

[733 to 734] Secret Cyst (Tiny, Small, Medium, or Large)

[735 to 736] Secret Grotto (Small or Medium)

[737 to 738] Secret Room (Tiny, Small, Medium, or Large)

[739 to 740] Secret Tomb (Small, Medium, or Large)

[741 to 743] Sepulcher / Sepulchre

[744 to 745] Sepulchral Cell (Tiny)

[746 to 747] Sepulchral Chapel (Small, Medium, or Large)

[748 to 750] Sepulchral Hall (Large or Huge)

[751 to 753] Sepulchral Heroum (Small or Medium, perhaps in a Medium, Large, or Huge surrounding space)

[754 to 755] Sewer (Small, Medium, Large, or Huge)

[756 to 758] Shrine (Small or Medium)

[759 to 760] Shrine Chamber (Small)

[761 to 762] Simmiltu (Tiny, Small, or Medium)

[763 to 765] Sinkhole (Small, Medium, Large, or Huge)

[766 to 768] Slaves' Tomb (Small, Medium, or Large)

[769 to 770] Sludge Pit (Tiny, Small, or Medium)

[771 to 772] Spiral Labyrinth (Medium, Large, or Huge)

[773 to 775] Stair Chamber (Small)

[776 to 777] Stairway Room (Medium)

[778 to 780] Statuary (Small, Medium, or Large)

[781 to 782] Storage Chamber (Small)

[783 to 785] Storage Room / Storeroom (Small or Medium)

[786 to 787] Storeroom – Box Room (Small or Medium)

[788 to 790] Storeroom – Ceremonial (Small or Medium)

[791 to 792] Storeroom – Char / Coal (Small or Medium)

[793 to 794] Storeroom – Construction (Small or Medium)

[795 to 796] Storeroom – Embalming (Small or Medium)

[797 to 799] Stricture (Tiny or Small)

[800 to 801] Strongroom (Small)

[802 to 804] Submerged Chamber (Small)

[805 to 806] Submerged Hall (Large or Huge)

[807 to 808] Submerged Room (Medium)

[809 to 811] Tar Pit (Small, Tiny, or Medium)

[812 to 814] Taum (Tiny, Small, or Medium)

[815 to 816] Teleportation Chamber (Tiny, Small, or Medium)

[817 to 818] Terminus (Tiny, Small, or Medium)

[819 to 820] Tholos (Small, Medium, or Large)

[821 to 823] Threshold (Tiny, Small, Medium, or Large)

[824 to 825] Tomb (Medium or Large)

[826 to 827] Tomb Chamber (Small)

[828 to 830] Tomb Shaft (Tiny, Small, or Medium)

[831 to 833] Treasure Chamber (Small or Medium)

[834 to 835] Treasure Vault (Medium or Large)

[836 to 837] Undercroft (Small, Medium, Large, or Huge)

[838 to 839] Underground Mausoleum (Huge)

[840 to 841] Underground Pyramid (Huge)

[842 to 843] Underground Ziggurat (Huge)

[844 to 846] Undervault (Large or Huge)

[847 to 848] Unfinished Chamber (Small)

[849 to 850] Unfinished Hall (Large or Huge)

[851 to 852] Unfinished Room (Medium)

[853 to 855] Unfinished Tomb (Small, Medium, or Large)

[856 to 857] Vault (Small, Medium, or Large)

[858 to 859] Vaulted Chamber (Small or Medium)

[860 to 861] Vaulted Hall (Large or Huge)

[862 to 863] Vaulted Room (Medium or Large)

[864 to 865] Vestibule (Small or Medium)

[866 to 867] Vestibulum (Small or Medium)

[868 to 869] Wadyt (Large or Huge)

[870 to 871] Walled-Up Chamber (Small)

[872 to 873] Walled-Up Corridor (Small or Medium)

[874 to 876] Walled-Up Room (Medium or Large)

[877 to 879] Warren (Tiny or Small)

[880 to 882] Warrens (Medium, Large, or Huge)

[883 to 885] Wasi (Small, Medium, or Large)

[886 to 888] Wda / Weda (Small or Medium)

[889 to 891] Winch Pit (Tiny or Small)

[892 to 894] Wndwt / Wenedewet (Small)

[895 to 897] Xnrt / Xeneret (Small or Medium)

[898 to 900] Xnty / Xenety (Small or Medium)

[901 to 909] Tomb Sub-Region: Funerary Grottoes. Roll on the Cave Room Table for the next 1D4+1 rooms (rerolling any results of 901 to 000), and then return to this table.

[910 to 915] Tomb Sub-Region: Sepulchral Caves. Roll on the Cave Room Table for the next 2D4 rooms (rerolling any results of 901 to 000), and then return to this table.

[916 to 918] Tomb Sub-Region: Cavern Crypts. Roll on the Cave Room Table for the next 2D6+1 rooms (rerolling any results of 901 to 000), and then return to this table.

[919 to 927] Tomb Sub-Region: Slave Chambers. Roll on the Dungeon Room Table for the next 1D4+1 rooms (rerolling any results of 901 to 000), and then return to this table.

[928 to 933] Tomb Sub-Region: Buried Slave Vaults. Roll on Dungeon Room Table for the next 2D4 rooms (rerolling any results of 901 to 000), and then return to this table.

[934 to 936] Tomb Sub-Region: Halls of the Servitors. Roll on Dungeon Room Table for the next 2D6+1 rooms (rerolling any results of 901 to 000), and then return to this table.

[937 to 945] Tomb Sub-Region: Gravekeepers' Chambers. Roll on the Manor House Room Table for the next 1D4+1 rooms (rerolling any results of 901 to 000), and then return to this table.

[946 to 951] Tomb Sub-Region: Death Priests' Vaults. Roll on the Manor House Room Table for the next 2D4 rooms (rerolling any results of 901 to 000), and then return to this table.

[952 to 954] Tomb Sub-Region: Necromancer's Manorial Halls. Roll on the Manor House Room Table for the next 2D6+1 rooms (rerolling any results of 901 to 000), and then return to this table.

[955 to 963] Tomb Sub-Region: Tomb Warders' Chambers. Roll on the Stronghold Room Table for the next 1D4+1 rooms (rerolling any results of 901 to 000), and then return to this table.

[964 to 969] Tomb Sub-Region: Tomb Guardians' Vaults. Roll on the Stronghold Room Table for the next 2D4 rooms (rerolling any results of 901 to 000), and then return to this table.

[970 to 972] Tomb Sub-Region: Underworld Holdfast. Roll on the Stronghold Room Table for the next 2D6+1

rooms (rerolling any results of 901 to 000), and then return to this table.

[973 to 981] Tomb Sub-Region: Sacred Undervaults. Roll on the Temple Room Table for the next 1D4+1 rooms (rerolling any results of 901 to 000), and then return to this table.

[982 to 987] Tomb Sub-Region: Funereal Fane. Roll on the Temple Room Table for the next 2D4 rooms (rerolling any results of 901 to 000), and then return to this table.

[988 to 990] Tomb Sub-Region: Great Funerary Temple. Roll on the Temple Room Table for the next 2D6+1 rooms (rerolling any results of 901 to 000), and then return to this table.

[991 to 995] Tomb Sub-Region: Enigmatic Crypts. Roll on the Evocative Random Rooms Table (refer to The Classic Dungeon Design Guide, Book I) for the next 1D4+1 rooms (rerolling any results of 901 to 000), and then return to this table.

[996 to 998] Tomb Sub-Region: Eldritch Ancestral Tombs. Roll on the Evocative Random Rooms Table (refer to The Classic Dungeon Design Guide, Book I) for the next 2D4 rooms (rerolling any results of 901 to 000), and then return to this table.

[999 to 000] Tomb Sub-Region: Sepulchral Aberrations. Roll on the Evocative Random Rooms Table (refer to The Classic Dungeon Design Guide, Book I) for the next 2D6+1 rooms (rerolling any results of 901 to 000), and then return to this table.

CHAPTER IV:

THE LABYRINTH LEXICON

A IS FOR ABATTOIR

Abattoir *(Small or Medium)*

A slaughterhouse room or locale, where beasts or monsters are slain (perhaps as a sacrifice).

Abreuvoir *(Medium, Large, or Huge)*

A water tank, or a partially flooded room, which has been designed to provide water for animals (mounts?) or (guardian?) monsters.

Absis *(Small)*

An ancient (Greek-themed) apse.

Abzu *(Huge)*

A great netherworld aquifer, underground lake, or subterranean sea. The term implies that it is (or was) sacred to a Mesopotamian civilization and may be supernaturally protected.

Access Cave *(Small or Medium)*

A narrow cave, likely with a controlled opening (covered with vines, guarded by spikes, etc.) leading into an important cavern.

Access Cavern *(Large)*

A large access cave. The cavern is likely to have multiple points of entry, but may have only a single exit leading deeper into the dungeon.

Access Chamber *(Small)*

A narrow room, likely with a secure door or gate, leading into an important room.

Access Room *(Medium)*

A large access chamber. There may be multiple points of access, controlled by a guard post, a set of doors or gates, etc.

Accommodation *(Small)*

A temporary place of lodging, typically for a servant, official, or guest.

Accommodations, plural

(Medium or Large)

Two or more accommodations in a room block. This may be an interconnected series of 10'x10', 10'x20', or 20'x20' rooms. The room block may be fairly large, but split into multiple sections by doors, archways, tapestries, etc.

Acidic Cave *(Small or Medium)*

Features a pool of ancient water, acidic vapor, or acidic mineralized water dripping down from stalactites. Note also that this would be an ideal defensive area for any adventurers (or denizens) who are assaulted by trolls or similar acid-vulnerable creatures.

Acidic Cavern *(Large)*

A large acidic cave. The cavern will likely have 1D4+1 acid pools.

Adamantite Delve *(Medium or Large)*

A place where adamantite ore can be mined (by dark elves, deep gnomes, dwarves, etc.). May be guarded, fought over, and/or partially depleted.

Adyton *(Small or Medium)*

An ancient (most likely Greek-themed) sanctum sanctorum.

Adytum *(Small or Medium)*

An ancient, classical (Roman-themed), and/or formal sanctum sanctorum.

Aerarium / Ancient Aerary

(Medium or Large)

An ancient (Roman-themed) treasure vault.

Aerarium Chamber *(Small or Medium)*

A small, ancient treasure vault. Alternately, this might be a succession of many 10' x 10' cubicles with adjoining doors; the doors are usually kept closed to keep treasures (or traps!) from flowing into one another.

Aerary *(Medium or Large)*

A medieval treasure vault, typically in a castle or temple. Medieval stronghold features such as portcullises, moat-works, or even drawbridges might be present.

Aerary Chamber *(Small)*

A small medieval treasure vault, typically in a castle or temple. There may be a single trap, but there is probably not enough room for multiple defensive systems to exist.

Af-Hus *(Tiny or Small)*

A Nordic-themed side room, or room of lesser importance.

Agiasterion *(Medium or Large)*

An ancient (Greek-themed) sanctuary featuring an ornate altar, and likely a basin for holy water.

Agiasterium *(Medium or Large)*

An ancient (Roman-themed) agiasterion.

Ah / Ahu *(Large or Huge)*

An Egyptian-themed temple.

Ah Hwt / Ahu Hewet *(Small or Medium)*

An ancient Egyptian-themed tomb or vertical tomb shaft. Very likely to be trapped, or at least secret. If neither, it is likely plundered.

Air Chamber *(Small)*

A small room specifically designed to serve as a junction for wind tunnels and/or air conduits and to provide air flow to remote areas. This room is almost certain to be breezy, or even windy, and the air flow may be assisted by magic (e.g., a permanent gust of wind spell, or even an imprisoned air elemental).

Refer also to the air speed and quality tables in *The Classic Dungeon Design, Book I* for more possible qualifications of this area.

Air Room *(Medium)*

A larger air chamber. There may be multiple exits, and air flow (ingress and egress) might be controlled by sub-walls or buttress structures of some kind.

Ala *(Tiny or Small)*

A Roman-themed alcove, perhaps featuring a bust, statue, or pedestal. Often found adjacent to an atrium.

Alae, plural *(Medium or Large)*

A long series of Roman-themed alcoves, for example on either side of a long hallway or narrow gallery.

Alcove *(Tiny or Small)*

A small recess adjoining a larger room. In game terms, these are likely 10'x10' (single-square), 5'x10', or 5'x5' indentations in a large room's walls. If an alcove is indicated as a standalone room, it is almost certainly either

(a) the bottom of a shaft, (b) the top of a shaft, (c) a connecting space between two nearly-adjacent rooms, or (d) the location of a concealed or secret door leading into a larger space. Rerolling is suggested if you cannot envision any of these options.

Alcove Succession *(Medium or Large)*

A long series of alcoves, for example on either side of a long hallway or narrow gallery.

Ale Cellar *(Small or Medium)*

An underground room used for the storage and aging of ale and/or mead.

Aleatorium *(Small or Medium)*

A gaming room, where dice games are played. Roman and medieval games are examples.

Alhacena *(Tiny or Small)*

An ornate alcove, featuring carvings, bas reliefs, or a statue, bust, etc.

Alhacena Succession *(Medium or Large)*

A long series of alhacenas, for example on either side of a long hallway or narrow gallery.

Alipterion *(Medium or Large)*

An ornate (Greek-themed) anointing room, where people (bathers, a lady, nobles, etc.) clean themselves with oils and unguents.

Alipterium *(Medium or Large)*

A Roman-themed alipterion. The room will almost always be adjacent to some form of baths (caldarium, tepidarium, etc.).

Almonerium *(Medium or Large)*

An ancient (Roman-themed) almonry.

Almonry *(Medium)*

A room where gold or other material goods are provided to the poor. Typically a part of a temple, but in the game this could also refer to (for example) a dungeon room where a great dragon's (or other powerful monster's) minions receive payment and offer tribute.

Almonry Chamber *(Small)*

A small almonry. A likely indicator that the overseen NPC or monster has fewer followers (than for a full almonry, above), and is therefore less powerful as well.

Almonry Hall *(Large)*

A large almonry. Likely an indication that this area is controlled by a very powerful dungeon personage or intelligent monster (such as an ancient dragon).

Altar Chamber *(Small)*

A small room featuring an altar as its centerpiece.

Altar Room *(Medium)*

A larger altar chamber. The altar may be located in a lower area, reached by a ring of descending steps.

Ambitus

(Medium or Large, with a Tiny or Small enclosure)

A hallowed room surrounding a smaller inner room; the smaller inner room is a crypt or tomb.

Ambry *(Small or Medium)*

A storeroom where food is kept in a preserved state, or in a controlled environment. Can also be used to store sacred vessels.

Ambry Chamber *(Tiny or Small)*

A small, and likely sealed, ambry.

Ambulatory *(Medium)*

A corridor-like area surrounding an inner room. This can be a surrounding enclosed hallway, a pillared walkway, etc. You should also roll the nature of the interior space (as a separate room location) at this time.

Amphithalamoi, plural *(Medium or Large)*

A succession of ancient and adjoining (Greek-themed) bedchambers. The chambers might well belong to NPCs of similar rank and standing; for example, a brotherhood of six level 3 fighters.

Amphithalamos *(Small or Medium)*

An ancient (Greek-themed) bedchamber.

Amphithalamus *(Small or Medium)*

An ancient (Roman-themed) bedchamber.

Amphitheater *(Large or Huge)*

A large, tiered hall meant for the observation of ceremonies. For a cavern region, this would be a carved and hewn amphitheater gallery hollowed out of the rock.

Anatomical Theater

(Medium, Large, or Huge)

A room of tiered seating surrounding a central rise or depression where a body is worked on surgically for educational purposes. In the game, this might be a mad archmage's monster laboratory for the training of apprentices, a monster hunter's lecture hall, or a necromancer's theater of undead minion creation.

Ancestral Chamber *(Small or Medium)*

A room (perhaps funerary in nature) where a specific bloodline is honored with mosaics, paintings, relics, statues, etc.

Ancestral Hall *(Large or Huge)*

A large ancestral chamber.

Anchorage *(Small)*

The bedchamber of a low-level priest (anchorite).

Anddyri *(Small, Medium, or Large)*

A Nordic-themed vestibule.

Andron *(Small or Medium)*

A room that provides quarters for men, to the exclusion of women. (Example denizens: priests, apprentices, monks.)

Angelic Shrine *(Small or Medium)*

A Shrine which is devoted to a deva, angel of the planetary spheres, or angel of the solar sphere.

Annex *(Tiny, Small, or Medium)*

Typically, a poorly-planned addition to an adjacent chamber.

Annex Labyrinth *(Large or Huge)*

A series of poorly-planned, unfinished and interconnected additions, leading off from an established adjacent chamber.

Annex Warren *(Tiny, Small, or Medium)*

A poorly-planned excavation (perhaps abandoned due to imminent collapse?) adjacent to a cave or cavern.

Anointing Chamber (*Small*)

A small anointing room, perhaps for the use of a single NPC (such as a high priest or priestess).

Anointing Room (*Medium*)

A room where people (bathers, laborers, guards, healers etc.) clean themselves with oils and unguents.

Antecabinet (*Small*)

An ornate and finely-furnished antechamber.

Antecavern (*Small or Medium*)

A relatively small cavern which opens into a much larger cavern. May be carved and ornate. This is a likely place for humanoid guards, or mercenary giants, or guardian beasts, or other protectors of the netherworld dominions.

Antechamber (*Small*)

A small chamber designed to restrict or control access into the next, larger, and more important room.

Antechapel (*Small or Medium*)

A chamber or room leading into an adjacent chapel.

Anteroom (*Medium*)

A large antechamber; a room serving as the entrance to a larger room, typically a hall.

Antrum (*Medium*)

A cave used by people in classical or ancient times. (It might have been merely a dwelling place, or used to hide treasure, or as a place of worship, etc.). There may be unusual markings or artwork here.

Antrum Cavern (*Small or Medium*)

A large antrum. If the antrum is ancient and/or has seen ancestral use, there might well be relics – or undead – buried beneath the floor.

Apartments, plural (*Medium or Large*)

A set of makeshift, interrelated living areas. In a medieval context, this would mean a room that is split into smaller areas by shoddy improvised walls; for example, a 30'x30' room split into rough 10'x10' cubicles to provide quarters for separate guards, servants, and/or humanoids. See also *The Masque of the Red Death*, by Edgar Allan Poe, for another potential inspiration.

Aperture (*Tiny*)

A very small area – perhaps 10' x 10' – that remains between larger constructed areas. The aperture is usually a blend of the other areas, featuring two archways or doors of passage.

Apodyterium (*Small or Medium*)

A disrobing room within or near a balnea, therma, or other bathing area. The bath should either be an adjacent room, or a location/pool within the current room.

Apotheca (*Small or Medium*)

A storeroom for consumable valuables (oils, grains, spices, wines, etc.).

Apothecarium (*Small or Medium*)

An ancient apothecary. The space has likely been put to other use, but interesting remnants (herbs, spices, perfumes, poisons, potions, etc.) may be hidden here.

Apothecary (*Small or Medium*)

The chamber, shop, or work area of an apothecary (an herbal chemist NPC, who may also work with poisons).

Apse (Small)

A small, semi-circular area with a domed ceiling. There will typically be an altar or shrine situated in the curved area. To explorers, this might look like the curved dead end to a corridor that splits off to the left and right.

Apse Cavelet (Small)

A small cave, used as an apse. The altar or shrine will probably be dedicated to an underworld god, demon, devil, or chthonic spirit of some kind.

Apse Room (Medium)

A room-sized apse; in game terms, probably a room in the shape of a half circle (with one straight wall and one curved wall, and likely two doors or passageways, one at each extremity).

Apsidal Chapel (Small)

A small, semi-circular chapel area; a combination of an apse and a chapel.

Aquarium (Medium, Large, or Huge)

A room, or series of rooms, devoted to the display and keeping of aquatic creatures or monsters.

Arboretum (Large)

A botanical garden devoted to the keeping and study of trees and shrubs. If situated underground, then magical light and water will be present.

Archive (Medium, Large, or Huge)

A room filled with historical books, tablets, and scrolls. There may be magical writings hidden somewhere ... perhaps even entire spell books.

Arcosolium (Tiny or Small)

In a temple or tomb, an arch-ceilinged recess or alcove built to partially enclose a sarcophagus and its side areas. In game terms, a perfect lair for the undead.

Arena (Medium, Large, or Huge)

A room (or even an amphitheater) where gladiatorial combatants fight to the death.

Arena Cave (Medium or Large)

A small arena cavern. An example would be situated next to a prison in an orc's lair, where captured adventurers would be forced to battle to the death against various monsters (unless, of course, they managed an in-battle escape).

Most challenges would be in an ascending order, with the less deadly monsters facing prisoners first and champions proceeding thereafter.

Arena Cavern (Huge)

A large naturally-shaped arena, used as a place of challenge by a tribe. Or, a similar place where prisoners are forced to fight to the death.

Armorial Chamber (Medium)

A small armorial hall. This might be the lair of a knight's guardian spirit, or perhaps an animated suit of armor.

Armorial Hall (Large or Huge)

A place where heraldic banners, pennants, statues, etc. are displayed. The statues might be animated guardians.

Armory (Medium)

A storeroom filled with armor and shields. Likely to be locked and/or guarded.

Armory and Forge (Large or Huge)

A place where metal armor is crafted; named as such (my own term) to differentiate it from an armory, where armor is stored. There might be an enslaved fire elemental here, or a dwarven master smith, or flame salamanders, etc.

Armory Chamber (Small)

A small armory. There might well be a hidden magical shield or suit of armor here.

Arryt (Large or Huge)

An Egyptian-themed hall of judgment, dedicated to one or more of the deities, and likely guarded by (summoned?) supernatural creatures.

Arsenal (Large)

A storeroom filled with weapons, perhaps including siege defenses (oil for boiling, prods for pushing off ladders, etc.). Likely to be locked and/or guarded.

Arsenal and Forge (Large or Huge)

A place where metal weapons are crafted; named as such (my own term) to differentiate it from an Arsenal, where weapons are stored. The place might be guarded by soaring animated weapons or something similar.

Arsenal Chamber (Small)

A small arsenal. There might well be a hidden magical weapon (miscellaneous or sword) here.

Art Gallery (Medium, Large, or Huge)

A gallery where various forms of art (drawings, paintings, sculpture, etc.) are displayed side by side. Typically a thematic collection belonging to someone powerful.

Artisan's Chamber (Small or Medium)

The shop, work area, or quarters of an artisan NPC (a worker who creates fine physical objects of some kind).

Artisan's Room (Medium or Large)

A slightly larger artisan's chamber. Likely to be inhabited by one or more artisan NPCs, who might be the crafters of magic items (along with their guards).

Ash Pit (Small or Medium)

A pit filled with ashes, and possibly bone chips as well (from cremated victims).

Ashen Abyss (Large or Huge)

A large ash pit, or a series of ash pits. This might be the lair of undead, burrowing beasts, ash worms, a dust elemental, or something worse.

Aslukku (Small or Medium)

An Akkadian- or Babylonian-themed storeroom of some kind; refer to the various storerooms types listed for ideas on a further specficiation.

Assemblage (Medium, Large, or Huge)

A room where priests and/or worshippers gather in preparation for a ceremony.

Assembly Chamber (Small or Medium)

A small assembly hall. Wandering monsters and random encounters (with patrolling guards, humanoid servants, guardian beasts, etc.) will be more common here.

Assembly Hall (Large or Huge)

In use, another name for a function hall. Technically, may infer that the functions held here will presage another event (for example, an assembly hall for announcements, wagers and greetings, before guests are seated in an arena to observe a gladiatorial battle).

Astrarium Chamber (Medium)

A small astrarium room. In addition to the celestial contraptions, the clockwork might pertain to a trap, alarm, elevator room, revolving room, or similar.

Astrarium Room (Large)

A room filled with clockwork that is used to calculate the movements of celestial bodies (sun, moon, planets, and possibly stars) for the prediction of holy days and prophetic events.

Asylum (Small, Medium, or Large)

A sanctuary of mercy, where it is forbidden to strike down anyone (regardless of alignment) who honors the appropriate god / goddess and begs for divine protection. In game terms, this is probably an area in an active temple; but if discovered in a dungeon, the place is probably desecrated and no longer powerful, but may well be cursed and/or haunted.

At Iwf / Atu Iwef (Medium or Large)

An Egyptian-themed ceremonial abattoir. This might be the lair of undead, flesh constructs, blood-feasting demons, or worse.

Atelier (Small or Medium)

An artisan's chamber where apprentices and/or workmen work on the fine arts: drawings, paintings, sculpture, etc.

Athanor Chamber (Small)

A small athanor room. There will almost certainly be an alchemist NPC present, along with unseen servants or a familiar servant of some kind.

Athanor Room (Medium or Large)

A workroom containing an alchemist's athanor, or charcoal furnace. If the alchemist is not present, the place might well be guarded by a summoned elemental of some kind (perhaps restricted in its movements to limit breakage or other disasters).

Atrium (Large or Huge)

A large, roofed, open space within a larger building or enclosure. A sacred courtyard. There may be a pool, fountain, etc. If discovered underground, the light (and plants and/or fungi, if they are present) will be magical.

Atrium Cave (Medium or Large)

A magical subterranean atrium. This is almost certainly the lair of monstrous fungi of some kind (shrieking fungi, violet, phycomorions, ascomideans, mushroom people, etc.

Atrium Cavern (Huge)

A large atrium cave; the likely lair of fungus men, giant beetles, sentient slime mold, an abomination, or something even more fantastical.

Atrium Chamber (Small or Medium)

A small atrium; perhaps the lair of shrieking fungi or some form of slime.

Attic (Medium or Large)

A low-ceilinged, or slant-ceilinged, area at the top of a house or mansion, immediately below the roof. Typically intended for storage, but see also garret. If this roll is not appropriate to the current elevation, a result of storeroom is suggested instead.

Attic Space (Small)

A small attic. If we follow the rules of cinema, this is the lair of a possessed doll, or features a cursed chest of some kind, or some form of magic circle protected by shadowry, etc.

Audience Cavern (*Large or Huge*)

A large, natural cavern which is used as an audience hall.

Audience Chamber (*Small*)

A small audience room; a small area where an NPC noble, ruler, leader, etc. addresses followers and guests (and perhaps, enemies). The room may feature magical wards if there is not enough space for bodyguards.

Audience Hall (*Large or Huge*)

A large area where a noble, ruler, leader, etc. addresses followers and guests; a place where visitors are formally received by the stronghold's ruler. The hall is likely to have columns, pillars, sculptures, tapestries, etc.

Audience Room (*Medium*)

A mid-sized audience hall. The place is likely guarded if the noble or leader NPC is not present.

Auditorium (*Huge*)

A very large audience hall. Rather than being merely a classroom, a classical auditorium would be used for audiences, lectures, oration, and justice proceedings.

Augury Cave (*Small or Medium*)

A natural cave used as an augury chamber. There may be a diviner NPC here, or this might be a "special" where adventurers can commune with a supernatural power.

Augury Chamber (*Small*)

A room where priests observe the flight of birds, small flying monsters, etc. to interpret

the will of the gods. (This is the specific definition of augury; more broadly, this could be a divination chamber.)

Augury Room (*Medium*)

A somewhat larger augury chamber. There will almost certainly be diviner NPCs of some kind present here (mystics, savants, priests, etc.).

Aula (*Medium or Large*)

An ancient (Greek-themed) hall.

Aula Regia (*Huge*)

An ancient (Greek- or Roman-themed) great hall. If a significant amount of time has passed, this might be the guardian lair of a dormant golem, a sleeping titan, an imprisoned Lernaean hydra held in stasis, etc.

Auxiliary Cave (*Small or Medium*)

A natural cave used as an auxiliary room. There is likely an interesting NPC or intelligent monster taking refuge here.

Auxiliary Chamber (*Tiny or Small*)

A small auxiliary room. There may be an NPC taking refuge here, or hiding nearby (perhaps behind a secret door, tapestry, etc.).

Auxiliary Room (*Medium*)

A reserve room intended for either future use, or emergency use by a sheltering person.

Axnwty / Axenwety

(*Small, Medium, or Large*)

An Egyptian-themed audience chamber. There might be spirits here, or visions of the past, or perhaps even a dangerous magical gate out to a dune sea (or Underworld of Apshai).

B IS FOR BARROW

Bailey *(Medium, Large, or Huge)*

An inner courtyard built for defense (i.e., a place to trap invaders and rain arrows down). In dungeon terms, this could be a subterranean approach chamber with arrow slits, where guards in the next room could fire arrows at invaders.

Bakery *(Small or Medium)*

A room where breads are baked. Almost certainly contains a fireplace and/or firepit, and perhaps some desirable material spell components (or even dried and preserved healing herbs).

Ballroom *(Large or Huge)*

A large festival hall where dances and masquerades are held. An ideal place for a vampire and his or her thralls, a demon holding court, jesters, illusionists and their creations, or something else quite extravagant to behold.

Balnea *(Small or Medium)*

A small therma. If no longer used as intended, this might be the lair of a slime or minor aquatic creature of some kind.

Balnearium *(Small or Medium)*

A small caldarium or washroom. In a ruin or dungeon, this might now be the lair of gremlins, fungi, giant rats, or something similar.

Banquet Hall *(Large or Huge)*

A large feast hall intended to host celebratory events and feasts.

Banquet Room *(Medium)*

A small and more intimate banquet hall.

Barag *(Small or Medium)*

A Sumerian-themed sanctum. This might be the lair of a magical (or summoned) guardian of some kind.

Barbican *(Large)*

A fortified gatehouse. In dungeon terms, this could be a subterranean chamber where a guarded portcullis blocks access to the next room.

Barracks *(Medium or Large)*

A place where troops (frequently demi-humans, normal men, or humanoids) are quartered.

Barracks Hall *(Huge)*

A very large barracks, possibly with its own guard stations. This is almost certainly the lair of men-at-arms, or humanoids, or both.

Barrow *(Small or Medium)*

A tomb created by packed earth being piled over the crypt. Barrows are surface structures, but in a dungeon this could refer to a tomb chamber beneath a hill (regardless of depth), or tombs that were once on the surface and then the shallower dungeon regions were built up over time.

Barrow Crypt *(Small, Medium, or Large)*

Technically speaking, a subterranean crypt which is situated beneath a surface barrow. More broadly, a subterranean barrow-like tomb.

Basalt Cave *(Small or Medium)*

A cave with basalt stone walls (ancient cooled lava).

Basalt Cavern *(Large or Huge)*

A large basalt cave. This might be the lair of troglodytes, a stone golem, amber behemoths (the floor clay is soft and malleable), or something worse.

Basement *(Medium or Large)*

An underground room typically used for storage and utilities (such as coal). The existence of a basement implies dungeon level 1; see also the sub-basement lexicon entry.

Basement Space *(Small)*

A small basement. An ideal lair for small scuttling creatures, such as rats, kobolds, gremlins, spiders, centipedes, etc.

Basilica *(Large or Huge)*

A hall of judgment within a temple. There may be a powerful guardian of Law here, perhaps an angel (good), devil (evil), or Nirvanan hierarch (neutral).

Bastion *(Medium or Large)*

A tower or room which juts out from the stronghold wall(s), allowing missile fire from another direction. In an underground stronghold, this may be a room with oddly-shaped walls where guards can fire missiles through arrow slits etc.

Bath *(Small, Medium, or Large)*

A room with one or more artificial pools constructed for bathing. In more technical terms, a caldarium, frigidarium, or tepidarium.

Bathhouse *(Medium or Large)*

A structure that houses a bath. In a subterranean context, this could mean a bath chamber that is enclosed within a larger room; for example, a large hall with an archwayed or enclosed pool structure in the middle.

Bath Room / Bathroom *(Small or Medium)*

In the game world, a modern bathroom-with-toilet will not exist; but this term may be used (for example) a small room that combines the functions of a caldarium and a washroom. See also garderobe.

Bawm *(Small, Medium, or Large)*

A well-fortified medieval room or enclosure. It may have locking interior doors, or dropping cages, or barred windows where archers can fire, etc.

Bay *(Tiny or Small)*

A small semi-circular space off of a larger hall or corridor. The space might be used for a statue, weapon rack, window, small table, etc.

Bay Succession *(Medium or Large)*

A long series of bays, for example flanking both sides of a long hall or corridor.

Beast Crypt *(Tiny, Small, or Medium)*

A crypt where animal remains have been interred. A perfect place to encounter skeletal or zombified animals, or some kind of monstrous scavengers.

Beast Pit *(Small or Medium)*

A pit occupied by imprisoned beasts (or at least a beast's corpse). The perfect lair for a chained guardian beast.

Bedchamber *(Small)*

A small bedroom, typically intended for one person (unique NPC). If plural, the rooms are adjoining and are used by people of similar station.

Bedroom *(Small or Medium)*

Accommodations for one or two people, including a bed, table, chair, etc. A likely place for an NPC encounter.

Belfry *(Medium or Large)*

A bell tower or bell chamber, typically used to mark the hours for holy days, ceremonies, etc. Or, an alert system utilized by dungeon guardians watching out for intruders. See also echo chamber.

Bell Tower *(Medium, Large, or Huge)*

A tower (typically attached to a church, temple, or stronghold barracks) where loud bells are housed near the summit.

Bema *(Medium or Large)*

A raised sanctuary, up a ramp or a flight of stairs. The bema may be a sub-room within another room.

Biaw *(Large or Huge)*

An Egyptian-themed mine or mine shaft; a likely place for hidden or buried treasure. There might be an undead protector or ancient automaton of some kind.

Bleeding Chamber *(Small)*

A small bleeding room. This might be the temporary home of a servile NPC, a wounded or sleeping victim of some kind, etc. There will probably be healing salves, herbs, bandages, honey (a medieval antibiotic), or similar valuable materials here.

Bleeding Room *(Medium)*

A room devoted to bloodletting and healing operations. The likely workroom of a cleric NPC of some kind.

Blocked Cave

(Small or Medium, but with accessible area Tiny)

A small blocked cavern. Likely a trap, but might have a half-buried skeleton with valuable gear or something similar.

Blocked Cavern

(Large or Huge, but with accessible area Small or Medium)

Either blocked off by a cave-in, or walled up to prevent something horrible from escaping.

Bodega *(Small)*

A small wine vault. A likely place for a small keg of wine (treasure), or perhaps even some form of magical pool or potion.

Bone House *(Large or Huge)*

A large secure room lined by, or containing, multiple ossuaries. Commonly, a lair for rats or undead.

Bone Pit *(Small or Medium)*

A pit filled with bones and skulls. Possibly the lair of undead, or gremlins, or snakes, etc.

Bone-Filled Cave *(Small or Medium)*

A small bone-filled cavern (below).

Bone-Filled Cavern *(Large or Huge)*

The lair of a predator (such as a badgerbear), or perhaps a sacrificial pit, a graveyard, etc. Filled with gnawed and/or crushed bones and skulls.

Boudoir (*Small or Medium*)

The private sitting room of a noble; the likely place to encounter an NPC noble or servant or some form of minor guardian.

Boulder Cave (*Small or Medium*)

A cave filled with boulders; or, a cave where one or more entrances have been blocked by boulders.

Boulder Cavern (*Large or Huge*)

A large boulder cave. This area would perhaps serve as a lair for stone giants, trolls, cyclopes, etc. who will be certain to use the boulders as weapons if they are given the chance to do so.

Bouleuterion (*Large or Huge*)

An ancient (Greek-themed) assembly hall. This large columned space will certainly have been repurposed as a lair of some kind if it is no longer relevant in its original purpose.

Bourse (*Small, Medium, or Large*)

A room or enclosure which serves as a merchants' exchange. In game terms, this may mean a place where humanoids bring their bounty to their leaders and receive payment, a place where guards and incoming troops exchange goods, etc.

Bower (*Small*)

A medieval bedchamber that serves as the residence of a single woman (not a man). The lair of a unique NPC.

Breezeway (*Medium or Large*)

An arched bridge connecting a tower to a stronghold or manor house. Could also exist in a large subterranean setting, with deadly drops to either side.

Brewery (*Medium, Large, or Huge*)

A room or outbuilding where alcoholic (and/or alchemical) beverages are made. This might be the common area for a small enclave of gnomes, or dwarves, or halflings.

Burial Chamber (*Tiny or Small*)

A small burial room. There is very likely a monster and/or treasure situated here. If the treasure is unguarded, it is probably cursed and/or trapped.

Burial Room (*Medium*)

A room where one or more persons are buried. The room may appear empty, with coffins below the stonework floor; or may have sarcophagi in the center; or may have alcoves around the walls where remains are kept.

Burial Vault (*Large or Huge*)

A large, and typically locked or sealed, burial room. The ceiling may be vaulted. This place will not have living creatures, but undead are likely, and the presence of treasure is a certainty if the locks and wards have not yet been disturbed.

Buried Longship (*Large or Huge*)

Mariner cultures may actually honor their fallen heroes or nobles by burying them in a ship beneath the earth. (Inspired by the Nydam Bog ship and similar Viking burials.) Likely the lair of draugr, wraiths, undead wolves, etc.

Burrow (*Tiny or Small*)

A tunnel and/or makeshift den created by a burrowing monster or beast.

Burrow Maze (*Huge*)

A very large, and labyrinthine, succession of adjoining burrows. The home of anhkhegs, or beetles, or rats, or something else.

Burrow Warren (*Large*)

A large succession of adjoining burrows, with encountered creatures being very likely as above.

Bursary (*Medium or Large*)

A treasure vault within a temple or university. In fantasy terms, this could also be the treasure vault of a scholomance (school of magic).

Buru (*Small or Medium*)

An Akkadian- or Babylonian-themed well room. There may be an aquatic encounter here, or drinking (random) monsters.

Butchery (*Small*)

A relatively small but well-kept abattoir. This might be adjacent to a kitchen, or it might be something far more grisly (for example, a hack-works belonging to an evil necromancer who is currently gathering "fresh materials" to create a corrupted flesh golem).

Buttery (*Small or Medium*)

A room where barrels of wine and/or spirits are stored. (No, it has nothing to do with butter; see dairy chamber.) Additionally, this would be an ideal location to have an alchemical bent. A buttery in a magical medieval setting might well be filled with bulk potion ingredients, steeping or aging potion ingredients, experimental potions, or magical liqueurs. Bulk ingredients would be in sealed barrels, distilling mixtures would be in smaller clay or ceramic jugs, and potions would be in crystal bottles or vials along the shelves.

C IS FOR CRYPT

Cabinet *(Small)*

Not a piece of furniture in this instance, but rather a small retreat or study. Perhaps the lair of a minor NPC.

Cache Chamber *(Small)*

A secure room where crucial supplies are kept. Typically used to provide emergency food and/or supplies when the stronghold is besieged.

Cache Room *(Medium or Large)*

A large cache chamber. This locale is likely to be guarded by men-at-arms, a magic mouth, warding magic, a guardian beast, or something similar.

Cage *(Tiny, Small, or Medium)*

A room with barred walls, typically surrounded by a corridor for use by observers, interrogators, and/or torturers. The likely location of a prisoner in need of rescue.

Cage Matrix *(Large or Huge)*

A very large room filled with cages, which are separated from one another by "walls" of metal bars. There may be space for different types of creatures, such as a large monster and a separate area for humanoids etc.

Caged Chantry *(Small, Medium, or Large)*

A chantry which is screened by filigree (pieces of solid, yet decorative, metal which can be seen through but not passed through).

Caged Chapel *(Small)*

A chapel which is screened by filigree (pieces of solid, yet decorative, metal which can be seen through but not passed through).

Caldarium *(Small, Medium, or Large)*

A room with a hot-water Roman bath. Likely heated from below by a Hypocaust Chamber.

Refer also to the other Roman bath types, tepidarium, frigidarium, etc. for associated information.

Calefactorium *(Small, Medium, or Large)*

An ancient calefactory. This might be a burial place for hidden treasure, or the ashes might be home to an undead spirit of some kind.

Calefactory *(Small, Medium, or Large)*

A warming room, intended to warm denizens who have cold quarters (monks, guards, soldiers, etc.); will include one or more fireplaces or firepits.

Camba *(Small or Medium)*

A kitchen-like (ancient?) room for brewing and baking. This might be the central area for a humanoid lair.

Cantoris *(Small)*

The bedchamber of a cantor or priest NPC.

Carcer *(Medium, Large, or Huge)*

A rough-and-tumble prison (perhaps run unjustly by humanoids, bandits, etc.).

Cartographer's Hall *(Large or Huge)*

A large map room. This one location could serve as the prime repository for all of the Game Master's desired campaign lore, adventure hooks, and dungeon maps if desired.

Cascade Hall *(Large or Huge)*

A hall with a holy font or running water. In game terms, this could be any large room with fountain(s) and/or pool(s). An ideal place for alchemical tricks, elemental magic, or aquatic encounters.

Cascade Room (Small)

A large room or hall featuring a large, artificially-constructed waterfall. Why? Perhaps magic; but that is for you to figure out. This might be a one-way gate exiting from the Elemental Plane of Water, or the terminus for an underground river leading downward into a subterranean sea, or whatever else you prefer.

Casemate (Small or Medium)

A protected chamber hollowed out of an existing wall. More generally, a heavily-protected vaulted chamber.

Catabulum (Medium or Large)

A stable room, perhaps internal or underground, where guardian beasts or beasts of burden are kept.

Catacomb (Tiny or Small)

A small burial chamber that is surrounded by labyrinthine passages and corridors. (A singular "Catacomb" is probably a room, while the plural "Catacombs" likely refers to the entire region of crypts and passageways.)

Catacombs, plural

(Medium, Large, or Huge)

A series of interconnected catacomb chambers. This is the perfect place for a series of building encounters with undead, cultists (of a secret society), humanoids, or some kind of hive-minded monsters who have turned the cells into colonial chambers.

Catacumba (Tiny or Small)

An ancient catacomb. The likely location of a hidden treasure, and/or some undead spirit (a wraith, spectre, or even a banshee).

Catacumbae, plural

(Medium, Large, or Huge)

An ancient series of catacombs. The ancient catacombs are likely plundered. If not, they are probably protected by deadly traps or powerful wards (such as teleporters or permanent illusions).

Cavaedium (Large or Huge)

An ancient atrium. This would be a good place to include murals, mosaics, illusions, or some other form of artwork that teaches adventurers about a lost culture, city, or realm.

Cave (Small or Medium)

Any natural subterranean hollow in earth or stone. According to your preference, this could be a featureless cave (the basic name implies there is not much there), or a nonesuch cave with some amazing and strange thing you need to devise (a magical effect, a strange form of stone, a monster lair, etc.)

Cave of Ancestors (Small or Medium)

A cave where ancestral remains are honored. The remains may be garbed or covered in talismans, the skulls may be wearing masks, etc. Likely considered a sacred place by the descendants (tribesmen, underworld demi-humans, shamanistic humanoids, etc.)

Cave of Ashes (Small or Medium)

A cave filled either with burned wood or cremated remains. There may be treasure buried here, and/or it might be a sinkhole trap (perhaps leading down to an even deeper dungeon level).

Cave of Bones (Small or Medium)

A cave filled with bones and skulls. Differentiated from a cave of ancestors (above) in that there is no religious or ceremonial aspect to the storage of the remains. Therefore, this might be a predator's lair, the deposit of a trap, a subterranean battleground, etc.

Cave of Columns (Small or Medium)

A cave with natural columns, which are pillars of stone reaching from floor to ceiling (as opposed to stalactites and stalagmites, which do not touch both surfaces).

Cave of Echoes (Small)

A cave with strong (natural) echo chamber qualities. If monsters lair here, they will use the confusion this place induces to their advantage ... potentially achieving surprise in any encounter.

Cave of Husks (Small or Medium)

A cave filled with molted remains (from growing arachnids, insects, snakes, etc.), or with the husks or desiccated victims.

Cave of Meetings (Small or Medium)

A cave where multiple tribes / factions regard one another under truce so that negotiations can take place.

Cave of Paintings (Small or Medium)

A cave covered with ancient paintings and pictograms (of hunting, warfare, exploration, worship, etc.); not necessarily manmade.

Cave of Pools (Small or Medium)

A wet, dripping cave with several pools of mineral water. A perfect place for slimes, rare crystals, or some form of aquatic encounter.

Cave of Residual Magic, Elemental Air

(Small, Medium, or Large)

A cave which still retains essence from the creation of the world. Air and wind spells will be enhanced here, and earth and darkness spells will be nullified.

Cave of Residual Magic, Elemental Earth

(Small, Medium, or Large)

A cave which still retains essence from the creation of the world. Earth and darkness spells will be enhanced here, and air and wind spells will be nullified.

Cave of Residual Magic, Elemental Fire

(Small, Medium, or Large)

A cave which still retains essence from the creation of the world. Fire and destructive spells will be enhanced here, and water and healing spells will be nullified.

Cave of Residual Magic, Elemental Water

(Small, Medium, or Large)

A cave which still retains essence from the creation of the world. Water and healing spells will be enhanced here, and fire and destructive spells will be nullified.

Cave of Skulls (Small or Medium)

A cave where decapitated skulls have deliberately been placed (on stakes, in niches, in a huge pile, etc.) as a grim warning to intruders.

Cave of Slaughter (Small or Medium)

A slaughterhouse cave, where enemies, beasts, or monsters are slain (for food, for sport, or as a warning, etc.).

Cave of Stalactites (Small or Medium)

A cave with many stalactites (fingers of stone descending from the ceiling). Likely to be the lair of flying or ceiling-crawling monsters.

Cave of Stalagmites (Small or Medium)

A cave with many stalactites (fingers of stone ascending from the floor). Likely to be the lair of climbing or camouflaged monsters.

Cave of the Dead (Small or Medium)

A naturally-shaped burial chamber. Differentiated from a cave of ancestors, because it probably only has one or two prepared burials.

Cave of Unmined Gemstones

(Small or Medium)

A cave where one or more types of gemstones can be seen in the walls, ready for mining. There may be a good reason (curse, evil spirits, guardians, threat of collapse, etc.) which the cave has not been mined

Cave of Unmined Metals, Adamantite

(Small or Medium)

A cave with untapped adamantite deposits and/or veins. Almost certainly guarded, because otherwise it would have been mined long ago. This might be the home of earth djinn, earth elementals, living statues, a great fire demon, etc.

Cave of Unmined Metals, Copper

(Small or Medium)

A cave with untapped copper deposits and/or veins.

Cave of Unmined Metals, Electrum (Gold and Silver)

(Small or Medium)

A cave with untapped electrum deposits and/or veins.

Cave of Unmined Metals, Gold

(Small or Medium)

A cave with untapped gold deposits and/or veins.

Cave of Unmined Metals, Iron

(Small or Medium)

A cave with untapped iron deposits and/or veins. Iron is usually found in banded formations along with chert (finely-grained silica).

Cave of Unmined Metals, Lead

(Small or Medium)

A cave with untapped lead deposits and/or veins. While the metal is largely worthless to adventurers, it is used by humans, demi-humans and humanoids for plumbing, construction, ceramics, cosmetics, decoration, etc.

Cave of Unmined Metals, Mithral

(Small or Medium)

A cave with untapped mithral deposits and/or veins. Refer to the adamantite cave entry, above, for ideas on the guardians that almost certainly reside here.

Cave of Unmined Metals, Platinum

(Small or Medium)

A cave with untapped platinum deposits and/or veins.

Cave of Unmined Metals, Silver

(Small or Medium)

A cave with untapped silver deposits and/or veins.

Cave of Unmined Metals, Tin

(Small or Medium)

A cave with untapped tin deposits and/or veins. While the metal is largely worthless to adventurers, it is used by humans, demi-humans, and humanoids for alloying and metalworking. It is needed for bronze working, and is highly coveted by deprived primitive cultures.

There are other metals which could be mined by a culture or monstrous population depending on utility or need; refer for example to the Game World Generator supplement for more possibly-mined resource types (and associated gems).

Cave of Unmined Metals, Various

(Small or Medium)

A cave with untapped deposits and/or veins of cobalt, mercury, nickel, zinc, etc. In the game, these more arcane metals are prized by underworld demi-humans, dwarves, gnomes, kobolds, mages, and alchemists. Some may also be useful as material spell components.

Cave Temple *(Small or Medium)*

A natural subterranean area being used as a temple. The deity or entity that is worshipped here would depend upon the race of the nearby denizens (Deep Ones, drow, humanoids, netherworld gnomes, trolls, etc.).

Cavea *(Small, Medium, or Large)*

A secured room, such as below an arena, where deadly beasts or monsters are held for a surprising release. In a dungeon, this might be a type of guarded room where guardian beasts can charge out (to the limit of their chains, etc.).

Cavelet *(Tiny or Small)*

A small cave. In game terms, probably no larger than 10'x20'. You can roll for features if you like, but it is probably too small to hold anything of considerable interest.

Cavern *(Large or Huge)*

A large cave. According to your preference, this could be a featureless cavern (the basic name implies there is not much there), or a nonesuch cavern with some amazing and strange thing you need to devise (a magical effect, a strange form of stone, a monster lair, etc.)

Cavern of Ancestral Memory

(Large or Huge)

A large cave of ancestors. Unless the former denizens are extinct, this would surely be a sacred place protected by the descendants (tribesmen, underworld demi-humans, shamanistic humanoids, etc.)

Cavern of Ashes *(Large or Huge)*

A large cave of ashes, as above. Alternately, this could a cavern filled with heated volcanic ash, making it a perfect lair for salamander men, fire serpents, or similar creatures.

Cavern of Bones *(Large or Huge)*

A large cave of bones. This could be the home of undead, or something terrible and far more monstrous, such as a dhole of the Dreamlands.

Cavern of Columns *(Large or Huge)*

A large cave of columns. This might be a place of aeries and ledges, where flying netherworld creatures reside (such as gargoyles, giant bats, hieracosphinxes, nightgaunts, wyverns, etc.).

Cavern of Echoes *(Large or Huge)*

A large cave of echoes. This might be considered a sacred (unholy) place by the denizens, and would then serve as a throne room, temple, domain of revelation, or something more profound.

Cavern of Husks (Large or Huge)

A large cave of husks. Very likely, a nightmarish lair of some kind. There might be a swarm of giant beetles, spiders, wasps, Apshai scarabs, or worse.

Cavern of Slaughter (Large or Huge)

A large cave of slaughter. This may be some form of ceremonial battleground, or an eternally-contested region between warring tribes.

Possible tribal inflicts could include: hobgoblins and gnolls; goblins and lizard men; or two rival orc clans.

Cavern of the Gatherings (Large or Huge)

A large cave of meetings, perhaps for multiple races (bugbears, troglodytes, trolls, etc.).

Cavern of the Piping Ones (Large or Huge)

A nightmarish Lovecraftian underworld that links the World of Oldskull to realms of horror via a planar gate, as described in the tale *The Festival*. Dangerous in the extreme.

Cavern Temple (Large or Huge)

A naturally-shaped sacred place of worship. There is latent and primal planar power here which attracts a specific race of protectors. A chaotic good cavern temple might be crystalline and defended by cave elves, while a lawful evil cavern temple might have magma and be protected by hobgoblins.

Cavity (Tiny, Small, Medium, or Large)

A soft-walled cave or hollow; or, a cave which has been suddenly corroded and hollowed out (such as due to trickling or pooling acid).

Celestial Hall (Large or Huge)

A hall either open to the sky, or decorated with sky-like patterns, in honor of the gods.

Cell (Tiny or Small)

In game mapping terms, a 10'x10' (or at most, 20'x20') room with a locked or barred door. The cell is usually, but not always, used as a prison; it could also represent stark living quarters (for a guard, humanoid, monk, etc.).

Cell Block (Medium or Large)

A corridor lined with multiple cells. In old school fashion, this is probably a long corridor with 10'x10' cells to either side.

Cella (Medium or Large)

A statue room within a temple or tomb, holding the image of a god.

Cella Olearia (Medium or Large)

An ancient (Roman-themed) storeroom for olives, olive oils, and similar products. There might be magical oils or potions stored here.

Cella Vinaria (Small, Medium, or Large)

An ancient (Roman-themed) wine cellar. Due to Roman technology and preservation techniques, some aged wines might still be valuable ... or perhaps even layered with some kind of magical potion in the same containers.

Cellae, plural (Medium or Large)

An ancient cell block. This area might be home to undead creatures, or perhaps the remains of prisoners have been repurposed by malefic Lovecraftian entities, or other horrific monsters from beyond.

Cellar (Small or Medium)

An underground chamber where something is stored, or intended for shelter. See for example Root Cellar, Salt Cellar, Storm Cellar, Wine Cellar. An undistinguished Cellar may have an ambiguous former use.

Cellarage (Large or Huge)

A large system of interconnected Cellars, likely separated by archways and/or narrow walls. Each Cellar is likely to have a different theme (Earth Cellar, Root Cellar, Wine Cellar, etc.).

Cellula (Tiny or Small)

A small sanctuary or secret room. This is the likely location of a shrine, trick, or enduring magical effect of some kind. Treasure is likely.

Cenaculum (Medium or Large)

An ancient dining room. Technically, this should only exist on the upper floor of an ancient manor house, but that definition is probably too exacting for use here.

Cenatio (Medium)

A fine Roman-themed dining room. There might be magical effects here, such as unseen servants who are "programmed" to serve food and drink … even if no one is left alive to enjoy it.

Cenotaph (Small)

An empty, ceremonial tomb. The remains have either been moved elsewhere; or, the room serves as a grave marker for someone whose remains could not be recovered.

Ceremonial Chamber (Small)

A small ceremonial room. Perhaps the lair of a minor cleric, mystic, or savant NPC.

Ceremonial Hall (Large or Huge)

A large ceremonial room. This might be the assemblage for a cult, priesthood, dwarven enclave, humanoid tribe, or something similar.

Ceremonial Room (Medium or Large)

A room where ceremonies are conducted. In game terms, this most likely means a room where a cleric (or other priest) worships a god(dess), but it could also be a room where (for example) a mage worships or consults with a demon or angel, or even a room where mock-traditional ceremonies are conducted for superstitious followers.

Ceroma (Small or Medium)

An ancient anointing room. This could be the location of a hidden magical treasure, such as a cache of potions, oils, or healing salves.

Cesspit (Tiny, Small, or Medium)

A pit filled with waste and trash. This would be a potential lair for something vile, such as a tentacle beast, tentacled centipede, beetle swarm, or worse.

Cesspit Cavern (Large or Huge)

A cavern with one or more cesspits. These deposits do not occur naturally and are a certain sign of monster habitation.

Cesspool (Tiny, Small, or Medium)

A pool filled with waste and refuse. This would be a potential lair for mudmen, corrupted reptilian things, aquatic ghasts or ghouls, etc.

Cesspool Cavern (Large or Huge)

A cavern with one or more cesspools. These deposits do not occur naturally and are a certain sign of monster habitation.

Chamber (Small)

A small general-purpose room. In mapping terms, this technically means a room covering 9 or fewer squares (no larger than 30'x30', and more commonly 20'x20' or something similar). As previously discussed, a chamber might have limited access (one entry), increased security (a locked door or portcullis), or passive security (reached through a concealed door, secret door, or trap door).

Chamber Barrow (Small)

A small barrow enclosure, likely featuring only a single room. A classic lair for a wight, spectre, banshee, Knight of Saigoth, or something more dire.

Chamber of Catafalques

(Small or Medium)

A former burial chamber, but the coffins and/or sarcophagi have been removed (by ghouls, robbers, nemeses of the buried species, etc.), leaving ominous stone pedestals. Very likely a lair for undead.

Chamber of Revelation (Small)

A private room where priests receive spells or visions from their god. There is probably a planar gate here of some kind, or a viewing gate (which shows visions of another world, without allowing passage in either direction).

Chamber Tomb (Small, Medium, or Large)

A technical archaeological classification for burials within prepared enclosed spaces. If you want to review a huge list of different subtypes found in the real world, look up the term "chamber tomb" on Wikipedia. (Those subtypes were not included in this guide, because the classifications tend to force you into a specific floor plan type in many instances.)

Chambers, plural

(Medium, Large, or Huge)

A series of several small, interconnected rooms. The plural appears here as a separate entry, because such clusters are common in underground areas and in manor houses.

Chancel (Small or Medium)

A private enclosed space surrounding an altar. Refer to *The Classic Dungeon Design Guide, Book II* for thousands of potential ideas concerning this space.

Chandlery (Small or Medium)

A place where candles are made and/or stored. This would be a good place to hide a small stash of Amberflame Candles, minor magical items which can be made to alight with a simple command word.

Chantier (Small, Medium, or Large)

A workshop for stonecutters. If designated as a lair, this could be home to dwarves, gnomes, pech, or some other kind of stone-working creatures. Or, it could feature a stone golem, caryatid columns, a living marble statue, etc.

Chantry (Medium or Large)

An echoing chapel intended for chanting and singing (and possibly spell casting).

Chapel

(Small or Medium, inside an enclosing Large or Huge area)

An enclosed place of worship. A small or medium-sized temple area within a larger structure; for example, a chapel with shrine within a castle, or even a private chapel for nobles within a manor house.

Chapel Hall

(Large, inside an enclosing Huge area)

A large chapel (temple area) within a larger structure. The area is probably guarded by under-priests, cultists, mercenaries, guardian beasts, warding spirits, or something else.

Chapter House (Medium, Large, or Huge)

An assembly and rooming hall or outbuilding for a fraternity, sorority, secret sect, brotherhood of clerics, etc. The term "house" can refer to a separate enclosure, or it can refer to an ancestral following or bloodline (House Sonoritas, House Tharien, etc.).

Chapter Room (Small or Medium)

A smaller chapter house, which is not situated in an outbuilding. This might well be the home of monk or mystic NPCs.

Char Cellar (Tiny, Small, or Medium)

A storeroom for coal dust, charcoal, burned alchemical powders, or similar dangerous substances.

Charnel House (Medium, Large, or Huge)

A vault filled haphazardly with piles of disarticulated skeletal remains. A likely lair for ghouls or giant rats. There may be incidental treasure here.

Charter Room (Small or Medium)

A space that is dedicated to the archival preservation of charters, which record the granting of rights, properties, titles, honorable stations, and so forth.

Chartophylacium

(Medium, Large, or Huge)

An ancient archive. Intended for the preservation of important scrolls, tablets, codices, etc.

Chasm (Large or Huge)

A deep natural rift in the earth. In a dungeon, a Chasm is likely to give (highly dangerous) access to multiple dungeon levels, and to allow wandering monsters free reign.

Cheese Cellar (Small or Medium)

A cool underground room where cheeses are kept. Perhaps guarded by somewhat friendly cheese-loving creatures! (Halflings and gnomes would be but two of the possible examples.)

Chiming Cave (Small or Medium)

A crystalline water cave, where dripping moisture creates beautiful chiming tones. A disruption of this sound might attract wandering monsters.

Chimney Corner (Tiny or Small)

A small heating / warming room located directly adjacent to a large fireplace with a chimney. Will be rare, but not impossible, beneath the surface.

Choir (Small or Medium)

A room where cult / priestly singers reside during ceremonies. Typically connected to a temple, but sometimes the singers are meant to be unseen.

Chrismographion (Small)

An ancient (Greek-themed) oracular chamber. A place of powerful divinatory magics, probably either deific or titanic.

Chrismographium (Small)

An ancient (Roman-themed) oracular chamber. The likely home of an oracle NPC, or his/her spirit.

Cimeliarch (Medium or Large)

An ancient treasure vault beneath, or within, a temple. The treasures found here might be cursed or divinely protected, which would explain why they have never been successfully plundered by raiders or adventurers.

Cinerarium *(Medium, Large, or Huge)*

A funerary room with many niches branching off of it, where sepulchral urns are kept. The room might also feature a central *cinerarium medianum*, which contains a large (haunted?) sarcophagus.

Cistern *(Small, Medium, Large, or Huge)*

A flooded / reservoir room, designed to store water for later use. Rainwater is typical, but in a deeper dungeon this might be a room designed to catch waters from an upper level to prevent flooding on the lower.

Cistern Room *(Small or Medium)*

A room above, or adjacent to, a cistern. Perhaps controlled by intelligent creatures, such as frogmen, lizard men, sea devils, etc.

Cistvaen *(Small or Medium)*

An ancient sepulchral chamber. This might be the lair of (for example) a Knight of Saigoth or vampiress trapped in stasis by impalement or a holy relic.

Classroom *(Medium or Large)*

A medium-sized or large room dedicated to education and instruction; in the game, this might include (for example) a room for the instruction of young magic-user apprentices, or even a room designed to train guild thieves how to pick pockets, etc.

Clay Cave *(Small or Medium)*

A soft-walled cave with usable clay deposits. An ideal lair for a clay golem, or mudmen, or salamander people, or perhaps giant worms.

Clay-Filled Cavern *(Large or Huge)*

A large clay cave. The deposits may also exist in the floor, potentially making walking rather difficult.

Clinic *(Medium or Large)*

A hall of healing, used by the stronghold's or temple's troops and servants. A clinic implies that the sick that are being cared for are devout and protected, or of a special respected importance.

Cloaca *(Medium, Large, or Huge)*

An ancient sewer. It may well be dry now, and used for another purpose (such as a lair or the entrance chamber to an escape tunnel). A likely lair for tentacle beasts, weevil men, swamp shamblers, a giant slug, etc.

Cloak Room *(Small or Medium)*

A room where cloaks and coats are stored. Typically found near to an entry or stairway, or the entrance to a sub-region.

Clockwork Room *(Small or Medium)*

In game terms, this is likely a chamber which houses the workings of a nearby mechanical trap, elevator, experiment, or (less likely) a large clock.

Cloister *(Medium, Large, or Huge)*

A hall with a vaulted ceiling, typically leading into an atrium or temple. There may be cleric, acolyte, neophyte, or follower (soldier) guardians here.

Closet *(Tiny)*

(This entry is primarily for completeness purposes for readers only, and does not necessarily appear on the random tables as a separate space.) A side Alcove for the storage of clothing and accoutrements. In game parlance with the focus on 10'x10' map grids, a closet would probably only fill 1/4th of a single square adjoining another room. See also, however, Walk-In Closet.

Coal Cave (Small or Medium)

A small coal cavern, likely with only a single coal seam which can be mined.

Coal Cavern (Large or Huge)

A cavern with unmined (and possibly dangerous) coal seams and deposits.

Coal Room (Small, Medium, or Large)

A room filled with coal (either piled on the floor, or in alcove-like coal bins). There might be minor monsters here, such as gremlins, rats, or beetles.

Coemeterium, plural Coemeteria

(Small or Medium)

A Roman-themed vaulted burial place. There might well be a buried magical item of honor here, such as a sword, helm, shield, or amulet of protection.

Coenaculum (Small or Medium)

A Roman-themed dining or feasting room. There might be a valuable object here (warded by magic?) such as a sculpture, decanter, or jeweled bowl.

Coenatio (Medium or Large)

A fine dining room that is reached by a lower staircase. The space is created for the viewing of entertainments or landscapes, perhaps (if the room is situated underground) magically.

Coldroom (Small or Medium)

A room that is kept cold (magically?) for storage purposes. Traditionally, this is a pantry or storeroom; but in a dungeon it could be far more sinister (for example, a room for the storage and preservation of dead bodies).

Collapsed Cavern (Large or Huge)

A cavern with a "new" roof, where the floor is covered with rubble (the "old" roof). Another collapse might be imminent, or might be started by violent conflict, magic, etc.

Collapsed Room

(Small, Medium, or Large, with the accessible area being Tiny or Small)

A partially impassible room which is filled with rubble due to a ceiling or wall collapse.

Colonnade Hall (Large or Huge)

A hall that is split into areas by one or more lines of evenly-placed columns. A good place for encounters with stony sentinels such as gargoyles, grotesques, or caryatid columns.

Colonnade Room (Medium)

A small colonnade hall, with a single series of columns. The columns might provide cover for archers, arbalesters, or skirmishers.

Columbarium (Large or Huge)

A room with many niches in the walls, where funerary urns are stored.

Combat Pit (Small or Medium)

A gladiatorial pit where monsters and/or victims are forced to do battle for the amusement of some powerful creature. If the monsters are not evil, and are intelligent, clever adventurers might well be able to create an alliance of necessity with the creatures in an attempt to escape the bloodthirsty captors.

Comfort Room (Tiny or Small)

A fine garderobe.

Commandery *(Medium or Large)*

A room / locale that is used for tactical and strategic discussion, and the coordination of defense. The room might be the headquarters of a knightly order, secret society, fighter's guild, etc.

Common Room *(Medium, Large, or Huge)*

A large informal lounge area, typically for a large number of denizens (guards, soldiers, minions, humanoids, etc.). Will likely feature benches, tables, barrels, fireplace(s) and/or firepit(s) and so forth.

Examples of relatively cultured humanoids who favor the use of common rooms in their lairs include: kobolds, goblins, hobgoblins, orcs, and gnolls.

Communal Quarters

(Medium, Large, or Huge)

The home of many lesser priests, soldiers, or minions. Refer to *The Classic Dungeon Design Guide, Book II* for hundreds of ideas concerning minion and troop types.

Compluvium Chamber *(Small)*

A room with a hole in the roof. The purpose of the hole is to allow air flow, and also to collect rainwater. If deep underground, the hole is a magical one-way portal, allowing the entry of gasses and liquids (air and water) but not solids (intruders). Note that this type of room must logically exist for deep dungeons to have air, although classic publications tend to gloss over this necessity.

Compluvium Hall *(Large)*

A very large compluvium chamber, likely with numerous ceiling holes. A very likely place for an aquatic encounter, or a water-themed source of magic (such as a sentient enchanted pool).

Compluvium Room *(Medium)*

A larger compluvium chamber, but smaller than a hall. Might well be protected by a serpentine water elemental, guards, giant amphibians, giant lizard guardian beasts, etc.

Concealed Cave *(Small or Medium)*

A cave whose entrance is shrouded by vines, a waterfall, etc.

Concealed Cavern *(Large or Huge)*

A large concealed cave. This may be the lair of a large intelligent monster, such as a shadow dragon, draconian lich, etc. Or, it might be the domain of many powerful monsters, such as the octopoid Thralls of Cthulhu or the eldritch Eyes of Azathoth.

Concealed Chamber *(Small)*

A small concealed room. This would be a good place for the Game Master to situate a valuable (but not necessarily monetary) treasure, such as a partial dungeon map, an adventurer's journal, a ring of keys, etc.

Concealed Room *(Medium or Large)*

A room which can only be reached through a concealed door. There might be a dark secret kept herein, especially if the concealed door is something quite disturbingly un-doorlike (such as a bricked-up wall).

Conclave *(Medium or Large)*

A room for secret meetings (typically by powerful NPCs). The room may be behind one or more concealed or secret doors.

Conclavium *(Medium or Large)*

An ancient conclave. By traditional definition, the room will be rectangular.

Conditivum (Small or Medium)

A large, ancient sepulcher. This would be the perfect lair for a powerful undead creature such as a lich, vampire lord, or one of the dread Knights of Saigoth.

Confessional (Tiny or Small)

A place for priests and worshippers to privately atone for sins done before their god.

Conjuring Chamber (Small or Medium)

A room where priests summon servitor beasts or monsters sacred to their god. This place almost certainly has a protective magic circle of some kind, and may also be protected by various arcane guards and wards. Or, there could be an imprisoned demon, devil, etc.

Conservatory (Medium or Large)

A room that serves as a greenhouse, preserving rare and/or exotic (monstrous?) plants. Typically glass- or crystal-roofed, but may also be illuminated by magical light.

Control Room (Small or Medium)

In the game, this would be a room filled with machinery or clockwork, likely designed to trigger traps and tricks, or remotely view other rooms and open/close doors in a mechanical and/or magical fashion. Slightly anachronistic, but consider (for example) the story Rogues in the House by Robert E. Howard; or even the charlatan Wizard of Oz.

Convocation Room (Medium or Large)

A room where priests gather in preparation for a ceremony. Similar to an assemblage, but typically excluding worshippers.

Copper Cave (Small or Medium)

A cave filled with partially-mined copper deposits. As opposed to an unmined cave, there will be equipment and possibly mine carts here.

Copper Cavern (Large or Huge)

A large copper cave. At least some of the miners are probably here. If the dungeon is too deep for them to be human, they might instead be dwarves, gnomes, goblins, or kobolds.

Corycaeum (Small, Medium, or Large)

A type of training room, where warriors strike hanging sacks that are filled with sand or seeds.

Council Chamber / Counsel Chamber (Small)

A small council room. It is likely that there will be several minor NPCs here.

Council Hall / Counsel Hall (Large)

A large council room. There will probably be several high-level NPCs situated here.

Council Room / Counsel Room (Medium)

A secure room where an NPC noble, leader, etc. listens to trusted advisors and makes plans. Refer to The Classic Dungeon Design Guide, Book II for the many relevant NPC archetypes.

Counting Room (Small or Medium)

A room designed for the counting of coins and other treasure. Likely located near a treasure vault and heavily guarded.

Court (Large or Huge)

A hall and/or throne room of judgment, where matters of justice and punishment are determined.

Courtyard

(Medium or Large if subterranean, otherwise Large or Huge)

An enclosed grassy or open area. In a dungeon, a courtyard might be a "Dungeon Court," a large pillar-bordered room with a central display of some kind (fungal garden, symmetrical fountains or pools, a glassteel maze, selection of petrified victims, etc.).

Crafter's Room *(Small or Medium)*

The room where a lesser artisan NPC (perhaps a leatherworker, potter, weaver, etc.) both works and resides.

Crawlspace *(Tiny, Small, or Medium)*

An underground storage and/or ventilation area, either a room or passageway, with a very low ceiling. This is probably the lair of several smaller monstrosities, such as giant rats, gremlins, centipedes, spiders, snakes, etc.

Crematorium *(Small or Medium)*

An incineration chamber where remains are turned into chips and ash. This may be a way to honor the dead, or it may be a trap, or even a torture chamber.

Crevice *(Tiny or Small)*

A narrow fracture in the rock. In this book's definitions, a crevice is a natural type of corridor, a vertical crevice is a type of level connector between dungeons, and a "room" crevice is a long narrow winding cave.

Crowde *(Tiny, Small, or Medium)*

An ancient cellar. The dangers here might include collapse, choking dust, a lack of breathable air, limited movement due to uncleared rubble, and so forth.

Crumbling Cave *(Small or Medium)*

A cave which is about to collapse. The collapse could be brought about by violence, powerful magic, or perhaps even loud noises.

Crumbling Cavern *(Large or Huge)*

A large crumbling cave. Particularly dangerous, because if adventurers are standing in the middle of the area they might not have enough time to safely escape a collapse.

Crypt *(Tiny, Small, or Medium)*

An underground funerary chamber. See burial crypt, monster crypt, secret crypt, etc. An undistinguished "crypt" is likely one that has been converted to a different use over the centuries by its current (or most recent) denizens.

Crystal Cave *(Small or Medium)*

A cave filled with beautiful, fragile crystal formations (which might well be valuable, and not only to the adventurers).

Crystal Garden *(Large or Huge)*

A large crystal cave. The crystals may be large enough to climb, fall from, ambush adventurers from, hide treasure under, etc. The temperature here may be quite hot, and the cavern might be fully or partially flooded.

Cubicle *(Tiny)*

In dungeon parlance, a 10'x10' room that is not a cell (meaning that it is not used as living quarters, or as a prison). Typically constructed to divide monster populations, to enforce secrecy, or to serve as a puzzle / siege / delaying area (especially when multiple cubicles are found in close succession). May have more than one door.

Cubicula, plural (Small, Medium, or Large)

A series of cubiculums. It is likely that at least some of them are occupied, either by prisoners or monsters.

Cubiculum (Tiny or Small)

A Roman-themed sleeping chamber or apartment. The small space is regarded as only a sleeping area, and therefore will be adjacent to a larger living area or common room.

Cubiculum Cineraria (Tiny)

An ancient cubicle, which serves as a funeral niche for ashes, an urn, a skull, or some similar form of remains.

Cul-de-Sac (Tiny or Small)

The "bottom of a bag," which typically means a dead end cave or partially-excavated chamber which was never finished. There may be discarded tools or equipment here.

Culina (Medium)

A fine, Roman-themed kitchen.

Cupboard (Tiny)

A small angular space under a flight of stairs (think Harry Potter).

Cyst (Small, Medium, or Large)

An unnatural hollow in the earth. Cysts can be caused by magic, burrowing monsters, infernal or elemental fire, the collapse of a portable hole or sphere of oblivion, etc. The creating source of the cyst is probably no longer evident. When one cyst is found, more are likely nearby; see secret cyst.

Cyzicene Hall (Large or Huge)

A formal ancient great hall, with some kind of viewing space to the north. (The direction of north is traditional, and likely even superstitious or reverential in nature.) Examples for the north end feature might include a grand view of wilderness, an entertainment (perhaps a stage or dueling cage), or even an elaborate programmed illusion of some dread spirit. Or is it an illusion at all?

D IS FOR DONJON

Dairy Chamber (Small or Medium)

The cold room where milk, butter, cheese, and similar foodstuffs are stored. Compare buttery.

Dairy Room (Medium or Large)

A large or compartmentalized dairy chamber. As with a cheese room, this might be guarded.

Dais Chamber (Small or Medium)

A room featuring a dais, which is a low raised area with steps leading up. The dais might feature a statue, throne, fountain, shrine, etc.

Dais Room (Medium or Large)

A large dais chamber. The surrounding area might be an art gallery, guardroom, temple surround, or something similar depending upon the dungeon setting.

Darkroom (Small, Medium, or Large)

A room that is intentionally kept dark due to specialized work. In the modern world this means photography, but in the game this likely refers to alchemy, or a mage's work with reagents, that requires dark conditions for the creation of magic items. It could also be the lair of shadows or a shadow dragon.

Dayroom (Small or Medium)

A room of comfort, used for daytime gatherings and recreation.

Dead End (Tiny or Small)

A small room, with no apparent exits, at the end of a corridor. This might be a portcullis trap, or the ambush site for nearby intelligent monsters.

Dead End Cave (Small)

A small cave, with no apparent exits, at the end of a tunnel. There may be a secret or concealed door here, perhaps hidden by a boulder.

Death Cavern (Large or Huge)

A large cave of the dead (see that entry, C).

Defiled Tomb (Small, Medium, or Large)

A tomb which has been desecrated and/or plundered. The violation of the sacred space may have left vengeful evil spirits, a curse, negative magic, etc.

Delubrum (Medium or Large)

An ancient sanctuary, which may be fairly large, or an area surrounding a smaller enclosed area (such as a sanctum sanctorum). There will probably be guardian NPCs here (such as clerics, cultists, etc.).

Delve (Large or Huge)

A deep and/or extensive mine, of the kind typically made by dwarves, kobolds, and the slaves of dark elves. Typical delve metals — worth digging deep for — are mithral, adamantite, platinum, and gold.

Den (Small or Medium)

[1] A comfortable multi-use family room. The word has two meanings; it can also mean [2] the resting lair of a beast or monster (such as a bear, or badgerbear). Use the definition most appropriate to your setting.

Depository (Medium or Large)

A place where goods (furs, wines, etc.) are taken in, counted, and secured for safekeeping. This place will have guards as well as treasure of the less-than-transportable variety.

Diaconia (Medium or Large)

An asylum or clinic within a temple. Technically, in the real world this would be run by a deacon (hence the name); in game terms, it would probably be under the control of a mid-level NPC cleric, healer, or shaman.

Diaconicon (Medium or Large)

An ancient (Greek-themed) sacristy for use by mid-level NPC clerics, healers, priests, etc. The NPCs would probably be followers of a Greek deity.

Diaconicum (Medium or Large)

An ancient (Roman-themed) diaconicon; therefore, the NPCs would be followers of a Roman deity.

Dining Chamber (Small)

A small room for eating and drinking.

Dining Hall (Large or Huge)

A large room for eating and drinking. NPCs and/or guards are likely present.

Dining Room (Medium)

A medium-sized room for eating and drinking.

Diorite Cave (Small or Medium)

A cave with surfaces of diorite, a black- and gray-hued igneous stone.

Diorite Cavern (Large or Huge)

A large diorite cave, probably the lair of some kind of monster which is capable of camouflage (gargoyles, giant lizards, stone giants, etc.).

Distillery (Medium or Large)

A room or locale where liquids are distilled. Generally, this means spirits; but in the game world, it could certainly be an alchemical location used in the production of potions.

Divination Chamber (Small)

A private room where priests perform magical rites (and typically cast spells or use magic items) to discern the will of their god.

Divination Hall (Large or Huge)

A very large divination chamber, the size of which implies that many priests / cultists / spell casters must be brought together to work powerful magics. Such places may involve the actual summoning of a deity, demon lord, arch-devil, etc.

Divination Room (Medium)

A larger divination chamber. This is probably the lair of a diviner NPC, such as a mystic, oracle, augur, sibyl, prophet, hermit, etc.

Domed Chamber (Small)

A small room with a high, curved ceiling. The dome is not necessarily special in any way; it might simply be an architectural structure that serves to keep the surrounding rooms from crumbling due to the omnipresent weight of stone. But if there is a monster here, a giant spider or tick would be ideal.

Domed Hall (Large or Huge)

A large room with a high-curved ceiling. See above for a possible monster lair idea.

Domed Room (Medium)

As above; a medium-sized room with a high, curved ceiling.

Domicile (Small or Medium)

The dwelling / bedroom of a minor NPC official (or mercenary).

Donjon

(Small, Medium, or Large, with Large implying multiple rooms and chambers)

Typically, the most secure tower or vault in the stronghold. Therefore, sometimes used to hold valuable prisoners (such as a demoness, knight, heir, high priest, or something else entirely ... not all prisoners are necessarily human-like in shape). The term "donjon" can also be used for any older subterranean prison or trap room.

Dormitory (Large or Huge)

Communal sleeping quarters for students, trainees, apprentices, etc. Refer to the minion section in *The Classic Dungeon Design Guide, Book II* for hundreds of minion ideas.

Dorter (Large or Huge)

A monastic or temple dormitory. The likely location of many low-level NPC monks, clerics, novitiates, or cultists.

Drawbridge / Drawbridge Chamber
(Small)

Either a water-filled moat outside the stronghold which can be crossed by a lowered bridge, or a fortified hall featuring a trench – possibly flooded, or even slime-filled – and a lowering bridge.

Drawing Chamber (Small)

A small drawing room.

Drawing Room (Medium)

A room designed for meeting with and entertaining guests.

Dressing Chamber (Small)

A small dressing room.

Dressing Room (Medium)

A medium-sized room for changing clothing (for example, for an official or noble who serves multiple functions).

Drill Hall (Large or Huge)

A room where troops practice. May feature target dummies, hay bales, sparring floors, wooden walls, etc. Encounters with men-at-arms, berserkers, or humanoids are very likely in spaces such as these.

Drowning Pool (Small or Medium)

A deep pool where victims are deliberately drowned as a sacrifice.

Dry Well

(Small or Medium, size being vertical)

A well that no longer contains water. The well shaft can be descended, and there will be a cave / chamber below.

Drying Room (Small or Medium)

A room where something is laid out to dry in organized fashion (food, laundry, leather, paintings, scrolls, etc.). Grimly, this could also be a drying place for mutilated flesh / food, used by cruel monsters such as minotaurs or ogres.

Dueling Pit (Small or Medium)

Similar to a combat pit, but the combatants are intended to survive (either so that they can be healed to fight repeatedly, or as a form of training / rite of passage).

There are probably gladiator NPCs (fighters and barbarians, for example) or monsters here. Monster duelists include ogres, cyclopes, and so forth.

Dueling Pit Matrix *(Small)*

A series of dueling pits, descending from a large hall filled with walkways and observation areas.

Dulli *(Small or Medium)*

An Akkadian- or Babylonian-themed workroom.

Dungeon

(Small, Medium, or Large, with Large implying multiple rooms and chambers)

In adventure games we tend to think of a dungeon as a multi-room and multi-level complex filled with monsters; but in reality, a dungeon is an underground prison and/or torture room.

A room might be termed a dungeon if, specifically, it is designed for the long-term incarceration of prisoners. A band of ogres, for example, might have a dungeon as their larder where wounded humans and demi-humans are thrown (fresh meat!).

Dungeon Court *(Large or Huge)*

See courtyard; a subterranean courtyard.

Dust Pit *(Tiny, Small, or Medium)*

A pit filled with dust, or a trap in which dust causes asphyxiation of falling victims.

E IS FOR EXCAVATION

Earth Cellar (Small, Medium, or Large)

A cellar where at least one wall surface is made of bare compressed earth, not fitted stone. Such places are likely to collapse if too many violent actions (from powerful spells, giant beasts, etc.) take place.

Echo Chamber (Small or Medium)

A room carefully created to enhance echoes; likely to reduce the chance of intruders being able to achieve surprise in the area. Noises here might attract wandering monsters.

Echoing Cave (Tiny, Small, or Medium)

A natural echo chamber; likely not specifically customized to serve in that alerting fashion, but it may still be used that way.

Echoing Cavern (Large or Huge)

A large echoing cave.

Echoing Vault (Small)

A large echo chamber.

Egg Chamber (Small, Medium, or Large)

A cave or room where egg-laying monsters (ants, beetles, harpies, perytons, etc.) lay and care for their eggs.

Elaeothesium (Small or Medium)

A storeroom for essences, oils, perfumes, and/or unguents.

Eldaskali (Large or Huge)

A Nordic-themed common hall, with firepits, benches, warming stones, tables, and so forth.

Electrum Cave (Small or Medium)

A cave filled with partially-mined electrum deposits. As opposed to an unmined cave, there will be equipment and possibly mine carts here. (Note that electrum is a naturally-occurring alloy of gold and silver.)

Electrum Cavern (Large or Huge)

A large electrum cave. (Note that electrum is a naturally-occurring alloy of gold and silver.)

Elemental Vortex, Air

(Tiny, Small, Medium, Large, or Huge)

A dangerous and aberrant gate between the planes, caused by a violent discharge of ancient magic. An air vortex will be the (possibly sentient) locale of a trick with air- and wind-themed spell powers.

Elemental Vortex, Ash

(Tiny, Small, Medium, Large, or Huge)

A dangerous and aberrant gate between the planes, caused by a violent discharge of ancient magic. An ash vortex will be the (possibly sentient) locale of a trick with wind- and fire-themed spell powers.

Elemental Vortex, Dust

(Tiny, Small, Medium, Large, or Huge)

A dangerous and aberrant gate between the planes, caused by a violent discharge of ancient magic. A dust vortex will be the (possibly sentient) locale of a trick with wind- and stone-themed spell powers.

Elemental Vortex, Earth

(Tiny, Small, Medium, Large, or Huge)

A dangerous and aberrant gate between the planes, caused by a violent discharge of ancient magic. An earth vortex will be the (possibly sentient) locale of a trick with earth- and darkness-themed spell powers.

Elemental Vortex, Fire

(Tiny, Small, Medium, Large, or Huge)

A dangerous and aberrant gate between the planes, caused by a violent discharge of ancient magic. A fire vortex will be the (possibly sentient) locale of a trick with fire- and destruction-themed spell powers.

Elemental Vortex, Ice

(Tiny, Small, Medium, Large, or Huge)

A dangerous and aberrant gate between the planes, caused by a violent discharge of ancient magic. An ice vortex will be the (possibly sentient) locale of a trick with frost- and water-themed spell powers.

Elemental Vortex, Lightning

(Tiny, Small, Medium, Large, or Huge)

A dangerous and aberrant gate between the planes, caused by a violent discharge of ancient magic. A lightning vortex will be the (possibly sentient) locale of a trick with electricity- and thunder-themed spell powers.

Elemental Vortex, Magma

(Tiny, Small, Medium, Large, or Huge)

A dangerous and aberrant gate between the planes, caused by a violent discharge of ancient magic. A magma vortex will be the (possibly sentient) locale of a trick with fire- and stone-themed spell powers.

Elemental Vortex, Mist

(Tiny, Small, Medium, Large, or Huge)

A dangerous and aberrant gate between the planes, caused by a violent discharge of ancient magic. A mist vortex will be the (possibly sentient) locale of a trick with earth- and water-themed spell powers.

Elemental Vortex, Steam

(Tiny, Small, Medium, Large, or Huge)

A dangerous and aberrant gate between the planes, caused by a violent discharge of ancient magic. A steam vortex will be the (possibly sentient) locale of a trick with fire- and water-themed spell powers.

Elemental Vortex, Water

(Tiny, Small, Medium, Large, or Huge)

A dangerous and aberrant gate between the planes, caused by a violent discharge of ancient magic. A water vortex will be the (possibly sentient) locale of a trick with water- and healing-themed spell powers.

Emasu *(Small or Medium)*

An Akkadian- or Babylonian-themed sanctuary.

Embalming Chamber *(Small or Medium)*

A place where dead bodies are ritualistically prepared for burial. And also, the classic place to put a mummy lair!

Embalming Room *(Large)*

A large embalming chamber, likely with ghouls, giant rats, or other monstrosities.

Enchanted Grotto *(Small, Medium, or Large)*

An artificially-carved cave with faerie magic or a magical trick of some kind.

Enclave *(Large or Huge)*

An isolated room, or series of rooms or caves, which serves as a lair / stronghold for demi-humans or humanoids. An enclave is likely to consist of 4D4 adjoining areas.

Enclosed Loggia (*Medium or Large*)

A long narrow hall with columns, pillars, bays, niches, or alcoves to one side. On the surface, a loggia has one long side open to the air; underground, the ornate side is likely to feature chests, frescoes, paintings, statues, etc.

Enclosure

(Small or Medium, with a Tiny internal space)

A small room inside a larger room. The classic dungeon example would be a 30'x30' room with a 10'x10' locked chamber in the center.

Enterclose (*Tiny or Small*)

A short passage-like archwayed room, situated between two larger rooms. There may be guards or a warding spell positioned here, depending on the dungeon theme.

Entertaining Room (*Medium or Large*)

A room that is intended for reclining or watching guests, and a central entertainment upon a dais (a juggler, fire-eater, singer, etc.).

Entrance Hall (*Medium, Large, or Huge*)

The first large space which leads into a structure from the outside; or, the entrance to a significant sub-section of a dungeon level which has a different theme than the rest of the level.

Entry / Entryway (*Small or Medium*)

Commonly a small room, guarded or empty, which serves as a mere widening transition between a corridor and a larger room beyond.

Entry Hall (*Medium or Large*)

A large entry chamber, leading somewhere important (a church, the ruler's rooms, a court, etc.)

Ephebeum (*Medium*)

A somewhat smaller Greek- or Roman-themed gymnasium.

Episcenium (*Tiny or Small*)

A room which contains machinery such as pulleys, levers, platforms, and so forth. It serves as the operating area for a drawbridge, elevator, supply pit, or similar.

Ersi (*Small or Medium*)

An Akkadian- or Babylonian-themed bedchamber for a priest or priestess NPC.

Ewery (*Tiny or Small*)

A room where bowls, dishes, and other vessels are stored.

Excavation (*Large or Huge*)

A large excavation room, with an interesting mix of angular and rough shapes (for example, a Hall which will be rectangular when finished, but which has only tunnels in the southwest quarter and an unfinished northeastern section).

Excavation Room (*Small or Medium*)

An underground room which is incomplete, and where rock is still being tunneled away. This may involve digging through walls, the floor, and/or the ceiling.

Excubitorium (*Small or Medium*)

A bedroom for guards. The idea is that a resting place is provided very near to a guard post, with quick and easy access to a point for defense or observation; so there might be (for example) a weapons rack next to the beds, an open door to the guard area, mobile defense works (e.g.. rolling walls) which can be moved into place, etc.

Execution Chamber (Small)

A small execution room. This room might feature one or more villainous NPCs, as well as a prisoner in urgent need of rescue.

Execution Hall (Large or Huge)

A large execution room, which implies an audience (of humans, demi-humans, humanoids, or intelligent monsters).

Execution Room (Medium)

A room where some kind of creatures are executed. In modern terms this would be in a prison, but in the game it is very likely (for example) that intelligent evil monsters would have an Execution Room where the killings of good humans and demi-humans are observed.

Exedra (Small or Medium)

A Greek- or Roman-themed entertaining room. Much of the area will be given over to seating. The room might be a semi-circle, or it might be circular with the speaker's pavilion in the center.

Exercise Room (Small, Medium, or Large)

A room where students, trainees, apprentices, monks, guards, etc. keep in shape and perhaps train in mock battle (depending on the size of the area).

Experimentation Chamber (Small)

A room where corpses, or living subjects, are experimented upon. A classic locale for a mad scientist mage, a golem, or the undead.

Experimentation Vault (Medium or Large)

A larger, and potentially more secure, experimentation chamber.

F IS FOR FANE

Fainting Room *(Small or Medium)*

A noblewoman's private retreat, allowing for the treatment of hysteria, madness, etc. away from prying eyes. (Could also be used by an afflicted nobleman; consider for example Roderick Usher.) Refer to *The Classic Dungeon Design Guide, Book II* for possible archetypes.

Fallen Angelic Shrine *(Small or Medium)*

An unholy shrine which is devoted to a fallen deva, or a fallen angel. The fallen angel might be neutral (and approachable), or evil (being quite intrigued by mortals, but also ready to destroy them if there is need.

False Tomb *(Small, Medium, or Large)*

A tomb where a commoner's body is kept, and/or where counterfeit treasures are stored. The purpose is to divert grave robbers away from the actual secret tomb.

False Treasure Room *(Small or Medium)*

A small false treasure vault, as below.

False Treasure Vault *(Medium or Large)*

A room filled with fake or low-value treasure (for example, gold-painted copper pieces); typically designed as a trap or to sound an alarm.

Family Room *(Small or Medium)*

A comfortable gathering place for family members.

Fane *(Medium or Large)*

An ancient temple. Technically, a fane is usually smaller (but not less powerful) than a temple.

Favissa *(Small, Medium, or Large)*

A cellar in or beneath a temple, where discarded remnants are kept (damaged furnishings, implements, vestments, containers, etc.).

Feast Hall *(Large or Huge)*

A large hall intended to host events and dinners for a considerable number of people. Similar to a banquet hall, but likely used with more frequency (or, read another way, more frequently than just special / momentous occasions).

Feretorium *(Small or Medium)*

A Roman-themed feretory, therefore dedicated to relics for a Roman deity.

Feretory *(Small or Medium)*

A room featuring a shrine, where relics are stored.

Firepit *(Tiny or Small)*

A pit that is filled by a bonfire, coals, firewood, etc.

Fissure *(Small, Medium, or Large)*

A narrow chasm (in the floor), or a room or cave dominated by a fissure.

Fissure, Ceiling *(Small, Medium, or Large)*

A dangerous chasm (in the ceiling), or a room or cave dominated by an above-head fissure. Such areas may collapse if violent magic or other action takes place.

Fissure, Wall / Fissure Vault

(Medium, Large, or Huge)

A wide crevice; a long, winding cave.

Flooded Cave *(Small or Medium)*

A cave that is partially filled with water. The depth of the water will force adventurers to wade, but not to swim (unless they are gnomes or halflings).

Flooded Cavern *(Large or Huge)*

A large flooded cave, which is very likely the lair for some form of aquatic beast.

Flooded Hall *(Large or Huge)*

A large flooded room, perfectly situated for an aquatic encounter.

Flooded Room *(Small or Medium)*

A room that is partially filled with water (probably not intended by the builders).

Food Cave *(Tiny, Small, or Medium)*

A cave where some kind of monster stashes food. (In a dungeon setting, this probably means dead bodies and/or badly wounded adventurers.) This behavior is exhibited by amber behemoths, crocutas, dimensional beasts, manticores, badgerbears, some dragons, and similar creatures.

Forbidden Chamber *(Small or Medium)*

A room which is intended to be entered only by a deity (or arch-devil or demon lord), his high priest, his beasts, or his monsters.

Forbidden Vault *(Large)*

A large forbidden chamber, which would be the lair of a high priest NPC, guardians, and perhaps also a summoned divine (or unholy) entity of some kind.

Forecourt *(Medium or Large)*

A courtyard near to the stronghold's entrance, or in front of a new region within the stronghold.

Forge *(Small, Medium, or Large)*

The place where weapons, armor and tools are made.

Formicary *(Large or Huge)*

A large giant ant or ant man colony.

Fornix Chamber *(Small)*

A room with a large gated archway.

Fornix Hall *(Large or Huge)*

A defensive hall which is divided twice (or perhaps more) by fornix archway gates.

Fornix Room *(Medium)*

A larger fornix chamber.

Foss *(Medium, Large, or Huge)*

A waterfall cavern with Nordic-themed carvings and/or decoration.

Fosse Chamber *(Small)*

A chamber intersected a narrow stream or watercourse enclosed by raised walls. The stream and walls serve as a defensive barrier and also provides water to defenders.

Fosse Room *(Medium)*

A larger fosse chamber, likely with more defensive works and defenders.

Foundry (*Small, Medium, or Large*)

A room or locale where metals are heated and melted down. Likely to be associated with a nearby forge.

Fountain Chamber (*Small*)

A small fountain room. Refer to *The Classic Dungeon Design Guide, Book II* for thousands of fountain-relevant design ideas.

Fountain Grotto (*Small, Medium, or Large*)

An artificial cave featuring a (magical?) sculpted fountain.

Fountain Hall (*Large or Huge*)

A large fountain room, likely including several fountains instead of just one.

Fountain Room (*Medium*)

A room that is dominated by a sculpted fountain. In the game, the waters are very likely enchanted, cursed, and/or inhabited.

Foyer (*Small or Medium*)

A more period-correct term for a formal lobby. While technically this means that the foyer is a crossing area between the outside and a building interior, in practice it can also mean the entrance to a dungeon or stronghold sub-section with a different theme. For example, a stronghold with outer areas guarded by low-level troops might have a Foyer which leads to the more secure rooms where commanders and/or nobles reside.

Frater (*Small, Medium, or Large*)

A refectory where only men (or male monsters) are allowed to gather.

Fresco Gallery (*Large*)

A room designed for the display of (magical?) artistic frescoes (wall paintings).

Fresco Room (*Small or Medium*)

A room painted with frescoes. The frescoes may actually be a map, a painted monster which animates, the covering to a secret door, a trick, etc.

Frigidarium (*Small, Medium, or Large*)

A bath hall (featuring one or more pools or fountains) for cold-water bathing and cleansing.

Front Room (*Small or Medium*)

A living room or lounge positioned toward the entry of a home.

Fumarium (*Tiny or Small*)

A room above a fireplace or firepit, where smoke is channeled through before rising and exiting. The smoke is used for purification, to dry wood, or to season food or drink (such as wine or cheese)

Fumigatory (*Tiny, Small, or Medium*)

A room where inanimate objects are purified with (magical?) smoke.

Function Hall (*Large or Huge*)

A large gathering hall intended to host celebratory events and functions (such as weddings or coronations).

Function Room (*Medium*)

A small function hall. A likely location for wandering monsters of minor NPC encounters.

Fundament (Small or Medium)

A room that is primarily a buttress, support, or column to hold up areas above the fundament (on upper levels). The fundament is the hollow area surrounding the large support.

Fundament Room (Medium or Large)

A room with more than one bulky support.

Funerary Chapel (Small or Medium)

A chapel that is meant to honor the dead. Unless the chapel is defiled, this would not be an undead lair, but rather a place to receive blessings or visions.

Funerary Workshop (Small or Medium)

A room similar to an embalming chamber, but probably devoted to other steps of internment and/or mummification (such as entrails extraction, curing of flesh, ornamentation, etc.).

Funereal Crowde (Small or Medium)

An ancient crypt, typically but not always beneath a temple.

Fungal Garden (Medium, Large, or Huge)

A room or cavern where fungi have flourished and grown to enormous sizes, due to magical energies and/or alchemical infusions. The fungi may be animated, deadly, edible, hallucinogenic, phosphorescent, etc.

Fungarium (Small, Medium, or Large)

A room devoted to the storing and study of fungi. In the game, the fungi are likely to be important (medicinal, spell reagents, and/or poisons), and/or monstrous.

G IS FOR GROTTO

Galininu *(Small or Medium)*

An Akkadian- or Babylonian-themed temple storeroom, perhaps for ceremonial objects or raiment. There may be a significant treasure hidden here – and perhaps an eternal guardian as well.

Galleria *(Medium, Large, or Huge)*

An ornate gallery (display).

Gallery (Cavern) *(Large or Huge)*

A cavern with impressive rock, crystal, and/or mineral formations.

Gallery (Display) *(Medium, Large, or Huge)*

A room devoted to the display of art. For specific examples see Fresco Gallery, Painting Gallery, Statuary, etc. An unspecified "gallery" is likely filled with a highly varied collection of artworks. And to be technical, a gallery is much longer than it is wide (from the perspective of the primary entrance).

Gambling Hall *(Large)*

A large room devoted to board, dice, and/or card games. See also aleatorium (A section).

Gambling Room *(Medium)*

A small gambling hall.

Game Room *(Small, Medium, or Large)*

A room devoted to board, dice, and/or card games. Distinguished from a gambling room by the fact that gambling is not allowed, or severely frowned upon.

Ganunmahu *(Small or Medium)*

An Akkadian- or Babylonian-themed storeroom, used for storing valuable goods (for example, spices or tapestries or weapons).

Gaol

(Small, Medium, or Large, with Large implying many cells)

A jail, typically including a guard room surrounded by cells. There will be many guard and prisoner NPCs here of course.

Garden *(Medium or Large)*

A place where plants are artificially encouraged and cultivated. Underground this will typically be a fungal garden (see that entry, under F), but other types of gardens (herb, poison, vegetable, etc.) are also possible with the influence of magic.

Garderobe *(Tiny or Small)*

A medieval toilet.

Garderobe Chamber *(Small or Medium)*

A room filled with multiple garderobe alcoves. Commonly found near barracks, quarters, etc.

Gardr *(Small, Medium, or Large)*

A Nordic-themed guardroom or lair.

Garret *(Tiny, Small, or Medium)*

An attic space which has been turned into a bedchamber or workspace. In a dungeon, this might also refer to a small annex situated above a cave or room (reached by a rope, ladder, etc.)

Garrison *(Medium or Large)*

A room where troops are stationed on guard. Typically larger / more populated than a guardroom.

Gas-Filled Cave *(Small or Medium)*

A cave that is filled with poisonous or magical gas. Refer to *The Book of Dungeon Traps* for many ideas to specify the gas and trap type.

Gas-Filled Cavern *(Large or Huge)*

A large gas-filled cave. Dangerous on its own, but it might also be the lair of one or more evil spores as well.

Gate Chamber *(Medium)*

A chamber where a massive gate (locked, rising / lowering, guarded, etc.) is situated.

Gate Room *(Large)*

A large and likely well-defended gate chamber.

Gatehouse *(Medium or Large)*

A gated entrance to a stronghold. Likely less secure than a Barbican. Underground, a gatehouse might be a fortified structure inside of a larger room which restricts passage through a guarded portcullis and corridor.

Gauntlet *(Medium or Large)*

A long room lined with traps or attackers, designed to kill or torture intruders. A variant is the summoning gauntlet, which is a long room that summons various monsters based on the pressure plates that are activated along the way.

Gem Lode *(Tiny or Small)*

A rich, partially-mined gemstone deposit. As opposed to an unmined cave, there will be equipment and possibly mine carts here.

Gemstone Cave *(Small or Medium)*

A cave with unmined, hidden, or protected gemstone deposits. As opposed to an unmined cave, there will be equipment and possibly mine carts here.

Gemstone Cavern *(Large or Huge)*

A large gemstone cave, perhaps a lair for earth genies, pech, or earth elementals.

Geode Cave *(Tiny or Small)*

A cave that features several unmined spherical geodes, hiding valuable crystals within.

Geode Cavern *(Medium or Large)*

A larger – and therefore more valuable – geode cave. Might be controlled but not yet exploited by miners, dwarves, gnomes, goblins, kobolds, etc.

Geode Mine

(Tiny, Small, Medium, or Large)

A cave that has been partially (but not entirely) mined of its precious geodes.

Geothermal Cave *(Small or Medium)*

A hot, steamy cave (which is probably directly adjacent to a geyser or hot water of some kind).

Geothermal Cavern *(Large or Huge)*

A large geothermal cave. There might be a planar gate here to one of the Elemental or Para-Elemental Planes (fire, water, mud, steam, etc.).

Geyser Cave *(Small or Medium)*

A cave with a dangerous spouting geyser in it.

Geyser Cavern *(Large or Huge)*

A large, and likely very dangerous, geyser cave.

Glittering Cave (Small or Medium)

A cave which casts radiant reflections when light is brought in (typically caused by fool's gold or crystals).

Glittering Gallery (Large or Huge)

A large glittering cave. This might be the lair of creatures that are entranced by dim light or reflections, such as amber behemoths, entanglers, giant beetles, purple worms, swamp (underworld) shamblers, troglodytes, etc.

Gold Cave (Small or Medium)

A cave filled with partially-mined gold deposits. As opposed to an unmined cave, there will be equipment and possibly mine carts here.

Gold Cavern (Large or Huge)

A large gold cave.

Goods Hall (Medium or Large)

A place where goods are received, counted and stored for common use; less secure than a depository.

Granary (Small or Medium)

A room or silo where grain is stored. If not well-protected, this might be a lair for beetles or rats.

Grand Aerarium (Large or Huge)

A large, ancient treasure vault. An ideal dragon's lair.

Grand Aerary (Large or Huge)

A large medieval treasure vault, typically in a castle or temple.

Grand Aquarium (Large or Huge)

A large aquarium. There will be an aquatic encounter here, either freshwater or saltwater depending upon the nature of the dungeon (and the aquarium's keepers).

Grand Arboretum (Large or Huge)

A large arboretum. Possibly a very good place to harvest rare material spell components, or other precious ingredients, reagents, etc.

Grand Arena (Huge)

A vast arena, which is certain to be a major encounter area (and not necessarily a voluntary one, either).

Grand Armory (Large or Huge)

A vast armory. There might well be magical armor and/or shields here, which are guarded.

Grand Armory and Forge (Large or Huge)

A large armory and forge area.

Grand Arsenal (Large or Huge)

A vast arsenal. A likely location for one or more types of magical weaponry.

Grand Arsenal and Forge (Large or Huge)

A large arsenal and forge area.

Grand Aviary (Large or Huge)

A large aviary, likely suited to either a large number of flying creatures / monsters, or a huge flying denizen of some kind. (Note that a smaller aviary could be found, but a grand aviary provides enough room for an aerial encounter. Feel free to alter this and treat as a Small or Medium aviary if that is more aligned with the dungeon's environment and keepers.)

Grand Cavern *(Huge)*

An enormous cavern, likely with one or more chasms, tiered ledges, and/or a very high vaulted ceiling.

Grand Gallery (Display) *(Small)*

A very large and exquisite (display) gallery, filled with hundreds of various items.

Grand Salon *(Large or Huge)*

A very formal and beautiful reception hall / salon. If monsters are encountered here, they will be quite sophisticated and rather open to parley (perhaps ogre magi, rakshasas, a vampire, a shape-shifted dragon, etc.)

Grapery *(Small, Medium, or Large)*

A greenhouse (or similar magical crystalline structure) where grapes are grown (typically for wine and/or potion brewing).

Great Abattoir *(Large or Huge)*

A large slaughterhouse room or hall, where beasts or monsters are slain.

Great Adamantite Delve *(Huge)*

A vast adamantite delve. A major source of conflict between rival dungeon populations to be sure.

Great Adyton *(Large or Huge)*

A large, ancient sanctum sanctorum.

Great Almonry *(Large)*

An almonry of considerable size. This place would be watched over by a powerful NPC or monster, likely protected by bodyguards and/or guardian beasts.

This overseer would be observing the proceedings of many minions, traders, and/or monstrous warders as appropriate to the dungeon environment.

Great Andron *(Large or Huge)*

A large andron. This would be the home of a major fighting men's brotherhood, priesthood, assassin's guild, etc.

Great Chamber *(Large or Huge)*

Not to be confused with a great hall (hereafter). Although somewhat confusing, this is a medieval term for a huge and more private room which is similar to a great hall but is intended for nobles' use. This distinction may mean (for example) that the entryway is protected by silence spells, or even that secret doors are needed to discover the great chamber.

Great Hall *(Large or Huge)*

The most impressive hall in a stronghold. May include the throne room, or serve as a court. The hall is almost certainly well-guarded.

Great Kitchen *(Large or Huge)*

A large room where food is prepared. In the game, this will include a great fireplace and/or firepit(s).

Great Room *(Large)*

A large and impressive room of comfort, combining the uses of a family room, a living room, and/or a study.

Greenhouse *(Small, Medium, or Large)*

Anachronistic. In game terms, this is likely a conservatory which is lit and/or watered by powerful magic. If situated underground, there will be crystal lenses which magically bring in sunlight.

Gren *(Tiny)*

A cramped lair for one or more small creatures (fox, gremlin, etc.).

Grinding Chamber *(Small)*

A small grinding room. There might be minor minions or humanoids working here.

Grinding Room *(Medium or Large)*

A grindstone room which serves (or which did serve) as a mill. Alternately, a room where jewelers and/or gem cutters work on their craft.

Grof *(Tiny or Small)*

A cavelet or pit with Nordic-themed carvings and/or decoration.

Grot *(Tiny or Small)*

A small grotto, or a sculpted feature within a larger space that has been sculpted to look like a cave (for ceremonial purposes?).

Grotto *(Medium or Large)*

An artificial cave, or an artificially-enhanced cave. There may be painted walls, carved rock formations, a fountain, reliquaries, etc.

Guano Cave *(Small or Medium)*

A cave filled with bats and bat droppings.

Guano Cavern *(Small)*

A guano cave of considerable size. This is probably the lair of giant bats or vampire bats. There may also be creatures feeding on the guano, such as giant beetles, slimes, or molds.

Guard Cave *(Small or Medium)*

A cave that is being used (likely by humanoids, giants, trolls, etc.) as a guardroom.

Guard Cavern *(Large or Huge)*

A large guard cave, with a considerable number of monstrous warders and defenders being present.

Guard Chamber *(Small)*

A minor guardroom. This might be stationed by demi-human warders, humanoids, men-at-arms, etc.

Guard Hall *(Large or Huge)*

A large hall where troops are kept in defense. The troops would likely be well-equipped, and backed up by fair numbers of war dogs or guardian beasts of some kind.

Guard Post *(Tiny or Small)*

A specific position where troops keep watch. As opposed to a guardroom, a guard post is usually in an archway, at a door, or in an intersection.

Guardroom *(Medium)*

A decent- or small-sized room where troops are stationed.

Guest Chamber *(Small)*

A small guestroom. The likely lair of a minor NPC, perhaps a dignitary or mercenary.

Guestroom *(Small or Medium)*

A sleeping room designed to host one or more guests in comfort. An NPC might be dwelling here, or perhaps a shape-shifter, doppelganger, or human-appearing monster (such as a gold dragon).

Guild Hall *(Large or Huge)*

A hall where a guild (an association of members of a profession, e.g. merchants, warriors, conjurers, thieves) assembles and convenes. In a dungeon, this might be the domain of a secret society or cabal (such as a pre-Illuminati sect of some kind).

Guild Room *(Medium)*

A smaller guild hall, with a lesser cadre of NPCs. Common guild rooms in dungeon environments would feature thieves, assassins, or templars (if the dungeon has a surviving good-aligned contingent of such warriors standing in defiance of evil).

You can roll randomly (D100) if desired:

- ❖ **[01-10]** Assassins
- ❖ **[11-35]** Fighters
- ❖ **[36-45]** Gonneslingers
- ❖ **[46-55]** Monks (a rogue sect, perhaps)
- ❖ **[56-65]** Serpent Folk (in disguise)
- ❖ **[66-70]** Templars (with Golgothan warbeasts)
- ❖ **[71-95]** Thieves
- ❖ **[96-98]** Winterbringers (in ritual)
- ❖ **[99-00]** Infiltrated Guild. Reroll as above, but also include serpent folk impostors.

Gymnasium *(Large)*

In the Greek and Roman sense, this is a large area designed for troops or nobles to exercise and wrestle to keep in fighting trim. Similar to an exercise room, but likely better-equipped (rings, swing ropes, climbing walls or nets, etc. May be located inside or adjacent to a therma area.

Gynaeceum *(Medium or Large)*

A room that provides quarters for women, to the exclusion of men. (Example denizens: priestesses, vestals, Amazon warriors.)

Gypsum Cave *(Small or Medium)*

A cave with gypsum surfaces, which is a form of crystal. The deposits might include sulfur, or the cave might be geothermal. There might be feasting earth elementals here.

Gypsum Cavern *(Large or Huge)*

A large gypsum cave. The crystals might be of immense size, or even magical in nature (as conduits of the Elemental Plane of Earth).

H is for Heroum

Hall (Large or Huge)

A very large room, typically with rows of columns or pillars, which is used by a great number of people. Examples include Banquet Halls, Mezzanine Halls, Reception Halls, Trophy Halls, etc. The generic "Hall" can also be used in a dungeon to indicate a large space that is used as a lair, but which had a former use that is now unknown.

Hall of Assembly (Large or Huge)

A large and ornate assemblage. There may be veteran guards here, in fine plate armor and with high-quality weaponry.

Hall of Bones (Large or Huge)

A great mortuary hall, filled floor-to-ceiling with niches and alcoves where skeletal remains are deposited.

Creatures which are likely to lair here would include: skeletons, zombies, ghouls, wights, shadows, wraiths, mummies, spectres, vampires, and so forth.

Hall of Challenge (Large or Huge)

A dueling hall where stronghold personages meet in (typically non-lethal) combat, either as a test of might or as the resolution of a legal / honor challenge.

Hall of Contemplation (Large or Huge)

A place where worshippers pray in silence, typically while holding hands or gathered closely.

Hall of Doors (Large or Huge)

A room with a large number of doors, typically the entrance to a labyrinth or otherwise designed to confuse intruders. The classic example exists in *Alice's Adventures in Wonderland*.

Hall of Healing (Large or Huge)

A hall where clerical magics are used to heal the faithful.

Hall of Honor (Large or Huge)

A place where the stronghold ruler's ancestral treasures are displayed. There will certainly be treasures here if the dungeon is not a ruin. However, they are probably magically warded ... or at least watched.

Hall of Immortal Judgment

(Large or Huge)

A hall of justice where judgment is passed not by mortals, but by the present avatar of a god or goddess.

Hall of Judgment (Large or Huge)

A large legal court. Legalities are aspects of law; therefore, if the hall is currently occupied there might be paladins (if the hall is sworn to good), devils (if evil), or Nirvanan servitors (if netural) present here.

Hall of Mirrors (Large or Huge)

A large hall filled with reflective surfaces, either to reflect light into otherwise-darkened rooms, or to serve as a confusing labyrinth.

Hall of Mourners (Large or Huge)

Similar to a hall of bones, but the emphasis is more on comfort for grievers than it is on storing remains. The dead will be concealed in urns, reliquaries, veiled niches, etc.

Hall of Offerings (Large or Huge)

A hall where priests and worshippers offer treasures or sacrifices to their god, or to ancestors.

Hall of Pools (Large or Huge)

A large pool room, likely including several pools instead of just one. A favorite great hall type preferred by alchemists and (mad?) wizards. Refer to *The Classic Dungeon Design Guide, Book II* for details on pools.

Hall of Repentance (Large or Huge)

Similar to a confessional, but intended for use by many persons at once. In some religions, confession is a public rather than a private ritual; in other religions, the hall will feature many confessional niches or sub-rooms.

Hall of Resurrection (Large or Huge)

A great sacred (or unholy?) hall where the faithful are brought back to life using divine (or infernal?) magics.

Hall of Reverence (Large or Huge)

A hall made to honor a mortal individual (such as an emperor), or a bloodline (such as a line of kings and queens). There will be statues, tapestries, paintings, mosaics, etc.

Hall of Runes (Large or Huge)

A hall covered in sacred writings. The hall is literally an "inhabitable book." Characters may need to climb stairs or crawl into alcoves to read all of the inscriptions (spells?) in sequence. Inspired by Egyptian funerary hieroglyphics.

Hall of Souls (Large or Huge)

A hall of bones where the spirits of the dead remain, rather than passing on; a prime locale for sacred spirits, or for evil undead.

Hall of Statuary (Large or Huge)

A hall filled with sacred or honorary statues.

Hall of Tapestries (Large or Huge)

A hall whose walls are covered with depictions of sieges, battles won, claimed kingship, etc. The tapestries might be treasure in and of themselves, or might be magically animated scenes.

Hall of the Dead (Large or Huge)

A hall of bones where the dead are interred in sarcophagi throughout the room, rather than in wall niches.

Hamr (Small or Medium)

A small Nordic-themed barracks. A perfect lair for Viking warriors, berserkers, barbarians, werewolves, etc.

Harem (Small, Medium, or Large)

A secure and guarded room for ladies in waiting, wives, concubines, etc. There will be two types of NPCs here, the women and the guards; but surely the women will be able to handle themselves if violence should break out (perhaps even more so than the guards).

Harness Chamber (Small)

A small harness room. This could be the lair of a tamed and stabled Golgothan war beast, griffon, hippogriff, nightmare, etc.

Harness Hall (Large or Huge)

A large harness hall. The space is probably divided into stables, sub-rooms, etc. where mounts (not necessarily horses) can be quickly prepared for battle.

Harness Room (Medium)

A storeroom for tack, harness, and saddles. See also tack room.

Hastarium (Medium)

An auctioning and bartering room. In a dungeon (for example), this might be a barter hall where troops are paid, or where supplies are traded between groups. The name implies "under the spear," which means the proceedings are watched and guarded.

Hatchery (Small, Medium, or Large)

A nursery where egg-laying monsters or denizens protect their young. Examples of egg-layers include dragons, giant ants, kobolds, lizard men, etc.

Haugr (Tiny, Small, Medium, or Large)

A Nordic-themed crypt or tomb.

Haven (Small or Medium)

A secret or sheltered room. Similar to a sanctuary, but the emphasis is less on worship and more on comfort and privacy.

Hearth Chamber (Small)

A small hearth room.

Hearth Hall (Large or Huge)

A large hearth room; there might even be room for two or three separate hearths, depending on the room layout and size.

Hearth Room (Medium)

A room dominated by a hearth (a large fireplace). There will be NPCs situated here, or otherwise lairing demi-humans, humanoids, etc.

Helieum (Large or Huge)

A temple room devoted to the divine sun, or a sun god / goddess. Actually found underground as well; probably due to nocturnal peoples praying for the sun to light

their way magically where it cannot do so naturally.

Hell Mouth (Medium, Large, or Huge)

A magical infernal portal, which leads to the Hells. It is likely an invasion point for devils and fiends; if one-way (leading to Hell and not back), it is an accursed place of mortal punishment. Almost certain to be defended by evil priests and/or diabolic creatures.

Hellir (Small, Medium, or Large)

A cave with Nordic-themed carvings and/or decoration.

Herbarium (Small or Medium)

A room devoted to the storing and study of herbs. In the game, the herbs are likely to be important (medicinal, spell reagents, and/or poisons).

Hermitage (Tiny, Small, or Medium)

The chamber where a hermit NPC dwells. The hermit is capable of taking care of himself, and will perhaps be a thief, mage, savant, monk, etc.

Heroum (Tiny, Small, or Medium)

A shrine chamber dedicated to a hero (a valorous mortal who performed deeds, as opposed to a demigod, god or goddess).

Hideout (Medium or Large)

A room where denizens hide to avoid detection.

Hiding Place (Tiny or Small)

Similar to a hideout, but smaller and more improvised.

Hieron *(Medium, Large, or Huge)*

An ancient sanctuary or temple, featuring a shrine.

Hole *(Tiny or Small)*

A small room with a very small unintended entrance, or a rough / collapsed floor. A "hole" implies a pitfall that has resulted either from structural degradation, an unfinished excavation, or the burrowing of some creature.

Holl *(Large or Huge)*

A large Nordic-themed hall.

Hollow *(Tiny or Small)*

A small, irregularly-shaped area. Not a planned room, just an open space that can be used. Examples include a collapsed cave wall which can be climbed into, a hollow tree, or a place where a large stone block has been removed to expose the earth.

Hollowed Trash Heap *(Large or Huge)*

These are piles of filth, rubble, stumps, dead trees, burned timber and various other types of debris. The trash heap is hollowed and used as a lair by creatures such as giant rats, gremlins, spiders, kobolds and so forth. Some are abandoned, but most are lairs. Any adventurer larger than a gnome or halfling will be reduced to crawling through the claustrophobic tunnels on hands and knees.

Hollowed Wall *(Tiny, Small, or Medium)*

A hollow within a very wide structural wall. The wider walls of Castle Oldskull (for example) still stand, although they are frequently crumbled into ruin at the points where siege damage or collapsed towers have created huge hills of rubble. Here, the opened walls are sometimes turned into small cave-like areas by industrious creatures.

Holr *(Small or Medium)*

A hollow with Nordic-themed carvings and/or decoration.

Horological Hall *(Large or Huge)*

A large horologium. Perhaps sacred to an Immortal of Time, or guarded by a time elemental.

Horologium *(Small or Medium)*

A room or locale containing a clock, sundial, or magical timepiece.

Horreum *(Small, Medium, or Large)*

A storeroom for grains or other dried foods.

Hospitalium *(Small)*

An ancient guest chamber.

Hospitium *(Medium)*

An ancient guestroom of respectable size.

Hostel *(Medium or Large)*

Outside of the modern definition, this is a combination kitchen and sleeping place, where travelers or transient visitors are served as needed. This might be (for example) an overflow kitchen / barracks in a stronghold, where more men are lodged and cared for while an army is amassing.

Hrt / Heret *(Large)*

A large Egyptian-themed tomb.

Hrt Ib / Heret Ib *(Large or Huge)*

An Egyptian-themed ceremonial hall.

Hunters' Hall *(Large or Huge)*

A hall filled with beast and monster trophies, famous and/or sundered weapons, pelts, skins, tusks, and (traditionally) a stuffed grizzly bear (or badgerbear?).

Hursu *(Tiny, Small, or Medium)*

An Akkadian- or Babylonian-themed larder, pantry, or storeroom for food.

Hus *(Small or Medium)*

A Nordic-themed dwelling room, or quarters.

Hwt / Hewet *(Large or Huge)*

An Egyptian-themed temple. There will likely be clerics here of one or more of the Egyptian Immortals. Supernatural guardians of some kind might also be present (sphinxes, winged uraeus serpents, Bennu hatchlings, etc.)

Hwt Ka / Hewet Ka *(Small or Medium)*

An Egyptian-themed funerary chapel.

Hylr *(Small or Medium)*

A Nordic-themed pool cave or pool room.

Hypocaust *(Medium)*

A large hypocaust chamber.

Hypocaust Chamber *(Tiny or Small)*

An underground room with burning materials (magical?), designed to heat the floor and space of the room above. May be situated below a caldarium, or simply used by a noble to heat an area during the winter etc.

Hypogeum *(Small, Medium, or Large)*

An ancient cellar, which may also be a tomb. The ceiling might be low, depending upon the dungeon level circumstances.

Hypostyle Hall *(Large or Huge)*

A hall with many ornate columns.

I is for Inquisition Chamber

Ibw / Ibiw (Tiny, Small, or Medium)

An Egyptian-themed refuge or shelter.

Ice Cave (Small or Medium)

A cave with surfaces made not of stone, but rather ice.

Ice Cavern (Large or Huge)

A large ice cave. This might be the lair of an ice elemental, frost giants, snow leopards, yeti, a polar worm, winter wolves, etc.

Ice Chamber (Small)

A small icehouse.

Icehouse (Medium)

A sealed vault where sawdust or magic are used to keep blocks of ice.

Idol Grotto (Small, Medium, or Large)

An artificial cave made to highlight a centerpiece idol, statue, or icon.

Idrt / Idret (Large or Huge)

An Egyptian-themed hall.

Ikw / Ikew (Large or Huge)

An Egyptian-themed quarry.

Illusory Chamber (Small)

A small illusory room.

Illusory Room (Medium or Large)

A room with illusionary features, typically designed to hide a trap or frighten intruders.

Imht / Imehet (Small or Medium)

An Egyptian-themed room of shadows, leading into the netherworld.

Immense Archive (Huge)

A very large archive; perhaps with multiple levels, ladders, stairs, etc.

Imnt / Imenet (Tiny, Small, or Medium)

An Egyptian-themed secret room. There may be a cursed and/or trapped treasure here.

Impluvium Chamber (Small)

A room dominated by a pool of drinking water. The water might be magically purified or warded.

Impluvium Hall (Large or Huge)

A grand room with multiple pools of drinking water.

Impluvium Room (Medium)

A larger impluvium chamber.

Infirmary (Medium or Large)

Similar to a hall of healing, but intended for long-term healing (and with less magical intervention in the process).

Inglenook (Tiny)

(This entry is primarily for completeness purposes for readers only, and does not necessarily appear on the random tables as a separate space.) A small alcove situated next to a fireplace or firepit.

Inner Chamber *(Tiny, Small, or Medium)*

A private room near to the main temple, where priests meet with one another.

Inner Ward *(Small or Medium)*

Similar to an inner chamber, but likely secret and/or fortified.

Inquisition / Inquisitorial Chamber

(Tiny, Small, or Medium)

A room where heretics are questioned (and perhaps given a chance to repent) prior to torture. See also interrogation chamber. Inquisitors are clerics; many inquisitors' servants are half-ogres, half-orcs, or humanoids.

Inscription Chamber *(Small)*

A room where scribes copy scrolls, tablets, etc. See also scriptorium.

Instrument Chamber *(Small)*

A smaller instrument room.

Instrument Room *(Medium)*

A room where delicate instruments (e.g., alchemical) are stored and/or used.

Internment Chamber

(Tiny, Small, or Medium)

The room where dead bodies are moved to their final burial places. Or, a small prison.

Interrogation Chamber *(Tiny or Small)*

A room where prisoners are questioned.

Interrogation Room *(Small or Medium)*

A larger interrogation chamber. These spaces are rarely large, as claustrophobia is an important factor in effective interrogations.

Ipa *(Small or Medium)*

An Egyptian-themed office, or bedchamber of an official.

Iron Cave *(Small or Medium)*

A cave with natural and partially-mined iron deposits. As opposed to an unmined cave, there will be equipment and possibly mine carts here.

Iron Cavern *(Large or Huge)*

A large iron cave. There could be guardian goblins, kobolds, dwarves, gnomes, etc.

Isi *(Medium or Large)*

An Egyptian-themed archive, council chamber, or workshop.

Isittu *(Small, Medium, or Large)*

An Akkadian- or Babylonian-themed treasure vault. If the (ancient?) treasures are still here, they may be guarded by a summoned protector, such as a lammasu or shedu.

Itima *(Small or Medium)*

A Sumerian-themed darkroom.

Iwnn / Iwenen *(Small or Medium)*

An Egyptian-themed sanctuary.

Iwnyt / Iwenyt *(Small)*

An Egyptian-themed pillared hall.

J IS FOR JEWEL CAVE

Jail *(Small, Medium, or Large, with Large implying many cells)*

Similar to a gaol, but more "modernized" (likely with reinforced bars and a more secure guardroom, and perhaps even magical wards or detections).

Jewel Cave *(Small or Medium)*

A gemstone cave with highly valuable deposits.

Jewel Cavern *(Large or Huge)*

A large jewel cave. This area is likely a major point of contention between rival dungeon populations.

Junk Room *(Small or Medium)*

A room filled with random discarded objects.

K IS FOR KEEP

Karmu *(Small, Medium, or Large)*

A Sumerian-themed ruined chamber or ruined room.

Keep *(Large or Huge)*

Typically the inmost fortified area of the stronghold. If there is a donjon, it is likely in the center of the keep. Underground, this will be a locked, guarded, and fortified region of the dungeon level.

Kelda *(Small or Medium)*

A Nordic-themed fountain room.

Kila *(Small, Medium, or Large)*

A Sumerian-themed excavation room.

Kimah *(Small, Medium, or Large)*

A Sumerian-themed tomb.

Kitchen *(Medium)*

A room where food is prepared. In gaming terms, will include a fireplace, cauldron, work tables, etc.

Kitchen Chamber *(Small)*

A small kitchen.

Kneipe *(Small or Medium)*

A drinking (and reveling) room.

Knights' Hall *(Medium, Large, or Huge)*

The hall where the stronghold's champions are honored, attended to, and possibly quartered.

Kosmeterion *(Tiny, Small, or Medium)*

An ancient (Greek-themed) robing room.

Kukku *(Small, Medium, or Large)*

An Akkadian- or Babylonian-themed room of shadows, leading into the netherworld.

Kummu *(Small or Medium)*

An Akkadian- or Babylonian-themed shrine.

Kunukku *(Small or Medium)*

An Akkadian- or Babylonian-themed storeroom, which is locked or sealed.

L IS FOR LABYRINTH

Laboratory (Alchemical)

(Small, Medium, or Large)

A room which is used for alchemical experimentation, meaning the creation and transmutation of solids, liquids, and gases. The room probably has magical potions, poisons, and/or material spell components in addition to laboratory equipment.

Laboratory (Magical)

(Small, Medium, or Large)

Similar to an alchemical laboratory, but the laboratory has additional space and features for the conjuration, control, and/or dismissal of magical creatures (such as a magical circle of protection). There may also be tools for the creation and protection of planar gates, such as planar tuning forks or resonant chimes.

Labyrinth *(Large or Huge)*

A maze which has a ceremonial, divine, or supernatural purpose.

Labyrinthine Cavern *(Large or Huge)*

A cavern with many columns and branching pathways, creating a maze-like natural space.

Labyrinthine Warrens *(Huge)*

A labyrinthine cavern which has been expanded by burrowing beasts, monsters, or humanoids.

Laconicum *(Small, Medium, or Large)*

A Roman-style sauna. The room is traditionally semi-circular in shape.

Lady's Chamber *(Small or Medium)*

A bedchamber, or salon, belonging solely to a noblewoman.

Lair *(Tiny, Small, Medium, Large, or Huge)*

The territorial domain of a monster or beast. There are thousands of different kinds, depending upon the type of monster and the specific characteristics of the dungeon. Refer for example to the *Oldskull Dungeon Bestiary* for many thousands of lair stocking ideas.

Landing *(Tiny or Small)*

An open space or room between two flights of stairs. By technical definition, this room would have stairs up and another flight of stairs down, but you can adjust this (or simply block off one flight with rubble, a magic gate, etc.) as needed for your floorplan.

Lararium *(Tiny or Small)*

A small Roman-themed netherworld shrine, dedicated to the Lares spirits.

Larder *(Medium)*

A cool room where preserved food is stored. The "food" might be horrific, in some cases; for examples, ogres have been known to keep "larders" which are basically prisons for humans and demi-humans with broken limbs.

Larder Chamber *(Small)*

A small larder.

Latrine *(Tiny)*

A crude communal garderobe.

Latrine Chamber *(Small or Medium)*

A room filled with multiple latrine alcoves.

Launderer's Room / Laundry Room

(Small or Medium)

A room where clothes are cleaned. Unlikely to exist in most places, but in the game it seems likely that nobles would use magic to clean their clothing and a room with servants would accommodate that function.

Lava / Magma Cave *(Small or Medium)*

A cave with exposed liquid magma; or, a cave (such as the nexus of several lava tubes) which was formed by lava, but then cooled over the centuries. In the latter instance, the source of magma is still close by. And as a scientific distinction, "lava" is magma that reaches the surface, while "magma" remains underground (without surface access).

Lava / Magma Cavern *(Large or Huge)*

A large lava cave. This is likely to be the lair of flame salamanders, fire elementals, pyro-hydras, or perhaps even an ancient red dragon.

Lavatorium *(Small or Medium)*

A Roman-themed lavatory.

Lavatory *(Small or Medium)*

A decent- or small-sized washroom.

Lazarette *(Tiny, Small, Medium, or Large)*

A secure room for the care, or confinement, of lazars (diseased people or creatures).

Leaching Cesspool

(Small, Medium, or Large)

A cesspool with underlying sewer works (submerged narrow passages), so that waste can flow out of the area.

Lead Cave *(Small or Medium)*

A cave filled with valuable and partially-mined lead deposits. As opposed to an unmined cave, there will be equipment and possibly mine carts here. Miners might include dwarves, gnomes, kobolds, goblins, etc.

Lead Cavern *(Large or Huge)*

A large lead cave. There may be a considerable demi-human clan or humanoid tribal presence here.

Leap *(Tiny, Small, or Medium)*

A good jumping-off point (for example, down into a pool below); or, grimly, can alternately mean the place where someone committed suicide.

Leprosarium *(Small, Medium, or Large)*

A secluded place where lepers are treated, or at least kept away from the rest of the populace. In a fantasy world, a leprosarium might feature a population that is cursed, lycanthropic, vampiric, etc.

Lesser Almonry *(Small)*

A small almonry.

Library *(Medium, Large, or Huge)*

A formal archive, where books, scrolls, and/or tablets are kept and organized. A perfect place to find new spells, curses, magic mouth alarums, bookworms, gremlins, secret passageways, etc.

Lightwell *(Tiny, Small, or Medium)*

An unroofed space which is not really a room, but which is created to allow sunlight into adjacent windowed rooms.

Limestone Cave *(Small or Medium)*

A solutional cave, created by the acid in groundwater decaying the stone in the immediate area.

Limestone Cavern *(Small or Medium)*

A large limestone cave.

Littered Cave *(Small or Medium)*

A cave whose floor is covered with trash, debris, husks, and/or the remains of prey.

Littered Cavern *(Large or Huge)*

A large littered cave.

Living Room *(Small or Medium)*

The room most intended for rest and comfort. Technically less private and more inviting to outsiders than a family room, although the distinction is often lost.

Lobby *(Small, Medium, or Large)*

(This entry is primarily for completeness purposes for readers only, and does not necessarily appear on the random tables as a separate space.) A large greeting room that leads outside. In the game, while too informal for a stronghold, a manor house might have a lobby if (for example) it is the residence of an archmage or alchemist who sells spells or identifies magic items for a price. Technically, a great inn (consider *The Shining* for haunted dungeon potential) or hunting lodge might have a lobby as well. If you would like to include such a space, you can do so without random selection.

Locutorium *(Small or Medium)*

A room in a temple, where priests, monks, acolytes, and/or the faithful converse. Typically designed as a gathering area so that ceremonial areas are kept formal and silent.

Loft *(Tiny, Small, or Medium)*

A room above ground level, converted to a bedroom or similar space, which was previously used for something else. In the game, for example, this might be a former storeroom in a castle which has been cleared to serve as temporary quarters for a new henchman or follower.

Lokrekkja *(Tiny)*

A cramped Nordic-themed sleeping alcove (space for one servant or warrior).

Long Gallery *(Large or Huge)*

A long, narrow room. By design, this is a living space or display space, so it is not a corridor or passageway. It is probably 20' long and has (for example) artwork, chairs, tables, etc.

Lookout *(Tiny, Small, or Medium)*

A room or locale which looks out over a lower area, as a place of vigil and/or to watch out for intruders.

Lopt *(Large or Huge)*

A Nordic-themed hall with a ceiling open to the sky.

Lord's Chamber *(Small or Medium)*

A bedchamber or salon intended for the exclusive use of a male noble. See also lady's chamber.

Lounge *(Small or Medium)*

A furnished room which serves as a waiting area. The term is rarely period-accurate, if that bothers you; but it does appear in dungeon modules from time to time.

Low-Ceilinged Cave *(Small or Medium)*

A cave with a ceiling height of less than 6'. An ideal guard post for dwarves, gnomes, goblins, kobolds, and so forth.

Low-Ceilinged Cavern *(Large or Huge)*

A large low-ceilinged cave.

Lumber Room *(Small or Medium)*

A storeroom for scrap wood, damaged furniture, and so forth. The lumber might be used as firewood, or it might be infested (by giant termites or weevils, for example).

Lyceum *(Large or Huge)*

A renowned hall of learning. This may be an ornate library, reception hall, amphitheater, etc.

M IS FOR MAUSOLEUM

Majestic Aerie *(Huge)*

A vast, high-ceilinged cavern with ledge(Small) used as a lair by flying creature(Small).

Makkuri *(Small, Medium, or Large)*

An Akkadian- or Babylonian-themed treasure vault.

Manufactorium *(Large or Huge)*

An ancient manufactory. The real world examples are chiefly Roman, and were for the mass production of boots, clothing, tools, etc.

Manufactory *(Large or Huge)*

The medieval term for a very large workshop (factory). This might be a place where humanoids, slaves, or servants make torches, traps, siege engines, doors, colossi, chains, or whatever.

Manzazu *(Small, Medium, or Large)*

A Sumerian-themed lair. (Examples of Sumerian monsters include demons, ghosts, griffons, lamassu, etc.)

Map Chamber *(Small)*

A small map room.

Map Room *(Medium)*

A room where maps, charts or even architectural models are studied displayed. Technically not an art gallery, so the maps are almost certainly used for planning and/or defense.

Martyrium *(Tiny, Small, or Medium)*

A sacred sanctuary or tomb, where the remains and/or relics of a martyr are kept.

Marw / Marew *(Small)*

An Egyptian-themed observation chamber.

Mass Grave *(Large or Huge)*

A room or cavern filled with many dead bodies, which were deposited quickly (after a battle, disaster, massacre, plague, etc.).

Massaku *(Small, Medium, or Large)*

An Akkadian- or Babylonian-themed chamber of general purpose. Likely dedicated to the veneration of themed divinities, demons, monsters, etc.

Mausoleum *(Large or Huge)*

A very large and ornate tomb. Technically, a nonesuch that is a free-standing building; but in the game, this could certainly be a complex or sub-level filled with guardian constructs, traps, treasures, etc.

Maze *(Large or Huge)*

A "room" comprised of many narrow corridors, designed to confuse, delay or trap intruders.

Mechanical Room *(Small or Medium)*

A room featuring some kind of contraption (steam works, or the gears below an automaton, or the under-works of a trap, or something similar).

Meditation Chamber *(Small or Medium)*

A room where priests pray to discern the will of their god.

Meeting Room (*Small or Medium*)

A place with tables and chairs, where minor officials or students gather to discuss their plans.

Megaron (*Large or Huge*)

An ancient, columned great hall. Traditionally, the setup would feature a square hall, a central hearth or firepit, and rows of columns.

Memorial Chamber (*Small or Medium*)

A room devoted to priests, heroes, and/or worshippers who have passed away.

Mesitu (*Tiny or Small*)

A narrow Akkadian- or Babylonian-themed storeroom.

Mess Hall (*Large or Huge*)

A general dining hall, used by the stronghold's troops and servants.

Mestaku (*Tiny*)

An Akkadian- or Babylonian-themed cell.

Metroon (*Small, Medium, or Large*)

An ancient sanctuary devoted to a forgotten goddess (the Matriarch of the Gods).

Mezzanine

(*Small or Medium, a subspace within an area that is Large or Huge*)

A raised mid-floor, typically reached by stairs, within a larger hall.

Mezzanine Hall (*Large or Huge*)

A hall with several mezzanines.

Mihat (*Small or Medium*)

An Egyptian-themed chapel or shrine room.

Mine (*Large or Huge*)

A hollowed-out area where minerals, metals, or gemstones are being extracted. The metal and/or gem type can be randomly rolled using the *Game World Generator* supplement if the Game Master so desires.

Mine Shaft (*Small or Medium*)

A vertical, or near-vertical, mine. Or, a sub-area within a larger mine.

Mined Cave (*Small or Medium*)

A cave which once had valuable deposits (gems, metals, etc.) which shows many signs of the work, but the resources has long since been depleted.

Mined Cavern (*Large or Huge*)

A large mined cave.

Misericord (*Small or Medium*)

A ceremonial dining room within a temple. Intended for the partaking of sacred foods; this might be a lovely place (where candied wafers dedicated to a goddess are taken) or an horrific one (where victims are eaten as sacrifices).

Misty Cave (*Small or Medium*)

A cave filled with condensation, mist, dripping water, etc. and with limited visibility.

Misty Cavern (*Large or Huge*)

A large misty cave.

Moat / Moat Vault (*Medium or Large*)

Either the ditch (typically flooded) which surrounds a stronghold, or a room featuring a flooded trench as a defensive measure.

Moat Hall (*Large or Huge*)

A vast moat vault, which might even be large enough to feature two concentric moats.

Mold-Filled Cave (*Small*)

A dangerous cave that is overgrown with a monstrous growth, such as yellow or umber mold.

Mold-Filled Cavern (*Medium or Large*)

A deadly and larger mold-filled cave.

Monastic Cell (*Tiny*)

In game terms, this would be a 10'x10' chamber designed as deliberately austere quarters for one denizen (monk, apprentice, henchman, knight bound by an oath of poverty, etc.). See *The Classic Dungeon Design Guide, Book II* for details on dungeon-dwelling monk NPCs.

Monster Crypt (*Tiny, Small, or Medium*)

A crypt where monster remains have been interred. This would be the ideal location of a monstrous skeleton lair; perhaps a giant king, a Knight of Saigoth and his undead war beasts, or even a great draconian lich.

Monument Hall (*Huge*)

A large monument chamber.

Monument Room (*Large*)

A room built to enclose a large sacred object (a meteor, petrified tree, large crystal outcropping, etc.)

Moot Hall (*Large or Huge*)

An archaic hall of judgment.

Morgue (*Small or Medium*)

An area where dead bodies are dissected, stored, and/or modified. The place might be cursed by one or more vengeful poltergeists.

Mortuary Chapel

(*Small, Medium, or Large*)

A chapel containing one or more tombs or sarcophagi.

Moss-Filled Cave (*Small or Medium*)

A cave filled with "moss," which is either a lush form of fungus, or a magically-cultivated growth (perhaps eaten by denizens).

Moss-Filled Cavern (*Large or Huge*)

A large moss-filed cave. This might be the domain of frogmen, swamp shamblers, giant beetles, giant snakes, a giant slug, etc.

Motte (*Medium, Large, or Huge*)

Generally, the hill on which a stronghold is built. But in terms of a single location, likely an open courtyard featuring an artificial hill for defensive purposes.

Msxn / Mesixen (*Small or Medium*)

An Egyptian-themed sanctum sanctorum. There may be sacred guardian beasts of some kind present here (baboons, cats, crocodiles, ibis birds, etc.), or their spirits.

Msxnt / Mesixenet (*Large or Huge*)

An Egyptian-themed necropolis.

Mtwn / Metwen *(Large or Huge)*

An Egyptian-themed arena.

Mud Cave *(Small or Medium)*

A cave with a mud pot, a boiling pool of geothermal mud.

Mud Cavern *(Large or Huge)*

A large mud cave.

Muniment Hall *(Large or Huge)*

A large muniment room.

Muniment Room *(Small or Medium)*

An archive where important historical documents are kept (deeds, titles, genealogies, laws, etc.).

Murder Room *(Tiny, Small, or Medium)*

A place where deadly attacks (arrows, oil, rocks, etc.) are rained down on intruders from above.

Museum *(Large or Huge)*

A hall where artifacts and historical pieces are displayed. In the game, a museum might include ancient armor and weapons, tapestries, fossils, dragon hides, statues of petrified medusa or basilisk victims, etc.

Mushroom Cave *(Small or Medium)*

A cave where naturally-growing or cultivated mushrooms are thriving. The mushrooms might be medicinal, hallucinogenic, poisonous, nutritious, monstrous, mold-infested, or simply cover for a lair of some kind (gremlins, changelings, Unseelie pixies, atomies, or whatever else the Game Master decides upon).

Mushroom Cellar *(Small or Medium)*

A temperature-controlled subterranean room where mushrooms are grown (likely as food or spell reagents).

Mushroom Forest *(Large or Huge)*

A large mushroom cave, and/or a cavern where giant fungi have grown due to unique conditions.

Music Chamber *(Small)*

A small music room. This could be the room of an NPC, or it could be haunted by a spirit, ghost, banshee, or something similar.

Music Room *(Medium)*

A room with excellent acoustic design, intended for the playing and practice of music. There may be a bardic treasure hidden here.

N IS FOR NETHERWORLD

Naos *(Medium, Large, or Huge)*

An ancient (Greek-themed) temple.

Narthex *(Medium, Large, or Huge)*

An enclosed hall connecting two major areas, such as an entrance hall and the main temple.

Naspaku *(Small or Medium)*

An Akkadian- or Babylonian-themed storeroom for oil or grain.

Nat *(Small or Medium)*

An Egyptian-themed weaving room.

Natatorium *(Large or Huge)*

A large room or cavern which features a deep pool.

Natural Amphitheater *(Large or Huge)*

A cavern with successive tiers and ledges leading down to a central "showpiece" area, creating an amphitheater-like space.

Naumachia *(Large or Huge)*

A water-based arena (for ships, rafts, "island" fights, etc.). Also, a term for the battles held there.

Nave *(Small or Medium)*

A hall which leads into the temple, but is meant only for priests or honored worshippers.

Necessarium *(Tiny or Small)*

A fine and well-kept privy.

Necropolis *(Large or Huge)*

A city of the dead; a vast sub-region, or sub-level, filled with many tombs and associated rooms.

Nest *(Tiny, Small, or Medium)*

The lair of an avian (or egg-laying) creature or monster.

Nether *(Large or Huge)*

A dark subterranean cave or chamber, with access to the deeper netherworld of the Under-Earth.

Netherworld *(Huge)*

An immense dark cavern, with access to the deeper Under-Earth.

Netherworld Descent *(Huge)*

A long, narrow – possibly widened – spiral descent that leads down into the Under-Earth.

Nht / Nehet *(Small)*

An Egyptian-themed refuge or shelter.

Niche *(Tiny)*

(This entry is primarily for completeness purposes for readers only, and does not necessarily appear on the random tables as a separate space.) A recess in a wall, typically for a statue, bookshelf, guard post, etc. A room will tend to have multiple niches if it has one at all.

Niched Cave *(Small or Medium)*

A cave with many natural or carved niches in the walls. The niches are likely to hold containers, minor treasures, remains of some kind, random tools, or elements of dungeon dressing (as noted in *The Classic Dungeon Design Guide, Books I and II*).

Niched Cavern (*Large or Huge*)

A large niched cave.

Niched Room (*Small or Medium*)

A room whose walls feature niches for statues, books, candelabras, windows, etc.

Nook (*Tiny*)

(This entry is primarily for completeness purposes for readers only, and does not necessarily appear on the random tables as a separate space.) A small alcove.

Novitiate (*Small*)

The quarters which are shared by the lowest-level priests (acolytes, initiates, etc.).

Nursery (*Small or Medium*)

A room where young denizens are raised. Human children are the first logical thing that comes to mind, but this is also very likely to be a room where monsters breed and protect their young!

Nymphaeum (*Small, Medium, or Large*)

A Roman-themed temple to the nymphs; typically featuring plants, statues, and running water.

If a nymph is present, she will probably be accompanied by a guardian creature, such as a giant serpent, hippocampus, ichthyocentaur, living statue, serpentine water elemental, etc.

O is for Ossuary

Obelisk Chamber *(Small or Medium)*

A room featuring a sacred obelisk.

Obelisk Hall *(Large or Huge)*

A large obelisk room.

Oblatorium *(Small)*

An apse that provides food, drink, or holy water. In the game world, this might be a magical area that conjures food or drink.

Observation Chamber *(Small or Medium)*

A room overlooking a major gathering area, such as the main temple or an amphitheater.

Observatory *(Small, Medium, or Large)*

A room where something is observed for research purposes. This could mean a place to watch the stars (for astrology and divination?), or the space could have a more mysterious or sinister purpose (such as a room for viewing remote worlds).

Occus *(Small)*

A relatively small dining chamber.

Oecus *(Medium or Large)*

A Roman- or Greek-themed living hall. Traditionally, the room is presided over by a matriarch, and is used by the matriarch and her lady servants most of the time and for banqueting during special or ceremonial occasions.

Offering Chamber *(Small)*

Similar to a hall of offerings, but smaller.

Offertorium *(Small)*

An offering chamber where bread, wine, or other victuals are placed upon an altar.

Office *(Tiny, Small, or Medium)*

A working room, typically for one individual.

Oil Cellar *(Small or Medium)*

A cool dry storeroom for the preservation of oils. In the game, this may include whale / dragon oil, olive oil, valuable netherworld-derived mineral oils, fungal oils, or similar substances.

Oil Press Room *(Small or Medium)*

A room where oils are extracted from some kind of material, either mechanically, magically, or both. Likely situated above an oil cellar.

Opisthodomos *(Small or Medium)*

An ancient and secret sanctum sanctorum; either situated in the most inaccessible part of a temple, or behind one or more secret doors. May well have been forgotten, walled up, and surrounded by completely inappropriate rooms by later builders ...

Oracular Cave *(Small or Medium)*

A cave used for purposes of divination. Historically, oracular caves sometimes had vents or chasms which gave off poisonous (and hallucinatory) gases.

Oracular Cavern *(Large or Huge)*

A large oracular cave.

Oracular Chamber *(Small or Medium)*

A room where visions from the gods are received by way of the environment. The classical version is a chasm giving off poisonous vapors, but could instead feature a talking statue, visionary crystal, magical waterfall, etc.

Oratory (Small or Medium)

A room where priests, outside of ceremonies, make proclamations to the worshippers. Can also be used to describe a small chapel.

Ossuary (Tiny)

A cramped container-like room, where the bones of the dead are placed. Or, this might be a chamber filled with multiple ossuaries. Note that an ossuary is a "bone box"; there is no room for an undead creature in the ossuary proper.

Ossuary Cave (Small or Medium)

A cave lined with ossuaries.

Ossuary Cavern (Large or Huge)

A large ossuary cave. There might be thousands of ossuaries present; some might be broken into (by scavengers, humanoids, etc.)

Ossuary Chamber (Small)

A small room lined with ossuaries.

Ossuary Room (Medium or Large)

A large ossuary room. There could be dozens or even hundreds of ossuary boxes here.

Oubliette (Tiny)

A very narrow pit, cell, or vertical shaft. Basically, a cell designed to slowly kill people. There could be a vengeful undead creature here, or a prisoner (in very bad shape) who could potentially be rescued by adventurers.

Oubliette Room (Small, Medium, or Large)

A room filled with narrow pits (hopefully covered), which are actually oubliettes.

Outpost (Small, Medium, or Large)

A garrison which is isolated from other guarded areas. (Example: in a tower in a courtyard, or in a dead-end series of rooms guarding a noble.)

Overlook (Small or Medium)

A room or cave which looks out over a lower room. For example, a chieftain's cave which is on a raised plateau over the tribal cavern.

P IS FOR PARTHENON

Painted Cavern (Large or Huge)

A large cave of paintings (see entry under C).

Painting Gallery (Large or Huge)

A hall where artistic paintings are displayed. The paintings might be magical, (for example) harboring undead or providing gateways to other lands.

Palatial Hall (Huge)

A large hall which serves as the primary space in a palace; or, a hall so sumptuously furnished that it is palace-like.

Pallet Chamber (Tiny or Small)

A servants' bedchamber.

Pantry (Small or Medium)

A cool room where food is stored. In medieval terms, can be distinguished from a larder in that a larder will only contain food, while a pantry might also include dishes, containers, and/or supplies.

Parakki (Small or Medium)

An Akkadian- or Babylonian-themed shrine chamber or dais chamber.

Parlatorium (Small or Medium)

An ancient (Roman-themed) parlor or reception room.

Parlor (Small or Medium)

A finely-appointed reception room.

Parthenon (Huge)

A great (Greek-themed) ancient temple.

Pastophorium (Small)

Most commonly, a small formal area leading into or out of an apse.

Pen

(Tiny, Small, or Medium, with Medium implying a number of pens in a single location)

A cage built from wooden stakes instead of bars.

Penaria (Small or Medium)

A general ancient (Roman-themed) storeroom.

Pergula (Tiny, Small, or Medium)

A later extension to a previously-existing ancient room.

Peristyle

(Small, Medium, or Large, surrounding a smaller interior)

A columned / pillared walkway surrounding a central area, typically a courtyard or garden. In a dungeon, a peristyle might surround a monster pit, fungal garden, pool, etc.

Peristylium

(Small, Medium, or Large, surrounding a smaller interior)

A Roman-themed peristyle.

Phosphorescent Cave (Small or Medium)

A cave filled with glowing fungi, glowworms, vapor, magic, water, etc.

Phosphorescent Cavern (Large or Huge)

A large phosphorescent cave.

Piristi *(Small or Medium)*

An Akkadian- or Babylonian-themed sanctum sanctorum.

Pit *(Tiny or Small)*

A perilous vertical shaft, usually meant as a trap, monster lair, hiding place, etc.

Pit Cave *(Small or Medium)*

A cave with a natural pit in the center.

Pit Cavern *(Large or Huge)*

A large pit cave, with one or more pits.

Pit Chamber *(Small)*

A room with a (covered?) pit in the center.

Pit Room *(Medium)*

A room featuring one or more pits.

Planetarium *(Large or Huge)*

An expensively-appointed room where the celestial spheres are presented, observed, and/or discussed. In an FRPG, this is probably the study of a sage, astrologer, and/or planetary adventurer (in the vein of John Carter and Carson Napier).

Planning Room *(Small or Medium)*

A room where leaders or officials make secret plans.

Platinum Cave *(Small or Medium)*

A cave filled with partially-mined platinum deposits. As opposed to an unmined cave, there will be equipment and possibly mine carts here.

Platinum Cavern *(Large or Huge)*

A large platinum cave.

Playroom *(Small or Medium)*

A secure room where children, or young monsters, play.

Ploutonion *(Small or Medium)*

A netherworld shrine that is devoted solely to Pluto or a similar immortal (Dis Pater, Orcus, etc.).

Plundered Tomb *(Small, Medium, or Large)*

A tomb which has been robbed and emptied of valuables.

Plundered Vault *(Medium, Large, or Huge)*

A treasure vault which has been robbed and emptied of valuables.

Plunge *(Small, Medium, or Large)*

A very long descent, possibly involving a natural pit, waterfall, magical vortex, etc.

Poison Garden *(Small, Medium, or Large)*

A garden filled with poisonous plants or fungi. The plants might have medicinal purposes, or spell effects, or they might be cultivated by an assassin or poisonous creature. Deadly plant- or soil-themed monsters are likely to dwell here as guardians.

Pool *(Tiny, Small, or Medium)*

A body of water, typically underground. The difference between a "pool" and a "pool room" is that there is no walkway around a pool, while a pool room indicates that the pool dominates the space without completely filling it.

Pool Cave *(Small or Medium)*

A cave with a (magical?) pool. The pool might be inhabited, holy water, enchanted, thermal, an illusion, etc.

Pool Cavern *(Large or Huge)*

A large pool cave. Or, a cavern with several pools.

Pool Chamber *(Small)*

A small pool room.

Pool Room *(Medium or Large)*

A room that is dominated by a pool (which might be ceremonial, for meditation, for scrying, etc.). In an FRPG, the waters are very likely enchanted, cursed, and/or inhabited.

Portcullis Chamber

(Tiny, Small, or Medium)

A room which narrows in the middle, and is divided by a portcullis (falling gate, gridded into squares of bars to prevent entry).

Potionry *(Small or Medium)*

A room where potions are created, distilled, prepared, and/or stored.

Pr Dwat / Per Dewat *(Small)*

An Egyptian-themed robing room.

Pr Hd / Per Hed *(Small, Medium, or Large)*

An Egyptian-themed treasure vault.

Pr Mdat / Per Medat *(Medium or Large)*

An Egyptian-themed library or archive (for papyri, scrolls, etc.).

Pr Nfr / Per Nefer *(Small or Medium)*

An Egyptian-themed embalming chamber or funerary workshop.

Priest Hole *(Tiny or Small)*

A secret room where religious fugitives can be hidden. In FRPG terms, this can be broadened to define any small secret room where some type of accosted denizen (cleric of the wrong alignment, good monster of a usually evil race, dark faerie exile being hunted by her parents, etc.) would be hidden and cared for.

Prison *(Small, Medium, or Large)*

A locked room, or at least a room featuring locked cells or cages, designed to keep prisoners. Refer to *The Classic Dungeon Design Guide, Book II* for prisoner ideas.

Prison Block *(Medium, Large, or Huge)*

In FRPG terms, this is likely a long 10' wide hallway lined with many individual prison cells. It could also be a grid or matrix of such areas.

Prison Cell *(Tiny)*

A very small prison, likely 10'x10' or smaller.

Prison Chamber *(Small)*

A cage-like room that is very secure.

Prison Hall *(Large or Huge)*

A large prison. Unlike a prison block, the prison hall is probably not divided into individual sub-areas.

Privy *(Tiny or Small)*

A small toilet area, and fairly nice as such things go.

Procoeton *(Small)*

An ancient (Greek-themed) antechamber.

Procoetum *(Small)*

An ancient (Roman-themed) antechamber.

Propylaeum *(Small or Medium)*

An entrance or vestibule in front of a sanctum.

Prostas *(Small or Medium)*

An ancient (Greek-themed) vestibule.

Protective Ditch *(Small, Medium, or Large)*

Typically a trench dug in an unexpected location to halt invaders; may be crossed by planks or something similar. A protective ditch could be dug in a cavern as well.

Prothyron *(Small or Medium)*

An ancient (Greek-themed) entry chamber and associated vestibule area.

Proving Ground, plural Proving Grounds

(Medium, Large, or Huge, with Huge being plural)

An arena where survivors are granted freedom; or, an extensive arena where an overlord or similarly powerful personage tests heroes who might be deserving of his legacy. The proving grounds might descend for multiple levels.

Psychomanteum *(Small or Medium)*

A private mirrored room where séances are held to make contact with the dead. In FRPG terms, this might be a room with a mage's crystal ball or scrying mirror, or a meditation chamber for an evil priest who summons psionic monsters or creates undead, etc.

Puffball Cave *(Small or Medium)*

A fungal cave filled with spores and puffballs.

Puffball Cavern *(Large or Huge)*

A large puffball cave.

Pulvinarium *(Medium or Large)*

A sacred hall for holy (or unholy) feasts, situated around a pulvinar, which is a symbolic reclining area for a worshipped Immortal.

Pump Room *(Small or Medium)*

Generally, a room which is designed to counter flooding, or to provide running water in a controlled fashion.

Purification Chamber *(Small or Medium)*

A room where defiled, cursed, or magically afflicted priests are cleansed with magic.

Puteus *(Small, Medium, or Large)*

A Roman-themed cistern or cistern room.

Pyre Chamber *(Small)*

A small room dominated by a funerary or sacrificial pyre, either prepared or already consumed.

Pyre Room *(Medium or Large)*

A large pyre chamber.

Q IS FOR QUARRY

Quarry *(Small, Medium, or Large)*

A cave or chamber where blocks of stone are mined / extracted.

Quarry Cavern *(Large or Huge)*

A large natural cavern being used as a quarry.

Quarry Shaft *(Small or Medium)*

A vertical or near-vertical quarry, which can also be considered a pit trap.

Quarters *(Small, Medium, or Large)*

Sparse accommodations for about three to ten denizens, including beds, table(s), chairs, etc. Compare with barracks, bedroom, and solitary quarters.

Refer to *The Classic Dungeon Design Guide, Book II* for hundreds of NPC types that could be designated to a dungeon's quarters depending upon the theme. In quarters, all denizens are likely to have the same archetypal class or profession, with examplars including (GM can roll D100 if desired, rerolling as necessary):

- ❖ **[01 to 04]** Anti-Paladins
- ❖ **[05 to 08]** Assassins
- ❖ **[09 to 12]** Barbarians
- ❖ **[13 to 16]** Bards
- ❖ **[17 to 20]** Brockfolk
- ❖ **[21 to 24]** Cavaliers
- ❖ **[25 to 28]** Clerics
- ❖ **[29 to 32]** Druids
- ❖ **[33 to 36]** Fighters
- ❖ **[37 to 40]** Gonneslingers
- ❖ **[41 to 44]** Hunters
- ❖ **[45 to 48]** Illusionists
- ❖ **[49 to 52]** Jesters
- ❖ **[53 to 56]** Magic-Users
- ❖ **[57 to 60]** Monks
- ❖ **[61 to 64]** Mountebanks
- ❖ **[65 to 68]** Mystics
- ❖ **[69 to 72]** Paladins
- ❖ **[73 to 76]** Plague Doctors
- ❖ **[77 to 80]** Rangers
- ❖ **[81 to 84]** Savants
- ❖ **[85 to 88]** Serpent Folk
- ❖ **[89 to 92]** Templars
- ❖ **[93 to 96]** Thieves
- ❖ **[97 to 00]** Winterbringers

Quarters, Solitary *(Tiny or Small)*

The (tight and confined, due to space) bedroom of an official, champion, advisor, etc.

There will probably be one NPC present here, with possibilities listed in the table prior. If the NPC is not currently present, there might be hidden and trapped treasure.

There might also be a small guardian beast (a war dog, as one example), or perhaps even a servant of some kind (gremlin, imp, familiar, etc.).

Quicksand Cave *(Small or Medium)*

A "trapped" cave, where part of the floor is wet quicksand.

Quicksand Cavern *(Large or Huge)*

A large quicksand cave. The cave might be completely covered in quicksand, or – more likely – there are several dangerous pools, and then also walkways which allow careful adventurers to avoid most of the perils as they cross the floor. Of course, any intelligent dungeon denizens would be quite familiar with this area, and able to quickly navigate the paths if necessary ... even if (*especially* if) pursued by the Player Characters!

Quicksand Pit *(Tiny, Small, or Medium)*

A sandpit / sinkhole that is either a trap, or is magical, monstrous, or extra-planar in nature, creating a (typically subterranean) quicksand hazard.

Quppu *(Tiny, Small, or Medium)*

A Sumerian-themed cage or prison chamber.

If this (ancient?) area is still in use as a prison, refer to *The Classic Dungeon Design Guide, Book II* for full details on creating prisoner NPCs.

R IS FOR REFLECTING POOL

Rdw / Redew *(Small or Medium)*

An Egyptian-themed stair chamber or stairway room.

Reading Chamber *(Tiny or Small)*

A small reading room.

Reading Room *(Small or Medium)*

A room where books are read and studied, as opposed to kept; likely adjacent to an archive or library.

Receiving Room *(Medium)*

A finely-appointed and ornate reception room.

Reception Chamber *(Small)*

A small reception room.

Reception Hall *(Large or Huge)*

[1] A large reception room. [2] Another name for a function hall; i.e., a large gathering hall intended to host celebratory events and functions (such as weddings).

Reception Room *(Small or Medium)*

A room designed for meeting guests. Sometimes distinguished from a drawing room if it is implied that after meeting in the reception room, the guests will be taken elsewhere to be entertained.

Recess

(Tiny or Small, with an adjacent Small, Medium, or Large space)

An indented area off of a larger room, typically secluded by tapestries, screens, etc.

Recreation Chamber *(Small)*

A small informal game room. Potential ancient and medieval games might include: knucklebones, latrunculin, micatio, par impar, pilae, trochus, and so forth. The Game Master can research historical examples if desired.

Recreation Hall *(Large or Huge)*

A large informal game room, perhaps also with aspects of a gymnasium.

Recreation Room *(Medium)*

An informal game room.

Redoubt *(Small, Medium, or Large)*

Outside, an earthen defensive structure. Inside, a room with a low wall which defenders (typically archers) can shelter behind.

Refectorium *(Small or Medium)*

An ancient room of restoration. This may be an ancient refectory, or retreat, or even a mediation room.

Refectory *(Small, Medium, or Large)*

In game terms, this will be a dining room or dining hall for clerics, druids, illusionist apprentices, magic-user apprentices, and/or monks. Traditionally, the space is divided into two naves by a central line of columns.

Reflecting Pool *(Tiny, Small, or Medium)*

A pool of holy or magical water. Refer to *The Classic Dungeon Design Guide, Book II* for full details on creating magical pool areas.

Reflecting Room *(Small or Medium)*

A room where priests gather to case ritual spells together (typically for purposes of divination).

Refuge *(Small, Medium, or Large)*

A hidden secure room that is used as a safe area during an assault or invasion.

Refuse Pit *(Tiny, Small, or Medium)*

A pit filled with non-liquid trash.

Reliquary *(Tiny, Small, or Medium)*

A room where holy treasures are kept.

Repository *(Small or Medium)*

A room where sorted objects or pieces of information are stored; this might be a combination archive / potionry, for example.

Reredorter *(Small or Medium)*

A long, narrow garderobe chamber.

Reservoir *(Large or Huge)*

A deep pool of fresh water, perhaps artificial.

Retreat *(Small or Medium)*

A private room (perhaps a study) where a house lord (or other noble) can rest and work, and likely only be interrupted by the most trusted servants.

Revolving Chamber *(Small or Medium)*

A mechanically rotating room, designed to confuse intruders (or to force them down a specific path).

Riding Hall *(Large or Huge)*

A large room with a sandy floor, designed for riding training and the indoor riding of mounts. In FRPGs this does not just imply horses, but also the possibility of dire wolves, giant boars, giant lizards, unicorns, etc.

Ritual Hall *(Large or Huge)*

A large room or fane where rituals are performed by priests, typically excluding worshippers. There will very likely be priest, mystic, or druid NPCs present here … and perhaps they are summoning something, or worshipping something forbidden.

Robing Room *(Tiny, Small, or Medium)*

A room for ceremonial dressing where a noble prepares before entering a Court or Great Hall; likely used by a Matriarch, Patriarch, King, Justiciar, etc.

Room *(Small or Medium)*

A shamelessly generic word for an enclosed space, which this book has been specifically designed to avoid the overuse of. Feel free to use the *Chaotic Descriptor Table* and the dungeon dressing tables (*The Classic Dungeon Design Guide, Books I* and *II*) to turn any featureless "room" into a quick and unique feature in your campaign.

Room of Pools *(Large or Huge)*

A room filled with different pools of magical or holy water.

Room of Slaughter

(Small, Medium, or Large)

A room filled with dead bodies, or one that is designed to kill people (such as with traps) for the pleasure of an observer.

Room of Unknown Purpose

(Tiny, Small, Medium, Large, or Huge)

Precisely that. Such spaces could be more precisely termed a Niche (Tiny), Chamber (Small), Room (Medium), Gallery (Large) and/or Hall (Huge).

Roost *(Tiny, Small, or Medium)*

The raised nesting area of a creature or monster.

Root Cellar *(Small or Medium)*

A cool underground room that is used for the long-term storage of fruit, vegetables, nuts, etc.

Rotating Room *(Small or Medium)*

A room that spins to connect with various other rooms; likely a trap, trick, magic and sentient, designed by a mad wizard, to protect a lair by confusing invaders, or something similar.

Rotting Chamber *(Small)*

A small rotting room.

Rotting Room *(Medium or Large)*

Grimly, either a room where remains are left before they can be buried, or a room filled with corpses (for example, at the bottom of a chute, or a walled-in chamber of the past).

Rotunda *(Small, Medium, or Large)*

A round room. Probably either ceremonial, or the central nexus of a dungeon level with many passageways, or a rotating room.

Royal Chamber / Noble's Chamber

(Small or Medium)

The bedroom of a noble, or the stronghold's ruler.

Royal Tomb *(Large or Huge)*

The tomb of a king or queen.

Rubble-Filled Cave *(Small or Medium)*

A cave with fallen boulders, stalactites, shattered columns, etc.

Rubble-Filled Cavern *(Large or Huge)*

A large rubble-filled cave. This would be the likely lair for a purple worm, or gargoyles, or amber behemoths, or perhaps something far more sinister (such as the drow and their monstrous allies.

Rubble-Filled Room / Ruined Room

(Small or Medium)

A room that is filled with blocks or shattered stones. Unlike a collapsed room, this room is used for storage of falling stones which have been removed from other areas. (Therefore, this room is probably sound and not in danger of collapse.)

Rugbu *(Tiny, Small, or Medium)*

An Akkadian- or Babylonian-themed loft.

Ruined Chamber *(Small)*

A small rubble-filled room.

Ruined Hall *(Large or Huge)*

A large rubble-filled room, which may be partially collapsed.

Rum *(Small or Medium)*

A Nordic-themed room of general (or random) purpose.

Runic Cave *(Small or Medium)*

A cave filled with runic engravings, which might be a warning, saga, or words of power.

Runic Cavern (Large or Huge)

A large runic cave. Some of the engravings might well be on or toward the ceiling, and difficult to read from floor level.

Runic Chamber (Small or Medium)

A room covered with magical or sacred writings.

Rwyt / Reweyet (Small)

An Egyptian-themed hall of judgment.

S IS FOR SANCTUARY

Sacrarium (Small or Medium)

A Roman-themed chapel or shrine in which holy / unholy objects are stored (probably meaning clerical magic items).

Sacred Abattoir (Small, Medium, or Large)

A slaughterhouse chamber, where beasts or monsters are slain as a ritual sacrifice.

Sacred Crypt (Small)

A crypt that has been protected by holy powers against the (rise of the) undead.

Sacred Tomb (Medium or Large)

A large sacred crypt.

Sacrificial Chamber (Small or Medium)

A room where mortal sacrifices are made to a deity, demon lord, or arch-devil.

Sacrificial Grotto (Small or Medium)

A grotto which serves as a sacrificial chamber.

Sacrificial Pool (Tiny, Small, or Medium)

A pool where sacrificial victims are drowned or slaughtered.

Sacrificial Vault (Large or Huge)

A vault where material sacrifices (typically treasure) are kept under protection for the honor of a deity, demon lord, or arch-devil. Plundering such a place may have unfortunate consequences.

Sacristy (Small or Medium)

A room where clerical vestments, vessels, and objects (holy or unholy) are stored.

Safe Room (Small or Medium)

A room with locking doors, intended to protect nobles or other important denizens during an invasion.

Salon (Small or Medium)

A formal and beautiful drawing room or reception room.

Salr (Large or Huge)

A Nordic-themed hall or common room. Likely guarded by berserkers, Norse warriors, etc.

Salt Cave (Small or Medium)

A cave with extensive salt deposits. The salt might be mined, or consumed, by creatures or monsters.

Salt Cavern (Large or Huge)

A large salt cave.

Salt Cellar (Small or Medium)

An underground room where salt blocks are stored. May also be used to store salted meats or preserves.

Salt Chamber (Small)

A locked, and/or above ground, salt cellar.

Salt Mine (Medium, Large, or Huge)

A natural area where salt is mined.

Salt Room (*Medium*)

A larger salt chamber.

Sanctuary (*Small or Medium*)

A room where only senior priests are allowed. By another definition, a place where those of a certain faith (alignment) are protected from harm.

Sanctum (*Small or Medium*)

A secret or private room within a temple; or, in a dungeon sense, the quarters, shrine, and/or scrying/meditation area of a cleric.

Sanctum Sanctorum (*Small or Medium*)

The forbidden place within a temple. This is where the god or power manifests, which is forbidden to all mortals (including the high priest). In the real world, this is where the god's sacred statue is likely to be; in an FRPG, this might even be the place where the god / demon lord / arch-devil etc. appears in avatar form to devout worshippers.

Sand Cave (*Small or Medium*)

A "trapped" cave, where part of the floor is quicksand. However, the sand is dry and dusty rather than wet and heavy.

Sand Cavern (*Large or Huge*)

A large sand cave.

Sandpit (*Small, Medium, or Large*)

A room dominated by a floor excavation which leads down to a dangerous sandy area (a sinkhole, sand trap, hidden tomb, crumbling stairway, etc.).

Sandstone Cave (*Small or Medium*)

A cave whose surfaces are made of relatively soft sandstone, which might be wind-sculpted, burrowed into, carved, etc.

Sandstone Cavern (*Large or Huge*)

A large sandstone cave.

Sarcophagus Chamber (*Small or Medium*)

A small room featuring a sarcophagus.

Sarcophagus Room (*Medium or Large*)

A room featuring one or more sarcophagi.

Sauna (*Small or Medium*)

A steam room, fed by underground fires and/or fireplaces, where smoke is minimized and steam presence is maximized (for health benefits).

Schola (*Small or Medium*)

The reclining chamber and study of a sage or philosopher.

Scrapheap (*Small, Medium, or Large*)

A room or cave that is dominated by a pile of trash.

Scriptorium (*Medium or Large*)

Similar to an inscription chamber, but larger.

Scullery (*Small or Medium*)

A room for food preparation.

Sealed Tomb (*Small, Medium, or Large*)

A tomb that has not yet been entered or violated.

Secret Crypt *(Small, Medium, or Large)*

A crypt which is hidden behind a secret door.

Secret Cyst *(Tiny, Small, Medium, or Large)*

A cyst which was completely sealed off by stone, but which harbored something valuable (unmined gems, adamantite, etc.). Clever monsters or underworld demi-humans created a secret door to reach the cyst and to plunder it. Secret cysts are commonly found in chains.

Secret Grotto *(Small or Medium)*

An artificial cave which is hidden behind a secret door.

Secret Guardroom *(Small or Medium)*

A place where elite guards are stationed, either to defend an important person's quarters or to stage counterattacks behind invaders.

Secret Room

(Tiny, Small, Medium, or Large)

A room that can only be accessed through a secret door. This is likely to be the location of a considerable amount of treasure. If guarded, there are lairing NPCs or monsters here that protect the treasure. If unguarded, the treasure is either well-hidden (such as by invisibility) or trapped, because otherwise it would have been plundered by now.

Secret Tomb *(Small, Medium, or Large)*

A tomb which is hidden behind a secret door.

Sellaria *(Large)*

A sizeable ancient reception room, with many stone sellae (stool-like seats).

Seminary *(Small or Medium)*

A schoolroom for mid-level priests.

Sepulcher / Sepulchre

(Small or Medium, perhaps in a Medium, Large, or Huge surrounding space)

A small free-standing tomb structure, in which someone (or something) is buried. In an interior setting, there will be a room surrounding the sepulcher structure.

Sepulchral Cell *(Tiny)*

A small and confined sepulcher space.

Sepulchral Chapel

(Small, Medium, or Large)

A mortuary chapel which branches off into several sepulchers.

Sepulchral Hall *(Large or Huge)*

A room or space featuring several (radiating?) sepulchers.

Sepulchral Heroum

(Small or Medium, perhaps in a Medium, Large, or Huge surrounding space)

The tomb of a hero (a valorous mortal who performed deeds, as opposed to a demigod, god or goddess).

Seraglio *(Small or Medium)*

A harem enjoyed by the stronghold's ruler, and possibly by the stronghold's champions or favored ones as well.

Servant's Quarters / Servants' Quarters

(Tiny, Small, or Medium)

In the singular, a pallet bedchamber for one servant. In the plural, a pallet or bunk bedchamber for several servants. Refer to *The Classic Dungeon Design Guide, Book II* for ideas on potential servant types.

Servants' Hall *(Medium, Large, or Huge)*

A large hall used by servants as a dining, gathering, assembly, and resting area.

Servery *(Tiny, Small, or Medium)*

A nearly-forgotten term for a room where food is prepared before being put into a dining room; or, a place food is served to a large number of people who then seat themselves elsewhere (for example, in a banquet hall).

Set *(Small or Medium)*

A Nordic-themed waiting room.

Sewer *(Small, Medium, Large, or Huge)*

A network of conduits, passageways and rooms meant for the transportation of waste and waste water away from living areas. In a dungeon setting, the sewer may be ancient (and dry); in a lived-in setting, the sewer may be impassable or partially impassable.

Sewing Room *(Small or Medium)*

A workroom intended for sewing and weaving.

Shaft Cave *(Small or Medium)*

A cave with several shelves, tiers, and steep vertical descents. Similar to a vertical cave (see that entry), but narrower, steeper, and more perilous and with fewer ledges.

Shaft Cavern *(Large or Huge)*

A large shaft cave. This could even be a dungeon sub-region; that is, a vertical sub-level with its own special rooms and guardians.

Shambles *(Small or Medium)*

A messy and chaotic abattoir.

Shanty / Shanties *(Tiny, Small, or Medium)*

Sometimes built within large halls / rooms by territorial dwellers. These are ramshackle dwellings created from wood, hides, metal and various junk. Single shanties are similar to stilt huts in regards to inhabitants, while clustered or interconnected shanties are typically used by bandits, humanoids, halflings and the like.

Shelter *(Tiny or Small)*

A haphazard, poorly-assembled dwelling place within a larger space; or, a room of some former purpose, quickly converted to serve as a refuge or living area.

Shop *(Small or Medium)*

A space devoted to mercantile activities. In a subterranean setting, this may be more of a trading area than a traditional floor-and-counter setup.

Shrine *(Small or Medium)*

A consecrated room, which is smaller than the main temple. Differentiated from a shrine room, as follows: a "shrine" implies that the entire room is sacred and covered with sacred writings, likely with icons and statuettes in wall niches; and a "shrine room" implies that there is a standing structure or descending area, which is sacred, with open space around it.

Shrine Chamber *(Small)*

A small room featuring a shrine. A shrine is a place of worship, and also a conduit of sacred (or unholy) power between an immortal and the World of Oldskull. Refer to *The Classic Dungeon Design Guide (Book II)* for complete details.

Shrine Room *(Medium or Large)*

A room featuring a shrine as its predominant, but not only, feature.

Shunned Cave *(Small or Medium)*

A cave that the area's denizens consider to be dangerous or horrifying (due to a curse, monster, undead, grim feature, memory, etc.).

Shunned Cavern *(Large or Huge)*

A large shunned cave.

Sibitti

(Small, Medium, or Large, with Large implying multiple cells)

An Akkadian- or Babylonian-themed prison or dungeon chamber.

Sick Chamber *(Small)*

A small sick room.

Sick Room *(Medium or Large)*

A carefully prepared and removed room where a diseased or wounded person can be kept.

Silver Cave *(Small or Medium)*

A cave filled with partially-mined silver deposits. As opposed to an unmined cave, there will be equipment and possibly mine carts here.

Silver Cavern *(Large or Huge)*

A large silver cave.

Simmiltu *(Tiny, Small, or Medium)*

An Akkadian- or Babylonian-themed stairway room or landing.

Sinkhole *(Small, Medium, Large, or Huge)*

A dangerous feature, where the floor has collapsed to create an open space and a plunge down into a lower cavern area.

Sitting Room *(Small or Medium)*

A more formal living room.

Skali *(Small, Medium, or Large)*

A Nordic-themed barracks or sleeping hall.

Skenotheke *(Small or Medium)*

An ancient (Greek-themed) storeroom containing theatrical equipment, ceremonial equipment, scenery, etc.

Skinning Room *(Small or Medium)*

A room where taxidermy specimens are prepared, later to be displayed in a taxidermy hall or trophy hall.

Skull Cavern *(Large or Huge)*

A large cave of skulls (refer to entry under C heading).

Slave Chamber *(Tiny, Small, or Medium)*

A room where slaves dwell, either under guard or in captivity.

Slave Pit *(Tiny, Small, or Medium)*

A vertical shaft where slaves dwell.

Slaves' Tomb *(Small, Medium, or Large)*

A tomb for many slaves; in some cultures, when a ruler would die all of his or her people were entombed as well.

Sleeping Chamber *(Small)*

A bedchamber with a heavy emphasis on sleeping; the living furnishings (table, desk, chair, wardrobe, etc.) are likely in an adjacent area. Or, the living furnishings are minimized, and kept in a collapsible trunk or similar contrivance.

Sleeping Hall *(Large)*

A large sleeping chamber for many people.

Sleeping Room *(Medium)*

A larger sleeping chamber, for one to three people (depending).

Slime Cave *(Small or Medium)*

A cave infested with slime. The slime might be phosphorescent, alchemical, poisonous, moldy, fungal, or monstrous (moving).

Slime Cavern *(Large or Huge)*

A large slime cave. The slime is very likely monstrous; it could be green, olive, gelatinous, ochre, etc. Or, this could even be the dread lair of a monstrous Shoggoth ... or Abhoth itself.

Sloping Cave *(Small or Medium)*

A cave with an uneven floor, which descends — not steeply, but in a noticeable fashion — in one direction.

Sloping Cavern *(Large or Huge)*

A large sloping cave.

Sludge Pit *(Tiny, Small, or Medium)*

A pit that is filled with thick mud. Different from a cesspit, in that a cesspit is filled with trash, and a sludge pit is an intentionally-fashioned death trap that is very difficult to get out of.

Smelter *(Small, Medium, or Large)*

A room where ore is smelted.

Smithy *(Small, Medium or Large)*

A blacksmith's work area. Typically less impressive than a forge.

Smoke Room *(Small or Medium)*

A room where smoke is deliberately funneled in, or kept in, to dry and cure flavored meats. In grim game terms, this might also imply that monsters with good taste are smoking the remains of adventurers and other victims!

Solar *(Small or Medium)*

A formal sunroom, perhaps even designed as a bedroom.

Solarium *(Small, Medium, or Large)*

An ancient sunroom, designed not only to bring in light, but also to worship the sacred sun.

This might well be the chamber of a druid hierarch, sphinx, shedu, lammasu, etc.

Spear Closet *(Tiny or Small)*

A space unintentionally created by poor planning or renovation. In a dungeon, this is likely a triangular space with two 10' long walls (i.e., a triangular half of one map square).

Spiral Labyrinth *(Medium, Large, or Huge)*

A ceremonial form of labyrinth, featuring tunnels which spiral into dead ends. This ritual setup with few branching paths is usually intended as a monster lair, or as the ceremonial area leading up to a shrine or gateway.

Spiral labyrinths are common in old school dungeons, but not all Game Masters are wise to the mythic underpinnings of the trope!

Spoliarium *(Small)*

A Roman-themed cloak room.

Alternately, depending on the setting this can be a grim "de-cloaking room," in which gladiators or other combatants are lain out when slain for removal of armor and gear.

Spur Cave *(Small or Medium)*

A cave which branches off in an unexpected direction, away from the majority of the cave system.

Spur Cavern *(Large or Huge)*

A large spur cave.

Squires' Hall *(Medium or Large)*

A place where the knights' or champions' apprentices gather, and are possibly quartered.

Stable *(Small, Medium, or Large)*

A place where warhorses or other mounts are kept ready. In an underground area, this could mean giant spiders, giant lizards, etc.

Stair Chamber *(Small)*

A small room at the top or bottom of a stairway.

Stairway Room *(Medium)*

A room at the top or bottom of a stairway (or more than one flight of stairs).

Stalactite Cave *(Small or Medium)*

A cave of stalactites, but with few or no stalagmites. There may also be floor-to-ceiling columns.

Stalactite Cavern *(Large or Huge)*

A large stalactite cave. Likely to be the lair of a colony of piercers (living stalactites).

Stalagmite Cave *(Small)*

A cave of stalagmites, but with few or no stalactites. There may also be floor-to-ceiling columns.

Stalagmite Cavern *(Large or Huge)*

A large stalagmite cave. May be the lair of entanglers, gargoyles, or similar creatures.

State Chamber *(Small or Medium)*

Similar to a council chamber, but also intended for the use of trusted visitors.

State Room *(Large or Huge)*

A grand great hall, designed primarily to intimidate or impress.

Statuary *(Small, Medium, or Large)*

A room or hall where busts, colossi, and/or statues are displayed. In a dungeon, this might be the lair of a petrifying monster.

Steam Cave *(Small or Medium)*

A geothermal cave filled with (dangerous?) steam.

Steam Cavern *(Large or Huge)*

A large steam cave.

Steinn *(Small, Medium, or Large)*

A Nordic-themed cave that is used as a dwelling or lair. Therefore, it would be a lair for berserkers, or trolls, etc.

Still Room *(Small or Medium)*

A distillery room used for the creation of beers, soaps, ointments, unguents, or something similar.

Stockpile Room *(Small or Medium)*

A place where many general supplies are kept. See also storeroom for various subtypes.

Stofa *(Small or Medium)*

A Nordic-themed sitting and warming room.

Storage Cave *(Small or Medium)*

A cave which is being used as a storeroom. See storeroom entries for various subtypes.

Storage Cavern *(Large or Huge)*

A large storage cave.

Storage Chamber *(Small)*

A place where supplies are kept, but the room is likely sealed for purposes of preservation, security, etc. In general, a small storeroom.

Storage Room / Storeroom

(Small or Medium)

A room where things are stored. (Examples include food storage, wine, leather goods, lumber, coal, supplies and sundries, textiles, etc.; see below.) A general "storeroom" without a describing adjective may either be filled with a random jumble of many things, or ruined, or currently empty (featuring only pallets, empty barrels, emptied boxes, etc.).

Storeroom – Alchemical

(Small or Medium)

A shelved storeroom with careful storage nooks for alchemical ingredients (not necessarily solids); some of which will be valuable, rare, exotic, and/or poisonous.

Storeroom – Alcohol / Wine

(Small or Medium)

A storeroom, and possibly an aging room, for alcoholic beverages.

Storeroom – Armor *(Small or Medium)*

A storage area for armor and shields. The armor will typically be kept in racks, or on pegs, or in trunks, or something similar.

Storeroom – Box Room *(Small or Medium)*

A storeroom with shelving or alcoves suited for boxes, chests, and trunks. What's in the containers, if anything, is quite another matter.

Storeroom – Butchered Meat

(Small or Medium)

A storeroom (possibly chilled) with hanging iron hooks and haunches of meat. Hopefully, the freshly-butchered meat is not of the adventurer variety …

Storeroom – Ceremonial

(Small or Medium)

A room which includes stage-works, "miracle" works (smoke bombs, glittering powder, etc.) and other trappings used in theatrical ceremonies. Can also include ritual objects, tapestries, etc.

Storeroom – Char / Coal

(Small or Medium)

A storeroom for forge and fireplace fuel. The room might be filled with coal, wood, sawdust, soot, charcoal, etc.

Storeroom – Cheese *(Small or Medium)*

A special storeroom where cheese is kept and aged.

Storeroom – Construction

(Small or Medium)

A storeroom with construction materials, including both some kind of raw material (lumber, cut stone, ornamentation, etc.) and some kind of tools (ropes and pulleys, hammers, saws, measures, etc.).

Storeroom – Drink *(Small or Medium)*

A storeroom for consumable, non-alcoholic liquids. The storeroom might be for cider, herbal waters, tea, juices, potion ingredients, pure water, etc.

Storeroom – Dry Goods

(Small or Medium)

Generally, "dry goods" implies textiles or textile products ...example include clothing, cotton bales, blankets, cloaks, yarn, tapestry material, canvas, leather, etc.

Storeroom – Embalming

(Small or Medium)

A room for embalming and corpse preservation instruments. May include (depending on culture) natron salts, canopic jars, scalpels, blood vases, stitching wire, etc.

Storeroom – Equipment Room

(Small or Medium)

In game parlance, this is a storeroom which is specifically filled with items that an adventuring party would find useful: spikes, poles, torches, picks, crowbars, perhaps even holy water vials, and so forth. Compare tool room.

Storeroom – Failed Experiments

(Small or Medium)

A classic "I'll fix it later when I know how" room for (mad?) magi; contents might include mis-transmogrified objects, invisible furniture, molten stone, petrified statues, twisted corpses, etc.

Storeroom – Foodstuffs

(Small or Medium)

A storeroom for foodstuffs. Most stored foods (without refrigeration) are dried, salted, preserved, or specially sealed.

Storeroom – Furniture *(Small or Medium)*

A storeroom for unused or broken (but fixable) furniture. Compare lumber room.

Storeroom – Herbs and Spices

(Small or Medium)

A room for storing healing herbs, special plants, valuable spices, etc. May be locked if the contents are expensive.

Storeroom – Ice *(Small or Medium)*

Non-magical ice storage in pre-electrical times is possible; consider clever advancements made by the ancient Persians and the Romans. It seems to require a closed area, sawdust, straw, reflective shields (if any sources of sunlight or fire are nearby) and clever structural evaporative cooling. Or, you can just use magic. This room features ice blocks, tongs, sawdust, rollers, and so forth.

Storeroom – Lumber *(Small or Medium)*

A storage area for timbers, and possibly for partially constructed or damaged pieces of wooden fortifications.

Storeroom – Masonry *(Small or Medium)*

A storage area for stone blocks, and possibly for stonecutters' tools or repair tools.

Storeroom – Oil *(Small or Medium)*

A storage area for flaming oil, cauldrons, handling equipment, pulleys, etc. As a more pleasant alternative, this could be a storage room for olive oil, kept in wax-sealed amphorae.

Storeroom – Reagents (Small or Medium)

In gaming parlance, reagents are material spell components. The contents might be valuable (gem powder), creeper (eye of newt, wing of bat type stuff), or obscure (crystal prisms, dried oak leaves, a spider with her webs being cultivated, etc.).

Storeroom – Salt (Small or Medium)

A storage area for salt and salt blocks, and possibly entire salted carcasses (siege meat).

Storeroom – Sundries (Small or Medium)

A storage area combining several specialized types of goods. If you need inspiration, roll 1D4+1 and select that number of specialized storeroom descriptions.

Storeroom – Tools and Gear

(Small or Medium)

A storeroom which might include hammers, mallets, wedges, crowbars, weights, shovels, pickaxes, block and tackle, etc.

Storeroom – Water (Small or Medium)

A storage area for casks of pure water. Similar to a drink storeroom, but there is no variety.

Storeroom – Weapons (Small or Medium)

Similar to an arsenal, but less secure (typically for quick and ready access). The weapons will be in racks, trunks, hanging from pegs, etc. The door is unlikely to be locked.

Storm Cellar (Small or Medium)

A reinforced underground retreat where a manor's residents can take shelter during a storm, fire, magical cataclysm, etc.

Stream Cave (Small or Medium)

A cave with a stream flowing through it, which might or might not be navigable.

Stream Cavern (Large or Huge)

A large stream cave. If you like, you can have this result mean that there is a full underground river present, but this is not a randomly provided option because that single choice will affect your entire dungeon layout.

Stricture (Tiny or Small)

A tunnel, enclosure, or corridor that is extremely narrow, either due to nature, accident, or design (perhaps an entrance to a kobold, cynocephalus, or goblin lair?).

Strongroom (Small)

A small locked treasure vault, or storeroom filled with valuables (such as reagents or spices).

Studio (Small)

A small workroom for an artisan (painter, sculptor, engraver, etc.).

Study (Small or Medium)

A library room where research and reading can be performed in peace.

Sub-Basement (Tiny, Small, or Medium)

A room beneath a basement; in FRPG terms, this would likely be on "dungeon level two," or deeper, beneath a manor house.

Sub-Cellar (Tiny, Small, or Medium)

A room beneath a cellar; in FRPG terms, this would likely be on "dungeon level two," or deeper, beneath a manor house.

Submerged Cave *(Small or Medium)*

A cave that is completely underwater.

Submerged Cavern *(Large or Huge)*

A large submerged cave.

Submerged Chamber *(Small)*

A small room that is completely underwater. This could be the result of flooding or an accident; or, it could be the lair of aquatic monsters.

Submerged Hall *(Large or Huge)*

A very large submerged chamber. Almost certainly the lair of some aquatic creature.

Submerged Room *(Medium)*

A larger submerged chamber.

Sudatorium *(Small, Medium, or Large)*

An ancient hot sauna with a vaulted ceiling.

Suite *(Medium)*

A finely-appointed bedroom.

Suite Chamber *(Small)*

A finely-appointed bedchamber.

Sulfur Cave *(Small or Medium)*

A dangerous sulfur-infused geothermal cave. There will be hot pools, a strong stench (as a warning), and a distinct lack of oxygen.

Sulfur Cavern *(Large or Huge)*

A larger sulfur cave.

Summoning Chamber *(Small)*

A small room where monsters are summoned or conjured.

Summoning Gauntlet

(Medium, Large, or Huge)

See gauntlet entry. A gauntlet where monsters are summoned to repel or destroy intruders.

Summoning Room *(Medium or Large)*

A larger summoning chamber.

Sunroom *(Small or Medium)*

In an FRPG, this is likely a term for a room which can actually be illuminated by sunlight for reading or comfort purposes. Common in manor houses, but underground this would be a special room lit by a long open chute, angled window chute, or reflecting mirrors.

Svefnhus *(Small or Medium)*

A Nordic-themed bedchamber.

T IS FOR TEMPLE

Tablinum (Small or Medium)

An ancient receiving room, bedroom, or study. Commonly attached as the entry to an atrium.

Tabulinum (Small)

A vestibule adjacent to an atrium.

Tack Room (Small or Medium)

A place where saddles, stirrups, reins, barding, and similar gear are stored. In an FRPG, the mounts which are equipped with such items might not necessarily be horses. A tack room could even be underground (for riding lizards, or rideable giant spiders, for example).

Tank (Small, Medium, Large, or Huge)

A chambered, well-structured, and/or relatively advanced cistern.

Tar Pit (Small, Tiny, or Medium)

A naturally-occurring asphalt pit, which can prove very dangerous to beasts ... and to adventurers as well.

Taum (Tiny, Small, or Medium)

An Akkadian- or Babylonian-themed secret room.

Taxidermy Hall (Small, Medium, or Large)

A room where stuffed creature and/or monster hides are displayed. See also hunters' hall, which is a variation in which (typically) the trophies have been gathered by hunters and/or champions associated with the hall and its environs.

Teleportation Chamber
(Tiny, Small, or Medium)

A type of trick created by magi, in which a room causes those who enter to teleport to another (identical-looking?) chamber. The purpose of the rooms, usually, is to confuse intruders, to allow the escape of important personages, and/or to hasten the response of guards to vulnerable areas.

Temple (Medium, Large, or Huge)

The main hall of worship, where a god, goddess, demigod, arch-devil, or demon lord is worshipped by reverent priests. There are almost certainly guardians here, and there may well be auras of divine or infernal magic as well.

Temple Cavern (Large or Huge)

A large cave temple.

Templum (Large or Huge)

An ancient (Roman-themed?) temple.

Tepidarium (Small, Medium, or Large)

A room with a warm-water Roman bath. If the complex has multiple bathes, the tepidarium is located between the frigidarium (cold bath) and caldarium (hot bath).

Terminus (Tiny, Small, or Medium)

A dead end to an ancient tunnel, or an ancient room which forms the end of a locale ("dungeon level").

Thalamium (Small or Medium)

An ancient (Greek- or Roman-themed) woman's bedchamber.

Thalamos *(Small or Medium)*

A Greek-themed sleeping room, typically for a woman.

Theater *(Large or Huge)*

A large room where seated or standing observers watch an entertainment of some kind.

Typically this means a play or dance, but more imaginatively might indicate observation of formal duels, illusions, acts of magic, torture, displays of thief craft or acrobatics, etc.

Therma *(Large or Huge)*

A large Roman bath complex of interconnected rooms. (Arguably, communal bathing was crucial to Roman health, longevity, and therefore learning and supremacy in a non-magical world.) Depending on the size of the area, this may include a caldarium, frigidarium, tepidarium, and/or a gymnasium.

Thermopolium *(Small or Medium)*

A room in which warm drinks are sold or provided (as to soldiers).

Tholos *(Small, Medium, or Large)*

A domed room or tomb.

Threshold *(Tiny, Small, Medium, or Large)*

A ceremonial area leading into a larger area, manifesting a transition in meaning or atmosphere. In dungeon design, this might mean (for example) the location where a tomb level leads into a temple sub-region. Or, it could mean that there is a magical field (dispel magic, for example) protecting the area before a great hall is reached, etc. As opposed to an entry, a threshold implies a major transition of meaning, security, wealth, or secrecy.

Throne Hall *(Huge)*

A very large hall where a guarded noble is seated upon a throne, holding audience with his or her subjects.

Throne Room *(Medium or Large)*

A smaller throne hall. Usually, a smaller throne room is used for more security, and a higher guard-to-visitor ratio.

Tomb *(Medium or Large)*

A room which is used to store the honored remains of the dead. A tomb is a "basic" room of burial. Compare variations such as sepulcher, oubliette, burial vault, crypt, etc.

Tomb Chamber *(Small)*

A small tomb. May be the lair of one or several undead creatures.

Tomb Shaft *(Tiny, Small, or Medium)*

A vertical tomb, or a room featuring shafts with vertical burials.

Tool Room *(Small or Medium)*

A room where tools are stored. The tools will typically belong to one type of work, with the worker's quarters or workroom nearby; examples include dyeing, leatherworking, paper making, pottery throwing, stonecutting, taxidermy, weaving, wood carving, etc.

Torcularium *(Small)*

A room situated around a wine or olive oil press.

Torture Chamber

(Small, Medium, or Large)

A room filled with implements (and as a traditional trope, an iron maiden) designed to physically punish prisoners.

Torture Pit(s)

(Small, Medium, or Large, with Large implying multiple pits)

A torture chamber with a low central floor, surrounded by an elevated observation area. For the perspective of someone entering through a door, the observation area would be the "floor" and the center of the room would be perhaps 10' or 20' below.

Refer also if needed to *The Classic Dungeon Design Guide, Book II* for torture room details.

Tower / Tower Chamber

(Small, Medium, Large, or Huge, with the Huge variant being almost wholly subterranean)

Outside, a tall, narrow fortification of several floors. Typically found at the corners of strongholds or fortified temples, but may also be found in a manor house or dilapidated mansion. Inside, likely a room or courtyard featuring a surprising tower fortification in the center for use by unreachable defenders. Some creatures (such as dark elves, netherworld gnomes, and dvergir) are known to make large subterranean areas with towers built up inside of them as well.

Training Hall *(Large or Huge)*

A large training room (or tower, as deemed appropriate). The size usually means that there is some form of mock combat occurring in the training area, and some safety measures to counteract haphazard activity.

Training Room *(Medium or Large)*

A room where important non-soldiers (spies, mages, scouts, rogues, etc.) practice their arts.

Treasure Cave *(Small or Medium)*

A cave where treasure is kept. Since caves can rarely be "sealed" (outside of the use of boulders and submerged tunnels), the existence of protective magic, traps, and/or guardian beasts is almost guaranteed.

Treasure Cavern *(Large or Huge)*

A large treasure cave, which means more treasure, and even more protective measures.

Treasure Chamber *(Small or Medium)*

A small treasure room. The use of "chamber" instead of "vault" may imply that the door is unlocked, probably because there is some more sinister form of protection for the place.

Treasure Vault *(Medium or Large)*

A room devoted solely to the protection of treasure; virtually certain to feature multiple locks, traps, and/or guardian monsters.

Treasury *(Medium or Large)*

The treasure vault belonging to the stronghold's ruler, or an important official.

Triclinium *(Small or Medium)*

A Roman-themed dining room. To be specific, a triclinium might be located away from a kitchen and/or preparatory areas, because it is intended as a place of quiet and relaxation … the servants / slaves are made to bring dishes to the triclinium location. The name "triclinium" implies that there is a central table surrounded by three dining couches.

Trophy Hall *(Large or Huge)*

A large room where trophies are displayed. In an FRPG, this is likely to include items from defeated monsters, such as mounted dragon heads, giant scorpion claws, acid mantis chitin, nightmare hooves, etc. Compare also hunter's hall; a trophy hall sometimes implies conquest and intimidation more than hunting for sport or territory control.

Trophy Room (Small or Medium)

A small trophy hall.

Tuppi (Small, Medium, or Large)

An Akkadian- or Babylonian-themed archive (for clay tablets).

Turret / Turret Vault

(Small, Medium, or Large)

A small tower, or a room with a raised enclosed center where troops can attack intruders (perhaps with pole arms).

A turret vault can also exist underground; see tower chamber (which implies a larger tower).

Turrinum *(Small, Medium, or Large)*

An Akkadian- or Babylonian-themed room of general purpose.

U IS FOR UNDERCROFT

Unctorium (Small)

A Roman-themed anointing room.

Unctuarium (Small or Medium)

A Roman-themed room for the storage and application of oils, unguents, and perfumes.

Undercroft

(Small, Medium, Large, or Huge)

A large, vaulted subterranean place. Typically beneath a church or a temple.

Undercroft (Special)

(Small, Medium, Large, or Huge)

An odd, specialized use of an undercroft. This might be a kitchen, prison, undead guard room, netherworld mount stable, or even a cattle-hold or shop (as we find historically attested).

Underground Lake (Large or Huge)

A natural body of freshwater in a subterranean locale. Deeper and larger than a pool.

Underground Mausoleum (Huge)

A vast hall in which an entire Mausoleum has been built as a separate structure (the room surrounds the edifice).

Underground Palace (Huge)

A (very rare) entire palatial structure built underground, either as a dungeon level, or inside of an immense cavern. Highly magical, and crafted through the application of great powers.

Examples include the legend heading this section, the iron city of Dis, the palace of Nergal in the netherworld, and the palace of Hades.

Underground Pyramid (Huge)

A vast hall in which an entire pyramid has been built as a separate structure (the room surrounds the edifice).

Underground River (Huge)

A large natural river flowing underground, connecting caverns and possibly dungeon levels. You will probably want to reroll if you don't want a water theme for your dungeon.

Underground Swamp (Huge)

A wet cavern with an unusual ecosystem, perhaps featuring water-holding fungi, quicksand, tar pits, magical moss, mud pits, giant mushrooms, and / or misty waterfalls.

Underground Ziggurat (Huge)

A vast hall in which an entire ziggurat has been built as a separate structure (the room surrounds the edifice).

Undervault (Large or Huge)

A large, secure subterranean room. It is probably protected by locks, magic, and/or small defensive structures built inside.

Underwater Cave (Small or Medium)

A submerged cave covered by deep water. Unlike a submerged cave, the underwater cave may have a (magical?) air pocket.

Underwater Cavern (Large or Huge)

A large submerged cave.

Unfinished Chamber *(Small)*

A room which is only partially-constructed. It may be lacking flagstones, columns, a door, all four walls, etc.

Unfinished Hall *(Large or Huge)*

A very large unfinished chamber.

Unfinished Room *(Medium)*

A larger unfinished chamber.

Unfinished Tomb

(Small, Medium, or Large)

An unfinished chamber or room, which is also a burial place.

Unstable Cave *(Small or Medium)*

A dangerous form of cave, perhaps filled with rubble, fractured, or subject to acidic decay. The ceiling, floor, and / or wall may be ready to collapse (particularly if there is violent magical combat in the area).

Unstable Cavern *(Large or Huge)*

A large unstable cave.

Urbatu *(Small)*

An Akkadian- or Babylonian-themed bedchamber.

Ursu *(Small or Medium)*

An Akkadian- or Babylonian-themed bedroom.

Usgidum *(Tiny or Small)*

A narrow Akkadian- or Babylonian-themed chamber.

Utility Chamber *(Small)*

A small utility room. There will probably be miscellaneous "dungeon dressing" items stowed here for adventurers to ponder over.

Utility Room *(Medium or Large)*

Similar to a workroom, but the room either (a) is used infrequently, (b) features heavy equipment (perhaps block and tackle), or (c) is a combination work and storage area.

V IS FOR VAULT

Vault (Small, Medium, or Large)

A room that is intentionally made difficult to access, and is used to secure valuable goods (e.g., treasure vault) or things that are not meant to be disturbed (e.g., burial vault). A "vault" without further description might be a room that is locked or sealed, but which does not contain things of obvious importance (the vault might be plundered, the treasure moved, or the coffins ransacked, etc.)

Vaulted Cave (Small or Medium)

A cave with a (naturally) high ceiling, beyond the usual 10-15'.

Vaulted Cavern (Large or Huge)

A large vaulted cave. Depending on the cavern's dimensions and composition, the ceiling might be between 50' and 100' high.

Vaulted Chamber (Small or Medium)

A chamber with a high ceiling, beyond the usual 10-15'. Compare with domed chamber; a dome is rounded, while a vault is usually angular.

Vaulted Hall (Large or Huge)

A very large vaulted chamber; a hall with a high ceiling.

Vaulted Room (Medium or Large)

A relatively large and/or high-ceilinged vaulted room.

Verdigris Cave (Small or Medium)

A cave covered in greenish verdigris (think, for example, of the Statue of Liberty). Verdigris is caused by the presence of copper and acid.

Verdigris Cavern (Large or Huge)

A large verdigris cave.

Vertical Cave (Small or Medium)

Technically, a cave that is higher / deeper than it is wider. From the entrant's perspective, the cave might go down, up, or both, in a series of ledges.

Vertical Cavern (Large or Huge)

A large (and dangerous) vertical cave, with much climbing required. Multiple successive precipices within the cavern might feature drops of 20-50'.

Vestiary (Tiny, Small, or Medium)

A room where sacred clothing is kept. Similar to a sacristy, but more narrow in purpose.

Vestibule (Small or Medium)

A small and formal antechamber, entry, or reception room. The term likely implies some feature of Roman architecture (perhaps two columns, or an arched entryway, or frescoed walls).

Vestibulum (Small or Medium)

An ancient vestibule.

Vestry (Small or Medium)

A robing room for clerics (or other priests). Compared to a "normal" robing room, the vestry is likely either (a) used by lower-level persons, or (b) partially used for storage (for example, for holy symbols and processional pieces).

Vigil (Tiny, Small, or Medium)

A formal guard post, lookout, or tomb sentry location (typically guarding against robbers or defilers), which is always occupied.

Vinery *(Small, Medium, or Large)*

A conservatory / greenhouse where vine-bearing plants (such as grapes) are grown. This could also be a place where deadly monstrous plants are cultivated.Underground, there will probably be magical light and/or water sources.

Volcanic Cave *(Small or Medium)*

A magma cave that is situated very near to, or is part of, a volcano. Alternately, this could be an older cave formed by volcanic processes where magma is no longer present, but that description can be misleading and is not encouraged here.

Volcanic Cavern *(Large or Huge)*

A large volcanic cave.

W IS FOR WATCHROOM

Wadyt (Large or Huge)

An Egyptian-themed hall of columns.

Waiting Chamber (Small)

A small waiting room.

Waiting Room (Medium or Large)

A place where people wait before moving on to some more important engagement. There is an implication that a paid, formal, or secret service is being waited for. In an FRPG, a waiting room would likely be situated before a reception room. Such a space could be needed by a wealthy and popular archmage, sage, duchess, high priest, etc.

Walk-In Closet (Tiny or Small)

A very large closet (comparatively); a small room intended for the storage of valuable clothing. In an FRPG, such a space would belong to a Count, Duke, Marchioness, etc., and would likely be 10'x10' or 10'x20', perhaps a bit larger.

Walled-Up Chamber (Small)

A chamber whose entrances have been sealed up with bricks and mortar. This might be a structural necessity, or it could be more sinister (hiding a body, protecting a trapped treasure, or keeping monsters inside from coming out).

Walled-Up Corridor (Small or Medium)

A former corridor which has been walled up (as above), creating a very narrow impromptu room.

Walled-Up Room (Medium or Large)

A larger walled-up chamber.

War Room (Medium or Large)

A planning room (see that entry, P) that is used solely for the planning and conduct of war. As you may know, no fighting is allowed here.

Ward (Medium or Large)

An open space which is smaller than a courtyard. See also the notes on subterranean spaces under that entry (C).

Wardrobe (Tiny)

A large armoire, featuring a door-like entry and a space for storing coats or clothing. A perfect place for a secret room or magical gateway, as a famous novel once noted.

Wardrobe Room (Small or Medium)

A room featuring one or more wardrobes (above).

Warming Room (Small, Medium, or Large)

A room heated by fire, steam, or magical heat, intended to warm denizens who have cold quarters (monks, guards, soldiers, etc.); will usually include one or more fireplaces or firepits. See also calefactory, which is an older term for the same concept; the distinction being that a calefactory is probably centuries old.

Warren (Tiny or Small)

A fairly large burrow, or a set of several interconnected burrows. See also plural entry.

Warrens (Medium, Large, or Huge)

A huge maze of interconnected burrows. Size of the tunnels can range from tiny (rabbits) to small (giant rats) to quite large (troglodytes), but rarely wider than 5' at most.

Washroom *(Tiny, Small, or Medium)*

A room with cold and hot water, for cleansing. May include, or be situated by, a garderobe. The water may be magical, but keep in mind that historically the Romans, Mycenaeans and Minoans had running water to varying degrees.

Wasi *(Small, Medium, or Large)*

An Egyptian-themed ruined chamber or ruined room.

Watchroom *(Tiny, Small, or Medium)*

A room where guards, or a noble, can observe passersby. A combination guardroom and overlook in purpose.

Water Cave *(Small or Medium)*

Similar to a cave of pools, but the water is separated into large puddles and/or rivulets, making walking here rather difficult.

Water Cavern *(Large or Huge)*

A large water cave.

Waterfall Cavern *(Large or Huge)*

A cave with a natural waterfall and river / stream.

Wda / Weda *(Small or Medium)*

An Egyptian-themed storeroom.

Weaving Room *(Small or Medium)*

A room where clothing is woven, perhaps doubling as a storeroom for textiles.

Webbed Cave *(Small or Medium)*

A cave covered in either (giant?) spider webs, or web-like mineral filaments.

Webbed Cavern *(Large or Huge)*

A large webbed cave. Almost certainly the lair of one or more giant spiders, or perhaps even the Spiders of Leng.

Well *(Tiny, Small, or Medium)*

A vertical shaft, usually with a rope and bucket, where water is drawn up for use. Compare well room; the terms are sometimes used interchangeably.

Well Room *(Small or Medium)*

A room with a well in it.

Wharf Cavern *(Large)*

A large cavern with an underground river or lake, a dock, and perhaps even a boat or two.

Whirlpool Cave *(Small or Medium)*

A dangerous cave along the route of an underground river, where the entire "floor" is taken up by a whirlpool.

Whirlpool Cavern *(Large or Huge)*

A large whirlpool cave. Since whirlpools have difficulty forming in broad waters, the cavern probably features an underground river course, a hollow with the whirlpool, and dry banks on one or both sides.

Winch Cavern *(Medium or Large)*

A cavern that is used as a winch room, with pits leading downward and machinery in place.

Winch Pit *(Tiny or Small)*

A pit with a block and tackle pulley system, so that barrels, boxes, crates, etc. can be lowered down to levels below. From adventurers' perspective, this will be a floor pit with a pulley over it, or a room with a hole in the ceiling and ropes hanging down. If ropes and pulleys are no longer present, this is simply a pit.

Winch Room (*Medium or Large*)

A room with one or more winch pits. Or, a room which controls machinery, perhaps for a drawbridge, gate, trap, covered well, etc.

Wine Cave (*Small or Medium*)

A cave where wine is stored, usually under carefully controlled circumstances (temperature, light, humidity, etc.).

Wine Cavern (*Large or Huge*)

A large wine cave.

Wine Cellar (*Small or Medium*)

An underground area, with a strictly-controlled temperature, where wine barrels are stored.

Wine Vault (*Small, Medium, or Large*)

A secure wine cellar, where valuable wines are stored.

Withdrawing Chamber (*Small*)

A small withdrawing room.

Withdrawing Room (*Medium*)

An older and more formal term for a drawing room; in the game, this likely means an historical place of long standing within a stronghold or manor house.

Wizard's Laboratory

(*Small, Medium, or Large*)

A magic-user's laboratory, which will likely feature potions, tools, alchemical mixtures, monster body parts, and/or partially-crafted magic items. Refer to *The Classic Dungeon Design Guide, Book II* for possible contents.

Wizard's Workroom (*Small or Medium*)

A magic-user's workroom, which will likely feature potions, material spell components, conjured monsters, and/or magical traps.

When there is a distinction between the two, a laboratory is used for experimentation and a workroom is used for the duplication of results leading to a finished product (scroll, potion, etc.).

Wndwt / Wenedewet (*Small*)

An Egyptian-themed hollow or pit.

Work Chamber (*Small*)

A small workroom.

Workers' Hall (*Large or Huge*)

A large workroom, or cluster of interconnected workrooms.

Workpit (*Tiny or Small*)

A pit where slaves or minions work on something unpleasant (mining, bailing water, hacking meat, etc.). Refer to *The Classic Dungeon Design Guide, Book II* for potential slave and minion types.

Workroom (*Medium or Large*)

A room devoted to work. This may be a noble's work area, but it more likely belongs to a tradesman or artisan. Examples: brewer, glazier, leather worker, scribe, weaver, etc.

Workshop (*Medium or Large*)

A secure area where work is done (perhaps the creation of armor and weapons, the repair of tools, construction of counter-siege works, etc.). As a point of distinction, a workshop is usually better equipped than a workroom, and implies more laborers might be present.

Wsxt / Wesixet (*Large or Huge*)

An Egyptian-themed hall.

X is for Xenodocheum

Xawt / Xawet (Small or Medium)

An Egyptian-themed altar chamber.

Xenodocheion (Small, Medium, or Large)

An ancient (Greek-themed) quarters area for guests, strangers, wanderers, etc. If no longer occupied, this area is likely haunted in some way.

Xenodocheum (Small, Medium, or Large)

A Roman-themed Xenodocheion.

Xnmt / Xenemet (Small, Medium, or Large)

An Egyptian-themed well room or cistern.

Xnr / Xener (Small or Medium)

An Egyptian-themed harem.

Xnrt / Xeneret (Small or Medium)

An Egyptian-themed locked chamber.

Xnty / Xenety (Small or Medium)

An Egyptian-themed entry chamber.

Z is for Ziggurat Hall

Zaggu (Small or Medium)

An Akkadian- or Babylonian-themed sanctum or sanctum sanctorum.

Ziggurat Cavern (Large or Huge)

A cavern in which an entire ziggurat has been built as a separate structure (the room surrounds the edifice). Or, the cavern might feature two or even three relatively small ziggurats.

Ziggurat Hall (Large or Huge)

Similar to a ziggurat cavern, above. An alternate classic dungeon trope is an inverted ziggurat hall, in which tiers of walkways lead down to a bottom reach which might be 40-60' below the entry level.

Zoo (or Menagerie) (Large or Huge)

A large area where fantastic beasts and/or monsters are held, typically for curiosity, experimentation, breeding, or as guardian beasts.

As always, room types can be further modified using *The Classic Dungeon Design Guide I & II*, as well as the *Chaotic Descriptor Table* GM options tome. Together, these books will provide you with an endless assemblage of room types for any type of dungeon that you might conceive of.

As with any random system, the tables and the Labyrinth Lexicon can break if you lean too hard on them. For example, if you roll a manor house using purely random rolls – instead of placing an entry at the front, stairs up leading to bedchambers, a pantry next to a kitchen, and so forth – you will need to work harder to justify the locations of rooms and chambers. But as a filling and finishing tool, this lexicon will serve you well.

Chapter V:
Methods to Madness

Making Sense of Unexpected Results

Due to the (perhaps daunting) extensiveness of this volume's Labyrinth Lexicon, you will find that there are some very obscure, archaic, and/or unusual rooms featured in the results.

This is by design. The tables are intended to maximize the amount of coherent variety that you can put into your dungeon designs to make them plausible as well as unique. However, due to massive set of potential results, the system will sometimes give you random results that are difficult to use or even entirely nonsensical.

The Lexicon generation system cannot prevent itself from (as but one example) putting an "entry chamber" within a dead end dungeon corner, or an Egyptian-themed storeroom in your classically Nordic setting. Therefore, if you roll up a cultural motif (Akkadian, Egyptian, Norse, etc.) that you do not think you can use, you can do one of two things: **[1]** Replace the cultural motif with the country from your own campaign where the dungeon is situated; **[2]** Revert the room type to standard (a "Nordic-themed guardroom" then becomes a "guardroom"); or, **[3]** replace the motif with a racial one of your preference (dwarven, elven, orcish, etc.) that suits the intent of your overall dungeon creation.

Similarly, from time to time the random rolls will — despite the thematic safeguards, which I have strived to make useful to you — insist upon giving you an unworkable or highly unexpected result. When this occurs, you can either reroll, or you can get creative and try to make the random result work no matter what. Do keep in mind that most dungeons in the World of Oldskull are ancient, rebuilt, damaged, refurbished, and magical places, where dozens if not hundreds of different factions vie for superiority over time. When you have (for example) a situation where an arena is adjacent to a bedroom, what does that actually mean?

The first solution is to once again consider the Original Room Usage vs. the Current Room Usage, as described earlier in this tome.

Perhaps the arena function is indeed still the Current Usage for room A, but it was actually built (centuries ago) as a ballroom. And the bedroom is the Original Usage of room B, which is now being used as an observation chamber. That situation makes a bit more sense, and some curious digging by the intrepid adventurers might reveal some odd items — say, a shattered dusty bed stuffed back into a corner — that will reveal some mysterious glimpses of the otherwise unknown past.

These examples of deep world building will make an impact upon your players. They will want to further explore your world, and to solves its mysteries, because every mystery leads to more paths of possibility in an endless realm that is filled with enigmas, unanswered questions, and darkly majestic wonders.

However, that world building approach can certainly take up a fair amount of Game Master creative time. Sometimes you will want a quicker fix while still paying attention to the random room aberrations in your design.

Therefore, the second potential solution is the "It's Magic" paradigm. Let us say that the arena is a real room, while the bedroom is an elaborate illusion cast over a guardroom. Does the illusion still make sense, or is it a vestige of the past which has become an oddity outside of time while the rest of the dungeon has moved on? (That, again, is for you to decide.)

Or conversely, depending on the setting you're devising, the bedroom might be real and the arena is an entertaining illusion created by the bored wizard who watches over the ballroom from his aerie. But in either of these design cases, the omnipresent existence of magic serves as a ready justification for the unusual dungeon settings and seemingly random juxtapositions of room types.

A third solution, should neither of these approaches appeal, is to reposition the anomalous result. Let's say that you like the arena where it is (in the center of the level map, perhaps), and you want to use a bedroom too, but the roll just doesn't make sense for the space that is close to the arena. In that case, you can use the created bedroom description and simply put it somewhere more appropriate. For example, you could position the bedroom in a cluster of small chambers of yet to be determined nature, up in the northeast corner of your map. Then you can reroll the bedroom result for the space adjacent to the arena until you find something more appropriate, such as a weapons room, or an observation chamber.

There are other unorthodox solutions that you might enjoy exploring too. Intuitively, a fourth potential workaround would be to create a built-over annex. For example, the arena might be the original space, and the bedroom is ancient and no longer used as such. This means that the lost bedroom might be walled in and forgotten, with (for example) an eldritch skeleton lying in inches of dust upon the ancient bed. The only way to get into this (treasure?) room is for the map-making adventurers to notice the "empty void" in their nearly-completed dungeon level map, and then for them to knock down a (strange-looking and poorly built?) wall, and crawl into the forgotten room to see what's actually there. Whichever solution you decide upon, you can always choose the one that works best for you in the moment. I do however recommend trying to work with odd random results whenever you can, because the justifications you need to devise to "make it work" will often get your creative juices flowing in your other dungeon design challenges as well.

THE OLDSKULL WORKSHOP:
A DETAILED EXAMPLE OF
RANDOM CAVE CREATION

If you are not yet experienced in improvisatory dungeon design, it might help to follow along with several demonstrative processes where I roll up random results and then work my way through the problems and opportunities as they arise.

In the following example, I will work with completely random rolls, very little preparation, no pre-existing dungeon map to speak of, and zero preconceptions. In other words, I will begin with almost nothing and then let the Labyrinth

Lexicon guide my thought process in designing a new and unique dungeon.

I will roll up 10 random rooms, consider their potential relation to one another, and illustrate how the justifications I come up with (for the stranger results) can be turned into cascading idea generators to spur my further design work.

I roll up ten random caves on the Cave System Room Table. They are as follows: Cavity, Steam Cave, Cesspit Cavern, Cave of Ancestors, Cave of Paintings, Boulder Cave, Cave of Stalactites, Mud Cave, Geyser Cavern, and Roost.

This unique selection already tells me quite a few things I didn't know about my cave system, as follows:

❖ **[1] My cave system is hot, muddy, and geothermal** (Steam Cave, Mud Cave, Geyser Cavern).

❖ **[2] My cave system has dangerous stone features** (Boulder Cave, Cave of Stalactites). This includes hollows made by pooling acid (Cavity).

❖ **[3] My cave system has an ancient tribal presence** (Cave of Ancestors, Cave of Paintings).

❖ **[4] My cave system is currently occupied by some kind of flying and/or intelligent monsters** (Cesspit Cavern, Cave of Stalactites notes concerning flying or ceiling-crawling monsters, and Roost).

And so from just these four general themes, I can already surmise the following: these caves are ancient, and have been occupied for a long time. Why would hot steamy caves be occupied by many generations of denizens? A good question. I can think of two reasons off the top of my head: **[1]** the heat is a feature, not a bug (meaning these hot caves are in an icy land, and coveted), and **[2]** the monsters dwelling here are fire-loving creatures of some kind. Let us use both of these ideas.

And what kind of monsters live here? I do not precisely know the answer yet, but they venerate their ancestors, they make cave paintings, and they (or their mounts, or their guardian beasts) fly and/or climb ceilings.

Now what do I do with that kind of emergent information? That really depends on the types of monsters I want to use, the experience levels of the Player Characters, and the types of creatures that are associated with the primary monster.

As a low-level example, I might decide that the ancestor-worshipping monsters are cultists, the ancestors are ghouls, and the roosting / climbing guardians are large red spiders. As a mid-level example, I decide the ancestor-worship monsters might be fire-breathing salamander men, the ancestors would perhaps be fire salamanders, and the roosting / climbing guardians would be giant pterodactyls. As an epic- or high-level example, the ancestor-worshipping monsters could perhaps be fire giants, the ancestors could be corrupted titans, and the roosting and climbing guardians could be chimeras and a pair of fire-breathing dragons. Any of these combinations can work just fine with the information provided.

And how do I start drawing a map, using just this core of ten vague room descriptions? First, we will take some advice from our good friend Yoda: *Unlearn what you have learned.*

Take a piece of graph paper, but instead of starting with the dungeon entrance, start with the middle of the main monster lair. And instead of starting in a corner, start your map in the middle of the paper. Choose the biggest random room result; in this selection, that is the Geyser Cavern, which is either Large or Huge. Draw a nice big Geyser Cavern in the middle of the paper. You can freehand it if you like, or you can search Google Images for "Geyser Cavern Map" and see what comes up. (You will see a selection of national park maps, game grids, some pictures of Yellowstone and a glimpse of Carlsbad Caverns, in the search I just did now. Some of this is background lore is useful, and some not. I bookmark some pictures of rainbow-hued geyser pools in Yellowstone to use as inspiration for my cave's pools and tiers.)

Make sure you have lots of pools, mud pots, descending and ascending tiers, and branching tunnels leading to other places. Maybe even put in a stalagmite throne, and a rickety bridge across one or more of the pools. Just assume that this "biggest" result is the most important center of your dungeon level, and go from there.

And why is the Geyser Cavern important here? Another good question. There could be lots of reasons. For one, it's probably the lair of the level's big monster. Using the above examples I provided, that's probably the salamander man chieftain and his shaman; or, the cultists and their Ur-ancestor the mud ghast (a monster I just made up); or, the fire giant thane and his two-headed giant guards.

Also, this room probably has the biggest treasure in the dungeon level too. Maybe it is a cauldron of molten gold, a standard trove, or a powerful ice scepter. Who knows? And if your dungeon is going to be more than one level, this room is probably one of the main ways down or up. There might be a sacrificial chasm, a magical gate to the Elemental Plane of Fire, or a winding calcite "stairway" up to sacred caverns higher up in the steam.

Once you have this core set up, you can decide where the other rooms should go. For the sake of example, I will say that the Geyser Cavern is the central base of the monsters, the "northern" reaches are claimed by these same monsters, the "southern" reaches are untamed and dangerous, the "eastern" reaches are partially abandoned, and the "western" reaches belong to rival monsters. Why? I'm simply using a Gygaxian design trick of variations on a theme, keeping the Geyser theme going while providing as much thematic variation as possible. Each of the five sub-regions of the level (NSEW / Center) is slightly different.

Using this general configuration, I split the other rooms up as follows:

❖ To the north, in the main monster lair area, there's the Cave of Ancestors and the Cave of Paintings. These places are made, revered, and maintained by the main monster type (cultists, salamander men, or fire giants).

❖ To the south, in the untamed area, are the hazardous obstruction caves. These are the Boulder Cave, the Mud Cave, and the Cavity (with nearby acid pools).

❖ To the east, in the abandoned area, are the refuse caves. This just includes the Cesspit Cavern for now, but that can be a huge place, filled with some kind of scavengers or carrion eaters.

❖ To the west, in the rival monster area, I'll put the Steam Cave and the Cave of Stalactites. I don't know what lives here yet, but they might be (for example) netherworld gnomes, pech, or even aquatic monsters of some kind.

This setup means I only have not placed the Roost. I decide that this belongs to guardian flying monsters (pterodactyls, chimeras, or perhaps giant bats for the cultists), and will be a defended area near the dungeon entrance. So because the strong monsters hold the northern reach and I want the PCs to fully explore the level, I will put the Roost and the dungeon entrance together toward the southern part of the map ... let's say the southeastern part, away from the rival monsters. The Roost through a series of guardian areas (not yet generated) will lead to the main Geyser Cave region.

From here, I can either design the rest of the dungeon level by myself using the information I've already discerned from the random results, or I can keep rolling to see what the dice and destiny want the dungeon to become.

This is a very crude setup, but nevertheless it shows how I have taken the 10 random results, clustered them thematically, made sense of the disparate pieces of information with pairings, and provided multiple solutions to the mix, based on my own preferences and the monster populations which will challenge my players' characters.

A SECOND EXAMPLE, OF RANDOM DUNGEON GENERATION

For an example of the creation of a "pure" iconic prison dungeon, I will make another ten random rolls. This time, I use the Dungeon Room Table and allow some rolls to go over 900 (which means that there will be some non-dungeon areas present, too). This gives me a bizarre and problematic set of random results to puzzle over, as follows: a Hideout, and then an Access Room, Kukku, Execution Hall, Hwt Ka, Grand Aquarium, Sludge Pit, Kimah, and then a Prison Block, and also a Submerged Chamber.

This is a rather tough set of results to easily justify, chiefly because there are three different cultures to work with here: Babylonian, Egyptian, and Sumerian.

But this is a good challenge to have because it will demand some creative thinking. So I am going to make this work! We're going to need to think outside of the box here about a lot of different things. We will see what I can learn first, from these 10 random room selections:

❖ **[1] There are three ancient Earth cultures to contend with** (Kukku, Hwt Ka, Kimah).

❖ **[2] There is an implication of water and water monsters** (Grand Aquarium, Sludge Pit, Submerged Chamber).

❖ **[3] There is an implied presence of an intelligent and unexpected personage** (Hideout, Access Room).

So how do I deal with this identified challenge? In the World of Oldskull – which is based on mythic and real-world Earth – it's not too difficult. Babylonia, Egypt, and Sumeria are all in the same general region (North Africa and the Middle East), and these cultures traded and warred with one another frequently enough that I can easily say there is a dungeon featuring all three cultures.

In a campaign world that is not the World of Oldskull, I would want to place this dungeon in an isolated arid desert, where the older civilizations (inspired by these three) are lost and forgotten beneath the sands. So I know that this is a dungeon, a prison (Prison Block), and a place of punishment. The Babylonian Kukku is a descent to the netherworld, the Egyptian Hwt Ka is a funerary chapel, and the Sumerian Kimah is a tomb.

Already, I can conceive that the dungeon and the caves beneath it were Babylonian in ancient times, and that a later generation (Sumerians) worshiped here and entombed their dead here, without fully understanding what the Babylonian presence was all about. (This situation is chronologically reversed from Earth's history, but that's no big deal for a pulp fantasy perspective.)

And we can continue to develop our themes by deciding that the Egyptians built a chapel here, but to put a variation on the theme I will say that the Egyptians came even later, that they knew the place was accursed, and that their funerary chapel is a holy shrine for guardians who are attempting to keep the Babylonian evil at bay. So already, I have changed the weakness in the random results (three disparate cultures to unify thematically) into a strength (I know three eras of the dungeon's history after about two minutes of justification).

I will decide that the water theme belongs to the middle Sumerian layer of the dungeon's history. Why? Because I have already decided that the Babylonians are the "villain guys," the Egyptians are the "lawful guys," and I haven't added anything interesting to the Sumerians yet. So they get water and the water rooms to keep them as interesting aspect of the cultural mix.

Now how do I use all of this new information? It takes a little bit of research to develop into something that has some heft.

First, I research several of the Babylonian gods of darkness, imprisonment, and evil. There is overlap with Sumeria and Akkad as I research the different cultures, but since we are already dealing with blended cultures, that's actually a good thing.

Good results include Ereshkigal and Dagon (mostly through his associations with the Deep Ones, via Howard Phillips Lovecraft). In this particular instance I decide that I do not want the Cthulhu Mythos to override my three already-crowded themes, so I instead choose Ereshkigal, the Queen of the Netherworld.

I decide that she will be the Immortal that the dungeon is dedicated to, and that she is the one who is worshipped in the Kukku locale and the netherworld below. Perhaps this is even the deep gateway to the Babylonian hell, and the "Prison Block" is actually the lair of the damned? That is actually quite interesting. This is not a dungeon to cage the living; it is a dungeon to cage the restless dead. Next, I research good Egyptian protector gods of the underworld. That is actually pretty easy, and I come up with ideas to include Anubis and Osiris right away. Osiris is more about resurrection and life after death, and Anubis is more about protection and ushering souls into the nether. So the good guys will be priests (and jackal men) of Anubis.

Lastly, I pause to consider Sumeria and the water theme. This leads me to the concept of the Abzu, the great mythic netherworld ocean in Sumerian mythology. The Abzu is sacred to Enki, the god of creation, magic, artifice and fertility.

So drawing these themes into a chronology, I come up with this: First, there was Ereshkigal in the netherworld. She called to men to worship her, and to bring her the damned ones to be judged. The ancient dungeon was built as a subterranean prison-temple to her, where the damned were imprisoned and executed. For some reason (perhaps war or cataclysm?) this practice only lasted a few centuries and then mostly died out, driven back underground.

A later culture, let us say the Sumerians of Enki, worshipped here and (as the Kimah room tells us) buried their dead here. They knew the dungeon harbored a descent to the Abzu nether sea, but did not know about the secret descent to Ereshkigal's palace. So they built their own tombs here. Let us say the spirit of Ereshkigal loathed this outrage, and eventually sent a wave of undead to wipe them out. The undead then spilled out onto the surface, and was put down by the Egyptians of Anubis. The priests of Anubis kept the dungeon sealed for generations, but now only a few elderly jackal priests survive. Enter the greedy treasure hunters into the picture …

So in this case, we've conceived of a lot of the dungeon from the room descriptions and their cultures, not necessarily their physical features. But in doing so, how do we draw the dungeon? We start in the middle again, with the largest and most important room. In this case, that's the Prison Block. I am going to make that the refuge of the imprisoned undead who serve Ereshkigal. If this is a low-level dungeon, they're skeletons and zombies. If it is a mid-level dungeon, they're ghuls and ghasts. And if it's a high level dungeon, they're wights and wraiths. Following the "split into sub-themes" trick again, let's give this dungeon level some sub-regions. The central part is Babylonian, the northern part is Sumerian, the eastern part is Egyptian, the western part is contested, and the southern part is mostly ruined and unclaimed. So here's how I split the rooms:

❖ **Central / Babylonian:** Kukku (leading down to the netherworld), Prison Block

❖ **Northern / Sumerian:** Grand Aquarium, Kimah, Submerged Chamber

❖ **Southern / Abandoned:** Access Room, Hideout

❖ **Eastern / Egyptian:** Hwt Ka (and also the dungeon entrance, which I decide on now because I want the PCs to have immediate access to potential allies before they explore this dangerous realm)

❖ **Western / Contested:** Execution Hall, Sludge Pit (and lots more random rolling needed, since I haven't fleshed out this idea very much)

This brings up a question I almost forgot: Who is in the hideout? That likely depends upon how much you want to intensify this already complex situation. I personally decide that I don't want to dilute the themes with any additional cultures or monster types, so the hideout belongs to one of the following people (my random ideas):

[1] If it's someone Egyptian, it's a good (but almost insane) high-level cleric who is trying to summon good spirits to keep the tomb sealed.

[2] If it's someone Babylonian, it's a powerful death priestess trying to break the Egyptian "tomb sealers" once and for all.

[3] If it's someone Sumerian, it's an intelligent water monster (like a water naga) that is the last remnant of its culture. I feel that any of these ideas could work, and any of them would give you a very different dungeon to design.

A THIRD EXAMPLE, OF HAUNTED MANSION CREATION

And now that we have covered the two most iconic subterranean environments (cave systems and prison dungeons), we can flex our creative muscles a bit by designing a manor house concept.

We begin with ten random rolls for room types, and the following ideas are revealed to us via the Labyrinth Lexicon: we have a Cenaculum, Cartographers' Hall, Peristyle, a Frigidarium, and then a Ceremonial Chamber, a Waiting Room, a Horological Hall, a Storeroom (Masonry subtype), Gynaeceum, and Icehouse.

There are a few easy associations that we can already devise just from these first idea generation seeds. Of course, I see the Frigidarium and the Icehouse go together right away. To keep things interesting and my creativity active, I'm going to cluster the Ceremonial Chamber into that group as well. The Cenaculum and Gynaeceum are both Roman-themed with their Latin names (in my campaign, that means ancient and venerated), so I will put them together too even though I'm not sure they fit with one another. The Peristyle strikes me as being ancient / ancestral too, so let's include it here for further thought.

The last group includes the oddballs: the Cartographers' Hall, Waiting Room, Horological Hall and Masonry Storeroom. None of those things have anything to do with one another. Oh well. Let's make it work! We'll come up with something strange, I'm sure.

The important thing to remember when designing a new manor house dungeon is that the space is instilled with the haunted essence of the bloodline that rules there, even if the bloodline was wiped out ... ghosts will remain if nothing else. So for each room theme, we will want to come up with a creepy mystery that tells the story of the accursed bloodline that lived (lives?) here.

First, we have the Frigidarium and the Icehouse. I'm going to say that this family loves cold, and that's why these very unusual rooms are here. What types of people love cold? Off the top of my head: Eskimos, Vikings, Skraelings, snow elves, and mountain dwarves.

I want to go with something regal, decadent, cultured and unusual for my dungeon, so we'll say that this mansion is home to an eccentric (and mad) ancestral line of snow elves. So why do they have this Frigidarium? That's where they purify themselves of curses and dark thoughts, in the manner of their homeland. And the Icehouse? That's where the magical ice comes from that they use to empower the Frigidarium and other forms of magic (maybe things like animated ice statues, or flying crystal weapons as "guards") throughout the entire mansion. How about the Ceremonial Chamber? That's where they have a shrine to their ice goddess (no clue who she is, but we can design her later using shrine generation material in *Book II*), and frescoes and statues that remind them of their homeland.

For the second group, we have a Cenaculum, a Gynaeceum, and a Peristyle. The Peristyle surrounds a courtyard or garden open to the sky. I'm going to say it surrounds a sacred garden filled with plants from the homeland, like ice lilies, snow jaws (cold-resistant man-eating flytraps), frost lotuses and icicle blossoms. I just made those things up off the top of my head; we can design them later. The garden is kept magically shielded from the sky and outside intrusion; to justify these design decisions, I decide now that the elven bloodline favors magic-users. The Cenaculum is an ancient dining room. That's fine; we'll just say that the Cenaculum is the oldest room in the house. In fact, it used to be the entire house, a thousand years ago when this magical mansion was just an inn. There will be some interesting and grisly trophies there for the PCs to marvel at, such as humongous ancient ice boars (now extinct), pale blue winter wolf pelts, and the skeleton of a white dragon forming the chandeliers. The bloodline is guarded by lesser elves, who are hunters and monster slayers. This is their trophy hall.

So what about the Gynaeceum? That's a Roman-style room where only women can quarter. Let's say this is a room where the hunters and monster slayers live. We will say that their clan is matriarchal, and all of them are female. They serve the magi fanatically, honoring a vow made centuries ago when the magi saved their ancestors in battle.

Moving on: the Cartographers' Hall is fairly easy to work with; it will show their homeland, the caves under the homeland where the monsters who drove them into exile dwell, and the surrounding borderlands. PCs will learn a lot about a hidden and dying elven kingdom here, and a netherworld of ice and geysers. How about the Waiting Room? The boring way to design this room would be to say that strangers enter the room, and then they sit and wait until servants get them to meet with the aristocratic elven magi. But a more interesting idea would be that the hunter clan, serving the snow magi, need to wait here before they can meet with their masters if they want any favors or extra gifts. They all line up once a year as supplicants, and they all stand in a circle trying to stay awake. They start hallucinating and babbling, and in the end only the most enduring hunter is left standing. That hunter (huntress, actually) is treated like a prince

/ princess for a month and has one wish (yes, magical) granted. That's a little messed up psychologically, but it's also cool and mysterious, which is what we're going for. If the PCs manage to ally with the huntresses, they will be included in the standing ritual if they want their own wish. The next yearly vigil is only thirteen nights away.

The Horological Hall has some kind of clock. We could make it a sundial or a grandfather clock if we're feeling boring. But this place is magical and eerie, so let's do something cooler: There is a majestic magical clock here carved from ice, with moving crystal gears, counting down to the day when all of the elves are going to return to their overrun homeland to engage in a suicide attack on the monsters who crawled out of the steaming earth. When that clock hits zero, the mansion will be abandoned to treasure seekers and vows will be fulfilled as the bloodline goes extinct in a hopeless war against impossible odds. (Unless, of course, high-level PCs decide to get involved and intervene.) When the mansion is first explored by outsiders, there's less than a year left on the thousand-year-old clock. The Masonry Storeroom is just a place where big blocks of stone are stored. But what if these blocks are covered in runes, and are being used to build a magical gateway back to the homeland? The gateway is almost complete.

So we have now what I feel is a really interesting and unique base of operations for the PCs, where they will learn about an odd, disturbing and sympathetic culture they never knew existed. That's the good news. The bad news is, that's not what I intended to design. I was planning on designing a rudimentary dungeon for you to use as an example! So now, I will turn my design into a dungeon with a few twists. Here we go:

[1] The bloodline is dying out. There are only 13 aristocrats left; they are all high-level wizards, illusionists and jesters. They are all insane to varying degrees (some harmless, some tragic, some sweet, some terrifying) and a few of them are violent. A couple of them hate one another. There are two battling factions in the mansion.

[2] The ever-obedient hunters have split into three groups. One of the groups serves faction A, a second serves faction B, and a third refuses to take sides and is hoping to heal their masters. (That group will want to ally with the PCs.)

[3] There are monsters here, and dungeons underneath the mansion. How? Well, let's say the strongest mad elf is an archmage, and he keeps summoning monsters he can't really control. He thinks he's already fighting back in the homeland, and he's summoning guardian monsters to take out all of the humanoids (actually his fellow elves) and enemy monsters (imagined?) that populate the house. He's slowly winning control of the mansion against his brethren, and there are rooms in the mansion where (for example) badgerbears nest in the stables, and wyverns roost in a crumbled tower. He dwells down in the cellar labyrinth, and neither of the major factions have managed to cure him or even contain him. And one of the factions doesn't even have the heart to kill them.

Enter the Player Characters, fleeing from a deadly blizzard in the mountains that wiped out their traveling caravan. The GM tells them, "A miracle of some kind hovers up from the snowy wasteland. A beautiful and ancient elven mansion perches in a hidden valley, its windows aglow with golden light and the promise of life-saving fireplaces. From inside echo song, laughter, and … was that a scream? Perhaps it was only an echo of the howling wind. You all take another 2D6 damage from frostbite, you can barely feel your legs."

And there you go. A new campaign setting, and a haunted house like no other in the world! Have fun with the idea. It's not what I set out to design, but that is the joy of serendipity. When you use random generation systems, you are giving your creativity a virtual feast of imaginary catalysts. The ways in which you filter, accept, and reject the offered information will lead you to design a dungeon more quickly than you might have ever imagined was possible. Embrace your creativity!

APPENDIX A:

TYPES OF STRONGHOLDS

There will be many times when you want to place your dungeon beneath a ruined castle, or you want to create a mad wizard's citadel and you really don't know how to make it feel like an integral part of the pre-existing game world. How do you know what type of castle to choose, and what are some real-world examples that you can research for deeper design advice?

Fortunately, there are many different kinds of strongholds, and many examples in the real world of those strongholds' various architectural stratagems and features.

However, remember that medieval castles might be very different in a fantasy world. Why? Simply because in the real world's medieval times, defenders did not ever need to contend with flying dragons, earth elementals, burrowing monsters, magical spells (such as earthquake) and invaders using powerful magical items. Historical castles were never built with aerial attacks in mind, outside of the considerations of catapults and trebuchets lobbing things over the walls. So you can use these historical stronghold types for inspiration and Google searches, but again, you don't need to be bound to the strictures of reality! Just find a floor plan or example that looks good to you, and modify it according to your needs.

If you are stuck for any realistic inspiration, I recommend rolling 1D100 on the following table to determine the type of stronghold that you should create for your next adventure.

TABLE 7

STRONGHOLD CLASSIFICATIONS

[01 to 02] Angular Blockhouse / Tower House: A small castle whose overall floor plan is in the shape of the letter L (one major 90-degree turn). The two extremities will have towers.

Examples to Guide Your Future Research: Culzean Castle, in Ayrshire; Muchalls Castle, in Scotland.

[03 to 04] Blockhouse / Tower House: A small castle with a square or circular floor plan.

Examples to Guide Your Future Research: Cromwell's Castle, in Sicily; Henrican Blockhouse, at Mount Edgcumbe.

[05 to 06] Bridge Castle: A castle built over both sides of a river, guarding the crossing.

Examples to Guide Your Future Research: Stari Most, in Mostar; Valeggio sul Mincio, in Italy.

[07 to 08] C-Plan Blockhouse / Tower House: A small castle whose overall floor plan is in the approximate shape of the letter C (two major 90-degree turns). The two extremities will have towers.

Example to Guide Your Future Research: Cragston, in Aberdeenshire.

[09 to 10] Cave Castle (German = Hohlenburg): A castle built into a large natural cavern, with only its foremost exterior facing out toward the surface world. The cave castle is probably elevated, in a cliff face etc.

Examples to Guide Your Future Research: Kropfenstein, in Switzerland; Marmels Castle, in Switzerland; Stein Castle, in Bavaria.

[11 to 12] Concentric Castle: A castle (not necessarily with a circular floor plan) with two or more curtain walls, one inside the other.

Examples to Guide Your Future Research: Beaumaris Castle, in Wales; Caerphilly Castle, in South Wales.

[13 to 14] Counter-Castle / Siege Castle: A castle built to defend against invaders from another castle, or built as a staging point to attack another castle. Found in tense, centuries-long border situations.

Examples to Guide Your Future Research: Caernarfon Castle, in Wales; Harlech Castle, in Wales.

[15 to 16] Crusader Castle: A castle occupied by a knightly order. In game terms, crusaders are probably of good alignment (possibly paladins) or neutral alignment (cavaliers), not evil.

Examples to Guide Your Future Research: Kerak Castle, in Jordan; Krak des Chevaliers, in Syria; Kyrenia Castle, in Cyprus.

[17 to 18] Enclosure Castle: Technically, this is a rather broad and abused term; but the best definition is probably a castle which features several buildings inside its walls, but no single dominant keep. This means that the walls and outer towers are the main areas of defense.

Examples to Guide Your Future Research: Clitheroe Castle, in England; Kenilworth Castle, in England; Ludlow Castle, in England.

[19 to 20] Fantastic Castle: A "fantasy" castle, built more as a folly / escape / madman's sanctuary than as a defensive edifice. A good prototype for the old school trope of the insane wizard's fortress.

Examples to Guide Your Future Research: Bishop Castle (modern), in Colorado; Neuschwanstein Castle, in Germany.

[21 to 22] Fortified Hunting Lodge (German = Jagdschloss): A combination castle / manor house; built as a resort location for a ruler to stay near hunting grounds.

Examples to Guide Your Future Research: Jagdschloss Gelbensande, in Germany; Jagdschloss Glienicke, in Germany.

[23 to 24] Fortified Manor House: A locale that was originally built as a manor house, but was fortified by later generations.

Examples to Guide Your Future Research: Kranzelstein, in Sarnthein; Schloss Hart, in Austria.

[25 to 26] Grotto Castle (German = Grottenburg): A variant of a Cave Castle, where the natural cavern has been artificially extended to allow more building room.

Example to Guide Your Future Research: Predjama Castle, in Slovenia. See also the Cave Castle entry.

[27 to 28] Hillside Castle: Simply, a castle built into the side of a hill for defensive purposes. A good design, because it means there are almost certainly subterranean areas.

Examples to Guide Your Future Research: Ehrenfels Castle, in Germany; Katz Castle, in Germany.

[29 to 30] Hilltop Castle: Similar to a Hillside Castle, but the castle is built on the highest crown of the hill so that there is no direction where it can be assailed from above.

Examples to Guide Your Future Research: Hohenzollern Castle, in Germany; Yilankale (Snake Castle), in Turkey.

[31 to 32] Imperial Castle (German = Reichsburg): A castle built by an emperor, which (in a fantasy world, instead of the real world's Holy Roman Empire) implies that the stronghold is even larger than other kinds of castles. The emperor which built it might have been overthrown centuries ago.

Examples to Guide Your Future Research: Imperial Castle of Munzenberg, in Germany; Imperial Castle of Nuremberg, in Germany.

[33 to 34] Island Castle (German = Inselburg): A castle built on an island.

Examples to Guide Your Future Research: Pfalzgraftenstein Castle, in Germany; Trakai Castle, in Lithuania.

[35 to 36] Lowland Castle / Plains Castle: A castle built in a plains / flatlands location. For defense, the castle will usually be bordered on at least one side by a river, and the bridge across the river is probably controlled by the castle's drawbridge. It probably has a moat as well.

Examples to Guide Your Future Research: Caerlaverock Castle, in Scotland; Warwick Castle, in England.

[37 to 38] Marsh Castle: A castle built in a swamp or other wetland, which makes it very difficult for armies or siege engines to attack. The castle might also be surrounded by a moat, very easy to create in these environs.

Examples to Guide Your Future Research: Calvorde Castle, in Saxony-Anhalt; Oebisfelde Castle, in Germany.

[39 to 40] Moat House / Moathouse: A small castle with a deep moat as its primary form of defense.

Example to Guide Your Future Research: Chiefly Gygaxian; refer to the Temple module for a fine example.

[41 to 43] Motte-and-Bailey Castle: The motte is a raised artificial hill which the castle resides on, and the bailey is a courtyard surrounded by the curtain wall. Basically, a hilltop castle upon an artificial hill.

Examples to Guide Your Future Research: Launceston Castle, in England; Windsor Castle, in England.

[44 to 45] Palace: A stronghold built less for defense, and more as a luxurious royal residence. Its protection will come mostly in the form of guards, traps, and powerful magic ... and if the palace ever falls, it will make a perfect dungeon setting.

Examples to Guide Your Future Research: Schwerin Palace, in Germany; Versailles (technically a chateau) in France.

[46 to 47] Pleasure Palace (German = Lustschloss): A small palace, built as a ruler's seasonal retreat away from state affairs.

Examples to Guide Your Future Research: Chateau de Madrid, in France; Schloss Favorite, in Germany.

[48 to 49] Quadrangular Castle: A square or rectangular castle, where the buildings are part of the outside walls and as a result there is no singular keep.

Examples to Guide Your Future Research: Bodiam Castle, in England; Bolton Castle, in England.

[50 to 51] Refuge Castle (German = Fliehburg, Volksburg): A crude defensive fortification which is built as a temporary retreat for villagers or townsmen in times of war. Very unglamorous, but there could well be a subterranean dungeon underneath. Also called "Giant Castle" (Hunenburg) because people believed they were built by giants, which in a fantasy world they could be.

Examples to Guide Your Future Research: Eresburg Fortress, in Germany; Raddusch Fort, in Germany.

[52 to 53] Ridge Castle: A castle built atop a ridge. Similar to a hilltop castle, but the castle is not built on a single isolated hill; it is built on a narrow height in a hill range or mountain range.

Examples to Guide Your Future Research: Beckov Castle, in Slovakia; Burghausen Castle, in Germany.

[54 to 55] Ringwork Castle: A castle with a courtyard and a single circular or oval curtain wall.

Examples to Guide Your Future Research: Andone Castrum, in France; Pennard Castle, in Wales.

[56 to 58] Rock Castle (German = Felsenburg): A castle which uses natural rock outcroppings as part of its defensive structure.

Examples to Guide Your Future Research: Castle of Mussomeli, in Sicily; Spangenburg Castle, in Germany.

[59 to 60] Shared Ancestral Castle (German = Ganerbenburg): A castle distinguished not by its structure but by its circumstances: it is home to more than one clan / family / ancestral bloodline. This creates interesting opportunities for role-play and adventure (for example, a castle which is half controlled and half haunted).

Examples to Guide Your Future Research: Altenstein, in Franconia; Eltz Castle, in Germany.

[61 to 62] Shell Keep: A slightly more advanced motte-and-bailey design, with a stone wall around the circumference of the motte (artificial hill), instead of a wooden wall.

Example to Guide Your Future Research: The Round Tower, at Windsor Castle.

[63 to 64] Sovereign Castle (German = Landesburg): A castle built by a lord (duke, marquis, count, etc.) to rule and control his territory.

Examples to Guide Your Future Research: Electoral Cologne's Landesburg at Linn, in Germany; Landesburg of Angermund, in Germany.

[65 to 66] Spur Castle: Similar to a rock castle, using the rock spur of a hilltop as part of its defense works.

Examples to Guide Your Future Research: The Citadel of Salah Ed-Din, in Syria; Montfort Castle, in Israel.

[67 to 68] Star Fort: An advanced form of angularly-walled fortification, giving artillery or archers (or spell casters!) maximum fields of fire against invaders. First appeared in the 1400s and refined in later centuries. These fortresses make for beautiful maps that are challenging to create.

Examples to Guide Your Future Research: The City of Palmanova, Italy; Fort Bourtange, in the Netherlands.

[69 to 70] Stockade: A crude wooden fort, with a wooden palisade wall and wooden structures. Typically square or rectangular.

Examples to Guide Your Future Research: Most frontier forts in America.

[71 to 72] T-Plan Blockhouse / Tower House: A small castle whose overall floor plan is in the approximate shape of the letter T. There will likely be one or two towers at the extremities.

Examples to Guide Your Future Research: Various examples in Scotland and elsewhere. Frequently conflated with manor houses, but can easily be blended with manorial source of inspiration.

[73 to 74] Toll Castle (German = Zollburg): A castle built specifically to defend an important trade route (such as a mountain pass), and demanding payment from all passersby.

Examples to Guide Your Future Research: Maus Castle, in Germany; Stahlech Castle, in Bacharach.

[75 to 77] Tower Castle: A small castle that has a single tower (instead of a keep and multiple towers along the wall).

Examples to Guide Your Future Research: Various examples in England and Germany, often conflated with manor houses (see note on T-Plan Blockhose classification, above).

[78 to 80] Tower House: A small castle which is basically a combination of a tower and living areas. Technically, a combination blockhouse / manor house. Not as fancy inside as one might think ... but magic can do pretty amazing things, yes?

Examples to Guide Your Future Research: The Tower of Hallbar, in Scotland; Vao Tower House, in Estonia.

[81 to 83] Underworld Castle: A fantasy type of castle, in which there is an immense castle built entirely underground.

Examples to Guide Your Future Research: Castle of the Queen of Hearts, in *Alice's Adventures in Wonderland*; Gygaxian, in the land of the dark elves; Palace of Hades, in Greek Mythology.

[84 to 86] Urban Castle (German = Stadtburg): A castle which is situated in a city, or is large enough to encompass an entire village. In game terms, this could also be a ruined castle surrounded by what remains of a ruined city.

Examples to Guide Your Future Research: Andernach, in Germany; The Gozzoburg, in Lower Austria.

[87 to 89] Water Castle: A castle that is entirely surrounded by moats; a large Moathouse. A variant is a seaside castle, with only a single narrow walkway leading out to the sea- or bay-surrounded castle.

Examples to Guide Your Future Research: Egeskov Castle, in Denmark; Inzlingen Castle, in Germany; Methoni Castle, Greece (variant).

[90 to 92] Wooden Fortress (Russian = Ostrog): A small castle, or steading, made entirely of heavy wood. Somewhat similar to a Stockade, but much more established.

Examples to Guide Your Future Research: Gygaxian hill giant structures; The

Tower of Ilimsky, in Irkutsk; The Tower of Yakutsky, in Siberia.

[93 to 95] Zigzag Blockhouse / Tower House: A small castle whose overall floor plan is in the approximate shape of the letter Z (two major 90-degree turns). The two extremities will have towers.

   Examples to Guide Your Future Research: Glenbuchat Castle, in Aberdeenshire; Hatton Castle, in Scotland.

[96 to 00] Hybrid Structure, Roll Twice

(You can reroll any paired architectural results that do not conceivably work together.)

APPENDIX B:

SEMI-REALISTIC DUNGEON LAYOUTS & FLOORPLANS

Sadly, realistic dungeons are not always as useful as you might think. The play of the game should always supersede any demands for realism over the glories of imagination. But there will nevertheless be times when you want to make your dungeon more plausible overall, more historically detailed, or more resonant with mythic themes. Or, you might just want to impress your readers with a truly epic dungeon for publication. All of these are valid reasons for research into useful real-world themes highlighted to empower your future dungeon designs.

As I noted in *Book I* of *The Classic Dungeon Design Guide*, you can find a spectacular array of premade dungeon maps and floor plans from four major sources: published dungeon modules, Google image searches, geomorphs, and online random dungeon generators. You can find hundreds of worthy examples of potential "dungeons" and other adventure interiors, which can either be used as is, or as inspiration for the development of your own custom dungeon maps (which I strongly recommend).

However, most of the easy maps to find and acquire are of classic fantasy dungeons. This is fine if you just want to play a game based on earlier games; but that's not necessarily the ideal old school paradigm. What do you do if, instead, you want realistic examples of inspiring castles, caves, manor houses, temples, and tombs? Is there any way to easily model real places for FRPG gaming purposes?

This chapter is devoted to showing you the best ways to navigate the bewildering array of real example floor plans in the world, along with a fairly substantial helping of images. These are not complete maps, mind you; you will still need to do the (fun!) design work yourself. But this chapter will alleviate a lot of the pain and research which would otherwise be required. I also provide you with some advice on how to turn your ideas for semi-realistic dungeons into reasonable series of rooms on a map, particularly for castles and other fortified structures.

ARRANGING ROOMS FOR A CAVE SYSTEM

(As an initial refresher, please refer to the discussion of realistic cave types found in The Classic Dungeon Design Guide, Book I.)

The first thing you need to know about cave systems is this: caves in a magical world built for gaming are very different from caves in a mundane world created by physical processes. We can emulate natural cave processes in the game, certainly, but we can also say "it's magic" when we need bigger spaces, more labyrinthine layouts, and — for the sake of GM sanity — relatively "flat" cave systems that all exist together on a linear dungeon level. Real caves are three-dimensional constructs, and are exceedingly complex with a great deal of verticality, overlapping spaces, tiny openings and unreachable areas. Further, the game presumes the existence of burrowing and mining monsters which expand natural caves with many warrens, grottoes, mines, fortifications and bizarre new expansions.

Despite the limitations with two-dimensional graph paper, and our vested interest in keeping the mapping players from going insane, we can still use and consider many of the real-world cave processes here.

Basically, caves are produced by erosion over a very long period of time. The erosion might be caused by acid, water, wind, gravity, melting ice, magma, or magical forces. The layout of the cave largely depends on the force(s) which caused the erosion, the type of rock(s) underground, the overall terrain, any seismic activity in the region, and the presence of intelligent monsters over time, if any.

The layout of a general cave system will — with some exceptions, such as magma caves — be dependent upon [1] the entrance location, [2] whether there is more than one entrance, and [3] the presence of flowing water. If there is only one entrance, the natural course of the cave system — before we consider the influence of magic and monsters — is probably somewhat linear. There will be an entrance at the high ground, a watercourse moving underground, and a series of open spaces following the water in various ways (descending stream banks, waterfall plunges, submerged caves beneath a pool, perhaps a rise in the tunnel and hidden areas with a limited air supply beyond, and so forth). If there is more than one entrance, the entrances are probably at different elevations and lead into very different places. The cave system will be an enormous labyrinth in many cases, reaching in all directions.

As a real world example, I am familiar with the Cave of the Winds system near Manitou Springs, Colorado, which has a few safe entrances toward the top of the cliff and some unsafe entrances hundreds of feet below, at the base of the cliff and the canyon floor. In game terms, this would probably mean that there would be three or four levels of caves, with the obvious entrances opening into dungeon level 1, and a lower entrance opening directly into dungeon level 4. With this layout, dungeon level 3 would actually be the most difficult location to enter, where the adventure would likely "end."

Caves can be strung together without apparent rhyme or reason, based on their size. Spaces can range from cavelet, to cave, to cavern, to majestic gallery, with every conceivable variation in between. "Corridors" between the caves can be tunnels, streams, sinkholes, chasms, plunges, pits, shafts, or gently descending tiers of stone in the form of a natural staircase.

The presence of monsters should then be considered too, whether the monsters are still there or not. Unintelligent burrowing monsters tend to enlarge caves, and to connect caves, because they are breeding and/or looking for food. Egg chambers are created far away from entrances and away from high-traffic areas where intruders might enter. Food sources might be fungi, in which case the monsters will be breaking into as many wet caves as possible; prey, in which case the monsters will burrow into other lairs; or minerals, in which case the monster burrows will follow the course of the mineral veins.

Intelligent monsters enlarge caves for many reasons, including defense, curiosity, exile (fleeing away from rivals, for example), worship, netherworld passage, exploration, or ancestral veneration. But the #1 cause of intelligent monster cave expansion is far more practical: treasure hunting. Mining monsters will follow seams of rich material, and will build vertical levels of artificial tunnels to reach deeper deposits. Treasure seekers will search for sealed vaults and tombs, and will build narrow tunnels to reach these areas. Dragon hunters will break into lairs from the back, trying to get at the treasure without alerting the dragon itself. (Fat chance!) And monsters which prey on other monsters will expand caves to improve their defenses, to provide multiple routes of invasion, and/or to establish dominance over weaker monsters will building bulwarks to protect against strong monsters.

To be more specific than this, we need to consider the different types of caves, as each cave type has its own rules of formation which you will want to research online. For example, solutional (acid-eaten) caves tend to descend in many levels, as gravity pulls the acidic water between layers of stone; while magma caves tend to be created from the underground on up toward the surface; and sea caves begin where the sea hollows out stone, and keep going horizontally inland as the tides find new surfaces to eat away.

As an example, you might want to review online map graphics which show the layout for Mammoth Cave of Kentucky. Feel free to look that up now if you would like to consider some of the aspects of an actual cave system, and how those features might translate into a fantasy role-playing game.

In Mammoth Cave, for example in the 1907 survey imagery, the primary cavern system entrance is shown at bottom left. The features near the entrance are **[1]** The Iron Gate (an installed artificial safety barrier, which we gamers would of course say was put there by evil dwarves or humanoids), and **[2]** Hutchins' Narrows (today call Houchins Narrows), named after a legend involving a bear hunter discovering the caves while on the hunt. Beyond these features is the system's first main cave, the Rotunda. This is a large overlook cave, looking down into the deeps, which you can find pictures of online.

From the Rotunda, the system splits in two directions. The spiral tunnel a bit above the Rotunda in the map is known as the Corkscrew, a perilous descent. In the other direction is Audubon Avenue, a subterranean canyon filled with sand deposits (from the ages long ago when this was a river).

Other major features that you can see on the map include Little Bat Avenue, Mammoth Dome, Styx and Lethe (named after the rivers in the Greek underworld, of course), Purgatory, Echo River, Gothic Avenue, Stevenson's Lost River, Gorin's Dome, The Ramble, Own Pit, Star Chamber, Welcome Avenue, Wright's Rotunda, Chief City, and the Chimney. Generally, the Avenues are tunnels between caves, and the Chimneys are vertical climbs between cave levels.

This is a natural system, which can be studied and viewed on Youtube. There is a useful video on Youtube — which is currently entitled "Mammoth Cave Exploration" — which shows you three-dimensional graphics of some of the detailed routes.

When considering the Mammoth Cave system in regards to FRPG dungeon exploration, the Game Master should keep in mind that underworld denizens would almost certainly expand these caves and conduits for their own uses. Even unintelligent monsters such as dholes, acid mantises, giant slugs, amber behemoths and burrowing behemoths would leave behind their own tunnels as they dig through the maze in search of tasty (screaming) prey. Intelligent monsters such as dark elves, dvergar, Deep Ones, trolls, troglodytes and bugbears would create warrens branching off of the main caves, expanding chambers, creating additional living areas, and connecting lairs to crucial supplies of fungi, drinking water, and breathable air. The warrens of course would be noted by adventurers are being free of stalactites, stalagmites, and other natural surface features.

By studying real caves, and imagining how monsters might expand the system over centuries, a Game Master can develop complex and reasonably realistic cave labyrinths. And I should also note that for those of you who might not know, the Mammoth Cave is also very important to the computerized Fantasy Role-Playing hobby. In the 1970s, programmer, spelunker, and D&D player Will Crowther used Mammoth Cave as the model for his seminal computer adventure game, ADVENT (aka Colossal Cave Adventure). And his work in

expanded and highly recreated form inspired the Zork series too. So if you like simple wireframe and flowchart maps, you can look up maps for Colossal Cave and Zork (especially Zork I) to see fantasy interpretations of how these caves might look after many generations of monstrous expansion.

ARRANGING ROOMS FOR AN ICONIC DUNGEON

If we define a dungeon as a prison, and the underworks associated with a surface stronghold of some kind, the arrangement of rooms is fairly straightforward. The complexity comes in when we consider the age of the place, and the effects of escape attempts, collapses, occupant death, undeath, and monster invasions over time.

The easy step involves considering the dungeon as it was first created. There was a surface stronghold, and the incarceration of prisoners underground. This means that there was one way down, probably a staircase; a guard room; and several branching tunnels. One tunnel would lead to water, food and equipment storage, another tunnel would lead to a mass-incarceration dungeon (where many prisoners would be thrown into the same place), and another tunnel would have many cells branching off of it (where more important prisoners could be isolated for intimidation, interrogation, awaiting ransom payment, and so forth). And really, that would be about the maximum extent of a realistic dungeon.

Then comes the fun part. What caused the dungeon to be expanded? You can choose your favorite option from many. If there was an escape attempt, there is probably a tunnel headed toward the surface. If there was a discovery of valuable minerals, there might have been a connection to nearby caves which were not detected during the initial construction, but which were found later using divination. If monsters invaded from below, they dug tunnels up into the dungeon and then the dungeon owners built defensive workers to deal with the invaders. If there was a natural disaster, then some dungeon chambers would be flooded or collapsed, and new ones would be created away from the disaster area. If the surface stronghold was abandoned, then it would later fill with monsters who would naturally expand their control to the underground areas later (and expand as needed). And if the surface stronghold was conquered, then the new owners might well imprison the older owners underground, where the tables-turned prisoners might know enough about the prison's layout to conceive of some ingenious escape on their own. They might even find a way to sneak back up to the surface, and to counter-invade the stronghold from within.

Once you rough out this brief history of the dungeon, the layout then tends to expand in unpredictable ways. This is because the monster populations are factionalized. For example, let us say that there was a dwarven castle, and the dwarves built a dungeon underground to keep orc and goblin prisoners. The goal was to convince the ever-encroaching tribes to stop attacking, or their imprisoned leaders and witch doctors would be wiped out. This worked for a time, but humanoids are resentful creatures and their grudges can last for generations and centuries. So the humanoids might have allied with kobolds who lived in a nearby cave system, and then tunneled into the dungeon and invaded the dwarven stronghold.

The dwarves were wiped out or forced to retreat, and the alliance of the humanoids — without their hatred to unite them — turned into an intense three-way faction rivalry. The orcs took the surface stronghold, while the goblins and the kobolds had a truce and split the underground area between them. The orcs would raid the surrounding lands, and occasionally hire the goblins and kobolds to raid for them. But then the kobolds got worse treatment (being smaller), and they rebelled against the orcs, and the goblins allied with the orcs once again. The kobolds were forced back into their caves. But there, they found that their caves had been taken over by slimes and amber behemoths ...

You can make all of this as complex as you like, although I actually discourage coming up with a fully detailed dungeon history. Your game should be based on creating future adventure sites for your players, not telling your players about the adventures that already occurred in your imagination. Keep developing a dungeon history in this manner to justify the arrangement of rooms underground, but don't make the

history so detailed that you're spending more time writing and less time playing!

There are quite a few dungeons and medieval prisons in the real world, and unfortunately I am here to report to you that the vast majority of them, collectively, are (a) ruined, (b) tiny and repetitive by design, (c) wishful thinking outside of the bounds of convincing archaeology, or (d) sensationalized as tourist traps.

Yet, my fellow Game Masters, do not despair! When this sort of thing happens to threaten our awesome imaginations, we simply need to crack open the history books and dig around in dirt a little. I've done quite a bit of the grungy ground work to get you started. So here are eight real examples that I believe are worthy of your further research. Naturally, you're going to learn a lot from these locations if you do some image searches and find the many excellent photographs, and links to high quality and out of print (read: expensive) hardcovers from days gone by. Also naturally, I can't repeat all of that copyrighted material here. Google Books, Google image search, Wikipedia and your local library will all serve you well in that regard. I simply want to bring some names to your attention, and to mention some of the interesting highlights for each place to whet your appetite for further research.

And down we go ...

The Bastille

The Bastille has a very long, dark, and storied history, but here we will focus on its use as a prison-stronghold with mysterious and evocative features.

Built originally as a fortress defending the eastern gates of Paris, the Bastille quickly became known as a prison where the Kings of France kept their most troublesome dissidents and political enemies ... particularly in the mid-1400s. The structure was secure, heavily guarded and difficult to breach, inside and out. A battle between rebels and royalists took place just outside of here in 1652. Accounts written by former prisoners in the 1700s turned the Bastille into a symbol of oppression for those opposing royalty, which led to the grim events of 1789.

The most infamous man ever imprisoned here was the Man in the Iron Mask. He was a real person, but to this day no one knows for certain why he was forced to wear the mask for the duration of his imprisonment. The favorite pulp theory, of course, is that he was the king's identical twin. This is the theory which was explored by author Alexandre Dumas in his novel *The Vicomte of Bragelonne: Ten Years Later*, which is basically Book III in *The Three Musketeers* series.

But the mysterious personage of legend has fallen away bit by bit, as historical research continues. It is more likely that he was a man who knew too much about the king's debaucheries, and that his mask was not to hide his identity but merely to make him humiliated and powerless. His name was likely Eustache Dauger de Cavoye, and he was no royal relation. He just pissed off the wrong powerful people and suffered a miserable lifetime for it. Sometimes, the legends are better than reality after all …

Other interesting features and historical bits concerning the Bastille include:

❖ The underground cachots. Under each of six towers was a cachot, or dungeon chamber. It is said that some of the more hated prisoners were forced to live in the cachots chained next to corpses or skeletons.

❖ A fortified interior drawbridge, which would be brought down to allow movement through the fortress during times of peace.

❖ Illegal goods and literature seized from criminals were stored in the Bastille in later years, which would certainly make for some interesting kinds of storerooms.

❖ An anarchist soldier named Latude, imprisoned, once escaped from his cell by climbing up a chimney and then deploying a rope-and-rag ladder which he had made.

❖ There may have been torturous oubliettes here, but an alternate theory says that the chambers were used for ice storage. Either option could be interesting, from a dungeon design perspective.

❖ Prisoners were frequently kept in accordance with their wealth. There might be temporarily-deposed nobles in their own rooms, with fine clothing and tapestries, and perhaps even a favored cat to control the vermin. Meanwhile, the poor would be in rags and practically left to die.

Bedlam

The world's most notorious insane asylum, established as a priory in 1247 AD, was more formally known as Saint Mary Bethlehem Royal Hospital. It eventually became a house of healing and then specialized more and more in mental disorders, beginning in the late 1300s or so.

In the medieval period, the insane could only be kept from hurting themselves and others until they became sane by themselves, or died. Therefore there would be stocks, manacles, chains, cages, prison cells and so forth to control the most violent members of the population. (My favorite portrayal of this mess is in Coppola's 1992 film version of Dracula.) This rather unfortunate reputation became deeply sensationalized in the 1600s. A famous song called *Tom o' Bedlam*, painting the image of a mad imprisoned anti-hero, spread the legend of the place far and wide.

Although conditions at Bedlam had improved by the time this song and its further chapters were being bawled out in English taverns, nevertheless the incessant "cryings, screechings, roarings, brawlings, shaking of chains, swearings, frettings, and chaffings" were still the relentless order of the day. The filth and conditions simply made matters worse, as did the frequent contact between disparate inmates with wildly different mental disabilities.

Blarney Castle

This is a fascinating medieval Irish castle, surrounded by enchanted druidic arbors and a poison garden. Below the fortress is a dangerous netherworld escape route, known as Badger's Cave. A magical stairway grants wishes. Nearby is the "Witch Stone," which looks like (or is?) the face of a petrified witch-giantess. The dungeon there is usually off limits these days, but it's there! It was a prison, likely with connected storerooms, and maybe an intruding army's sapping tunnel too.

The most intriguing feature here is the Blarney Stone. This thing has a huge amount of legends and superstition built up that Americans only partially understand, so I'll strip all that away and get to my own campaign's interpretation of the medieval origin:

This is a holy shrine in the form of a crude limestone block, sacred to the goddess Cliodhna (domains of power: beauty, beguiling, faeries, and banshees; Chaotic Neutral). It is guarded by invisible sprites. If threatened by the unworthy or destructive evil, the shrine summons a guardian banshee. It grants the worthy the "gift of gab," a permanent increase of +1 or +2 Charisma. The +2 is reserved for Bards and Mountebanks. To get this power, you need to kiss the stone, which — they rarely tell you this — involves climbing the castle summit and leaning over a crumbling parapet, while a buddy holds you by the ankles in the hope that you don't fall to your terrible death.

As you can see, Blarney Castle is a perfect example of blending many different dungeon themes into a single evocative locale.

Pontrefact Castle (Castle Pomfret)

This Yorkshire castle was built in the 11th century, and was later reinforced with a magnificent donjon keep. It was used as a major defense center by the Royalists during the English Civil War. Many of its subterranean cellars, hundreds of years old by then, were used to store arms and armor. There is very little of this castle left, because it was leveled c. 1649 to prevent it from being used as a fortress ever again. As such, it is an ideal real example of a ruined castle with extensive dungeons, armories, and secret storerooms underneath.

In the 1200s and 1300s apparently, the dungeons were used to house many prisoners in absolute darkness. They scratched their names into the walls so that history would not forget their terror. King Richard II may have been murdered or starved to death in these same dungeons in 1400, although no one really knows ... he was simply never seen alive again. Shakespeare gave his imagined death seen a

much more heroic bent, which may be of interest to GMs seeking to give a dungeon the legacy of a fallen hero which the PCs can rediscover. The ruins of the castle above the dungeon could be quite interesting to explore as well. Some of the towers were 60' high, and the massive kitchen had two ovens and four fireplaces. Imagine how many giant spiders you could fit in that ruined mess ...

The Tower of London

The tower of London is mostly an arsenal and fortress, but because it was so secure it also served as a prison for the most important personages ... particularly in the 1400s to 1600s. It's a quintessential example of a princess prison (young Elizabeth I), and of a prison where politically dangerous individuals were kept until the day of execution. War spies were executed there as recently as World War II. There are actually lots of towers and connecting walls, but the most significant structure is the donjon keep known as the White Tower. Other interesting locales include(d) a drawbridge, chapel, crypt, ward, protective ditch, and the Crown Jewels (a trapped and protected dungeon treasure idea if there ever was one). Further intriguing and disconcerting details include:

❖ The first person imprisoned there was a cleric, Bishop Ranulf Flambard. He was kept in luxury, but was a prisoner nonetheless. He escaped by getting the guards drunk during a feast and using a hidden rope. For all his flawless craftiness, he was accused of dark magic tricks and witchcraft, not to mention being a bad sport.

❖ Hundreds of people were imprisoned there for coin clipping, which is the crime (against the king) of shearing off little pieces of gold or silver for later melting, while using the lightweight coin at face value somewhere else. Imagine the fun that could be had if you created a dungeon filled with merchants and petty thieves, all proclaiming their innocence to the PCs!

❖ Enormous intelligent ravens dwell here.

❖ After the Battle of Agincourt, defeated noble knights were kept here for ransom.

❖ At least one king, and two princes, were cruelly murdered here.

❖ There is a deep, adjacent Roman graveyard filled with bones and relics.

❖ Many people were tortured here, either for punishment or to extract confessions. Perhaps the most notorious was the most excellent Guy Fawkes, whose mask is now associated with Anonymous and V for Vendetta.

❖ To this day, ghosts of the accursed are said to wander here.

Despite being an "on the surface" locale, and technically a stronghold, the Tower of London is arguably the coolest dungeon in existence.

~

I hope you have found this sampling of real dungeon-like settings to be inspiring. I also encourage you not to overlook the potential of surface prisons and gaols as adventuring locales, particularly if they are controlled by evil forces, or abandoned and repurposed. A medieval prison would be a perfect place to justify the existence of locked doors, iron bars between rooms, perilous pits and oubliettes, and lots of secret escape tunnels … many of which go nowhere and end in bloodstains, or a skeleton's grisly rest.

The common thread in adventure-themed medieval prisons is that they are difficult to break into or out of, and dangerous foes will try to prevent such activities … so it is the GM's task to devise scenarios revolving around those activities.

(Usually, that involves PCs rescuing NPC prisoners; but if your group is skilled and willing, you could devise an unforgettable scenario involving the PCs' capture and their attempt to break out without armor or magic items.) The problem with most prisons of course — from the players' savvy perspective — is the lack of treasure incentive, so the mission should be either compelled (failure to break out meaning long imprisonment or death) or well-rewarded (breaking out a valued rebel, noble or personage and being paid handsomely for the difficult work).

ARRANGING ROOMS FOR A

MANOR HOUSE

A manor house, in game terms, is a basically a fantasy version of a late medieval mansion. This means that we can follow the general rules for modern house design, with a few nods toward both medieval sensibilities and the gothic tropes of the haunted house genre of adventure fiction.

Manor houses typically have a large winged primary structure, and several outbuildings. The outbuildings might include (for example) stables, a coach house, a mill, a shrine, latrines, a family crypt, and garden locales … perhaps even including, if you have a sense of humor and appreciative players, the ever-dreaded monstrous gazebo. Other outdoor locales which are not technically rooms, but which are useful to an adventure design, can include a hedge maze, a pool, a fountain, and surrounding patios and pavilions.

Inside the house will be centered on the great hall proper. There will be an elaborate main entry, likely gated, surrounded by columns inside and out. There will be an entry, foyer, a cloak room, approaches to the main hall, sweeping stairs leading upward, and subtle tapestried approaches to the ubiquitous serving rooms and servants' quarters. Very generally, the ground floor will feature entertaining rooms, perhaps including a ballroom, sitting room, library, dining room, and so forth. The presence of dining implies that the kitchen, scullery, buttery and related areas will be located on the ground floor or immediately below. There will probably be servants' entries and egress areas toward the back of the main house, and perhaps even separate areas for guards and patrols.

Below ground, the house will feature a mix of cellars, storerooms, coal rooms, and warming rooms. Above ground will be the private living areas, the bedchambers, the studies, the private discussion chambers, and perhaps even secret areas of worship or esoteric learning.

If you're into adding classic dark fantasy tropes to this type of locale (and you should be!) there will be lots of opportunities to add sliding walls, secret passageways, walking suits of animated armor, magical paintings, a ghost, a chapel, a confessional, and perhaps even experimentation chambers, a mad scientist's lair and cells for imprisoned victims. Just think of every great haunted house concept you've ever wanted to use, and make it more medieval. The house will have a lot of stone, ancestral memory, shuttered windows, dark passageways, crude timepieces, creaking stairs and perhaps even guardian beasts.

The layout in the wings can depend on how big the ancestral family is, how big the house is, and the purpose of your design. For example, if the house is shared by more than one bloodline (refer to the "Ganerbenberg" entry in the stronghold table, later in this chapter), then the less influential bloodline probably lives in one of the more rundown wings of the house. If the house's wealth was built on collections, artwork, or some kind of museum, those collections would probably be housed in another more secure wing. If the house serves as a guesthouse for many loyal subjects, they might get their own wing to. And if the owners are highly militant or devout, there could be an entire wing devoted to servant-soldiers, apprentice priests, or some other kind of guardians.

If you need more examples from fiction or real life, they are plentiful. My personal favorite manor house floor plan is Judges Guild's *Tegel Manor*, which remains under copyright. The real world Winchester Mystery House is interesting as well if you'd like to take a look at the tour plans. And the king of all manor houses (technically a chateau, or palace) is Versailles, of which there are many fascinating floorplans available online which you can explore as you like.

But there are many other types of manor houses beyond Versailles that we can consider too.

I could write an entire book about manor houses, and their potential to service as epic haunted dungeon-mansions in the old school FRPG ... and perhaps I shall. But for now, I can give you a quick raven's-level view of what types of manor houses exist, and where to learn more, and why you should be interested in them.

I have three truly excellent books in my personal design library, which cover the topic in exhaustive detail and are very atmospheric and inspiring. They can be expensive and hard to find, but you can try the library before Amazon

and decide if you want to plunk down the cold hard cash to add these beauties to your collection. But I promise you they are all very much worth the money. These titles are:

[1] Design and Plan in the Country House: From Castle Donjons to Palladian Boxes, by Andor Gomme and Alison Maguire. This is the most important book for a Game Master, because it has hundreds of dungeon-like floor plans with keyed rooms all listed by type. The major and most common rooms included here, for your reference, are: Anteroom, Buttery, Chamber, Closet, Common Parlour, Chapel, Dressing Room, Gallery, Great Chamber, Great Dining Room, Great Parlour, Hall, Kitchen, Kitchen / Winter Parlour, Larder, Little Parlour, Pantry, Steward's Closet, Scullery, Vestibule, and Withdrawing Room. You can literally flip through this book, pick a floor plan, and turn it into a dungeon directly inspired by a real world manor house in a matter of minutes. How cool is that? Just grab a house idea and start populating the rooms. And the detail in the 338-page accompanying text is positively fearsome.

[2] The English Country House: A Grand Tour, by Gervase Jackson-Stops and James Pipkin. The strengths of this book are threefold: **[1]** Great photos. **[2]** The text is thematic, with chapters teaching you everything you want to know — with examples — about Halls, Stairs, Great Chambers, Bedchambers, and so forth. **[3]** There's a tiny but excellent Gazeteer in the back, with some outstanding floor plans I wish I could show you. Kedleston Hall and especially Blenheim Palace will blow your mind.

[3] The English Manor House: From the Archives of Country Life, by Jeremy Musson. The text of this book is quite excellent, but its real strength lies in its exclusive photographs of gardens and period interiors ... including armor, chapels, Gothic chandeliers, monolithic fireplaces and serene secret chambers. Just paging through this book will give you hundreds of ideas.

~

There are three major traditions which I recommend you learn about first, the English, the French, and the German. (Other countries such as Spain and Portugal and Russia also have beautiful examples, but I recommend researching these three traditions first.) The English manor house is to me the most iconic; the French (chateau and manoir) are the most romantic and ethereal; and the German (gutshaus, rittergut, etc.) are the most stark and authoritarian ... but sadly also the hardest to find good information on in English. Fortunately the Google image search term "German manor house interior" tends to give some fairly high quality results in very little time.

Each house as you will find possesses its own unique floor plan, largely determined by (a) when it was built, (b) whether it started life as a castle, (c) whether it later became fortified, (d) where it was built and (e) how much money the family had to commit to majestic architecture. You can find a good list of world locations for manor houses, although it's necessarily dominated by English examples, at Wikipedia, "List of Manor Houses."

As you look through the many floor plans, you will see that the houses tend to be quite similar to one another. There's an impressive entrance surrounded by comforting rooms, a major staircase leading up to bedchambers, servants' quarters hidden away in all the nooks and crannies, unmarked rooms which can be assumed to be storerooms and pantries and general purpose nooks, and so forth. The most unusual and unique houses tend to have an old section replete with ominous solid stone walls, surrounded by a larger plan of later rooms which are much more delicate, wide-reaching and livable by comparison.

I've included a fair number of the best floor plans herein, and if you combine those with the work by Gomme and Maguire you'll be set for life.

The most important manor house information for a GM, however, is a bit harder to classify and convey: it's the atmosphere. You need to soak this up yourself to get it infused in your brain; if I just give you a list of haunted house tropes, it would be of cliché and surface "Scooby Doo" quality, and nothing more. You've got to *feel* it! Don't worry, I'm going to give you a very high quality reading list that will keep you busy and inspired and creeped out for months to come. If you aren't inspired to design a haunted house dungeon just yet, you soon will be.

As mentioned earlier, you'll want to check out the TVTropes pages beginning at the Haunted House, Haunted Castle, and Old Dark House pages for general ideas on elements and themes.

But to get really inspired (and scared!) you'll also want to read *The Fall of the House of Usher* (Edgar Allan Poe), *The Masque of the Red Death* (Poe), *The Rats in the Walls* (H. P. Lovecraft), *The Shunned House* (Lovecraft), *House of Leaves* (Mark Z. Danielewski), *Salem's Lot* (Stephen King), *The Shining* (King), *The Haunting of Hill House* (Shirley Jackson), *We Have Always Lived in the Castle* (Jackson), *The Turn of the Screw* (Henry James), *The Mystery of Chimney Rock* (Edward Packard, *Choose Your Own Adventure*), *The Yellow Wallpaper* (Charlotte Perkins Gilman), and my personal favorite, *The House on the Borderland* (William Hope Hodgson).

And for movies that emphasize the psychological over gore, I recommend the following: *Poltergeist, The Others, The Innocents, The Conjuring, Crimson Peak* (flawed but still gorgeous), *The Orphanage, In the Mouth of Madness* (limited house scenes, granted, but very much in the vein), and *The Haunting* (but dear gods don't watch the 1999 version, it's so terrible). I also have a particular soft spot for the 1999 version of *House on Haunted Hill*, which is by no means a good movie ... but if you watch it from a Game Master's dungeon designer perspective, it's pretty spectacular.

ARRANGING ROOMS FOR A STRONGHOLD

(Refer to Appendix A for a detailed overview of stronghold types.)

So how do you design a somewhat realistic castle or other fortified structure?

Very generally, a stronghold (particularly a castle) is designed as follows. Please keep in mind that these attributes apply most to surface locales, since subterranean castles are mostly fantasy; but the general principles can be applied to the rooms and tunnels in subterranean fortifications as well.

At the outermost extremity (on the surface), there is a series of towers, or bastions. These are elevated and relatively narrow structures, which are designed to allow the stronghold's defenders to repel besiegers from positions of relative safety. The towers can be accessed from the inside, but not from the outside. If there are counter-siege engines (such as catapults or ballistas, or bastions for spell casting), they are probably positioned on the tops of the towers.

Between the towers there are curtain walls, which are very high (and difficult to scale) barriers that connect the towers to one another to form a cohesive unit that cannot be breached. These walls might be "hollow," allowing defenders to traverse through multiple levels and to repel enemies through outward-facing windows and/or arrow slits. These types of hollow walls are easier to defend when the castle is housing a large army, but the walls are also of course not fully solid ... which makes them narrower and easier to knock down. The curtain walls probably have an upper walkway, protected by battlements, whether the interiors of the walls are hollow or not. Troops can be funneled through the towers to the adjoining walkways wherever there is need, and as casualties among the defending forces mount.

The walls and towers however are only the first line of defense. Access from the exterior of the castle to the interior is typically further protected by a gatehouse, or barbican. There may also be a moat (either dry and steep, or filled with water) outside of the curtain walls. If there is indeed a moat, a descending drawbridge will be attached to the gatehouse. In a magical castle, the "drawbridge" might actually be a shimmering plane of energy instead of a solid surface. The gatehouse will probably feature both an inner and outer gate, or portcullis (plural portcullises). Urban castles and palaces might have more than one gatehouse for access, but in a strictly defensive structure this is a definite no-no.

Inside and beyond the walls, there will be one or more wards, or courtyards. These are grassy areas where people can walk freely. Very generally, a courtyard is typically a peaceful place meant for walking and gatherings; while a ward is an inner defended court overlooked by more inner walls or fortifications.

If the castle is especially well-protected, it may well be a concentric castle. This means that there is an outer set of walls, a set of outer wards, and then another set of inner walls, and then a set of inner wards, and finally the castle keep at the center.

The wards and/or courtyards of the castle will probably be lined with outbuildings, roofed areas, or separate shops for various purposes. Example structures of this type include chapels, granaries, inns, smithies, stables, storerooms, warehouses, and wells. The ground levels of towers — opening near to these interior structures — will probably include guardrooms, barracks, and/or armories where additional defenses can be mustered if the outer walls are ever breached.

The keep, if there is one, will be the largest and best-protected structure in the center of the castle. Here there will be more armories, arsenals, barracks, halls (perhaps with a singular great hall and/or throne room), kitchens, servants' quarters, and so forth. Above ground level in the keep will be apartments (which are separated chambers for officials of importance), the lady's chambers, the lord's chambers, council and meeting halls, and so forth. If there is a treasury, it is probably far above ground and only accessible from the lord's chambers.

There will also be a donjon, or dungeon. These terms are frequently confused. In game terms, I would recommend that a donjon is the most secure above-ground room within the keep, while the dungeon is the series of cells and prisons found below ground. That's not quite a technical distinction, but it's a good guideline for gaming and to avoid further confusion.

Considering all of the above, there are also palaces. A palace is basically a stronghold which is designed more for living in luxury, and less for warfare and defense. A fortified palace would have a good mix of rooms (perhaps 2/3rds "stronghold" rooms and 1/3rd "manor house" rooms, in terms of the Labyrinth Lexicon). An ancestral palace would become a bit more decadent over time (perhaps 1/2 stronghold rooms and 1/2 manor house rooms), while a refurbished palace would be a former stronghold turned into a massive mansion (perhaps 1/3rd stronghold rooms and 2/3rds manor house rooms). These guidelines of course presume that the palace is still serving as a palace, and is not a monster-infested ruin.

In a fantasy game, a palace is not necessarily more vulnerable than a stronghold; it just has a less militant nature and atmosphere with more creature comforts and wealth on open display. The fantasy palace might well be further protected by magics, summoned monsters, traps, illusions, and so forth.

Further, keep in mind that all of these tactical and architectural concerns are only general guidelines for your use. Stronghold-themed dungeons — especially those fortifications which exist underground — are typically centuries old, and have been repurposed many times by various denizens. There is no reason why your stronghold cannot feature two throne rooms (one ancient and one newer, hosting an upstart humanoid chieftain), multiple lords' chambers, secret rooms, collapsed areas, magical areas, and so forth. The information provided here is to help you "break the rules" in an intelligent fashion. Use the guidelines that you need, and ignore the ones you don't. Be creative!

Arranging Rooms for a Temple

This is one of the most difficult sections in this book for me to write, because the conception of FRPG temples is based more on fantasy dungeons than it is on real world temples and other sacred buildings. For that reason, I need to bring forth some themes concerning ancient, classical and pagan temples while downplaying modern structures. I also need to broaden the definition of "temple" to also include elements from some other types of reverent buildings: cathedrals, churches, monasteries, abbeys, nunneries, priories, and — I kid you not — epic bathhouses, a forgotten-yet-amazing favorite of the ostentatious Roman Emperors.

There is no real way for me to turn this conglomeration of different structures into a single cohesive narrative involving room flow. But I can tell you that very abstractly, sacred buildings tend to have several shared elements of room-to-room procedure and design.

There is usually an entryway which is elaborate and impressive, while also serving to siphon worshippers into a narrow conduit which controls their (in)ability to reach private areas in the pagan temple. This is because the temple space is shared by two very different populations:

[1] the priests, who might indeed live there, and who are of a higher social caste that rarely humors frequent disturbances induced by lesser folk; and, [2] the worshippers, who don't live there, visit all the time, tend to be of lower caste, and who don't stop to think that the "house of the god" might also be somebody's home and place of business. I realize that this is a rather jaded way of looking at things, but it is beneficial for us to consider the truth: A pagan and / or medieval-themed temple is a vast shared space that belongs to two very different populations, who typically only meet in large areas that are relatively close to the holy / unholy altar.

Areas open to the worshippers in such a design would include the entry; the main temple; rooms of worship, singing, prayer, and sacrifice; and galleries filled with story-enhancing relics, light, views, mosaics, frescoes and / or statuary. Areas open only to the priests would include treasuries, bedchambers, meditation rooms, summoning rooms, bell towers (if any), divination pools, vestment and ceremonial storerooms, temple servant quarters, and the sanctum sanctorum (holy of holies).

Most "realistic" temple floor plans that I've seen in FRPGs over the decades tend to be modeled after Christian cathedrals ... probably because the architecture is immense, stunning and serves as a "common language" to the church-informed imaginations of Americans and Europeans. The temples that I most recommend for GM research purposes, however, are Egyptian (very much so) and Roman (less so). (You might think Greek as well, but massive Greek structures such as the Parthenon were actually open-aired, simple and accessible to all ... very admirable, but not very useful in terms of labyrinthine FRPG dungeon design.)

There are more different temple types than there are religions, so it is impossible to be comprehensive here. But I can go over the cultures which are most popularly used in dungeon modules, old school pulp fantasy, and classic campaigns to give you some general ideas.

~

Babylonian / Mesopotamian: The major temples were ziggurats, which were elaborate step pyramids. In real life, ziggurats are ominous yet disappointing structures with no major shrines to speak of. As far as we can tell, rituals and ceremonies were held on the summit so that the priests and worshippers could be as close to the (sky) deities as possible. In an FRPG, of course, the ziggurat will probably be a massive hollow structure that is entered through the top, with dungeon level 1 being small (toward the summit) and deeper dungeon levels becoming successively larger until the floor plans are found underground beneath the structure.

Celtic: Despite the amazing surface circles of standing stones, in regards to interior temples of the Celts we unfortunately know very little because so little has survived. There is a sub-theme which is now termed the Romano-Celtic temple; these were structures built by the Romans in reverence to Celtic deities in the farther provinces. My favorite example is the Temple of Nodens which is barely preserved at Lydney Park, because much of foundation has survived and we can discern the temple outline. These temples were relatively simple and small affairs, although of course an enterprising GM can solve this by tying the Celtic temple directly to the Celtic netherworld. That's where your dungeons will be.

Central American / Aztec / Mayan: The majestic Aztec temples were call "Teocalli," or "Houses of the Gods." They tend to be massive step pyramids, and unlike ziggurats many of them have internal chambers of prayer, sacrifice, and subterranean access. Mayan pyramids tend to be steep, with celestial themes and engravings. For such temples you can use the "ziggurat approach" to dungeon design, as I mentioned in the Babylonian section above. It's also likely that Mayan temples existed in cave systems as well, which can serve as further inspiration.

Egyptian: Egyptian temple floor plans are very useful, because they're monolithic, pagan, relatively rectangular with few curved surfaces (good for transitioning to graph paper), and many are still in existence. This means that we can find information on their plans online and their surveyed sites in accessible books.

~

See for example the Temple of Hathor, with the plan appearing on the following page. You can see that this interesting design is built for processions, and that the entryway leads directly

— through a succession of pillared halls — into the central shrine.

All of the many priests' rooms, ceremonial chambers, storerooms, stairs, and guard rooms form a periphery around this central in-and-out conduit. This can be an interesting floor plan to emulate in a game, where your players are expecting the "big bad" to be hidden away in a deep and secret corner ... but the truth (and dangerous circumstances) are something quite different from what they will be anticipating.

A more detailed example is the temple of Ammon (Amun Re) at Karnak. This is one of the largest ancient temple structures in existence, and it holds many features which can be inspiring to a dungeon designer. I will give you a whirlwind tour of the highlights here. The temple was apparently designed as a sacred microcosm, emulating all that was good in the Egyptian world. The ceilings depicted the sky, sacred waters reflected the architecture, and the columns were designed to look like immense palms, lotus flowers, and papyrus stalks. The outlying areas along the Nile were deliberately designed to flood, further underlining the crucial theme of reverence for water, plants, creation, life, endurance, and divine being.

The front courtyard featured a massive obelisk, and a walkway between columns and pylons. The inner Great Court (see plan hereafter) led into the Great Hypostyle Hall, but also featured lesser temples devoted to Ramses and Sethos. The Great Hypostyle Hall has 134 colossal columns made of sandstone. It featured clerestory lighting, which means that daylight was allowed to filter down from high above so that not all of the illumination would be artificial.

Beyond the Great Hall was the Central Court, a major thoroughfare between temple grounds. Deeper into the structure were mortuary temples. Priests' rooms, side halls, storerooms, and many ceremonial chambers.

If you are thinking of designing a mega-temple, this one will give you a good idea of how to structure your ideas. You could also of course include a huge funerary netherworld beneath the temple too.

~

Greek: Greek temples are gorgeous, but they don't make for very good dungeon settings. This is because they were open, simple, and designed for maximum access. Good for worshippers, but bad for dramatic adventures and exploration! You can find some good (yet disappointing) floor plans of Greek temples online if you need them. The major elements of such a temple include the Stereobate (the stone substructure the temple is built on), Stylobate (entrance floor), Peristyle (column perimeter), Pronaos (the "front porch"), Cella (main temple room) and Opisthodomos ("back porch"). And that's pretty much it: one room and two half-open rooms, surrounded by columns.

Norse: Norse temples range from crude caves, to mountaintop vistas, to the beautiful wooden stave churches at sites like Heddal. They have very few rooms, but they do have dramatic architecture, soaring ceilings, fantastic decorations and interesting grounds. If you choose to make a Norse-themed temple, I would recommend that you have most of the "interesting bits" underground, and the traditional spaces up top for atmosphere. Do an image search for "Heddal stave church" if you want to see what one of these fascinating structures looks like.

Roman: Second only to the Egyptians, the Romans are a great source of inspiration for temple dungeon design. This is because the Romans had a culture of monumental architecture, which was mostly falling into ruins in medieval times ... and regarded with superstitious fascination. Most of the dungeons in my Castle Oldskull campaign (featuring a magical medieval version of Earth) are found under Roman ruins.

~

However, I should warn you that the Romans by Imperial times were a rather civic yet cynical people. Unlike the Egyptians who lived for the gods, and who looked to the afterlife as the true life beyond mortal existence, the Romans were more interested in business, warfare, ceremony and the finer points of civilized life. So while they could build beautiful temples (and later churches), they were also obsessed with grandiose structures for government, rulers, games and gladiatorial matches, entertainment (amphitheaters) and public discourse. This means that the best Roman floor plans you will find are not for temples, really; they are for bathhouses, palaces, and marketplace quarters.

I heartily recommend stealing all of the Roman floor plans that you can find and using them as temples in your game. (I've tried using bathhouses and senate buildings in my own campaign, but the players just have too much trouble equating such spaces with adventure and taking them seriously. Whatever cultural imagination of legends and fairytales we collectively share within our minds, it's far more firmly rooted in castles and tombs than it is in saunas and senate chambers!)

I have included a fair number of Roman rooms in the Lexicon in this volume, particularly types of baths and treasure chambers and so forth. People tend to forget that in ancient times, health was power. A simple sword cut could become infected and lead to horrible death long after the battle was over. Entire civilizations were wiped out by plague, parasites, contact with foreign peoples (with different immunities) and unknown illnesses.

The Romans' ability to keep their people clean (baths) and well fed (granaries) with lots of healthy drinking water (aqueducts) and efficient cloacas (sewers) meant everything: Rome was unconquerable because its people lived longer, stronger, and healthier, and instead of struggling for day-to-day survival they were free to write, create art, develop law, share ideas, and to wage war on disorganized neighboring tribes with ruthless efficiency.

But despite all of this, today's FRPG players just don't appreciate this magnificent culture for what it was. They want ruins, caves, castles, temples, and tombs, all filled with monsters and with little care about the ways of the world, and that's actually fine. It is a game. But that's all my long-winded way of reminding you: if your players are like mine, don't try to emulate Rome itself when you're digging for floor plans; take the floor plans that you find and repurpose them, fitting them into the existing tropes of the fantasy game for maximum effect.

ARRANGING ROOMS FOR A TOMB

Many of the problems that we run into when researching tombs, I've already explained to you in previous sections. Namely: **[1]** Much like real dungeons, real tombs tend to be tiny, overhyped, or sensationalized for tourists. **[2]** Much like real caves, most of the good tomb maps and surveys were created after 1923 ... so we run into the dreaded copyright monster once again. I can't show you everything I want to show you.

But as an easily seen example, I would invite you to perform a Google image search for the topic "catacombs of Saint Callixtus map." Those catacombs provide some truly revelatory information on a potential tomb dungeon that I am sure you will be interested to take in.

There are several things that I find striking about this floor plan. First, there are broken and inaccessible sections. This implies to me that there are multiple surface entrances into this complex, but not all of the tunnels meet up with one another. This would be a perfect chance for a GM to include secret tunnels, teleporters, and magical gateways to connect the entire system and to make it fully coherent.

Second is the fact that tunnels run off the map edges, leading to entirely separate catacomb sections (different dungeons) further on. And lastly, there are very few plain old corridors here. If you watch videos of people walking the catacombs, you'll see that virtually every tunnel has alcoves, grave niches, bones, skulls, and so forth. The dead are everywhere. Woe be to the adventurers if necromancers are at work in the catacombs they discover ...

There are some other excellent catacomb maps for real world places, some of which are absolutely terrifying to conceptualize. To my mind, the most intimidating tomb-like system in the real world (from a mapping perspective) is comprised by the mined Odessa Catacombs. You can find partial maps online if you would like to take a look, but I would warn you that you might see some upsetting things as well if your Safe Search is not on when you go exploring.

As you can well imagine from the information that is available on the Odess Catacombs, people would get lost and die from dehydration and starvation before they ever found an exit. Odessa

has some pretty stories associated with these tunnels. Feel free to poke around online for more details, but I will warn you that you'll probably see some dead bodies and other recent unpleasantness if you dig a bit too deeply.

The Catacombs of Paris are very interesting as well. They are vast, and filled with millions of skeletons. Grim features that would translate well into a game include: collapsing walls of piled bones; pools of filthy water leading down into lost rooms; organized crime hideouts (rumored over the centuries); the bodies of murder victims; the remains of bunkers and shelters; and people allegedly sneaking in, going crazy, and never being heard from again.

Despite the discomfort of the subject, catacombs are a very beneficial research topic for Game Masters. This is because the catacombs comprise the real world settings that are closest to what most people imagine when they envision a "real" FRPG dungeon. The features which you can emphasize that will make an impression on your players include: the endless piles of bones, the nameless rows of skulls, dust, dripping water, cracking and rumbling stone, the scent of decay, limited air, strange smells from incense and candles, echoing sounds, circling tunnels which lead back upon themselves, limited light, and confined quarters. You can create some pretty grim psychological effects too, by constantly reminding players of the adventurers' claustrophobia, fear of getting lost, the omnipresent sense of death and disease, limited sight lines, limited opportunities to use ranged weapons, and dramatic shadows shifting wildly up from carried light sources.

~

Despite these intriguing inspirations, I should point out a rather disappointing reality as you research further options: Most tombs are boring. There are stairs down, an entryway (probably sealed up by a wall), a tomb room, and that's about it. There may be some interesting inscriptions, paintings, mosaics or hieroglyphics depending upon the culture. Things tend to get more elaborate when the interred person was important and revered; then you might actually have multiple treasure vaults, a room for entombed slaves, and even secret rooms (treasures hidden behind less valuable treasures, in a futile attempt to fool many centuries' worth of thieves).

Honestly, however, to make interesting tomb dungeons you will probably need to combine a catacomb floor plan layout with tombs for several (if not a dozen) different personages. If you take the Tomb of Qa above as representative, and repeat that kind of layout ten or so times in a catacomb layout similar to the Saint Calixtus floor plan, you will end up with an intriguing and sufficiently huge dungeon which the PCs can explore to their hearts' content.

AFTERWORD

And with all of that said, I feel that this is a good time to bring the Classic Dungeon Design Guide trilogy to a close. If you have enjoyed this deep exploration of dungeon creation, do not despair. I have written over 50 books on the topic of fantasy role-playing games, and if you choose to explore further you will see that I have interlaced them all into a single coherent narrative that touches on many related subjects (such as monster lairs, treasures, artifacts, demon lords, the World of Oldskull, and the mega-dungeon setting of Castle Oldskull proper). Thank you for coming along on the journey!

ABOUT THE AUTHOR

Beginning play as a chaotic neutral normal human with one measly hit point to his name, KENT DAVID KELLY eventually became apprenticed to a magic-user of ill repute ... a foul man who dwelt in the steamy deeps of the Ivory Cloud Mountain. After this mentor carelessly misplaced an intelligent soul-sucking sword and then died under suspicious circumstances, his former henchman Mr. Kelly escaped to the deeper underground and there began playing Satanic role-playing games. This, the legends tell us, occurred in the year 1981. Hoary wizard-priests who inspired Mr. Kelly in his netherworldly machinations included the peerless Gygax, Carr, Arneson, Cook, Hammack, Jaquays, Bledsaw, Moldvay, Kuntz, Schick and Ward. Sadly, a misguided made-for-the-basements movie entitled *Mazes and Monsters* gave Mr. Kelly's parents conniptions in 1982. As a result of that blasphemous Tom Hanks debacle (and other more personal lapses in judgment), Mr. Kelly was eventually forbidden from playing his favorite game for a considerable length of time. Nonplussed but not defeated, he used this enforced exile to escape to a friend's alehouse, and there indulged himself in now-classic computer RPGs such as Zork, Telengard, Temple of Apshai, Ultima, Tunnels of Doom, The Bard's Tale, Phantasie, Pool of Radiance, Wizard's Crown and Wasteland. He then went on to write computer versions of his own FRPGs, which led to his obsession with coupling creative design elements with random dungeons and unpredictable adventure generation. Mr. Kelly wrote and submitted his first adventure for Dungeon Magazine #1 in 1986. Unfortunately, one Mr. Moore decided that his submission was far too "Lovecraftian, horrific and unfair" to ever serve that worthy periodical as a publishable adventure. Mr. Kelly, it must be said, took this rejection as a very good sign of things to come. In the late 80s and 90s, Mr. Kelly wrote short stories, poems and essays ... some of which have been published under the Wonderland Imprints banner. He wrote several dark fantasy and horror novels as well. Concurrently, he ran Dark Angel Collectibles, selling classic FRPG materials as Darkseraphim, and assisted the Acaeum with the creation of the Valuation Board and other minor research projects. At this time, Mr. Kelly and his entourage of evil gnomes are rumored to dwell in the dread and deathly under-halls of the Acaeum, Dragonsfoot, ENWorld, Grognardia, Knights & Knaves, ODD, and even more nefarious levels deep down in the mega-dungeon of the Web. There he remains in vigil, his vampiric sword yet shivering in his hand. When not being sought outright for answers to halfling riddles or other more sundry sage advice, he is to be avoided by sane individuals *at all costs*.

MORE TOOLS OF THE MAD GOD

The Castle Oldskull line of fantasy role-playing supplements is forever expanding, with topics ranging from monster design to campaign creation. You should be able to find the entire line of available tomes wherever you purchased this book.

Castle Oldskull gaming supplements are published at various websites including CastleOldskull.com, Amazon.com (including Kindle and unillustrated paperback versions), DriveThruRPG.com (PDFs), Itch.io (PDFs), Lulu.com (PDFs and fully illustrated paperback versions), and elsewhere. As of this writing, the full line of available supplements (and related titles) stands as follows:

❖ *1,000 Rooms of Chaos*

❖ *1,000 Rooms of Chaos II*

❖ *1977 Bestiary*

❖ *333 Realms of Entropy*

❖ *Advanced OSR Character Record*

❖ *Adventurer's Arsenal*

❖ *Bloodbath Bunnies*

❖ *The Book of Dungeon Traps*

❖ *Captains of the Scarlet Tabard*

❖ *Chaotic Descriptor Table*

❖ *Character Creation*

❖ *City State Encounters*

❖ *The Classic Dungeon Design Guide I*

❖ *The Classic Dungeon Design Guide II*

❖ *The Classic Dungeon Design Guide III*

❖ *Dungeon Delver Enhancer*

❖ *Game World Generator*

❖ *Game World Generator – Deluxe Edition*

❖ *Hawk & Moor Book I: The Dragon Rises*

❖ *Hawk & Moor Book II: The Dungeons Deep*

❖ *Hawk & Moor Book III: Lands and Worlds Afar*

❖ *Hawk & Moor Book IV: Of Demons and Fallen Idols*

❖ *Hawk & Moor Book V: Age of Glory*

❖ *Hawk & Moor: The Steam Tunnel Incident*

❖ *The King in Yellow Rises*

❖ *Lords of Oldskull Book I: Krampus*

❖ *Monsters & Treasures Level 1*

❖ *Necronomicon: The Cthulhu Revelations*

❖ *Oldskull Adventure Generator*

❖ *Oldskull Anti-Paladins*

❖ *Oldskull D100 NPC Generator*

❖ *The Oldskull Deck of Strangest Things*

❖ *Oldskull Dragons*

❖ *Oldskull Dungeon Bestiary*

❖ *Oldskull Dungeon Encounters Book I*

❖ *Oldskull Dungeon Generator*

❖ *Oldskull Dungeon Tools*

❖ *Oldskull Gonneslingers*

❖ *Oldskull Grid War*

❖ *Oldskull Half-Ogres*

❖ *Oldskull Knights*

❖ *Oldskull Monster Generator*

❖ *The Oldskull Necronomicon I*

❖ *Oldskull Plague Doctors*

❖ *Oldskull Treasure Trove*

❖ *Oldskull Trolls*

❖ *Oldskull Tyrrhenia Map Pack*

❖ *Oldskull Warriors*

❖ *The Order of the Scarlet Tabard*

❖ *The Pegana Mythos*

❖ *Serpentine: Oldskull Serpent Folk*

❖ *Turn Tracker*

LEGAL

Open Game Content

Open Game Content may only be Used under and in terms of the Open Game License (OGL).

This entire work is designated as Open Game Content under the OGL, with the exception of the trademarks "Castle Oldskull," "Wonderland Imprints," "Only the Finest Works of Fantasy," and with the exception of all artwork. These trademarks, artwork, and the Trade Dress of this work (font, layout, style of artwork, etc.) are reserved as Product Identity.

Open Game License

OPEN GAME LICENSE Version 1.0a

The following text is the property of Wizards of the Coast, Inc. and is Copyright 2000 Wizards of the Coast, Inc. ("Wizards"). All Rights Reserved.

1. Definitions: (a) "Contributors" means the copyright and/or trademark owners who have contributed Open Game Content; (b) "Derivative Material" means copyrighted material including derivative works and translations (including into other computer languages), potation, modification, correction, addition, extension, upgrade, improvement, compilation, abridgment or other form in which an existing work may be recast, transformed or adapted; (c) "Distribute" means to reproduce, license, rent, lease, sell, broadcast, publicly display, transmit or otherwise distribute; (d) "Open Game Content" means the game mechanic and includes the methods, procedures, processes and routines to the extent such content does not embody the Product Identity and is an enhancement over the prior art and any additional content clearly identified as Open Game Content by the Contributor, and means any work covered by this License, including translations and derivative works under copyright law, but specifically excludes Product Identity. (e) "Product Identity" means product and product line names, logos and identifying marks including trade dress; artifacts; creatures characters; stories, storylines, plots, thematic elements, dialogue, incidents, language, artwork, symbols, designs, depictions, likenesses, formats, poses, concepts, themes and graphic, photographic and other visual or audio representations; names and descriptions of characters, spells, enchantments, personalities, teams, personas, likenesses and special abilities; places, locations, environments, creatures, equipment, magical or supernatural abilities or effects, logos, symbols, or graphic designs; and any other trademark or registered trademark clearly identified as Product identity by the owner of the Product Identity, and which specifically excludes the Open Game Content; (f) "Trademark" means the logos, names, mark, sign, motto, designs that are used by a Contributor to identify itself or its products or the associated products contributed to the Open Game License by the Contributor (g) "Use", "Used" or "Using" means to use, Distribute, copy, edit, format, modify, translate and otherwise create Derivative Material of Open Game Content. (h) "You" or "Your" means the licensee in terms of this agreement.

2. The License: This License applies to any Open Game Content that contains a notice indicating that the Open Game Content may only be Used under and in terms of this License. You must affix such a notice to any Open Game Content that you Use. No terms may be added to or subtracted from this License except as described by the License itself. No other terms or conditions may be applied to any Open Game Content distributed using this License.

3. Offer and Acceptance: By Using the Open Game Content You indicate Your acceptance of the terms of this License.

4. Grant and Consideration: In consideration for agreeing to use this License, the Contributors grant You a perpetual, worldwide, royalty-free, non-exclusive license with the exact terms of this License to Use, the Open Game Content.

5. Representation of Authority to Contribute: If You are contributing original material as Open Game Content, You represent that Your Contributions are Your original creation and/or You have sufficient rights to grant the rights conveyed by this License.

6. Notice of License Copyright: You must update the COPYRIGHT NOTICE portion of this License to include the exact text of the COPYRIGHT NOTICE of any Open Game

Made in United States
Troutdale, OR
03/27/2025